# The Last Westerner

## Other Novels by Chilton Williamson, Jr.

*Desert Light*

*The Homestead*

*Jerusalem, Jerusalem!*

*Mexico Way*

*The Education of of Héctor Villa*

# The Last Westerner

CHILTON WILLIAMSON, JR.

ST. AUGUSTINE'S PRESS
South Bend, Indiana

Manufactured in the United States of America.

1 2 3 4 5 6 30 29 28 27 26 25

**Library of Congress Control Number: 2025939479**

Paperback ISBN: 978-1-58731-448-3
Ebook ISBN: 978-1-58731-447-6

∞ The paper used in this publication meets the minimum requirements of the American National Standard for Information Sciences – Permanence of Paper for Printed Materials, ANSI Z39.48-1984.

St. Augustine's Press
www.staugustine.net

For
Maureen McCaffrey Williamson,
and in memory of my friend Edward Abbey,
who I hope would have enjoyed this book

"...He fares well who obeys the commands of love, and whatever he does is pardonable, but he is the coward who does not dare."

— Chrétien de Troyes, *Lancelot*

# TABLE OF CONTENTS

## ACKNOWLEDGEMENTS

The author wishes to thank his good friend Brooke Cadwallader for his expert help with the Spanish language employed in this book, and also Karen L. Myers who read the text through and offered many valuable editorial suggestions.

# BOOK I
## JODY

My father had beautiful manners, and his father before him. I don't believe either of them cared for people very much, but they both adored women. For them women were the whole world and the promise of it, men being hardly more than rivals in love to be challenged and defeated. Romantic love, I suppose, was the only kind of love they ever knew, or even recognized. So far as they were concerned, men were the second sex and women superior and infinitely fascinating creatures worthy of an entire lifetime devoted to pleasing them. When my father was still a very young man a male acquaintance, attempting to console him for the fickleness of a woman, counseled him to relax and "play the game." My father's reply to this advice was that love isn't a game to be played, it's simply the most important thing there is.

Personally, I never hoped for anything more in life than a good wife to please, and to please me, and a son to raise up to be a good man, the way a good man should. It could be I haven't a lot to offer a woman. Women nowadays love intensity in a man and after that expressiveness; the strong silent type belongs to history and Grade B Westerns from the Fifties. My Southern heritage gave me intensity enough, while my Western upbringing covered it over and disguised it with reticence and that dry, I guess laconic manner that used to drive women wild. My second wife called me a stick the night before she left me, and I still have trouble forgetting that.

Lydia was an Eastern lady. East and West don't lie well together, according to a saying out here. She came out from L.A. to Montana with her first husband, who she met in California after moving West from New York City. He was a movie man, a producer, and she was a failed actress after only three years in Hollywood. They had plenty of money and their friends were people like Whoopi Goldberg, Elizabeth Ashley, and a writer fellow named Tom McGuane. I liked Tom; he bred the best cutting horses in the country and was a hell of a hand when it came to working them, too. The others I did not like so much. I went to work as ranch foreman for her husband with not a lot to do besides watching his bison herd spread brucellosis around the neighboring cattle ranches. In addition to growing bison they made movies, too; one time they put me in one. I played Buffalo Bill Cody, growing out my hair behind and a chin beard in front to look the part. The movie was never released; in fact it wasn't even finished, but I kept the beard and the longish hair after Lydia's husband died suddenly of a heart attack and I became, after a not exactly appropriate interval, the proprietor of a beautiful wife, six sections of land, and three-hundred-fifty-six head of buffalo.

It is just possible that nobody really falls in love again after the age of forty but everybody has to believe in love, especially me, and so I did. It seemed as if at my age I was getting a final chance. The marriage went along all right, as marriages go these days, for a couple of years and then Lydia met a talkative young screenwriter with no money and I became a stick. I moved down to Wyoming where I spent another couple of years working as a range detective, and when I got tired of having potshots taken at me by rustlers and poachers from Salt Lake City I went on the road in a three-quarter-ton Ford pickup with a camper set in the bed.

I had been traveling for a year and a half when I met Jody James, and although I was only fifty-one years old the world I had been born into a short half-century before had already ceased to exist. Our meeting occurred at a horse show in Moab, Utah on the afternoon of a late winter day in the February thaw with a chinook blowing up from the Gulf of California a thousand miles away. The wind lifted the horses' tails as they waited to enter the arena and I put my hand on my hat in time. She accepted the movement as a greeting and put her horse forward several steps.

"Do I know you?"

"No, ma'am. Not as I can recall."

"I know I've seen that hair and goatee somewhere."

I did not say anything. Mounted, she looked tall and willowy, with a supple long waist I could have spanned with my hands. And wanted to.

"Are you showing?"

"No."

"I could see you know horses from the way you watched Cortez set his feet. Will you have a drink with me when this next class is over?"

"This is Mormon country."

"You aren't Mormon are you?"

"No."

"I have a bottle of Johnny Walker Black under the bunk bed in the trailer. I'll see you back here in half an hour then."

She placed second in a class of fourteen entrants. The horse was a stallion, black bay, strong looking but not tall, with a strange paddling gait that seemed to throw his front feet to the side, tortoisewise. We had a drink in the changing room up front of the horse trailer and a couple more before supper at the restaurant in Moab. The restaurant was the former home of the first wildcatter to make a big strike back in the Fifties. Supported by stilts, it hung on the side of a steep hill above the town. I helped her out of her coat, drew the chair back from the table, and pushed it in again when she was seated.

"You do have such nice manners," Jody James said.

Seated at table against the plate glass window we drank whiskey and soda while the slickrock cliffs flared in hues of glowing rose and pink and subsided in folds of purple shadow. She was a tallish hardlimbed cowgirl with high cheekbones, sea-green eyes, and straw-colored hair cut off at the shoulder blades and sun-split in the ends. She had what was left of a good tan, which stopped approximately where her shirt-collar and cuffs did. Her teeth were white and small and her expression demure but knowing, a thing I find irresistible in a woman. I complimented her on the stallion, which she had paid a lot of money for in Phoenix last summer. He was a Peruvian Paso with a gait that appeared from the ground to have the smooth action of a jackhammer but was, she insisted, actually quite level and floating.

"You can take him for a spin if you like," Jody offered. "Nobody but me and the trainer has ever ridden him."

We ate a green salad and beefsteaks with home-fried potatoes while sharing a bottle of California red wine.

"What a gorgeous sunset," Jody said. "It looks like the end of the world. Don't you get lonely wandering about with your house on your back, like a turtle?"

"It's better than having no house at all."

"Haven't you ever been married?"

"Years ago."

"What happened?"

"The same thing that happens with every divorce. A world died. That's all."

"You sound bitter. Are you?"

"No," I said. "I'm not bitter."

The waiter brought two heated cognacs and we drank them with coffee for dessert. When we had finished I brought the truck around to the front of the restaurant and got out to hold the passenger door. In town the shadowed bungalows crouched under the bare hanging branches of the cottonwoods and the brushy Navajo willows. The glare of the passing arc lights lit the near hemisphere of her face for seconds at a time before letting it relapse into shadow in the darkness between the light poles.

"Are you always so communicative with women?" Jody James asked.

"I'm sorry. I didn't mean to be unfriendly."

"You're not unfriendly."

"It's been a long time. That's all."

She directed me across Spanish Valley to the house where she was staying over, one of those modular homes they ship in slices like the two halves of a cake and glue together on location. There was a light on beside the door and a ristra hanging above it.

"Ristras up here in Moab? And Christmas was months ago."

"Ristras are a matter of the heart, not of geography. You can have ristras anywhere you want them, anytime."

"What about mistletoe?"

"So far as I know," Jody said, "I don't have a drop of Spanish blood in my veins, but I'm terribly responsive to ristras."

We shared our first kiss under a cluster of dried red chili peppers rustling on a warm wind out of Mexico and then I drove back into town and across the Colorado River. I found a jeep trail winding into the deeper canyons and followed it for a mile or so before parking the truck in a salt cedar thicket. A thousand feet in the sky the pudding shaped Navajo sandstone glowed pale against the stars in the moonlight. I climbed up in the camper, got under the woolen blanket on the bunk bed, and lay there, thinking. After a while, listening to the early tree frogs croaking in the cottonwoods beside the creek, I fell asleep.

I can be gabby as a politician at a Chamber of Commerce banquet if I don't have to talk about myself. Look around you, if you can bear it, and see what is happening in the world. I don't understand it all myself, but I feel more than I understand, and I know that at the heart of it is the relationship between men and women. Everywhere you look there is a huge sadness and even suffering, especially among people who do not know that they are sad and suffering. Everywhere people are lonely and alone, and those who are most alone are those who cannot understand that they are lonely. Everywhere they are confused, and their confusion tells them they have nothing to be confused about. They are unhappy with themselves, and with each other. Love has grown hateful as hate is elevated to a form of love. Chivalry is considered oppression, and valor something that earns you five million bucks a year working for the Denver Broncos. God is still love if you want Him to be, I guess, but there isn't any question that love has been made God. The great cities are growing back into wilderness, and the wilderness is being bulldozed and paved for multimillion-dollar playgrounds for the wealthy and suburban lots and highways for everyone else. Even nature has been thrown out of balance to produce blizzards in July and drought in winter time. The only good I can see in all this is that I'm not a young man anymore, though young enough still to please Jody James—in the short run, anyway. And even that's good enough.

Only a little snow fell in southeastern Utah that year and most of that little melted out of the mountains by the second week in April except for the cols high on the northern aspects of the tallest peaks. The melted snow soaked into the talus slopes until it found the solid rock and ran downhill beneath the scree to the edge of the rockfall where it burst in waterspouts into the streambeds carved out of the tundra among sparse stunted trees. Sluicing through ravines shaded by the tall pines the water reached the aspen forests and spread itself in shallow torrents, washing the thin soil from around the roots and suckers and tearing out whole colonies of the tender trees. Below the aspen the flood recovered its channels as it entered the piñon and juniper covered foothills, undercutting banks and engorging toppled masses of red clay and sand until the water thickened at last to a flow of liquid mud, meandering across sagebrush flats toward the canyon of the Colorado and dropping by a series of tepid falls until at last it poured itself out into the great river. And so the house and power boaters on Lake Powell, the water skiers and striped bass fisherman, had enough water to play in, for one more summer at least.

Even before the drought, what we had instead of winter in the Southwest meant that when spring arrived it left you with a feeling of not having earned it, although I didn't know this—having been raised on a cattle ranch in the Animas Valley of the New Mexico bootheel where my grandfather, Charles Jamieson Ryder, knew George Scarborough and Pat Garrett, and met John Wesley Hardin and John Henry Selden on occasion—until I had lived up north for some time. There are exceptions, like the Sangre de Cristo Mountains in northern New Mexico and the San Francisco Mountains above Flagstaff, Arizona; still, the Southwest, as a general rule, doesn't have a winter, only an eerie monotony of weather and temperature rising gradually from midwinter into late spring by which time, like the frog in the saucepan, you're cooked without having been made aware of the fact, if you haven't already been worn to a toothpick by the sandstorms.

You would have said to look at it that the Bar Nun Ranch belonged to a Hollywood movie star. The house was a two-story timber and stucco affair with a skylight in the pitched roof, a portal running on three sides, and a flagstone patio behind. The lawns extended as far as the apple orchard between the house and the creek, and the bunkhouse off by itself beneath the aged cottonwoods. Beyond the bunkhouse were the barns, the stables, the horse corrals, and a riding arena surrounded by a low stucco wall, white-painted and sweeping up to make an enclosing frame for the heavy wooden entrance gate. The blue mountains went straight up behind the house which faced across the green valley to the sheer vermilion cliffs falling fifteen hundred feet. Herds of Angus and Brangus cattle grazed in the valley and now, in spring, flocks of boattailed grackles settled on the freshly turned alfalfa fields. Fifteen years before, Jody and her husband, the late Mr. James, purchased the spread from the old-timer who had been born on it and, for a half-century or more, ran a few poor head of cattle while hauling logs from the mountains in winter time. For nearly ten years they lived in a two-room cabin built from the unsold logs while the two of them, working alone, reclaimed the surrounding fields from the salinity produced by the old man's lousy irrigation practices. It took them a year and a half to build the new house which was completed ten months before Mr. James was killed when the horse he was breaking fell over backwards with him.

By now the Bar Nun had become the most prosperous and financially sound outfit in southeastern Utah, and every millionaire tourist from California had advised the James's answering machine that he had fallen in love with the property at first sight and must have it, adding that money was no obstacle for him at all. In the more than two years since her husband's death Jody had been hanging on with the help of Dago O'Grady, a dour Irishman and professional cowboy who had worked as the Bar Nun's foreman for eighteen months before the accident, and an octogenarian sheepherder called Whitey who wore his beard as far down as his waist. Dago won his nickname by sticking a shiv between the ribs of the man the prosecution claimed was trying to move in on Dago's girlfriend; I never learned what his real name was. A black Irishman, short and stocky, with the temperament of a rattlesnake or a little man with a big gun, he made a competent foreman, getting seriously drunk only three or four times a year in a calculated and deliberate manner, the way some people visit spas or go on religious retreats. When I asked Jody why Dago didn't care for me she said it was a remark I had made about Brangus cows, which you couldn't give me for an April Fool's Day present. I had been living on the Bar Nun for a week when I backed the pickup into a shed, drained the water pipes and the tank in the camper, unscrewed the gas lines, slid the unit from the truck bed, and left it resting on two-by-fours on the packed dirt floor with only the mice and the snakes for company.

This late spring day we were up before daybreak and on the way to the barns while the sun was still trying to get above the headwall and the canyon lay submerged in a substantial twilight that was more like water than air. In the light of a naked sixty-watt bulb we threw down hay bales from the loft, cut the string with my pocketknife, and stuck the separate flakes under the long faces of the horses waiting in their box stalls along the cement runway. Jody helped Whitey nurse the bum lambs while I carried away the carcasses of the ones that had died during the night and fed the dogs, the half-feral ones hanging back and watching with slit yellow eyes as I set the food out in iron pans. We looked at the calves in the calf pens, and then I made Jody show me the fainting goats. The goats lived in a shed of their own at a distance from the barns, away from surprises. They stood close together watching us approach and when I yelled BOOOOO! three or four would keel over in terror and lie unconscious on the ground for several minutes before they woke up screaming with fright, while the rest milled and bleated. The fainting goats were always the best part of early morning. After visiting with them we returned to the house for breakfast, which we had on the patio with our backs to the climbing sun. We ate a light meal, scrambled eggs with green chili, toast and jam, some kind of fresh fruit, and black coffee with a shot of whiskey. Before we could finish eating the slickrock cliffs glared red above the house, radiating a dry heat across the valley.

We were in the saddle until early afternoon when we had lunch and a short siesta before doing paperwork and making phone calls. Jody, who was feuding with the government men in Monticello, did the calling while I reviewed the books with a pocket calculator. It was more or less like trying to catch a bank examiner out in a trivial error. In those several months I uncovered only two or three mistakes, one of which turned out on closer inspection to be my own. We ate supper at six, washed up the dishes, did the chores, and sat on the patio in the evening cool to drink whiskey and listen to the purple vetch growing in the meadow while the sun went down behind the Henry Mountains a hundred miles away, the bullbats dived at our heads, and the early mosquitoes whined. Some evenings I would bring out the nickel-plated harmonica and play or sing the old Irish songs—The Harp that Once Thro' Tara's Halls," "The Green Isle of Erin," and "Kathleen Mavourneen," which Jody liked the best.

"It's such a sad song," she said. "But what does it mean?"

"No one knows that I ever heard of. My thinking is an Irish politician has been summoned to London expecting to be put in the Tower and maybe have his head cut off. He is up early and goes to look at his wife who is sleeping still in a fourposter bed in her separate room—grateful for her peace of mind but hurt because she hasn't awakened early to tell him goodbye. 'It may be for years, and it may be forever,' he says."

"It's the saddest song I think I ever heard. It makes me want to cry whenever you play it."

"If you wish, I'll work on playing and singing it for you at the same time."

For two months we didn't go into town at all and we were hardly ever out of one another's company. Jody gave me her Stephen King novels to read and I taught her to back braid rope. Finally she cut my hair and insisted that I shave my beard after I had allowed both to start growing back.

"You look just exactly like Buffalo Bill," she complained. "In his later years."

"Is that bad? Lydia liked it."

"You've given me one more good reason why I don't."

"I actually look more like my namesake, the Confederate cavalry officer Jeb Stuart."

"I didn't even know who the guy was until you told me, but the name goes well with Ryder. And why would the two of you men want to look like environmentalists, anyway?"

We were in love, Jody with the wild infatuation of her lingering youth, me in my cautious middle-aged way that comes from having learned—too late, perhaps—that love always exacts patience and hard work in addition to gratitude and contentment. If it sounds like a dull life, then probably both of us should have been watching television instead.

The early heat brought the snakes out of hibernation and into the shrubbery and the flower beds. We were always coming across them sunning themselves on the patio and coiled against the supporting posts of the portal. On a rare morning when Jody was sleeping in I discovered an old rattler, over five feet long and as big around as my thigh at the middle, dozing under a chaise longue when I came outside to drink a cup of coffee. I kicked the chair and he oiled slowly from beneath it, testing with his tongue ahead of himself and swaying his dusty head from side to side. A garden rake stood against the house wall. I went for it and hazed him gently across the warming flagstone.

"Get along now," I told the snake. "I don't want you making unnecessary trouble in this place. It's a good life here and I won't stand for anything messing it up."

His yellow eyes glinted as he went in thick doubling and redoubling curves toward the grass.

"Keep going" I said, "and for as long as you behave yourself and don't come around here making mischief I won't hurt you. You can take that as a promise. You understand?"

He slipped off the edge of the patio and into the long grass beyond the fence and I returned the rake to its place against the wall. I saw him several times again that spring, never on the patio or anywhere very close to the house.

In the weeks before we took the cattle up to the hills Dago O'Grady spent much of his time on a bench above the side canyon south of the ranch, dragging together the skeletons of the piñon pines he'd chained two years before and firing them in piles. By now the reddish-brown boughs were volatile as kerosene. Several days out of the week the thick blue smoke rose in nearly straight columns into a sky of a deeper blue, paling through shades of gray before thinning away in the glare of the spring sun overhead. Each day around noon the columns tilted suddenly, bulged, and toppled to the east as the afternoon winds hit them, then diminished sharply when Dago damped the fires. On an afternoon in the second week the columns instead of dying back continued rolling higher and thicker in separating coils that flattened finally to lay a pall of smoke over the bench, a lake of smoke extending almost to the base of the mountains. Jody stepped out of the house to view the smoke from the back yard. Then she tried paging Dago on the cell phone. "Damn it," she exclaimed, "I've told him a hundred times to carry the phone with him when he leaves the truck. You can bet he's packing iron though. Would you drive up there, Jeb, and tell him to damp those fires immediately? If the forest gestapo were to see that they'd snatch my burn permit, pronto."

I eased the truck through her flock of prize bantam chickens, taking care not to flatten any of them, and across the ford south of the house. The water still ran high and fast in the creek, rising into the wheel wells and soaking the brakes. I drove slow for a mile in the sandy road while I pumped them dry. The canyon floor, stretching wide at the mouth, was green with the new spring grasses and the freshened prickly pear. Desert flowers bloomed between the spaced sage bushes: Indian paintbrush, purple gentian, something egg-yellow and sticky looking I didn't know the name of. The road followed in the dry wash a few miles before climbing out and switchbacking through sandstone rubble up to the bench. Ahead a couple of miles still Dago's inferno continued to send billows of smoke against the mountain front. I stepped on the accelerator pedal and ran a golden eagle off the carcass of a yearling deer it had been feeding on. In the tow mirror I watched as he climbed out over the abyss of the canyon, circled back, and lighted on the carcass again.

Dago O'Grady sat at a distance from his truck on a red jerry can, observing the nearest fire. He raised his hand as if to wave as I drove up and pulled his hat brim over his eyes. I set the parking brake and climbed out of the truck.

"Morning, Dago."

"Afternoon."

"Jody tried calling you on the cell phone."

"Forgot it, I guess, this mornin when I was leavin the house."

The flames were bent nearly parallel with the ground and overhead the smoke was thick with sparks.

"I've been asked to request you to damp the fires down. Wind's up," I added, in case he hadn't noticed.

"Don't she know we're puttin cows up here in less'n a week?

"I would assume she does. They're her cows."

He rose suddenly and stood scowling at the fire.

"Hell," O'Grady said contemptuously, "There ain't no danger in it."

"If you had the cell phone with you, you could call and discuss it with her."

O'Grady lifted the jerry can and held it a little forward as he stared longingly into the fire. "They's another ex-tinguisher in back of the truck," he said finally.

We damped the fires and cleared the ground surrounding them of duff and twigs. I brought my canteen from the pickup and offered it to him.

"Water?"

O'Grady gave the canteen a suspicious look before accepting it and taking a long drink. He wiped his mouth on his sleeve and handed it back.

"I need to be getting back," I said.

"To where? Wyomin?"

"Home," I told him.

His eyes burned holes in the back of my head as I walked to the truck. The man resented me—more accurately, he resented my presence on the Bar Nun Ranch—and I hadn't been able yet to figure why, not that I cared a tart's last trick. I steered a tight circle around a boulder and into the single-track without looking back. The eagle flew up from the dead deer beside the road and the lake of smoke, pushed by the wind, had started to spread around the mountain. No one patrolling out here for the Bureau of Land Management or the Forest Service could miss seeing it.

---

The heat came too soon again in early May. The creek dried up except for a trickle meandering between pools of water, the snow vanished from the mountains, and on the desert the surface water disappeared except in the most protected places. The sun, rising well north of the mountains, poured itself into the canyon each morning, flooding it with a terrific heat.

We were at the barns well before five now to finish the chores in the cool dawn and in bed an hour past sunset, taking with us a bottle of chilled wine and two glasses. The coolness came quickly after the sun was down and we would lie in bed with the swamp cooler shut off and the casement windows pushed out, drinking wine and listening to the sounds of crickets in the flower beds, the tree frogs in the cottonwoods along the dried-up creek, and the coyotes having hysterics in the foothills. We would talk for a while, going over the day and enjoying the wine until it was no longer cold, and then put out the lights and enjoy each other beneath the single sheet. Afterward we slept close and well until just before first light, when I went to the kitchen to start the coffee pot and Jody showered. Being friends in addition to the other thing we had got beyond the ecstasy and settled down to being happy—not the sort of happiness that makes you fear an unexpected diagnosis of cancer but happiness of the serene kind, the kind that comes from a sense of the wholeness, the absolute rightness, of it all. The monsoon season was more than a month off still and the weather, in spite of the heat, continued perfect. Except for the drought we had no worries, and no bad thoughts at all to think.

Jody worked the show horse three-quarters of an hour daily in the walled arena beside the house. Cortez knew nothing about cows and gave every sign of not wanting to know anything. Jody said Peruvian Pasos and Pasos Finos were becoming very popular in the Southwestern United States; she was considering establishing a bloodline of her own and realizing a profit on it. When I failed to light up like a Christmas angel at the idea she took me down to the stables for a test drive. The rotating shoulder blades and the forelegs paddling sideways were, if anything, more disconcerting from the saddle than when viewed from the ground, but she had been right about the smoothgaitedness. The comparison with the land tortoise miffed her at first but it also amused her, and pretty soon she was using it herself to the point where Tortuga became the horse's nickname, outside of his hearing. Not, it seemed to me, that he gave a damn. I accompanied them when she showed. By the Fourth of July the three of us had traveled some thousands of miles together into Colorado, Arizona, and New Mexico, sharing, Jody and I, the bunk bed in the horse trailer and later, when we became tired of sleeping on top of each other, renting a motel room while Tortuga boarded at a local stables. Dago O'Grady in our absence, with the help of seasonal Navajos hired from Tohatchi, New Mexico, on the reservation, kept the home fires burning. Though Jody insisted that Dago was entirely responsible, after two or three days away from the Bar Nun she seemed eager to be getting home again, and I was usually ready myself. When you've spent as many years of your life wandering as I have, just being on the road doesn't seem like a world cruise anymore.

There are no holidays in the ranching business and almost no vacations either. Some days you find ways to enjoy the work a little more than other days, and always you're on the lookout for the opportunity to put business together with pleasure. On a morning before or after Memorial Day Jody packed a picnic dinner and a magnum bottle of red wine and we drove into the mountains to supply Whitey up in sheep camp and have a look at the cattle ponds. I drove slowly in the dirt track, stopping now and then to allow Jody to glass for stragglers and measure the height of the grasses after the cattle had been through. The Bar Nun's grazing lease out here went until July first, but she was already worrying the cows might have to come off well before then on account of the drought.

Sheep camp was in a park among aspen, above the black timber. In the high country the white trunks surmounted by trembling green leaves rose straight into the blue sky from a carpet of arrowleaf balsam flowering yellow on the moist purple ground. The musky odor of balsam mixed with the rank one of the sheep milling through the trees and across the park, tended by the dogs. Whitey's old horse, under saddle and with the bridle and reins hanging from the saddle horn, stood tied off to the hay wagon. It turned to look over its shoulder at the truck grinding uphill in the steep trail, and then away. Blue smoke trailed from the wired chimney in the roof of the herder's wagon. I stopped a few feet from the wagon and Jody and I began taking boxes of canned goods from the truck bed. The horse, showing a renewed interest in the supply operation, looked around again and nickered. Everything was unloaded on the ground in front of the wagon when the wagon door opened and Whitey peered out. He had on antique chaps over torn blue jeans and his beard showed very white against the front of his purple shirt.

"Hello Whitey."

"'Lo."

"You didn't hear us drive up?"

He cupped a hand behind one ear.

"What?"

He held a blackened pipe between his teeth and, in the other hand, a book.

"Where do you want these supplies to go?"

Whitey took the hand away from his ear.

"Bring em on in here."

"Okay, boss," I told him.

He stood away from the door while we carried the boxes in. There wasn't room enough in the wagon for everything we had brought. We set the rest of the supplies in the balsam plants underneath the wagon and covered them with a tarpaulin to keep the rain from getting in, if there ever was any rain.

"How are you, Whitey?"

"Okay."

"Getting lonely for you up here yet?"

"Nope."

"What are you reading?"

"Book about me."

Twenty years ago when he was still on the rodeo circuit a journalist from Denver had interviewed him for a book he was writing called *The Last Cowboys*. When the book was eventually published the author sent Whitey a copy inscribed with his signature and a page notation to look up. All that had been saved from the one-hour interview was a paragraph where Whitey, expressing contempt for animal rights activists back East, proposed that they be traded to the ayatollah for the American hostages in Iran. Jacketless and rain-spotted, its pages dog-eared, thumb-worn, and already yellowing, the book was the sole worldly possession, beyond his horse, his rifle, and the cracked and stiffened chaps, that the old man showed any attachment to.

"Is that the only book you ever read in your life, Whitey?"

"I don't remember."

He took his finger from the pages and laid the book carefully on top of the bunk bed.

Whitey gave us what was left of the coffee he had been keeping warm on the wood stove. The coffee was mostly grounds, strong enough to tan leather and tasting like sheep dip. Obviously he was hoping we would keep company with him a while, but Jody was impatient to investigate the cattle ponds. As we were going he took a bundle of pelts tied up with rawhide from under the bed and handed them to her.

"The bounty on coyotes isn't much these days, Whitey."

"Hold onto em till it goes up again then."

Jody accepted the pelts with a sick expression and we went outside and got in the truck. Whitey stood watching from the wagon door as we drove off down the mountain. The pelts between us on the seat smelled terrible.

"What's he bother skinning out the damn coyotes for?" I asked.

"They're supposed to be his whiskey money next fall."

"If he makes a fair trade the whiskey's going to be pretty terrible."

It was midafternoon when we reached the ponds, bulldozed depressions half-filled with stale red water impounded behind earthen cofferdams. The ponds were dug in a series of connecting parks among juniper forests overlooked by turrets and spires of purple sandstone eroded to fantastical shapes. Dusty and hot from driving at ten miles an hour with the windows down, we spent the rest of the afternoon checking the dams. Jody's face and her bare throat were rimed with salt from the evaporated perspiration.

"They should hold through next spring at the very least, don't you think?"

"They better."

"Unless we have an unusually wet winter this year."

"It isn't going to be a wet winter."

"How do you know?"

"The yellowjackets are building their nests close to the ground this year."

"Last year they built them high up and we still didn't get any snow to speak of."

"Ask the weather man then."

"I will not. They're all environmentalist stooges."

"Environmentalist" was the worst thing Jody could think to say about a person. Having a fairly wide green streak myself I prefer to keep to the center of the road, but it's no good trying to argue it with ranchers. Loving someone is being able to hold your tongue about the one thing in a hundred you disagree on. A lot of folks don't seem up to it, though.

Six miles ahead a trail branching from the main track went west across the meadow toward a ragged line of trees. Beyond the meadow the forest pressed close against the trail on both sides. The trees grew thickly but so low you could look above them to the horizon where the sun was descending through shades of purple, gold, and copper. Pine boughs dragged on the truck doors and Jody drew her elbow in through the window. The trees thinned and then we were beyond the forest, riding on caprock that ended abruptly thirty yards ahead. I stopped the truck and looked at her.

"Follow along the rim and I'll tell you when to stop."

She called halt at a stricken pine tree leaning from a fracture in the rimrock and we got out and unloaded the picnic boxes.

"I must look a mess, Jody said.

"Yes ma'am. You do."

"You're no Beau Brummel yourself. We need to wash up before we eat."

"We can't wash. I didn't bring the water barrel."

"We don't need the water barrel. Come on. I'm going to show you something."

"What are you going to show me?"

"Something you'll like. Don't sound so apprehensive."

"I'm not apprehensive. I just don't like to be surprised."

Jody led me to the cliff edge and pointed.

"Look down there."

The cliff formed the headwall of a narrow box canyon arranged in levels of opposing terraces with box elder, scrub oak, and ponderosa pine growing close against the sheer rock walls. The canyon, cutting raggedly west, became lost in the maze of red and purple slickrock, swales and domes of yellow and white sandstone, and the wilderness of wild forms carved from the level plateau stretching along the horizon.

"Where?"

"Down there—a little to the right of that bush. See it?"

"I don't see anything."

"It doesn't show very well from up here. You can see better from the ledge."

"What ledge?"

"The one just below us."

"You're going to climb down *there*?"

"I am," she said, "and you are too."

A game trail several inches wide, scored with the tracks of deer and small rodents, descended ahead of us, a scratch on the cliff face.

"You go ahead," Jody suggested, "and I'll follow you."

Carefully setting one boot ahead of the other I started down, clutching at small bushes and rock outcrops.

"You're off the trail!" Jody called when I had descended fifty or sixty feet.

I looked up thoughtlessly, out and down—and after that I didn't look again but held my eyes on the faint, almost illusory trace beneath my shuffling boots. Jody was behind me somewhere, dainty and surefooted as a desert pig. Love can be downhill work sometimes, especially in cowboy boots. The polished leather soles slid and slipped on the loose gravel. I caught hold of a bush growing from a fissure above my head and swung outward like a window cleaner hanging from a skyscraper as my feet searched to recover the firm ground.

"Jeb!" Jody cried, "be careful!"

I had a sickening view of treetops revolving slowly on the canyon floor a thousand feet below before I found the trail again and let go the bush, which snapped back with a cracking sound.

"Go on," Jody urged. "Just a few more yards and you'll be there."

She caught up on the edge of the tinaja. Vaulted by the sweating rock and holding water to a depth of about two feet it was a natural bath tub sunk in the floor of a shallow cave. Jody pushed forward from behind, unfastening her jeans at the waist and beginning to unbutton her blouse. She shucked her clothes on the stone floor and sat on the edge of the basin with her white legs in the water.

"It's delicious," she said, and slipped all the way in.

When I joined her in the pool she splashed water over my head and rubbed my shoulders and back with a vigorous circular motion. I worked her over the same way and she ducked her head below the surface of the water and came up after nearly half a minute blowing, laughing, and shaking her hair out. She looked very lovely, her eyes green behind the darkened fringe of her wet hair, and I reached for her and kissed her and held her hard against me and kissed her again while we relaxed together in the water which felt cool and fresh, infinitely pleasant. The waves made a plashing sound within the echoing chamber of the cave. I let her go finally and lay back with my shoulders fitted to the curving edge of the tinaja while Jody traced my collarbone with the tip of one finger.

"You're awfully *white* for a New Mexican," she said.

"If you're from southern New Mexico and you're not Spanish, Mexican, or Indian, you're a blue-eyed, red-blond, peckerwood redneck like me."

"I'm sorry."

"After the Civil War, the Federal troops and the Yankee carpetbaggers from the North chased Southerners like my family west of the Mississippi and the Red Rivers. We kept going and moved in on the Mexicans and Indians beyond the Pecos."

"You know a lot about history, don't you?"

"Only what I learned from my father—and his father. They read more than most college graduates."

"What is it about people who don't know their history…?"

"Are condemned to repeat it. And the people who do know history are condemned to foresee it." An even more terrifying idea, when you think about it.

"I wish we'd thought to bring the wine with us," Jody said.

"I had my hands plenty full as it was getting down, thank you."

"And I was thinking you'd do anything for me, Jeb."

"Anything is a big word, my dear."

She stepped up from the basin and stood erect under the overhang, her wet body gleaming like bronze in the red light of the setting sun.

"I'm almost dry already," she said. "I don't need a towel."

Jody combed her hair out straight and we pulled our clothes on. I picked up one boot and looked at it. Then I reached for the other.

"I'm carrying these up."

"If you think it will make it easier for you. Don't step on a prickly pear."

While she unpacked supper I gathered wood from the juniper forest and built a fire on the caprock at the edge of the cliff. When it was burning well I brought the magnum of wine from the picnic box and drew the cork. The wine was dry as the desert air, fragrant as juniper smoke. I poured two tin cups full and passed one of them to Jody.

"Thank you," she said. "You smell somewhat better than you did an hour ago."

"You always smell good."

"You're a liar. But always such a gentleman."

We drank the wine and I filled the cups again. Jody uncovered the food and served supper. She had brought cold lamb, pinto beans in gravy, potato salad, and a loaf of French bread she had wrapped in foil to warm on the coals. Sitting on folding camp stools to eat, our feet braced on the bare rock, we held the sagging paper plates between our knees, taking care not to spill any of the wine. When we were through eating I built the fire back and set the pot to boil for coffee. I poured the last of the magnum bottle and we carried the cups to the cliff edge and sat with our legs hanging over while we waited for the water to boil. The track of the vanished sun was still bright in the sky, the evening star gleamed, and a cool breeze sprang up, fanning the fire until I heard the sparks shoot up to meet the falling darkness.

Jody placed her hand on my knee.

"I don't suppose you thought to bring your harmonica."

"Of course I did."

"Really?"

"I'll get it from the truck."

She lay on the rock with her head in my lap while I played "The Meeting of the Waters," one of the most beautiful songs I know, and "The Bard of Armagh," which made her cry. I played "Jeannie with the Light Brown Hair" and "Sweetly She Sleeps, My Alice Fair," also by Foster, and then Jody wanted "Kathleen Mavourneen."

"I want to hear the words," she said.

"I'll sing them for you then, if you'll get off my diaphragm first."

You can't handle "Kathleen Mavourneen" from a sitting position; a song like that takes guts to sing. I stood up, blew B-flat on the harmonica, and began.

Kathleen Mavourneen! the grey dawn is breaking,
The horn of the hunter is heard on the hill;
The lark from her light wing the bright dew is shaking,
Kathleen Mavourneen! what, slumb'ring still?

O, hast thou forgotten how soon we must sever?
Oh, hast thou forgotten this day we must part?
It may be for years, and it may be forever;
Oh, why art thou silent, thou voice of my heart?

It may be for years, and it may be forever;
Then why art thou silent, Kathleen Mavourneen?

"You sing that so beautifully," Jody said.

"It's too beautiful a song to spoil. And too beautiful a night."

"Do we have any wine left?"

"It's all gone. Jeb Stuart sang that song the morning he was killed at Yellow Tavern."

"He must have been a very brave man, General Stuart. Were you really related to him?"

"I don't think so."

"Did you have any close calls when you worked as a range detective?"

"One fairly close one, anyway."

Her head was in my lap again.

"Tell me."

"I was investigating the disappearance of some cattle from a ranch in Elko, Nevada. They were being cut out of the herd by a rider from Wyoming who was shipping them home to his ranch, where his wife and her mother would alter the brands and turn them out with their own herds. The girl knew I was onto them."

"What happened?"

"We rode out together to have a look at the herd. She was getting ready to shoot me when the brand inspector showed up."

"How did you know she was going to shoot you?"

"I just knew it."

"You're a brave man, aren't you, Jeb Ryder?"

"As brave as I have to be. Bravery is just ignoring feelings that ought to be ignored."

"I love you so for being brave. You *would* do anything for me—wouldn't you, Jeb?"

"I'd do my best, anyway."

"I know it, darling," Jody said.

---

For the Fourth of July Jody and I pulled Tortuga over to Cortez, Colorado where he was entered in the show there. We left the ranch at a little before eight in the morning when the sun was burning the dew from the grass and the canyon smelled of warming rock and the wet alfalfa. She had on black jeans that fitted her like pantyhose, the silver concho belt I had bought for her in Durango, and a green silk shirt. Her straw-colored hair was pulled back and fastened with a black ribbon at the nape and a new straw hat came down over one eye like a long wink. From behind the steering wheel Jody leaned across the truck seat, took the hair at the back of my neck between her fingers, and pulled gently.

"Your hair's growing out again behind," she said. "Otherwise you look very handsome this morning."

Then she kissed me and started the engine.

Tortuga ran the hundred miles to Cortez in place, causing the truck to ride as if there was water in the gas line or the fuel pump was about to go. We climbed out of the canyons onto the bench and turned east at Monticello across the Great Sage Plain with the sun in our eyes, and in the summer haze above the rolling pinto bean fields and cedar forests. At Dove Creek, birds roosted away from the heat in the tops of the grain elevators standing over the quiet town where only the taverns and package stores and a couple of gas stations were open for business.

Celebrating the Fourth is like admiring photographs of an aging beauty queen before she became a courtesan and began to put on weight. In Cortez they had flags suspended from the iron lamp posts and there was a serious traffic jam along the main street. Tour buses going to Mesa Verde waited at the stoplights and the street was crowded with tourists crossing from one side to the other to visit the shops and restaurants. Tourists of every age were dressed in short-pants, T-shirts, and sneakers with ankle socks as if it was some kind of uniform, and quite a few of them wore fanny packs under their stomachs. Every summer now is a kind of invasion, and in the winter time there are the skiers. Someday I'm going to run off and live with the Indians.

"Look at all the kangaroos," I said.

"You know— that's *exactly* what they look like, kangaroos."

"Kangaroos with weak legs."

"Kangaroos with no legs at all."

We followed the secondary streets back to the highway and drove to the showgrounds east of town. The parking area was already crowded. Good-looking girls exercising their horses raised clouds of dust outside the arena and Jody drove carefully to avoid the animals being worked around by their owners as they stood snubbed beside the trailers. We unloaded Tortuga away from the crowd where the sagebrush began, and while Jody curried him down I brought him a drink from the water barrel and began fitting the Powder River panels together. Before I had the pen finished Jody was warming the horse up in an open field beyond the parking lot. Blue smoke drifting over from the concession stands carried the smells of hotdogs, hamburgers, and fry bread.

"We're on our way over to the arena now," Jody said as she rode up.

"I'll be along when I get the pen together."

"Hurry, then. And don't forget the videocam."

The video camera was the closest thing there was to a sore point between us. I detest cameras generally, video-cameras in particular. Cameras encourage people to forget what it was they were supposed to be looking at, while video-cameras protect them from seeing anything at all. My previous effort at taping an equine event had produced an hour-long docudrama whose highlights included a Big Mac box tacking about on the ground under a stiff breeze, the open beer can I held in my left hand, and finally—for three or four uninterrupted minutes—my shirted armpit. Jody had given me careful instruction since then, so I was expected to do better this morning. When I had the panels in place finally I took the video-camera from the truck, walked over to the stands, and climbed to the top bench for a clear view of the arena. The painted board, blistered by the sun, was already uncomfortably warm. I spread my bandana handkerchief on it and sat looking away to the mountains over in Colorado. The mountains were streaked with snow still, the thin sky above them was pale and cold-looking, and suddenly, for the first time in years, I missed the Southwest—the real Southwest—with its blue piñon-juniper forests, yucca flats, sandstorms, and the terrible dry heat. A few people, not many, were taking seats lower down in the stands. Peruvian Paso classes are a lot like amateur theatrics, attended mostly by friends and relatives of the performers. Just beyond the entrance gate Jody sat Tortuga proudly, the two of them looking magnificent. The horse had been fired a few minutes before by the mares but she had managed to get him relatively calm again. I settled the video-camera on my right shoulder and attempted to hold them in focus as they maneuvered in the arena with the other contestants, the sleek horsehair coats and elaborate saddles ornamented with Spanish American silver shining under the hot sun. When they halted the judge announced, and Jody and Tortuga had won first place. I climbed down from the stands and met them at the exit. Jody looked exultant while the horse, wearing the blue ribbon against his cheek, appeared bored.

"His first win," Jody said. "Aren't you just so proud of us both, Jeb?"

I gave her thigh a squeeze and slapped the glossy neck.

"Good old Tortuga."

"He's not Tortuga, he's a Spanish grandee. A conquistador."

"I thought he was named for the town," I told her.

A handsome woman, another of the contestants, with bright black eyes and a thin nose, wearing her black hair in a thick braid down her back, smiled as she rode past on a fine-looking gray with a red ribbon pinned on the cheek strap.

"She's Indian," I said when the woman was out of hearing.

"You've seen Indians before, haven't you?"

"Not on one of these fancy land tortoises. I thought the Indians had better sense."

"She has plenty of sense. Probably she drives a newer model truck than you do, too."

Jody unsaddled the horse, brushed him, and put him into the Powder River pen. We sat together on the dropped tailgate of the truck to eat the lunch she had brought and afterward felt sleepy from the sun and the wine we had drunk.

"I'm ready for a nap," Jody suggested.

"We could go ahead and check into the motel now."

"I wouldn't want to leave Cortez alone here in the pen."

"We can drive by the stables and drop him there, if you wish."

"His next class is at three o'clock. That's only two hours from now."

"You brought the padlock, didn't you?"

"A lot of good that would do if someone wanted him badly enough."

"He'll be all right for a couple of hours. I'll leave the radio going in the dressing room."

"Let's go then. I really could use a nap."

At the motel they gave us a room on the second floor where the housekeeping carts stood along the row of open doors around the balcony while the maids finished making up inside. Jody hung the Do Not Disturb sign on the outside handle of the door and drew the curtains. Her body in the half-light looked pale and diffuse as if I was seeing her underwater.

"You don't have a spare ounce of flesh anywhere."

"Am I too skinny, do you think?"

"Of course you're not too skinny."

"Perhaps someday I'll want you to get me fat. If I'm ever going to have a child it will have to be soon now. But not too soon, darling. I have enough to do at this point in my life just keeping the Bar Nun safe from the farm credit agent."

We slept for an hour and a half and dressed in the airconditioned chill.

"I'm glad we don't have to drive home tonight," Jody said. "I want to eat a big dinner and go dancing. Will you take me out dancing, Jeb? I want to have fun, and get drunk."

When we left the motel the glaring heat seemed to rise up from the ground. The No Vacancy sign out front had been switched on and the traffic was heavy in both directions along the thoroughfare. Getting back to the show grounds took time on account of the cars slowing to turn out at the fast food joints and the Indian jewelry stores. By the time we arrived there Jody's face under the straw hat was damp with perspiration and she looked exasperated. The kangaroos wandered everywhere, patting the horses and trying to offer them things to eat.

"Oh *damn*!" she exclaimed as we approached the trailer.

Two people, a man and a boy about sixteen, stood with Tortuga inside the pen. The boy had one hand on the horse's withers and the other on his chest, while the man stood back several paces, holding his chin in his hand to observe the horse. Both of them were Indians.

"What do they think they're *doing*?" Jody cried.

"You there," I shouted, "come away from that horse!"

The Indians looked at us, and at each other. Then, moving deliberately, they climbed over the top of the pen and began to walk slowly away without having said a word.

"What's the big interest in the horse?" I called after them.

The man stopped and turned about, while the boy kept walking. The kid wore short-pants and had his cap on backwards, like any American teenager.

"Nice horse," he said. "Just looking."

"Well, you do your looking from the outside, please. His owner doesn't want anyone in the pen with him. He's a stallion. If he was to kick you, she'd be the one held responsible."

The Indian faced me, deadpan behind mirror sunglasses. Even without the glasses his eyes would be as expressionless as the rest of his face, which was small and rather narrow for a Navajo.

"Horse looks perfectly gentle to me," he said.

He turned on his heel and walked away after the boy, not hurrying.

"What gall," Jody said as she got out of the truck.

"Probably they were just curious. They never saw anything like Tortuga before."

"He doesn't look that different from any other horse when he's standing still."

"Who knows what's different to an Indian?"

"Poor Cortez," she said, rubbing the long face. "He took his first blue ribbon and now he's like any other celebrity—his fans won't leave him in peace anymore."

She refused to leave the horse by himself in the pen and I went alone to watch Dago O'Grady ride in a bronc-busting event. The bronc-riding was interrupted when a cowboy from the Bronx got stepped on and had to be removed from the arena by ambulance after receiving emergency medical treatment. Dago himself came off well before the buzzer sounded. I walked around to the chutes and found him seated on a step of the stairs going up to the announcer's box, punching up the crown of his old felt hat with his fist.

"The New Yorker's horse was Number 32," Dago said.

"Was it?"

"I drew Number 31."

"You were lucky."

"Naw," Dago told me, "I'd of busted that horse, all right. I'd of ridden him to the buzzer and past it."

"Maybe you'll get lucky again and draw him yourself tomorrow," I suggested, and watched as the sarcasm flew over his head like a hat in a windstorm.

Jody had the pen apart and stacked when I got back. While she loaded the horse I mounted the panels on the trailer and then we drove to the boarding stables. The stables were under a mile from the showgrounds within sight of the highway. For twenty dollars a night you had a clean dry pen, a half-bale of alfalfa hay, and a can of sweet grain. Jody led Tortuga into one of the corner pens, slipped the halter, and kissed him on the nose. "¡Hasta luego!" she told him.

We showered at the motel and had a drink from the bottle of whiskey I had brought along. Then we dressed in fresh clothes. Jody asked me to fasten the buttons up the back of her blouse. I did up the buttons, then undid them all the way down again and set my mouth on her bare shoulder.

"What are you doing, Jeb?" she asked.

"Let's not go out tonight."

"But I'm hungry. Aren't you?"

"Very hungry. We can order out later and eat. Afterward."

"Absolutely not. We're going to meet Dago downtown and have a wonderful supper and watch the fireworks. And then you're going to take me dancing."

"A trained bear looks better than I do on the dance floor."

"Fake it then. That's what other men do."

We ate at Nero's because Jody said they served real Italian food there. Dago O'Grady was waiting for us at the bar as we arrived, drinking Jack Daniels on the rocks and trying to make time with the barmaid. While the waitress was still taking our drink order Dago picked up the menu and opened it.

"I can't eat this wop food," Dago told her. "Can I get just a steak here?"

"Have another drink first, Dago," Jody told him. "Jeb and I are going to have one, maybe two drinks before we even think about eating, the way civilized people do."

He sat looking like the Dying Gaul as we drank, and ignored our conversation. The wide brim of his hat kept brushing the head of the woman seated behind him until she rose and changed her place at the table, giving Dago a killing look as she did it. Finally we ordered supper. I had veal piccata, Jody had spaghetti with pesto sauce and pine nuts, and Dago ate the twenty-four-ounce steak with fried potatoes and onions. We were sitting afterward over coffee and brandy when a party of German tourists dressed like Hopalong Cassidy sat at the table next to ours and one of the men asked Dago if he had ever been down into the Grand Canyon.

"Hell, no," Dago told him. "What would I ever want to do a thing like that for?"

I paid for the three of us and we left the restaurant. People standing in the vestibule, waiting for a table, stepped aside for us as we passed. Obviously Cortez had been what they call discovered since I saw it first thirty years ago. Outdoors it was warm still and the sky behind Ute Mountain had a wash of color in it. Jody put her arm through mine and leaned into me as we went around the corner to the truck, followed by Dago. Her breath smelled of whiskey and she was already a little drunk.

We drove out to the fairgrounds with Dago on the end of the bench seat and Jody squeezed in between us on top of the floor shift. Men stood in the road at the entrance to the field swinging flashlights in wide descending arcs like trainmen to direct the traffic. I found a parking place on a height of ground a little above the field and we sat in the truck with the lights switched off, passing a bottle of schnapps between us in the darkness. The first rocket to burst caught Jody with her head thrown back and her lips around the long neck of the bottle. Her face faded into shadow as petals of fire drifted down and then there was a thud and whiz before the second clap of sound, the glare, and the colored lights raining out of the black sky.

"That one was a beauty," Jody said.

One rocket followed another up and burst, singly at first, then in clusters, the oriental firestorm building to a climax above the invisible desert that had been home to the mysterious Anasazi and later roamed by the more or less peaceable Utes before being conquered by bearded invaders wearing steel suits and riding horses. Now the conquistadores too were gone and we were celebrating the end of a story growing out of the jungles of Yucatan and the darkness of unrecorded time—if it was the end. I felt Jody's hand on my knee and a violent flash of light revealed Dago O'Grady, his face a livid green, scowling ahead through the windshield.

"Look, how lovely!" Jody exclaimed. "Is that normal?" she added in a doubtful voice as a spear of white light broadened suddenly at its base and then exploded into a mushroom cloud of orange and yellow fire.

"The fire department just blowed theirselves up," Dago announced in a satisfied voice.

I pressed the truck through the rubberneckers and got away from the field before the emergency vehicles arrived. The main stockpile had failed to go up and already the flames were subsiding. In town I found space on a side street around the corner from the bar and parked there.

"I'll leave you folks here and get on back to the motel," Dago said.

"Don't be silly," Jody told him. "We appreciate your company, Dago. Besides, it's only just past eleven."

A drugstore cowboy seated on a stool inside the door took fifteen dollars apiece from us before stamping the backs of our hands with ultraviolet ink. The bar was the forward part of a much larger room running from the street all the way to the alley behind the building. We worked past it through the crowd to a table beneath the stage at the back of the room where the Western swing band was taking a break. I pulled Jody's chair out for her and she took a seat at the table between Dago and me. The band was three men dressed in cowboy clothes and a girl in a long calico dress wearing her long mahogany hair piled on her head. The girl was extremely pretty. Dago said something I couldn't hear to her from the floor but she gave him a blank stare and turned away again to her colleagues. When the waitress came with the drinks Jody took her purse out and paid for them. She was still wearing the straw hat over one eye in a sort of Western imitation of Veronica Lake. All the men at the tables around us were looking at her.

"They're a really great band," Jody said. "The girl plays a mean fiddle."

"That's nice of her. But not really necessary."

"You'd love to take that long hair down, wouldn't you? One pin after the other."

"She wouldn't need to wear a thing else."

"You're not trying to make me jealous, are you?"

"It might keep you from noticing I have two left feet."

Jody leaned to brush my cheek with her mouth.

"It doesn't matter to me how you dance. You do everything else so marvelously well. For me, you're absolutely the perfect man."

Out on the dance floor couples were dancing to rock music being disc-jockeyed by the bartender. The music on top of the human roar made it difficult to hear what anyone was saying and I was beginning to wish we were out of here already and home in bed, which is the only kind of dancing I ever cared about. The musicians took their positions on the stage finally and the bartender killed the rock music. In addition to the fiddle were an accordion and the two acoustic guitars. While the lead singer introduced the set I went to the bar for another round of drinks. Jody and O'Grady were talking with their heads close together as I returned to the table, but he shut up before I got back there. Jody acted tired and had circles under her eyes. She closed them when the band started playing and swayed her shoulders in time to the music while Dago drew up an empty chair with the toe of one boot and rested his crossed heels on the seat. At the beginning of the third number Jody put her face against mine.

"Will you dance this one with me?" she requested.

She took me by the hand and led me onto the dance floor among the swirling, dipping couples.

"This is an easy one," Jody said as I felt for her waist. " We practiced this step over Memorial Day—remember?"

A ladies' man I knew in the service used to say that dancing is the way to a woman's heart, and I have been afraid ever since he might be right. We started off together and I was just beginning to feel the rhythm, a little, when the music stopped.

"You're doing beautifully," Jody encouraged.

The swing band really was wonderful and I could have sat comfortably at the table all night, drinking scotch and listening to—and watching—that girl play the fiddle. They began a new number and Jody led me patiently through a series of complicated calisthenics I didn't know from a Highland Fling or a Watusi war dance.

"I told you you really were a dancer, didn't I?" she demanded when the torture ended finally. "Do you mind if we sit down for a minute? It's awfully hot and stuffy under these lights."

We found Dago O'Grady, still with his boots up, behind a fresh drink. "I didn't know if you folks was wantin another," he said, "so I didn't order."

"There's plenty of single women here tonight," Jody told him. "Why don't you take one of them out on the floor?"

He looked glum. "I don't feel like dancin."

"The trouble with you is, you need to be married. We're all of us too old to have to break the ice again every night."

Dago took a long drink of the whiskey and set the glass down hard on the table.

"Guy I used to know in Vegas," he said. "Had all the money in the world, millions and millions of dollars. Spent his summers on a ranch up in Montana, near Bozeman. Ever weekend he used to send a Lear jet to bring a call girl out from Vegas. Cost several thousand bucks for the plane, another couple thousand for the girl. Most beautiful girls in the world. Guy said to me one time, says, 'Dago, I don't pay these girls to come out here. I pay em to leave.'"

Jody and I danced again and it went better this time. The guitars strummed rocking on their heels, the accordion swayed from side to side crunching out the notes, and the fiddle sawed the air with her elbow and tapped the toe of her little black boot peeking out from under the flouncing hem of her skirt. The girl's face glistened with perspiration under the hot lights as her hair began to come apart behind her ears. Jody's step slowed and she felt heavy in my arms.

"Let's go sit," she suggested. "I need to rest again."

I offered to buy her another drink but she refused it. Jody drank the melted ice water at the bottom of the glass and I gave her a look.

"Yes," she agreed, "I suppose we should go."

Then she turned to Dago.

"Dance this last one with me, Dago, before they finish the set."

Jody snatched the straw hat from her head and dropped it on its crown at the center of the table among the empty glasses. She did not look wilted anymore but erect and vibrant. She led Dago onto the dance floor, faced him, and offered him her hand. They were off on the downbeat, swinging, spinning, reeling, and bowing among the other swaying couples. Like a fine horse and rider or a loving couple joined in love they moved as a single body, taking possession of the floor until the fiddler, inclining her body and leaning out above the fiddle, appeared to address herself and her music to them alone. The dance went on, a rush of music and motion and passion that felt as if it would continue forever until, suddenly, it stopped. For a long moment Jody and Dago stood facing one another—she the taller of the two by nearly a head—before she let go his hands and returned ahead of him to the table. The silk shirt stuck to her back between the shoulder blades, her green eyes were bright, and she was breathing hard. Jody swept up the hat from the table and clamped it down straight on the back of her head.

"Now we can go," she said.

We undressed quickly in the room and got in bed together under the top sheet with our bodies touching all the way down.

"Marry me," I said.

"I'm not certain I want to be married again, Jeb."

"You told me I was your perfect man."

"Well. I suppose you are."

"You asked me to be your stud. I want to have a child. Or two."

"We don't have to be married for you to give me a child."

It shocked me, of course. Ranchers are usually conservative people, the women especially. But this is 1999. So all I said was, "It would look a hell of a lot better on the pedigree."

"I don't know. It isn't something we have to decide right now tonight, is it?"

"I suppose not."

"I'm drunk," Jody said. "Do you still want to make love to a drunk woman, Jeb?"

"I always want to make love to you."

"Then go put something on. You're not going to be a stud tonight, anyway."

"All right."

"*Is* it all right?"

"I'm going," I said.

---

In the morning there was an overcast. Jody woke up with a headache and went into the shower without saying a word. She stayed under for twenty-five minutes and emerged with her hair wrapped in a towel and another one around her middle. Silently she dried and combed her hair, made up, and dressed while I watched the weather channel on the television. They were forecasting the return of hot weather later in the week, with severe afternoon and evening storms.

"Just in time for my second cutting," Jody remarked in a voice like deadly nightshade growing underneath a rock.

We went for breakfast downtown at a diner where the food was all grease and salt and the girls skidded the heated plates at you along the counter the way waitresses used to do in the movies back when I was a kid. The fried eggs and ham tasted wonderful and there wasn't a health faddist, jogger, or mountain biker in the place. The coffee was strong enough to galvanize a Basque sheepherder three weeks dead. When I suggested to Jody that she drink some she barked at me, saying that coffee only made her feel worse. She ate an enormous breakfast and drank a glass of soda water afterward.

The overcast had lowered until it appeared balanced on the cone of Ute Mountain and the day began to look like rain. I waited at the curb while Jody unlocked the passenger door and got up beside her in the truck.

"Are we ready to go for Tortuga now?"

"His name is Cortez—damn it!"

I could tell from the way she said it she was starting to feel better.

Every stoplight on the way out of town turned red when she looked at it. The traffic was awful and people crowded the crosswalks. Beyond the big new motels that had been cow pasture a couple of years ago we came up behind a tour bus grinding along and spraying exhaust. When Jody pulled out to pass the driver accelerated suddenly, forcing her to drop behind again.

"You dirty sonofabitch," she said.

The bus was ahead of us as we approached the turnoff, the stables plainly visible from the highway behind a row of Navajo willows. Jody pulled off and drove slowly up the dirt track. Dust clouds raised by the loading horses obscured the pens and the horse trailers backed around in the ranch yard. When we were still a hundred yards from the stables she stopped the truck and set the parking brake.

"I'm not getting myself into another traffic jam. Are you coming with me? Or would you prefer to wait here?"

"I'm coming with you, of course."

She took the halter and lead from the seat and we walked on together toward the pens. Many of them were vacant already behind the swung-out gates. The dust rising all around made it difficult to see anything clearly.

"Where is Cortez?" Jody asked suddenly, in a voice that sounded completely unlike her.

"He's there somewhere. You can't see the pen from here."

"I can see it," she insisted. "He isn't there, I tell you. He's gone."

"Are you certain?"

"Someone took him," Jody said.

She began running as I followed at a slower pace. The gate of the pen stood open and the fresh tracks of the horse led through it and mixed with the confusion of tracks beyond.

Jody said, "The Indians took him."

She looked as if she were going to cry.

"You used the padlock, didn't you?"

"Of course I did. The padlock's gone."

I put my arm around her shoulders.

"Maybe Dago pulled him home with his horse."

"Dago wouldn't do a thing like that without telling me. He doesn't have a key, anyway."

Jody threw the lead and halter in the dust and kicked them. Her face caved in and collapsed altogether, and then she did cry.

I embraced her, holding her rigid body hard against me until she grew calmer and relaxed somewhat in my arms. Then I put one hand beneath her chin and raised her ruined face to mine.

"I'll go after him for you and find him and bring him back, if it takes the rest of the summer to do it."

"You'll never find him. He doesn't even carry a brand."

"It's what I used to do for a living," I said, staring across her shoulder toward the dry desert cliffs. "You remember?"

---

The summer sun squeezed suddenly above the horizon and it kept coming, and coming, and coming. We got up in the chill of the desert night and drove for an hour before stopping for breakfast at a roadside café or an Indian trading post, and when we finished eating the sky was glaring blue and empty. The sky filled with small white clouds as noon approached. The clouds swelled and turned dark on the bottoms, and by midafternoon they had piled themselves into overbalancing columns of shining vapor, sharp against the ultraviolet sky. Electric stingers pricked the dark veils lowering beneath the advancing storms, and sometimes there was the smell of rain. But the rain evaporated between the clouds and the overshadowed plateaus and tablelands, leaving the arroyos and the deeper canyons dusty and dry, undisturbed except by the scouring winds.

We rode with the windows down and the canteen between us on the seat. Jody kept her hair pulled behind her ears and fastened in a bun above the nape. She wore loose-fitting sleeveless blouses instead of the denim shirts she used for work, and each morning she applied a heavy coating of sunblock to her face, neck, arms, and shoulders until the farmer's tan spread itself around and she became a smooth brown all over like a tourist. Finally she pulled the shirttails from her jeans and knotted them between her belly-button and breasts.

"And you can honestly sit there and tell me you still don't believe in air conditioning?"

"If God had meant for us to be airconditioned He'd have given us Freon to breathe instead of oxygen. Airconditioning is for potted plants, housecats, tourists, and dead fish."

"Why in God's name couldn't we have taken my truck instead?"

"I told you why. The camper won't go into a half-ton bed."

"Please. I don't want to listen to that ridiculous story again."

In just ten days we had been north to Price, Utah, east to Grand Junction, Colorado, and south as far as Montrose and Durango. We had gone west to Flagstaff, Arizona and east again to Gallup, New Mexico, stopping for every horse show and livestock sale—even rodeos, though Tortuga knew as much about barrel-racing or team-roping as a college graduate knows about unsticking a plugged toilet and the cowboys would have laughed themselves to death just watching him come out of a horse trailer. We would camp for a couple of nights, following a jeep trail or wagon track away from the highway and building a campfire beside the truck; the third night we took a motel room to let Jody shower and shampoo her hair. Except for the pressure and Jody's distress at losing the horse it was like a vacation for me, heating pork and beans on the propane stove and sleeping out on the ground beside the dying fire. In the morning we tamped the coals and soaked them with water, threw the sleeping bags in the camper, and got back on the highway. It was how I had lived for eighteen months, except now I had Jody with me. Having a woman around makes all the difference in the world, which is the way it ought to be.

The weather was cooler in the high cedar breaks around Gallup. Route 66 through town was mobbed with kangaroos shopping for Navajo rugs and pottery, jewelry, and Hopi kachina dolls, while across the Santa Fe tracks the Indians tried to talk the supermarket checkers into selling them booze. Gallup at least doesn't change very much, if it changes at all. A hand-lettered sign in a market in Holbrook had advertised a horse show for the afternoon but the showgrounds were deserted except for a couple of Indians drinking blackberry brandy from a bottle wrapped in a torn paper sack. Neither one of them understood English, and they did not offer me a drink of the blackberry brandy. They had on muscle shirts and the standard black felt reservation hats and their bloodshot eyes looked hopeless and very sad. We spent another hour in Gallup sniffing around, and I telephoned one of the local brand inspectors. The inspector, whose name was Wilson Bill, said he had never heard of a Peruvian Paso and why hadn't I put a brand on my horse if I didn't want to lose him? Now the rustlers had him and I would never see the horse again, he assured me.

"What did he say?" Jody wanted to know when I got off the phone.

"Nothing," I told her. "The Indians have problems enough of their own without worrying about the white man's horse."

I agreed with him about the brand part but figured there wasn't any mileage to be had from saying so.

From Gallup we followed the interstate east to Grants. The slickrock cliffs ran north of the highway, facing toward the dark green uplands of western New Mexico rolling south. Shadowed by a cloud mass towering gold and rose in the light of the evening sun, Mt. Taylor stood blue against the eastern sky.

"I am so tired," Jody said.

"Do you want to look for a place to stay in Grants?"

"Let's go one more night. Motels along the interstate are going to be awfully expensive."

Beyond the malpaís a line of hills ran on the eastern side of the valley. We followed the sandy road south a few miles and made camp in the cedar trees between the hills and the lava field covering the valley floor. While Jody went to gather wood I dug the firepit and surrounded it with chunks of volcanic rubble.

"I'm not sleeping out tonight," she said when she returned with an armload of branches. "This place is positively crawling with snakes."

"There were plenty around last night, too."

"I didn't see any snakes. Why didn't you warn me?"

"Because you didn't see any."

"Always the gentleman, aren't you. You know I'm not afraid of snakes. I just don't want them in my sleeping bag, thank you very much."

I brought the whiskey bottle and we had a couple of stiff drinks apiece, seated on the camp stools away from the heat of the fire. Afterward we grilled two thick steaks on the coals and ate them with cob corn and beefsteak tomatoes sliced thickly. The storm over Mt. Taylor broke as we were finishing supper and dragged away to the east, uncovering the golden peaks surrounding the central bowl sunk deep in the mountain's purple heart.

"The gods of the sacred mountain," I said. "*They* know where to find him."

"I still think they were Ute Indians, not Navajos."

"They were Navajos."

"How do you know?"

"I know Navajos when I see them."

"You know everything, don't you?"

The lights of the town came on at the base of the mountain and across the malpaís the savage outline of the western range stretched beneath the sunset clouds.

"What mountains are those?" Jody wanted to know.

"Those are the Zuni Mountains."

"God," she said. "We really are surrounded, aren't we?"

We took a walk in the remaining daylight. It felt good to be out of the truck and working the cramped muscles in my legs and back, drawing the cooling air of the desert through my lungs. The malpaís was infested with rattlesnakes emerging from their dens to hunt. As we walked I picked up rocks and threw them out among the twisted junipers growing from the lava field, where each rock provoked an angry buzz. We were returning to camp when a rattler sounded off a few yards away. Jody hung on my arm while I found the snake with the flashlight, coiled to strike within a bowl of lava rock. Holding the light steady I took up a rock chip and tossed it underhand at him.

"Get along, old man," I said. "We have a gentleman's agreement. You remember?"

"Don't turn that light off," Jody ordered as we started forward again. "What do you mean, talking to a snake?"

"I wanted him to know I'm still around. That's all."

In camp she wanted a drink. I poured nightcaps after building the fire back and we sat closer on the stools to feel the warmth of the orange flames on our faces and knees. The smoke, rising thinly from the clean-burning cedar, had the smell of all the Southwest in it.

"I'm so discouraged, Jeb," Jody said.

"Don't be discouraged. This is only the beginning."

"I do love you so for not giving up."

"If I find Tortuga for you, will you marry me?"

I meant it as a joke, of course.

"I'll be thinking about it while you're looking for him," she agreed, and laughed. That's how I remember it, anyway.

# BOOK II
## JOHN-WAYNE

Shipwreck, New Mexico, would be more like it: the flotsam and jetsam of a foundered small civilization loosely scattered on the dry desert floor above the San Juan River, nowadays a sour green rivulet trickling in slow exhausted curves toward the once great Colorado. I crossed the simple truss bridge and stopped at a convenience store for gas and to use the public telephone at the back, past the counter display of Indian jewelry and the livid pottery created for the tourist trade by native artisans working with their eyes shut from shame and humiliation. The next step down would be simple prostitution, but a person has to make a living somehow.

That morning I had kissed Jody goodbye after waiting for her to come around again on the tractor, smelling freshly of perspiration, new-cut alfalfa, and diesel smoke, and got on the road to Kayenta, Arizona. I had been driving for less than an hour when, for absolutely no reason at all, I thought suddenly of the Indian woman riding past on her gray Paso at the Fourth of July show. I thought about her some more and at Monticello, rather than continuing south to the Utah line and the Big Reservation, I turned east across the Great Sage Plain into Colorado instead.

In Cortez I inquired at the city hall and then with the show committee, and made some calls. The woman responsible for organizing the Paso events had the names of the entrants, their addresses and telephone numbers on her Rolodex. I explained that I had been impressed by the second-place winner and was interested in making an offer on him, or another horse of the same bloodlines. She said yes, he was a beautiful horse wasn't he and the judge in her opinion should have awarded him first place rather than the horse that actually won it, and looked up the names of the owners and their address. They were Sam and Lena Begay of Lukachukai, Arizona, no phone number given. I said I was definitely in the market for a blue-ribbon winner and thanked her for her time. Jody and O'Grady had not come in to dinner when I called the house. I hung up without leaving a message on the machine and drove down to Shiprock. It was a long drive over the mountains on reservation roads to Lukachukai where someone might or might not have a telephone in working order, and so I was hoping very much to get through to her from Shiprock. This time she picked up at the second ring.

"Hello. It's me."

"Where are you?"

"I'm in Shiprock."

"I thought you were going to Kayenta."

"I had a better idea, suddenly."

I told her how it had occurred to me the Indian woman might be helpful and that I had her name and event from one of the show committee.

"You think *she's* the horsethief? That's awfully prejudiced of you, Jeb."

"I think she knows every Indian in four states who has an interest in Peruvian Pasos. For the same reason that a blue-eyed, golden-haired Indian who played Bach on the harpsichord would know every other golden-haired, blue-eyed Indian harpsichordist in the Four Corners area."

"Oh," Jody said. "It was clever of you to think of it, wasn't it?"

"It dawned on me while I was driving to Monticello this morning."

"You're going on over to Lukachukai then?"

"As soon as I get off the phone with you."

"Remember," she said, "you're looking for a horse. Not a blonde blue-eyed Indian playing the harpsichord."

"I'm going now. I love you."

"I love you too. Call me when you get to Lukachukai."

"I will if I can find a phone, mavourneen," I said.

In the government developments the laundry flapped flat out on lines connecting the single-family units, the faded garments turning a uniform color in the blowing dust as the wind, sweeping down from the Chuska Mountains, scoured the desert and drove a blizzard of paper and plastic trash against the barbwire fence along the highway. Past the Shiprock monolith the road going over to Lukachukai crossed the yellow upslope rising to the dark rugged mountains. The pavement ended as it wound into the foothills and up to a saddle grown with tall Ponderosa pine. From this place the Shiprock monolith was visible below, a gray-masted image in basalt rising eighteen hundred feet above the desert floor of the vessels that four centuries before had changed the life of the Navajo people forever.

It was much cooler in the mountains, where the wind as it came pouring through the pass sounded far off and lonely in the tops of the trees. Below the saddle on the downhill side I met a truck grinding uphill in low gear over the boulders and exposed rock ledges. The driver, an Indian cop, passed me without taking his eyes from the road. Dropping below the pine forest the road turned to soft dust where it entered a narrow canyon grown up with live oak. Four Indians in a pickup truck had stopped around a sharp curve to observe three or four horses drinking down in the creek. They watched without seeming to see me as I squeezed by them—that slow unrecognizing stare between beings from neighboring but mutually impenetrable worlds. Past the opening of the canyon I came to a silver water tower with LUKACHUKAI painted in black letters around it standing above a few houses, the Indian boarding school, and a green-painted shack with torn screens in the doors and windows and a sign in front identifying it as the local senior citizens' center. In the Totsoh Trading Post they were selling saddles and saddleblankets, lariats and halters, sheep shears, salt blocks, sack flour, automotive supplies, canned goods, Navajo blankets, chicken pellets, dry dog and cat food, onions, potatoes, and pears, dyed woolens, the Navajo newspapers, ironware kettles made in Saltillo, Mexico, tin plates and cups (also from Saltillo), audio tapes and video movies, and soft drinks, among other items. I bought fifteen dollars and ninety-two cents' worth of unleaded gas and read the posted notice for a dance ceremony the Mescalero Apaches were holding in southeastern New Mexico, several hundred miles away. It sounded like a good time.

Lake Wheatfield was a manmade lake filled with tepid water reflecting the banded Chuska Mountains in broad strokes of primary color and surrounded by a soft purple beach littered with mutton bones. I made camp in a grove of tall pines, beneath a pair of ravens having a domestic argument in the treetops. Not very far away at the edge of a meadow a laughing Indian family played at horseshoes. The ground beneath the trees was dry—too dry for a fire. I opened a can of beans with my knife and ate them cold with a loaf of French bread I shared with the squirrels. A little whiskey remained in the bottle. I drank it, lying on my back on the long pine needles and watching the fiery clouds drift rapidly eastward through the deepening sky above the spires of the trees. The Indians packed up the remains of their picnic supper and left and the grove was quiet except for a light wind in the pine branches and the ravens, who hadn't made their minds up on a divorce yet. I forget whether ravens mean good luck or bad for Navajos. After a time, when it was getting toward dusk, I heard a vehicle moving over by the lake and the intermittent sound of a horn. Leaving the whiskey bottle standing against a tree I walked down to the beach where a woman in a new pickup was driving slowly, herding the sheep home for the night.

The truck advanced and stopped as the passenger door came alongside. The driver's hair fanned about her shoulders and her stomach pushed against the steering wheel, partly enfolding it. The lenses of her sunglasses were like black pennies stuck into her enormous face, while her mouth above the three chins was entirely expressionless.

"Ya tah-ay," I said.

She stared at me, or seemed to, saying nothing.

"I'm looking for Sam and Lena Begay. Do you know them?"

Except for the rise and fall of her belly against the wheel she remained absolutely motionless. A coiled lasso rested beside her on the seat, along with *Cosmopolitan* and *Woman's Day.*

"You speak English?" I asked, pointing to the magazines.

Still she did not say anything.

"¿Habla español?"

"No," the woman said.

"Muchas gracias," I told her. "Goodnight."

I brought the sleeping bag from the camper and unrolled it on the needle carpet beneath the pine trees. The stars had begun to point through the dark branches and the Indian dogs were already talking back to the coyotes in the mountains across the lake when I fell asleep.

I woke at dawn and lay looking up at the green sky beyond the trees and the sun trying to get above the Chuska Mountains. It was already warm in the bag when I crawled out, stirred instant coffee into a cup of cool water, and drank it while I ate a stick of jerkied beef and a handful of raisins. I was still having my breakfast when an Indian driving a green pickup with the seal of the Navajo Nation on the door stopped and asked to see my camp permit. The official was a goodlooking young man, trim and neat in his dark green uniform. I didn't have any permit, but he accepted my dollar politely and filled out a permit form, which he carefully backdated. Then he looked at my license plate as if he wanted to remember it.

"There is much rain where you come from?" the young man asked finally.

"Not very much. The Forest Service takes most of what we do get and freezes it to snow."

He looked puzzled.

"But you have the rain forests?"

"That's Washington State you're thinking of."

The Indian looked at me. He had no idea what I was talking about but he grinned anyway. If I had had real coffee to give him I'd have offered him a cup. He seemed to be a very nice man.

"Can you tell me how to find Sam Begay's place?" I asked.

"Sure," the Indian said.

The Begay house was out a few miles on the Chinle road beside a blue-painted hogan with a new timbered roof. About an acre of red dirt surrounded the house and beyond it juniper trees growing in clumps where the grass began. A windmill whirling like a silver pinwheel on the stiff breeze stood over the brush corrals, a collection of rusting automobiles that looked as if they had been sitting there since before the Navajo code-talkers left for World War Two, and a post-and-rail corral built against a low sandstone cliff. Six head of horses, including a handsome gray, stood end to end in the shade of the cliff, resting their chins on each other's croups. I turned into the drive and stopped when I was a hundred feet from the house. As reservation houses go, it was a nice house. A satellite dish had been installed off to the right and two four-wheelers sat parked in front. I cut the engine and sat behind the wheel, waiting. When I had waited three or four minutes a woman walked through the door of the house and across the turnaround toward the truck.

She had on a long velvet skirt and white blouse and I didn't recognize her at once as the elegant lady in the embroidered vest and tight-fitting jeans riding the fine-looking horse. She came fast, appearing to float just above the ground, her movement all forward without any up-and-down in the way that only people wearing moccasins can move. Her hair was pulled back from her face, the braid piled and covered with a black scarf knotted behind. She seemed to slow as she approached the truck and when she stopped she was still nearly ten feet away.

"Ya tah-ay," I said.

"Good afternoon," the woman told me in perfect English. Her voice was soft but dignified, proud almost.

Cumulonimbus had begun to form overhead, rising high into the sky like gods peering to see what might be going on on the other side of the world.

"It's looking as if we might have rain later on in the day."

"Perhaps," she agreed. "Is there anything I can do for you this morning?"

"I'm looking to talk to somebody about a horse."

"Is that supposed to be funny?"

"I didn't mean it to be. The Paso you have in the corral over there is a fine-looking animal."

"Which one?"

"The gray."

"He's not for sale," the woman said.

I tried to look disappointed.

"They told me at the show over the Fourth that you were wanting to sell."

"In Cortez?" Her voice was sharp now.

"Uh-huh."

"Well I'm not. Who is 'they?'"

"Two men. Dineh."

She moved closer to the truck.

"A young man and an older one?"

"I think so."

"They made an offer on Ganado." Mrs. Begay laughed. "When I told them what a good Paso is worth they looked at each other and went away."

"What is he worth?"

"It doesn't matter because he isn't for sale." She glanced at the sky. "Now I have to move the sheep up to pasture."

"Do you know who the men were?" I asked.

"Just some Indians from over by Tuba City. Maybe horse traders. Probably they never saw a Paso before." Mrs. Begay looked disgusted. "One of them wanted to know how he got his feet under him when he gets up."

An old woman came to the door of the house and stood there. Mrs. Begay saw me look, turned, and called to her in Navajo before facing round to me again.

"Goodbye," she said. "I'm sorry you came all the way out here for nothing on account of two Indians from Tuba City."

The women were hiking their skirts to climb onto the four-wheelers as I backed down the drive, and before I could get straightened out in the road they were gone after the sheep, bucking across the hummocks of salt grass and sage in a cloud of dust and gasoline smoke toward the cedar breaks beyond the red sandstone cliffs.

At Canyon de Chelly the kangaroos, Japanese tourists, and park rangers seemed to have the Navajos buffaloed more completely than Kit Carson ever dreamed of doing, while convincing them that the industrial tourism business was all their idea to begin with. In Ganado they had a new high school sports center half as big as the town, which crowded against it the way medieval villages clustered around their cathedrals and churches. A few more years and there won't be any Indians left to run away to. I stopped to add three quarts of oil to the engine after the emergency light came on and continued west across a wide valley drawing down from the Chuska Mountains where horses, still "those that men live by" to the Navajos, grazed the lush blue grass standing above their pasterns. Beyond the valley the highway climbed up to a high plateau, blue and cool looking in its sagebrush and juniper cover. It dropped down into Keams Canyon and climbed again toward the Three Mesas of the Hopi Nation while the building clouds slid steadily eastward and the sun, coming between them, burned through the windshield beneath the sun visor. The road skirted the base of First Mesa where the outhouses of Walpi hung their backsides over the cliff edge hundreds of feet above the desert floor and ran on across a sweep of golden-green grass broken by carefully tended patches of Indian corn, the young plants jetting like green flames from the pink sand. Far out on the desert kerchiefed figures herded their animals beneath high-tension wires supported by a line of silver pylons striding away to the horizon, but west from Oraibi Village what had been choice grassland many generations ago was bitten down and ruined now by the sheep and cattle. In Tuba City the sand dunes advanced on the outlying houses and trash was blowing in the streets. Besides the Indians there were plenty of tourists around, on their way to see the Grand Canyon which showed in cross-section on the western horizon. At the service station where I stopped again to check the oil level a man wearing sandals, a Hawaiian shirt, and a golf cap wanted to take my photograph.

"Mister," he asked as he brought his camera up, "Are you a real cowboy?"

"I'm a cowboy, I guess. I never have been able to tell whether I'm real or not."

He looked puzzled. "I mean—do you ride a horse, and...?"

"I can ride a horse."

"Good," the man said. He seemed relieved. "I don't make slides that aren't authentic, one hundred percent. I'll remember and write on the back of it that you're for real."

I filled the tank while I was at it and went inside to pay for the gas. When I came out the tourist with the camera was waiting for me.

"Say, mister," he said, "is it okay if I ask you a question?"

"Sure."

He looked cautiously around before asking in a lowered voice, "Is it a safe thing to camp on the reservation?"

"It is so long as you're camped in a safe place."

"The Indians won't try and—you know—rip you off?"

"Don't believe everything you hear about Indians," I told him. "An Indian won't steal except on one condition."

"What's that, sir?"

"He has good reason to. Just like anybody else."

The man nodded.

"Under 'cowboy' I'm going to put 'and crackerbarrel philosopher,'" he said.

I went for a late dinner to a restaurant run by the Indians for the tourists and called the local brand inspector from the payphone while they were bringing up my order from the kitchen. The inspector was out, for a change, and I hung up without leaving a message. When I was through eating I asked the waitress for another pot of coffee and drank it as I read the local shoppers. None of them carried any livestock listings beyond an upcoming horse auction at the fairgrounds. I paid the bill, which was twice what the meal was worth, and put down an oversize tip on top of it. Outside it was hot enough to boil rocks. I drove to the Ya Tah-Ay shopping mall and parked around on the shady side. Bland impassive faces under the wide black hats stared through me as I entered the supermarket which was stocked to satisfy a Beverly Hills starlet. A community bulletin board up front of the store carried notices of upcoming events and for-sale items. I wrote down several of them in my pocket notebook, and left. I was almost to the truck when a kid walked out of a video store around the corner from the market and crossed straight in front of me as if I was invisible. Trying to sidestep I lost my balance and fell against him. He walked on without saying a word or even looking at me—an adolescent Navajo boy, sixteen or seventeen years old, dressed in sneakers and socks, Bum shorts, a long black T-shirt hanging out, and a black cap. I was about to call after him to ask had he been raised in a barn when the sight of his retreating back nearly made me lose my balance again. I knew that round-shouldered stoop, those bare brown legs stalking rapidly away, the black cap worn with the bill pointing backward. Only the other time he had not been alone.

I almost lost him leaving the parking lot. The kid was driving a red Toyota truck with tinted windows. He paused on the apron to let traffic pass, made a hard left turn without signaling, and drove off in the eastbound lane, accelerating fast.

Two Indians in a pickup pulling a gooseneck trailer and several head of horses cut me off as they made a wide turn from the street into the parking area. By the time they were clear the red truck had already passed through the junction where the road coming from Moencopi intersects with the one going north to Kayenta. I caught sight of it again from the crossroads, dipping and climbing ahead among the sand hills, and took the left fork. Indian kids drive the way they used to ride horses fifty years ago. I kept my foot to the floor, caught up with the truck, and followed it at a comfortable distance. The kid tore along for fifteen miles or so. Then he braked hard and swerved left onto a reservation road headed straight across the desert to White Mesa. The washboard clay had a wide borrow pit running on each side of it and soft, high shoulders above the pits. The kid had slowed some but he continued to drive very fast, holding the left wheels in the borrow pit and the right ones on the shoulder and towing a parachute of dust behind him. I kept to the washboard until I felt my teeth floated by an eighth of an inch and my tailbone compressed to a stump. Then I steered out of the road and straddled the ditch, the truck canted over at an angle of nearly fifteen degrees while the cab filled with the fine sifting dust that filled my lungs until they felt scratchy as the inside of a vacuum cleaner bag. The gallon canteen beside me was empty; I had neglected to have it filled at the restaurant in Tuba City.

Brake lights showed suddenly in the traveling cloud of dust ahead and the truck veered right into a wagon track running toward a house and outbuildings isolated in a grove of cottonwood trees half a mile out from the cliff. The kid never slowed again until he was through the gate, and then the truck went down hard on its front suspension, the rear end came around, and it skidded to a stop in a storm of dust in front of the house. Following more slowly I drove across the cattle guard and stopped behind him. He was out of the truck already and leaning against the driver's door with his sunglasses hanging from an elastic cord around his neck and his arms folded on his chest, watching me.

"You followed me out here from town," the kid said.

"It wasn't easy," I admitted.

When he grinned, his Mongolian eyes nearly disappeared behind his round cheeks.

"The white man don't know how to drive on reservation roads. I could of lost you if I wanted to, but I didn't want to."

"Why didn't you want to?"

He removed his cap, turned it so that the bill pointed forward, and clapped it onto his head again. His hair, a smooth black mane, fell below his shoulders, covering them like a mantle.

"Wanted to see who you was," he told me, still grinning from under the cap.

"Who am I?"

"You're the guy walked into me outside of the video store at the mall."

He hadn't recognized me, apparently.

"I didn't think you noticed," I said.

"You come all this way to fight me about it?"

The house was a frame affair with two rooms and a tin roof, stuccoed. Behind it were a hogan in poor repair and a couple of barns, a brush corral, and a newer, post-and-rail one. Both of the corrals were empty.

"No," I told him. "Though a polite apology wouldn't hurt my feelings any."

"You apologize to me?"

"You apologize to me, of course."

"Hey, Dude," the kid said, "I had my shades on, okay? I didn't see you comin. I was temporarily blinded—you know?"

"That's an apology of sorts," I said. "I accept it. What were you doing at a video store anyway? There's no electricity out here."

"I watch movies with my grandmother when I'm at her house. My grandmother lives in town."

"And where do you live?"

"In town, except when I have to herd sheep."

"Whose sheep are those?"

"They're my grandmother's. This is her place."

He looked around at the house and outbuildings and sideways at me again, grinning from the corners of his eyes. The T-shirt was printed with the words WE ARE THE OVERLORDS in red letters across the back.

"It's a nice place."

"I think its borin."

"Why boring?"

"Without no video, without no cruisin, without no place to hang out. Without no shower. Nothin to do but chase sheep and kill snakes."

"My name's Jeb," I told him.

"I'm John-Wayne. That's one name. John-Wayne."

We shook hands.

"I could use a drink of water,' I added.

"The white man is thirsty," John-Wayne said. "Come on in the house, Dude. You can have all the sody-pop you want."

Inside it was dark in the shade of the big cottonwoods, and pleasantly cool. The house smelled of kerosene and old rope, sweated saddleblankets and mutton grease. There was some furniture, not much; Indian rugs on the floor and cartons of supplies, mostly canned food and soft drinks, stacked against the walls. A handpump clamped on to a corner of the battered enamel sink. I told John-Wayne I would as soon drink water as pop, but he explained that the well water was seventy-five percent alkali and the rest of it salt. He opened two cans of Mountain Dew and we carried them outside and sat on a bench against the front wall of the house, drinking warm soda pop and watching the great trees turn over on a strong wind that had arisen suddenly ahead of a late afternoon storm. The sky behind White Mesa was black and though we could hear the distant thunder and smell the dry smell of alkali dust sharpened by the scent of rain, no rain fell and the storm appeared stalled in space somewhere between the earth and the sky. I asked John-Wayne where the sheep were now and he said out on the desert with his cousin and the dogs, not very far away. In the morning the cousin would drive them on to the house and take the red truck back to town while he, John-Wayne, moved the sheep onto the desert again.

"Two days and two nights without my honey," he said in a grudging voice.

"So you have a girlfriend?"

"She's my honey. There ain't no mutton-gut on *that* girl."

He gave me a challenging look as if I would contradict him.

"Why don't you invite her to help you out with the sheep?"

"Because. She don't know sheep."

"What does she know?"

"She knows horses," John-Wayne said.

Scattered raindrops struck in the turnaround beyond the protecting circle of the trees as gray fingers poked down from the seething clouds overhead. The drops were absorbed instantly by the heavy dust and the rain stopped.

"I bet you know something about horses yourself," I told him.

He tried looking modest.

"My dad's an expert. I learned from him."

"You guys teamrope?"

"He don't ride since he got sick three years ago. He's an alchyholic." He added proudly, "I'm the only man in my family not to be an alchyholic yet."

"I was thinking I saw you ride in Cortez over the Fourth. It must have been someone else, I guess."

"I was there," John-Wayne said, "with my cousin. But we didn't either one of us do no ridin."

The desert was gray and dark-looking for miles around but away to the south and in the east patches of color showed where the sun shone at the edges of the storm. The clouds moved out fast above the mesa, but down on the desert the air was still again and the swallows swooped and dived against the cliff wall after insects.

"You live up in Wyomin?" John-Wayne asked.

"No."

"License plates say you're from Wyomin."

"It's where I lived for a while. That truck was home sweet home to me for eighteen months."

"You're lucky, Dude," John-Wayne told me. "I wish I lived like that: Phoenix, Vegas, Reno—noplace, you know what I mean? That way I wouldn't be bored all the time. Anytime I got bored I'd just drive to the next place, and I wouldn't be bored no more. You ever been to Reno?"

"Not for a long time."

"It's way up in Utah somewhere on a big lake. It costs a thousand dollars a day to stay there but guys with funny names that speak funny and carry guns under their arms from New York give you the money to pay for it and there's thousands of beautiful women you can marry anytime you want to. I rented the movie from the video store on the mall where I ran into you."

"Well," I said, "that sounds like Reno, all right. It's a strange place. In northern Nevada, by the way. The question is, Which came first? The city or the movie?"

He went into the house and came out with two more cans of Mountain Dew.

"Are you startin to be bored yet?" he asked as he seated himself again on the bench.

"Not me. I'm never bored."

John-Wayne shook his head disbelievingly.

"You're lucky, man."

The sky was black in the east now while the sun's rays spoked above the mesa, rising high into the ultraviolet deep of the western sky.

"You can camp here tonight if you want to," he offered. "That way, it won't be so borin."

For supper I broiled a couple of steaks I found in the freezer compartment and John-Wayne brought canned corn and beans from the house.

While I worked over the stove he tried the bunk beds, ran the water in the sink, and urinated in the chemical toilet. When the food was ready I filled the plates and we carried two folding chairs outside and ate supper from our laps as whippoorwills called from the deepening dusk and the canyon wrens sounded their liquid wind-down song.

"I'm glad you showed up, Dude," John-Wayne said. "Corn and beans for supper is really borin."

I brought the propane lantern from the truck and we continued sitting out after dark while moths dived and spun around the glowing chimney. The lantern light drew the gray trunks and thick lower limbs of the cottonwoods from the darkness and illuminated the front wall of the house. When John-Wayne wanted to go for a soda I told him to take the lantern with him. I watched as he walked on to the house, holding the light out ahead, and as soon as he was inside I heard him yell. From the doorway I saw him holding the lantern above his head as he prodded with a long stick at the big rattlesnake writhing on the dirt floor. The end of the stick was a fork holding the rattler pinned just behind the thick wedge-shaped head.

"Cut his head off!" John-Wayne shouted. "The knife is behind you, where you're standin."

A second pole with a cleaver bound to the end of it rested against the wall of the house. Its length made it unwieldy but the weight of the blade gave it momentum and accuracy. The neck severed easily and the thick body, as big around as my thigh and six or seven feet in length, continued to thrash and whip about as John-Wayne, laughing delightedly, inserted one of the tines of the fork between the open jaws, which snapped down on it.

"I killed six snakes in the house last week," he said. "The witchcrafters make them come to us." I lifted the body, still twisting, from the floor and cut away the buttons with my pocketknife.

"He was an old fellow," I said. "The rattles are yours if you want them."

"Navajos aren't supposed to even look at a rattlesnake. You keep em, Dude."

I slipped the rattles into my shirt pocket. Then I carried the snake outside and threw him into the brush behind the cottonwood trees, and John-Wayne pitched the head after it. We walked back together to the truck and he set the lantern on the ground between the two chairs. Crickets sang from the darkness and I heard the whippoorwill again.

"I'm going to bed," I said. "Take the other bunk if you feel like it."

"I always sleep outside. Up on a platform, to be away from snakes."

"Good idea," I told him.

I made him take the lantern when he went. Then I undressed inside the camper and got in bed. The chill of the desert night came through the open door and the scrape of the crickets, mournful and alone for their brief summer lives. Turning on my side I drew the pillow against my chest and put one arm around it. A pillow isn't much to take to bed, but it's better than nothing. After what seemed only a little while I fell asleep.

---

I was still sleeping when I heard somebody somewhere shouting, "My sheep are comin! Here come my sheep!" Turning over in bed I clutched the pillow tighter, trying to escape into sleep again, but when I heard the doves calling from the trees I knew I was already awake.

John-Wayne urged me to dress quickly. I was still buttoning my shirt as he led me around the house to the edge of the trees. It was barely past dawn and I saw nothing in the vague light of early morning but the indefinable line where the pale sky touched the gray sagebrush desert.

"There they are! Can you see them?"

"No."

At last, following his pointed finger, I made out a thickening along the horizon a mile or so east from the mesa.

"I see them now," I told him. "Will your cousin wish to eat breakfast with us?"

"We don't stop to eat when we're herdin sheep."

"Come on then," I said. "We have time for coffee and a bite before they get here."

I fried up Jody's fresh bacon with the bristles still in the rind and scrambled green chili into half a dozen eggs. We ate breakfast at the little table under the pop-out window. John-Wayne looked through the window all the while he was eating and went outside immediately when he had finished, leaving me to clean up. He was sitting on the bench against the house as I walked over, securing a pair of rusted spurs to the heels of his boots.

"What's the Navajo word for boring?" I asked him.

He thought for a moment, and told me.

"How come you want to know, man?"

"Because you don't look very however-you-say-it to me."

The kid grinned widely under the dusty felt hat he was wearing instead of the cap, and this time his eyes disappeared entirely behind his cheeks.

"Let's go, Dude," he said in a voice that was suddenly almost a man's. "I'm goin to show you my sheep now."

The band was a quarter-mile away, pushed by a single rider on horseback and kept together by the dogs stretched out low along the ground as they ran and carrying their tails down like foxes while they worked to head off stragglers. Already we could hear the bleating of the lambs and smell the pungent stench as the sheep pressed forward in a small storm of dust. John-Wayne removed his hat and waved it at the rider, who waved back.

The sheep arrived in backflows and eddies like a slow tide moving up a beach. The rider had pushed them hard, and even the dogs were tired. They stood in the shade of the trees with their heads down and their tongues out, or lay flat on their bellies in the dust while the sheep milled and bleated, the animals in the rear of the band rising on their hind legs to plant their forefeet on the backs of those ahead as John-Wayne's cousin pressed them from behind. At last he turned the horse and rode around the band to the edge of the trees where he drew rein, slipped down from the saddle, and tied up to a cottonwood limb. He hadn't gone ten steps when I recognized the slightly forward shoulders and the arms hanging straight and a little ahead of the hips. John-Wayne hailed him in Navajo and his cousin greeted him the same way. If you can learn the Navajo language after twenty or thirty years of fairly regular exposure, you could probably master the Zulu Click in a semester or two at your local community college.

The cousin was the taller of the two and narrower, though he did not appear to be much older, nineteen perhaps or twenty. The dark skin stretched tight across his meager face which seemed too small for him with its thin purple mouth and the sharp nose coming between the two halves of his mirror shades. John-Wayne did not introduce us. Instead he began a conversation with his cousin, the two of them speaking in low intense voices and gesturing in the direction the sheep had arrived from. When they had talked for a while John-Wayne switched abruptly to English and was joined by the older man—and then I recognized the voice, too.

"This is Shorty," the kid told me. "He's my cousin," he added proudly.

Shorty and I shook hands. His was thin and long for a Navajo, the fingers prehensile, the palm horny and dry. Attempting to meet his gaze behind the glasses I saw my own reflection instead, doubled in the shiny twin lenses.

John-Wayne glanced at the sky.

"Sody-pop is goin to taste like horse piss in about an hour," he suggested.

Shorty left the dogs to tend the sheep while we sat against the house drinking Mountain Dew. The pop was already warm and it tasted awful. I sat on one end of the bench, Shorty on the other, and John-Wayne was in between us. The kid and I rested our shoulderblades against the wall and our heels in the dust while Shorty sat up very straight with his feet hanging beneath him as he faced directly ahead of himself, keeping his chin lifted. No one said anything. At last Shorty stood, dropped the empty can in the dust, and put his heel on it. He and John-Wayne spoke briefly again in their own language and then Shorty went over to the horse which had been resting on three legs, half asleep in the shade. He untied his bedroll from the saddlestrings, lifted the canteen from the horn, and threw them onto the seat of the truck. Finally he got in behind the wheel and drove away in a cloud of dust without waving goodbye.

"My cousin don't like you," John-Wayne said.

"Why doesn't he like me?"

"Because you're the white man."

I asked him where his cousin lived and he said near Red Lake in the government housing there. The cousin had made a lot of money working construction on a chocolate factory in Vegas and now the government wanted him to move out in order to make room for someone who really was poor. John-Wayne said Shorty had enough money to set up as a horse trader, working from his great-uncle Yazzie's ranch at Kaibito where he kept the horses he had bought and was trying to sell.

"Why doesn't he live on the ranch?"

"Because it's haunted. That's why."

"Haunted by who?"

"My great-uncle," the kid said.

He wanted me to herd sheep for two days before I reminded him that there was only the one horse between us. Then he suggested I remain at the house—as camp cook, I guessed. I explained that I had business to attend to in town but promised to return to the ranch that evening, or early the next morning.

He was shortening the stirrup leathers and whistling up the dogs as I left, standing with his feet apart and his stomach out while the dogs rose from their bellies in the shade and the sheep stirred apprehensively with their legs folded under them, and no one that I could see looked bored at all, except the horse.

I was half way to Kaibito already when the late morning wind got up, hot as the Devil on Easter Sunday. Covered by low piñon and juniper forest the plateau country stretched, green and monotonous, under the scorching sun. At the trading post where I stopped to ask directions I waited nearly five minutes for the clerk, who was outdoors working on his girlfriend's old sedan, to come inside. The clerk was a big, soft-looking kid wearing his hair tied in a ponytail behind. He held his hands, which were black with grease, helplessly in front of himself as if he thought they might never be any use to him again and seemed relieved to learn that I did not wish to buy anything from the store. The clerk couldn't tell me how to find the Yazzie place but said perhaps his girlfriend would know. Together we went out to the car where the girlfriend, sitting sideways on the front seat behind the steering wheel with her bare legs hanging through the open door, gave me directions while she drank soda pop through a straw. A tow rope connected the car with the boy's pickup truck ahead of it. When I left he was leaning on his blackened hands beneath the raised hood, staring into the engine compartment.

The Yazzie ranch lay ten miles north approximately on the road going to the Indian school at Navajo Mountain. The girl had said to look for a couple of vacant mobile homes set on blocks east of the highway and take the next left turn after that. I drove for ten miles on the odometer, seeing only the low forest all around, the blue mountain ahead, and every couple of miles a house, set far back from the road among the trees. Less than a mile past the abandoned trailer houses a dirt track went left across a narrow meadow and into the trees beyond. I stopped across the cattle guard and got out in the road. Truck tires passing in the hardened ruts had pulverized the outer layer of clay, leaving a fine dust printed with a heavy tread. I drove on slowly into the forest where bluebirds jinked among the trees and the air smelled of heated resin, until buildings appeared in a clearing in the woods ahead. Then I shut off the engine and went the rest of the way on foot.

Old man Yazzie having died at home, his house had been sealed up to prevent his chindi from escaping. The cinderblock walls and tarpaper roof were strong yet, but the tin outbuildings tilted and bulged and the wood and tarpaper roof of the hogan was fallen in. Someone had removed the arc light from the tall post above the turnaround and the pump and wheel were missing from the windmill behind the house. In the broken-down corrals grass and weeds grew high from the manured soil mulched with old straw. The tire marks went as far as the house and continued past it, across the clearing into the deeper woods beyond.

It was hot in the woods, and very still. I walked on, following the old wagon road where the grass lay flattened in parallel tracks. A horsefly made a couple of passes around my head and settled on my bare neck above the shirt collar. I slapped at it, crushed the fly between my finger ends, and dropped it in the road as I went. When I had gone another hundred yards I smelled horses, and stopped. In the silence I heard their measured stamp, felt the vibration of hooves striking ground—almost. I stood still, listening, for perhaps a minute. Then I started forward again, moving carefully.

The horses were penned in a corral made of unbarked poles nailed to the trunks of living trees. I counted nine, standing head to tail along the fence on the shaded side of the corral, all of them good-looking animals. The tire tracks became confused at a new Powder River gate and a row of plastic water barrels across the fence from a watering trough made from half of an old boiler unit, then ran on around the corral to a hayrick covered by a plastic tarpaulin guyed with ropes. Tortuga rolled an eye at me as I approached, and resumed scratching his back against a pine branch overhanging the fence. He had lost weight but looked in good shape otherwise, except for the brand someone had burned onto his right hip. The scab had mostly fallen away already, exposing the new skin, pink as raw steak, underneath. The horses in the corral with him were geldings, I saw, so that life for him at Yazzie's was no romantic interlude.

Two horseflies pursued me from the corral, through the woods past the sealed-up house in the clearing. I succeeded in killing one, but missed the other. The grass sprang back from under my boots as I hurried in the wagon track and where it stopped, using a fresh pine bough I brushed over the prints in the dusty road between the house and the truck. Driving out to the highway I saw the red Toyota truck around every curve, but met no one.

At the trading post the young man still labored under the hood of the sick automobile while his lady, having finished the pop, was working on a bag of fried pork rinds. From the oil that covered the front of his T-shirt and barred his face like warpaint, I guessed that he had been beneath the chassis also. He looked weary when I asked him for permission to use the telephone, and nodded without saying anything.

Jody was out. I left a message telling her I had found the horse, that there were complications, and I would call back tomorrow when I had the chance. I put down a five-dollar bill to pay for the call, and the nuisance, and went outside where the thunderheads accumulated already with no scent of rain. The kid was under the car again, only his feet and ankles showing beneath the rocker panel, while the girl twirled the dials on the radio. I wondered if she understood she had discovered the Pearl of Great Price at the advanced age of sixteen or seventeen and, if so, what she was expecting to do with it.

John-Wayne was still away with the sheep when I returned to the ranch at White Mesa. I mixed a couple of stiff whiskeys and drank them, seated in one of the folding chairs on the turnaround while the black clouds played out the daily farce above the mesa, beginning with the strong winds and ending in veils of hanging dust. Toward sundown I ate the last steak from the little refrigerator, washed up the supper dishes, and sat with a nightcap listening to the bullbats grunt as they pulled out of their dives and watching night come on. Afterward I found a big rattler under the truck and killed him with a shot from the .22 pistol in the glove box. I dragged him out with a stick, carried him to the house, and coiled him up, looking very natural, on the daybed. When I had the snake arranged just right I felt ready to turn in.

The wind returned in gusts, rocking the camper like a boat at sea as I lay still in the darkness thinking about John-Wayne. He seemed like a good kid, certainly no horsethief. Yet he had stolen the horse—or helped steal it. I thought some more and decided not to hold it against him, much. The Navajo have made a living stealing horses for more than four hundred years. You can't expect anyone to change overnight.

---

John-Wayne did not return the next morning and he was still away by early afternoon. I changed the engine oil in the truck and went climbing on White Mesa, taking the canteen and the revolver loaded with snake shot. Several good arches buttressed the cliff wall, which rose sheer and white into the blue sky and appeared to be falling backward as wisps of white cloud trailed from behind it. I climbed up carefully, working from one tree to the next and sending down falls of the loose rock underfoot. When I had climbed a third of the way I stopped to drink water and let the wind stiffen my soaked shirt. From here the cottonwood grove looked like a clump of bushes with a doghouse set in the middle of it. The water tasted terrible, and it was very refreshing. I climbed a hundred yards more to a perpendicular rock face and edged sideways along the base of it, searching for a way up. The rock was smooth as if it had been cut with a knife, no vents or handholds. I was about to abandon the attempt to scale White Mesa when a shear opened in the face of the cliff, a natural staircase ascending the cliff at an angle of forty-five degrees.

I went up it on all fours over stony rubble, squeezed in the narrow chute, until the pitch increased and I climbed hand over hand to the terrace above, a hanging garden in the wall of the mesa. Seated on the grass in the shade of a juniper tree, surrounded by wildflowers and prickly pear, I drank some more of the stale-tasting water while watching a bluebird balance expertly in the swaying top of one of the little trees. The sun had dropped behind the mesa so that it was cool already here in this small shaded paradise, lifted hundreds of feet above the desert floor and protected by an overhang of rock. I left enough water in the canteen for the descent, wondering as I screwed the cap back on what the water source was that kept this place alive. For no reason at all I decided to have a look.

Trees grew against the backwall beneath the overhang where a variety of small, water-loving plants were scattered on the freshened grass. I kneeled and touched the ground. It felt cool under my spread hand but not damp. I was still on one knee when I spied a recess in the cliff wall, not over five feet above the ground and concealed almost entirely by the screen of trees. The opening was seven feet or eight feet wide and about four in height, formed by wind erosion and the leaching moisture. Huck Finn wouldn't have hesitated for a second, and I didn't either.

Something was inside the cave. I thought an animal before I recognized the position, as if it had awakened suddenly and sat up like the princess in the fairy tale. Gazing out through the cave mouth and across the infinite world beyond, the wizened face had a commanding look that seemed both impersonal and intimate as if its message was addressed to humanity in general and each human being individually, demanding some terrible and impossible thing. The mummy was almost childsized, but the long black hair partially shrouding the corpse and the shrunken paps pasted against the hollow chest had once been a woman's pride. Shaken, and feeling somewhat embarrassed, I backed away from the cave through the trees and descended the way I had come to the plain below.

From halfway down I saw John-Wayne and the sheep some miles out from the house and, on the turnaround, the red Toyota truck. Next to it a vehicle I didn't recognize, hitched to a stock trailer, stood parked. The radio was turned up full blast as I approached the house and the snake lay flung out in the dust near the camper, covered with bluebottle flies and beginning to stink already. I washed up, had a whiskey and water, and napped until John-Wayne returned with the band at around seven o'clock. Then I walked over to the house where the cousins sat out together with a third man, drinking pop. John-Wayne had his knees wide apart and his heels together as he rested the back of his head against the wall of the house. He opened his eyes as I came up and grinned wearily.

"Hello, Dude."

"Howdy," I told him.

Shorty did not say anything. As far as he was concerned, I wasn't there at all. It hadn't occurred to me he would make it out here first and find the snake but good enough for him, I thought. No one offered to make introductions with the other fellow.

"Tired?" I asked.

"I'm dead," John-Wayne said. He was covered all over with the pale dust and looked exactly like a mudhead kachina.

"Better shake a leg if you're going to take your honey dancing tonight."

"The white man is very funny."

"You'll feel better after a shower."

"No water at the house since yesterday morning," Shorty told him.

"No water *shit*," John-Wayne said, and closed his eyes again.

"You can wash up in the camper if you wish," I offered. "There's a little water left in the tank."

He shook his head.

"I'll shower at Bette's. I was wantin to introduce you anyway, Dude."

The cousins conferred briefly with the third Indian. I understood them to be discussing where the graze was good, and where it wasn't. Then Shorty went to tend to the horse and John-Wayne threw his bedroll into the red truck.

"Take it easy," I warned him. "This isn't the Indy Five Hundred, remember."

Horses grazed along the airport runway beyond the picture window in the end of the grandmother's house trailer in Tuba City. Mrs. Bilagody was a large woman wearing a heavy blue velvet skirt and an elaborately stitched ivory blouse with a lot of heavy jewelry. The knob of silver hair behind her head moved up and down and her dark face smiled broadly while her grandson translated for her, explaining that I was invited to leave the truck in the yard overnight. John-Wayne found clean clothes and a toothbrush and we drove together in his Toyota to the girlfriend's house. Bette lived with her family in a mobile home two miles west of town on Route 160. She was a tall broad-shouldered Amazon with high cheek bones and a coppery skin, smooth as an ironwood statue and with plenty of curve to her except at the belly, which was flat as a man's hand under the tight-buttoned jeans.

"This here's my girl, Bette," John-Wayne said proudly.

She was smiling as she held out her hand to me.

"My name is Bette Atcitty," Bette said. "And I'm not anybody's girl."

John-Wayne was embarrassed.

"All I meant is, she's my girlfriend. She ain't anybody else's."

"I know what you meant," I told him. Then I smiled at Bette. "I know what she means, too."

The Atcittys were away for the evening attending a Baptist revival meeting in Kayenta. While John-Wayne showered Bette took me out to the corrals to see her show horse. He was a tall Appaloosa, strong and well-conformed, but she explained that he was past twenty now and she intended to buy a young horse as soon as she had saved the money for a good one. When John-Wayne came from the bathroom wearing clean pants and a shirt and his damp hair slicked back she said he looked better now, and offered to give us supper. Seated at the oilcloth table in the kitchen area we ate fried eggs, bacon, and thick rounds of fry bread. After we had finished supper we moved up to the sitting room, where John-Wayne sat beside Bette on the sofa with his arm around her shoulders. When he tried kissing her she told him to behave himself and slapped at the hand he placed on her thigh.

"What do you think, Dude?" Shane asked as we drove back to town.

"She's a lovely girl. Too good for an old sheepherder like you."

"I'm a lucky guy, huh?"

"You'll be lucky, if you can keep her. About sixty years from now you can say for sure."

"Sixty years is a long time, man."

"It is a long time. It goes fast, though."

"She's goin to look like her mom in sixty years."

"What do you think you're going to look like?"

"I don't know. Better than that."

In Tuba City the NO VACANCY signs were on and the tourist cars had the fast food restaurants surrounded. John-Wayne drove up the wide main street, turned right, and continued past the end of the airstrip where a mule and two horses, illuminated by the red and white landing lights, stood staring on the tarmac.

"Do you know where I could find a horse to buy?" I asked.

"You want to buy a horse?" John-Wayne was surprised.

"Sure."

"What kind of a horse?"

"A good horse."

I could feel his mind at work there in the dark beside me.

"Me and Shorty will sell you a horse, Dude," John-Wayne said at last in a confident voice.

---

A relative who had offered to repair the water line to the trailer failed to show up the next morning. With the swamp cooler shut down the heat was almost intolerable by ten o'clock and Mrs. Bilagody went to shop at the supermarket, having instructed John-Wayne to haul the garbage to the city dump. I helped load the truck and rode with him to the landfill, where an aged crone sat wrapped in blankets in a chair atop a pile of refuse sniffing an empty nail-polish bottle while a middle-aged man climbed around below in search—John-Wayne explained—of copper to pay the bootlegger with. After leaving the dump he drove to Bette's house where we found no one at home and the Appaloosa missing from his pen. He was so glum at not finding her that I bought him an ice-cream cone at the ice-cream parlor in town.

"She didn't say she had no trainer's appointment this morning," John-Wayne said when I asked what the trouble was.

"Probably she forgot to tell you."

"That girl don't never forget nothin."

"You forget to tell her things, don't you?"

"Not unless I have a reason to forget. I'm goin to kill that fat Paiute, next time I see him."

"What fat Paiute?"

"The trainer. He gives her a lesson ever week."

"You're jealous of the horse trainer?"

John-Wayne did not answer. Instead he stared at me as if he suspected me of training barrel-racers also.

"What are you jealous of him for if he's fat?"

"He ain't fat," John-Wayne growled.

He was still brooding when we left the ice-cream parlor.

"It's no good being jealous," I told him. "Women react badly to jealous men, and I can't say as I blame them. King Arthur wasn't jealous of Lancelot for loving Guenevere."

"Who you talkin about, Dude?"

"King Arthur was a king of ancient Britain. His wife, Queen Guenevere, was loved by Arthur's greatest knight, Sir Lancelot. He married her even after being warned by Merlin, the enchanter, that she was going to be unfaithful to him with Lancelot."

It's strange all you remember from childhood. My grandfather must have read aloud about the Knights of the Round Table a thousand times to me, seated in his lap while the smoke from his cherrywood pipe went up my nose and the gray tobacco ash settled on my forehead and over the printed page.

"How come he didn't make the witchcrafter put a spell on Lancelot so he got sick and died?"

"That wouldn't have been considered the chivalrous thing for him to do in those days."

"He'd of been shiverous all right if he'd been hangin around tryin to hit on *my* woman," John-Wayne said.

We spent the afternoon in the sweltering house with the windows closed on the west side against the blowing dust, watching videos with Mrs. Bilagody while she packed for a trip to visit relatives in San Diego. The hot weather seemed not to bother her in spite of the heavy clothing. Most of the dialogue was incomprehensible to her but she followed the action carefully, nodding approvingly to the actors and laughing at the sight gags. When John-Wayne fell asleep in a sitting position on the sofa with his cap pulled over his eyes I went outside and sat in the door of the camper to finish *The Old Man and the Sea,* a book by Ernest Hemingway. *The Old Man and the Sea* is not a very long book but I had been working at it for almost a month already. Being in love doesn't leave much time for reading.

After supper we loaded the empty water barrels in the bed of the Toyota and filled them at the service station. The sun hung above the edge of the Grand Canyon as we were leaving town and the wind blew like a red typhoon out of the fiery sunset. At Red Lake a work crew struggled to erect a revival tent, the canvas bulging and flapping around them as they worked. The wind caught the straw hat belonging to one of the men and sent it bowling across the highway ahead of the truck.

"Do you have wind where you live in Wyomin?" John-Wayne asked.

"Every time it gets a chance to blow."

"Wind makes me angry, sometimes."

"That's because of the positive ions," I explained.

"What does that mean?"

"I don't know."

At the trading post at Kaibito the sedan stood attached still behind the boyfriend's truck. The hood was up and various engine parts lay spread around on the ground, along with a few tools. John-Wayne stopped to buy himself a soda pop. He was in the store a long time and when he came out finally I asked him what the delay was about.

"There's a real fox in there," John-Wayne said.

"A fox?"

"A girl, man. A real cool chick."

"Well?"

"I asked her for her name and address and she gave em to me. Just like that."

"What about Bette?"

"What about her?"

"You really know how to play the game, don't you."

"Why not, Dude?"

John-Wayne quit grinning and was silent for a little while. Finally he said, "You know, a girl like that can have everthin she wants. *Everthin*."

"Of course she can. Pretty women lead charmed lives in this world."

"It kind of makes you mad almost, don't it?"

"Not if you have any sense," I promised him.

We passed the mobile homes on blocks and came to the road in to Yazzie's. Noticing the fresh tire marks I was about to comment when I stopped myself in time. It was already dusk in the forest and only a little brighter in the clearing where the abandoned house stood.

"When did your grandfather die?" I asked.

"I don't want to talk about it here," John-Wayne whispered.

"Why not?"

"I don't want to be haunted."

He drove past the house without looking at it and into the tunnel of grass between the trees. The horses were on the way over already as we came in sight of the corral, nodding their lowered heads and switching their tails.

John-Wayne backed the truck around to the gate and we began taking the water barrels down from bed. The barrels were heavy and hard to take a hold on, leaking water down their plastic sides.

"We got one missin!" John-Wayne exclaimed.

Grappling with the barrels I had seen the milling horses without really looking at them. Now I did look. I had a one-in-nine chance of being the loser, and of course I lost.

"Shorty stoled my horse," John-Wayne said in a shocked voice. He looked as if he was going to cry.

---

He took it as a doublecross and I wished I could have told him differently, knowing that Shorty had driven to Kaibito the evening before and taken the horse not out of treachery but from panic at recognizing me as the man who had challenged him at the fairground in Cortez. Guessing that John-Wayne would have told me about the corral of rustled horses in the pine woods guarded by the falling-down house and old Yazzie's chindi, he had arranged for a friend to herd the sheep at White Mesa while he took the man's rig to Kaibito for Tortuga. Naturally I said nothing to John-Wayne about any of this. That was how I acquired a partner in my work: a sixteen-year-old Indian kid who had agreed to pay five hundred dollars on the installment plan for a stolen horse of the breed his girlfriend wanted without her being able to afford it, in the hope and expectation of winning her love forever at the expense of his rival, the Paiute horse trainer. Love, like war, makes strange bedfellows.

I counted on catching up with the horse within several days, a week at most with John-Wayne's help. Shorty would want to get rid of him fast—on the res, where many of the traders (like plenty elsewhere) weren't terribly particular when it came to identifying altered brands or asking questions about new ones. Letting your horse go without a brand is equivalent to leaving your car unlocked with the key in the ignition, and the brand Shorty had put on him was the single greatest obstacle to recovering Tortuga, amounting as it did to a claim at least as valid as his papers and the brand inspection—which described him as a maverick, of course. After that the big problem was going to be the Navajo police, who I did not expect to confiscate a branded horse from a tribal member for the purpose of handing him over to a belagaana from Wyoming. So I had not notified the police at all. We were looking for a beige 1973 GMC pickup pulling what John-Wayne described as a gray WW stock trailer with the nose stove in, both vehicles registered to a Mr. Johnson Sam of Tuba City, Arizona. I was worried Mrs. Bilagody would insist on her grandson staying home to tend the sheep, but she gave him permission to go for a few days with the white man who had so generously offered to find the stolen horse for him. John-Wayne explained that she could easily find a replacement before she had to leave for San Diego, the Bilagodys being a cooperative family as well as a large one.

"Except for Shorty," he said. "He was always one of them *bad* Indians."

We had my truck with us now, hitched to a bunged-up, rusted-out, single-horse trailer—a kind of loading-chute on wheels—I had bought at a trading post for twenty-five dollars.

"I already paid him seventy-five bucks. What percentage of five hundred dollars do I have left to pay?"

"That would amount to about five-sixths of the selling price."

"So the sonofabitch stoled one-sixth of my horse," John-Wayne said. "And I told him I'd pay him another fifty in a couple weeks."

"That's fifty good bucks you didn't throw after bad anyway."

"It don't matter,' he said darkly. "Because I'm goin to find where he took that horse and steal him back. The whole six-sixths of him. You see if I don't, Dude."

It was late in July now, a season of blasting heat, false lightning, dry thunder, and wind. As Jody and I had done only a couple of weeks before we camped up dirt trails, cooked an early supper over the campfire, and lay down with the sun, stretched on top of the bags spread on the desert hardpan. Waking long past midnight I watched the stars spin from cold white through alternating shades of pink, gold, and green and back to white again, feeling the hard earth under my shoulderblades and on my face the night breeze fanning the heat murmur above the dying coals of the fire. When I phoned Jody from Tuba City she had sounded interested but a little distant. Late summer is always a busy and worrisome time for ranchers. I know, having been in the business myself.

The fourth day a trader out of Cameron nodded when I described Johnson Sam's outfit. He was a small, thin hosteen, his eyes weary but farseeing, his gray hair combed straight back from the red bandana he wore folded over and knotted about his head. A tall eagle feather stood up from the bandana behind the left ear.

"Remember the horse. Gaited like a duck. I don't handle canners."

The old man had given Sam the name of a trader who did sell to the slaughterhouses, a Mr. Jake Thompson from Holbrook.

"Belagaana," the old man said. "White guy," he added without embarrassment, looking directly at me.

According to the hosteen this Thompson would buy any horse that was offered to him and sold how and when he could. He interest was volume and he cared as much for the horses themselves as he would for so many junk cars. Thompson, he went on, had men working for him around the res buying up old, broken down, and half-starved Indian horses and corralling them until Thompson came through and picked them up. One of these buyers lived at Cedar Ridge. It was this man, the hosteen said, he had recommended to Johnson Sam.

"He was in a big hurry to get rid of that horse," the old man said. "When I asked him who put the raw brand on him, seemed like he was in an even bigger one."

John-Wayne was enthusiastic on the drive up to Cedar Ridge. He had become discouraged and finally bored the last two days, but the conversation with the hosteen had boosted his spirits considerably.

"We'll cut him out of the corral after dark, load him right up, and man—we're out of there! I can see Bette's face when I bring him over in the mornin. The Paiute can put his head between his legs and kiss his ass goodbye."

"Don't Navajos have a saying about not counting your chickens, and so forth?"

John-Wayne blew out his cheeks in scorn. "Navajos don't take their luck, man. They make it."

"Well, make enough luck for us to get back to Tuba City tonight for a shower, then."

He had on the T-shirt, the baggy shorts, and rolled socks he had been wearing for four days now and his bare legs were dusty and streaked with sweat.

"You tryin to tell me I stink, Dude?"

"I'm not trying to tell you anything."

"White men smell funny to Indians, did you know that?"

"You don't smell funny at all to me. Just bad."

"I *am* bad," John-Wayne agreed, grinning until his eyes disappeared.

The village of Cedar Ridge straddled the highway where it ran in a valley between a yellow ridge crested with cedars and a line of tall red cliffs facing west. Following the hosteen's directions we found the buyer's house out a dirt road going north of town against the base of the cliff.

"Ain't nobody home," John-Wayne said. "Why don't we just go ahead and take him now?"

"How do you know there's no one home?"

"Don't see nobody around nowhere."

"We're going to do this thing as we planned it," I told him, "and wait until after dark."

We bought hamburgers at a fry-bread stand along the highway and ate supper in the camper while starving horses grazed the yellow stubble between the fence and the road and women went on foot among the cedars driving the sheep home. The western ridge stretched black against the molten sky; across the valley the red opposing cliffs glowed in the deepening twilight scented with cedar smoke from the cook fires. It was getting on to dark as we drove across town again and followed the dirt road north. When we were still a quarter-mile from the house I stopped and cut the lights and at full dark we started walking, taking with us a bridle and reins, a lead rope, and a can of oats.

The wind died and except for the rush of cars on the highway away off the night was soundless. We stepped briskly, sensing the road beneath our feet rather than seeing it, watching the house light draw in closer.

"Who gets to ride behind?" John-Wayne whispered.

"You do."

"But he's my horse!"

"And I'm the white man."

"*Sheesh*!" he exclaimed in a low voice, kicking up a cloud of the ghostly dust from the road.

We had been going seven or eight minutes when we made out the house and outbuildings. One of these was full of light and surrounded by automobiles.

"They're holding a ceremony," Shane whispered.

"They won't be paying attention to what's going on at the corrals, then."

Outside the hogan people stood in clusters, illuminated by the interior light. The corrals were off to one side a couple of hundred yards, strongly made, about five feet in height. The light from the hogan did not reach as far as the corrals where the horses appeared to stand quietly, not allowing the ceremony to disturb their rest. We ducked through the wire fence beside the road and circled round until we had the corrals between us and the hogan. In the darkness the darker mass of gathered horseflesh showed behind the heavy posts at the near end of the corral. I reached for the miniature flashlight I was carrying in my pocket.

The horses were a poor-looking bunch on their way to the glue factory, something a junkyard dog would turn up his nose at. I played the light around carefully and discovered Tortuga, looking like a little bit of a poor keeper himself as he tried to mount a mare too old and tired to resist him. Made nervous by our presence they lacked the energy for real alarm, shifting their weight uneasily and flinching in the beam of the tiny light. John-Wayne was over the fence already. I dropped down after him and walked up to the horses, holding the can out and shaking it to make a noise like an oat. They ignored the can and were backing off skittishly when Tortuga climbed off the mare and trotted forward with his head down.

I killed the light and put the lead around his neck as John-Wayne ran to unlatch the gate. While he chewed oats I slipped the headstall over his ears and slid the bit between his teeth.

"Let's go, horse," I said.

John-Wayne stood watching with his hand on the gate. Behind us the horses, their ancestral memories revived, were moving up for the oats, trying to gather courage enough to push in. When the lead horse came within reach Tortuga kicked him. The leader squealed and the animals behind him fell back, milling.

"Let's go," I said again—to John-Wayne this time.

I set my hands on the withers, vaulted up, and rode out through the gate as he swung it open narrowly. John-Wayne was up behind me before the dogs arrived in a pack, giving tongue as they moiled and ran in at the horse's heels. Tortuga had little familiarity with dogs. He kicked at them with his back hoofs and struck at them with his front ones, squealing. Shouts came from the direction of the hogan and running boots sounded on the packed ground as I turned the horse and heeled him in the flanks, aiming for the kidneys.

The dogs were in full voice now and in the corral the glue herd ran the fence, whinnying. The arc light went on above the turnaround and when Tortuga, harassed by the dogs, began to spin and commenced finally to buck, I gave him my heels as hard as I was able and let him have his head. At the sound of the first shot he bolted with the bit in his teeth and then we were going at full gallop in the darkness. As the dogs and the shouting fell behind more shots came at our back, hard on the crack of a bullet into sandstone.

John-Wayne held tight behind, moving with me and with the horse with that preternatural horsemanship Indians have as I lay forward over the withers working to reach the dragging right rein before Tortuga could step on it and throw himself. Around the night was a blur of blackness in varying shades beneath a faintly luminous sky on which some starkly massive thing showed ahead. I shouted, and then a shaggy resistant claw struck a terrific blow from above, sweeping us backward off the horse over the croup. Lying on my back with the wind knocked out of me I heard the horse run clattering away into the desert and John-Wayne gasping to get his breath back in the deeper dark of the cedar grove.

"Can you run?"

"I...can't—breathe."

"You don't need to breathe. Just get up and run like hell."

We ran together a way. Then, perceiving we were not being followed, we dropped back to a dogtrot. Rising from behind the cliff the moon poured itself into the valley; by its light we picked up the fenceline running back to the clay road where the truck stood parked. We approached carefully on the chance someone might be waiting for us there, but no one was.

"What do you think of the range detective business?" I asked.

John-Wayne's bare arms were abraded and striped with dried blood. His cap was missing.

"Pretty exciting," he admitted. "I ain't exackly dressed for it, though."

---

In Page I rented a motel room from the sleepy clerk who answered the night bell and we fell asleep across the beds without stopping to take our clothes off. John-Wayne was still sleeping when I woke around nine and telephoned Jake Thompson in Holbrook. He was in Gallup but planned on bringing a load of horses from Cedar Ridge on Saturday, his wife or whoever it was answered the phone said. Today was Friday. Because Tortuga was thoroughly farmerized and completely without survival skills, I was betting that he had come in from the desert this morning at feeding time and was safely back in the buyer's pen. I was as certain of him being on the truck to Holbrook Saturday afternoon as if I'd paid for his ticket myself.

When John-Wayne and I were through in the shower the water had dropped a foot behind Glen Canyon Dam and six inches of sediment were added to the deteriorating environment of Lake Powell. We went for a big breakfast, had our ears lifted at the barbershop, and then I took John-Wayne to a western wear store where I had him outfitted in jeans, a denim jacket and blue-denim snapbutton shirt, boots, a strong belt with an ornate silver buckle the size of a dinner plate, two red bandana handkerchiefs, and a wide straw hat with a black ribbon around the base of its vented crown. He dressed in the changing room and left his old clothes in a pile on the floor.

"Pick up your clothes so the young lady doesn't have to do it," I told him.

"Nice potato chip," John-Wayne said, and grinned as he took the frontal brim of the new hat between his thumb and forefinger, admiring himself in the long mirror. "I look just like the white man now."

"You look pretty darn much like an Indian still to me."

"*I* think he just looks western," the girl said as she toted up the bill.

We drove north from the dam a way for a look at the lake. The water which appeared blue from a distance when viewed close up was brown with silt and stagnant-looking beneath the small waves glinting dully under a hazy sun. Far out on the lake the big power boats swung their water-skiers like square-dance partners in foaming circles, while bass boats hugged the watermark around the shoreline. Between the highway and the near shore an army of RVs and camper trailers overlooked a flotilla of houseboats tied up at the marina. A sunken houseboat rested against the pilings of one of the piers, only her top deck rising above the oily water. A charcoal grill and several chairs remaining on deck suggested she had gone down fast, interrupting someone's barbecue supper. Good enough for him, I thought.

"Did you ever fish for striped bass?" I asked.

"I never went fishin for nothin."

"Never went fishing?"

"I was raised in a desert," John-Wayne explained coldly, with a touch of pride.

"We'll have to fix that," I promised him. "The best place for bass is the Sea of Cortez in Mexico. They have the best desert fishing you ever saw."

Small deltas of the fine red sand filled in the corners of the motel and around the door frames. I left John-Wayne sitting stiffly in his new clothes on the bed watching something on television and went around to call Jody, using the pay telephone.

"Hello?"

"Hello."

"Hello! Where *are* you?"

"We're in Page."

"'We?'"

I explained about John-Wayne, leaving out the part having to do with Bette's gift horse.

"Like Tonto and the Lone Ranger? That might work. When is he going to find my horse for me?"

I said I expected to pick him up from a man in Holbrook in a couple of days.

"God, I hope so. This business has been dragging on for weeks now. How are you otherwise?"

"I'm all right. I miss you."

"I miss you too."

"What's happening on the place?"

"We're haying still. The crop is thin because of the drought but at least the cuttings don't get rained on. The hay is full of rattlesnakes."

"O'Grady's behaving himself?"

"Of course. Dago's the perfect gentleman."

"He is like hell."

"Anyway he's a hand."

"If you say so."

"Why are you down on Dago today?"

"I'm not down on him. I'm glad he's there to defend you with his trusty stiletto."

"I don't need defending by anyone," Jody said.

"I know you don't. You're a brave girl. That's only one of the many reasons why I love you so much."

"I love you too."

"I'll be seeing you in a couple of days, then."

"That doesn't sound like a long time to wait."

"You can spend it thinking what I'm going to do with you when I do see you."

"*Please* don't talk about it," she begged.

John-Wayne was sitting propped with a pillow against the headboard of the bed when I returned to the room.

"Did you call your girlfriend?" he asked.

"How did you know I have a girlfriend?"

"Everyone has a girlfriend," he answered simply.

He had been mooning over the photo of Bette he carried in his wallet, lying open beside him on the bed.

"I'm goin to call mine in a couple minutes."

"You're way too young to be serious about a woman," I told him.

"I ain't serious."

"You could have fooled me. Her too, probably."

"I'm in love."

"That's serious," I said. "For you anyway."

"Not really." John-Wayne grinned. "It's fun."

One of the trailer tires was low when we came out. There was no spare. We went looking for someone to fix a tire and found an old man living on the edge of town in a cinderblock house surrounded by automobiles in various stages of disassembly. The old man did not speak English and he was very deaf. John-Wayne had to yell to make himself understood; finally he was able to tell me to go ahead and jack the trailer up and take the wheel off. The old man did not look at me while he patched the leak and sealed it, but he spoke volubly to John-Wayne.

"He was a talkative old bird," I remarked when I had paid the man five dollars and we were on our way south again. "What did he have to say?"

"He said to be careful hangin around with you."

"Why?"

"Cause if I ain't, I might let myself get corrupted," John-Wayne said.

He protested when we came to the junction with 160 and I turned east toward Tuba City.

"This ain't the fast way to Holbrook."

"I know it."

"Where we goin, Dude?"

"To your grandmother's."

"What for, man?"

"She'll be missing you after five days."

"Missin me like a bad headache. That's what *she* says."

"All grandmothers talk that way. I know mine did."

"She's gone to San Diego, anyway."

"You told me this morning she wasn't leaving until Monday," I reminded him. With any luck she would want to send him to Red Lake to herd sheep while she was in California, allowing me to get away to Holbrook alone and pick up the horse from Thompson. John-Wayne was a good kid but the truth was I didn't need him anymore. The opposite, in fact.

Instead of Mrs. Bilagody's car a new-model Dodge truck stood parked beside the trailer.

"Jesus," John-Wayne said when he saw the pickup.

"Who is it?"

"My grandfather."

"He lives here, doesn't he?"

"Only when my grandmother don't. That's how come she went to California already."

We sat in the truck with the engine switched off, watching the white truck shiny with new paint and the trailer house beyond it. The front door was pulled shut behind the aluminum screen and the blinds had been let down behind the windows.

"Isn't he going to come out?" I asked.

"He's drunked up," John-Wayne said. "He don't even know we're settin out here, man."

"Are we going in, then?"

He didn't answer at once.

"We got to," he said at last. "*I* got to."

He stepped onto the porch to ring the bell, and stepped back off it again. When no one answered he rang a second time. The bell made a chiming sound somewhere within the house. After nearly a minute John-Wayne stepped up again and tried the door. The door was unlocked. He pushed it open slowly and we went on in together.

It was dark inside the house, deep twilight behind the closed-up blinds, and stifling, almost suffocatingly hot. There was a smell too, staley sweet and fetid like the breath of a hundred drunks panhandling for quarters in the men's room in a Greyhound bus station. The smell seemed to have a definite source that was impossible to locate in the darkness where the separate shadows were already beginning to merge.

"Granpa," John-Wayne said. "It's me, John-Wayne."

He paused, waiting, and when nothing happened he spoke again, this time in the Navajo language. Then he switched on the overhead light.

The old man sat watching us from a basket chair across the room between the television set and Mrs. Bilagody's good Navajo rug hanging on the wall. He was a short, still strong-looking man, pudding-faced, and he bared his strangely-white teeth as he glared with reddened unseeing eyes. In fact those eyes saw plenty though it was not us they were focused on but something behind or rather beyond us, not in space but in some other dimension I had never looked into—and never wanted to, either. An empty glass rested on the table beside him and a whiskey bottle stood upright on the floor by his feet, but it wasn't the glass or the bottle that had my attention. Sitting forward with his knees apart as if he were about to spring from the chair the old man gripped a hatchet—not a lethal-looking war hatchet trimmed with ribbons but one of the garden variety, the kind sold by Walmart or Alco to Yellowstone campers and worm fishermen. Not that I cared where the old codger bought his equipment: From the business-like way in which he fingered the handle I guessed he knew well enough how to use it. I knew a Blackfoot up in Montana who could have removed your appendix with a well-honed hatchet without you ever having been made aware of the fact. John-Wayne addressed his grandfather again in Navajo, at which the hosteen blinked once but said nothing.

"Granpa," he said once more, and took a step toward the chair.

A rattlesnake doesn't strike faster than that old man did, squatted down in the chair like a toad, and rattlesnakes don't have a whiskey habit. I hardly saw his arm come up and I never saw the hatchet at all, just heard the chink as the blade bit into the dry-wall lining of the aluminum skin beside the front door. I don't know who he was aiming at, but to come as close to either one of us as he did was like almost winning a dart game throwing pencils. Then at last the hosteen spoke. It sounded like a single word, harsh and guttural, evil-sounding. A curse perhaps, but something more than a curse: a designation, an evil naming.

"Let's go," I said, taking the kid by the elbow. It was going to mean complications, maybe even trouble, but you can't leave a sixteen-year-old boy alone to face that.

We drove thirty miles toward Holbrook in silence before John-Wayne spoke.

"My granpa used to be a good man before he got to be a drunk. He never made me go to school when my grandmother was away. He used to let me have the keys to the truck when he was drunk. When I was little he used to hold me on his knee and call me his Honey Lamb."

"He throws a mean hatchet, that's for sure. Kit Carson wouldn't have stood a chance against your grandfather."

"That's why the white man gave the red man his whiskey. He didn't know that even a drunk Indian is still a man. As good as him, or better. Like my grandfather."

We were almost to Flagstaff when I asked, "What was it he said after he threw the hatchet?"

"He was crazy drunk. He thought we were skinwalkers, come to kill him."

"It sounded awful the way he said it."

"It is awful," John-Wayne said. "There's things happen on the reservation the white man don't know nothin about. And never will, neither."

---

In the long rays of the late afternoon sun slanting across dust clouds raised by dry thunderheads above Holbrook, Arizona, the town looked more gritty and depressing even than I remembered it. I checked us into a motel behind the package liquor stores and the Indian crafts shops in the old business district south of the interstate exchange. The motel was a single-story stucco building with a tile roof, plain but clean looking, advertising single rooms for eighteen-ninety-five.

"They don't have no TV," John-Wayne said in an ominous voice.

"Of course they have TV."

"The sign don't say they do."

"It doesn't need to. Every motel in America has TV nowadays. Unfortunately."

"Not for eighteen-ninety-five they don't."

"It'll be more than that for two people," I assured him.

The on-duty clerk, a kid from India, seventeen or eighteen years old, lay prone on an Indian blanket thrown over a sofa, watching television. He got up off the sofa reluctantly as we entered and went behind the narrow office desk. If he understood the English language the way he spoke it, he wasn't enjoying the television show very much. The place smelled of curry and there was the hiss of food frying in the manager's apartment behind the beaded curtain covering the door space. The kid ran my credit card as if he had been born doing it and handed me an oldfashioned latchkey attached to a piece of board with the room number burned into it.

On the way across the parking area we passed two Mexican families sitting outside in folding chairs around a barbecue grill, smoking cigarettes and drinking beer as they listened to a Spanish-language program through the open door to their room.

"Buenas tardes," I told them.

"Buenas tardes," the men replied.

The room, which was plain and barely furnished, smelled of fresh paint, the cheap new carpeting, and immigrant earnestness. A black-and-white Motorola TV set, resting on a flimsy chest of drawers, faced toward the bed.

"You see?" I asked John-Wayne. "They may not give you very much for eighteen ninety-five but you do get your goddamn TV."

He switched on the set and went into the bathroom to shower. I switched it off again and lay down on one of the beds with two pillows under my head.

"You goin to call your woman tonight?" John-Wayne asked, emerging from the bathroom a full quarter of an hour later with a towel around his waist.

"No. Did you wish to call yours?"

"I do, but I ain't got no change left."

"You don't want to be calling her all the time anyhow," I advised him. "That way, she won't be in such a hurry to get rid of you."

We went for supper at the Desert Sun. It advertised itself as a steakhouse, the vehicles parked around were pickup trucks rather than minivans and Cadillacs, and I was surprised to find what looked like a hefty-looking wine list on the table.

"Let me see that," John-Wayne said after we had given the waitress our order.

"You want to see the wine list?"

"It ain't wine, it's kereoke."

"We're going," I said, pushing back in the chair.

"But we already ordered!"

"That's all right. Someone else can choke on it."

"I want to *stay*!" he cried. "There ain't no kereoke on the res!"

I drank two double whiskeys before the food came and a half-bottle of red wine with the meal. The singers were country-western wannabes and a couple of choir tenors; also a young lady, dressed beyond the occasion, who obviously enjoyed a rich fantasy life and had what must have been the worst voice between Needles, California and Nashville.

"She stinks," John-Wayne observed.

"She does, indeed."

"I guess I'm goin to have to show them all, now."

He reached beneath the chair for his hat and stood up.

"I didn't know you were a singer."

He grinned.

"You watch me, Dude."

John-Wayne clapped the hat down over his ears and swaggered to the podium where he sang "Achey-Breaky Heart" in a roaring voice, keeping his eyes screwed shut and his forehead creased while he held his arms out rigidly before him, the fists tightly clenched. He received a tremendous hand when he finished and returned, grinning, to the table.

"I sounded good, huh?"

He removed his hat and wiped his sweating forehead with his sleeve.

"You sounded loud. Lots of feeling."

"That's what music is all about, man—feelin."

The Mexicans were sitting out still when we returned to the motel, the ends of their cigarettes burning in the darkness. I raised my hand to them in passing.

"Buenas noches."

"Buenas noches, señor."

I thought about calling Jody but John-Wayne would have guessed what I was up to. I slept badly that night, waking for the last time around six when I lay under the thin sheet in the coming light listening to John-Wayne's snores and thinking that today finally we would have the horse back and I could go home to Jody James and resume the life we were making together in the beautiful green valley with the tree-lined creek running in it, the red cliffs, and the tall blue mountains rising above. John-Wayne quit snoring and woke all at once with enthusiasm, like a whale breaking water.

"Hey Dude."

"Hey yourself."

"Did you sleep good?"

"No."

"I didn't sleep good either."

"The hell you didn't. You never stopped snoring from the time your head hit the pillow until right now."

"I didn't say I didn't sleep. I said I didn't sleep *good*."

"And you're going to be a successful Washington attorney when you grow up."

"Today's the day we get my horse back, man."

"*If* we're lucky."

"You know what? I had a dream last night."

"About what?"

"About Bette tellin the Paiute to go chase himself."

The Mexicans were lifting the chairs and the outdoor grill into one of two already overloaded pickup trucks as we went for breakfast. We walked the couple of blocks to the café and I bought a paper from a vending machine. It was a long time since I had looked at a newspaper and when I finished reading the first page I felt sorry to have broken my track record. After breakfast we looked around downtown in the stores, which were having their summer sales. We spent over an hour in the hardware and sporting goods emporium, starting with the miniature tractors and power mowers up front behind the plate glass window and working our way back through the gasoline-powered chainsaws, dangerous-looking in their sharp paint jobs, the polished helves of axes and black bit-heads, silver chain in varying strengths and sizes wound on spools, coils of hemp and yellow nylon rope, and the stacked trays of bolts and nails each with its diameter neatly inscribed on a card beneath it. The plank floors and stamped tin ceiling reminded me of my boyhood, and so did the sharp exciting smell of unstained metal and new paint, the chemical ones of rubber and plastic. The firearms stood racked across the back of the store, behind the antique wood and glass cases displaying small arms and boxes of ammunition. The shotguns began on the left and worked over to the large-caliber rifles, ranked in descending size down to the .22-250s and .22s. The guns looked tall and competent and dangerous, waiting to be handled and used—beautiful. Big yellow tickets with the sale prices written on them in bold numbers stood out against the heavy walnut stocks and the blued steel.

"Have you ever owned a rifle?" I asked John-Wayne.

"Just a little-bitty twenty-two. My grandfather was goin to give me his old four-ten for my fourteenth birthday, but he ain't done it yet."

"What would be your choice, if you were buying?"

He went around the end of the counter and commenced studying the arsenal, beginning with the shotguns. When he came to the rifles he slowed up and studied them carefully for some time before lifting one from the rack. He handled it in a tentative way—less from respect, I thought, than disbelief. It was a Winchester Model 94 .30-30 lever-action equipped with iron sights, and the distinctive high Winchester comb. John-Wayne brought the rifle up and sighted along the barrel. When he lowered it I made him shoulder the gun again and showed him how to support the forward weight properly under the forestock.

"Why the lever-action?"

He shrugged. "It looks cool."

"Meaning that's what you've seen in the movies," I said.

John-Wayne racked the Winchester reluctantly. He turned the price-tag over and read it. Then he turned it back again.

"If that's what you want, that's what you're going to have one of these days."

"I was fourteen two and a half years ago, and I still ain't got no four-ten."

"Never mind," I told him. "Hope is supposed to be a virtue."

When we were ready to leave I borrowed a telephone directory from the store clerk and looked up Jake Thompson's address in the listings. We checked out of the motel, ate lunch, and killed the rest of the day poking around in the Indian and Mexican import stores. The evening shadows were already lengthening toward six o'clock when we got on the road going south to Snowflake and Show Low. The Thompson place was several miles out of town, a dusty doublewide with extensive corrals off to one side and the open haysheds behind them. Among the heavy equipment standing around was a long silver stock trailer with THOMPSON LAND & LIVESTOCK printed in black letters on the front of it.

"Looks like he made it home from his glue-run already," I said.

The near corral had many horses in it, all of them standing still to observe the one who would not stand run the fence, back and forth, at a well-collected trot, holding his neck arched and his tail up in the show position.

"There he is!" John-Wayne shouted. "They got my horse!"

A young girl hanging on the outside of the fence watched him also. She looked around when she heard us coming in the truck.

"Hello," I told her. "Is Mr. Thompson your dad?"

"Yes he is."

"Is he home?"

"No," she said, "he ain't."

I guessed her age at about twelve or thirteen years old, certainly not above fourteen.

"I need to have a talk with him."

The girl looked scared.

"Did he do anything wrong?"

"Not that I know about."

"He's at the casino in Show Low."

"Is your mother inside?"

"My mom's dead."

"I'm sorry to hear it. When do you expect your father home?"

"I don't know. Some time, I guess."

I caught Tortuga's eye as he came along the fence, flaring his nostrils and blowing. He didn't look surprised to see me at all. Or interested, for that matter.

"That's a good-looking horse," I said.

"Oh yes," she exclaimed, "he is. He's a *beautiful* horse." Her voice sounded eager and sad at the same time.

"Well," I said, "I guess I'll just have to try again in the morning, then."

"He'll be here," the girl said, "unless he has a winning streak. It don't happen very often though."

We made camp on the desert at a near distance from Thompson Land & Livestock. I sent John-Wayne to gather wood for a fire and we cooked our supper outside and ate it while the evening storm clouds drifted eastward into the rising darkness and the sun dropped behind the triangular outline of the San Francisco Mountains.

"This time tomorrow," John-Wayne said, "my honey's going to love me. And *only* me."

"Look there," I said, pointing toward a cloud of golden dust moiling far out on the desert dotted with the dark cedar trees: "wild horses."

The desert at dawn stretched dun-colored under a gray sky. John-Wayne was still asleep in the bunk bed when I awoke. I rose quietly, dressed, and went out to build back the fire with the wood we had gathered the evening before. The coals were warm still but lifeless beneath a blanket of feathered ash. I laid a shaggy juniper branch on them and touched off the browned needles with a match. The branch exploded in flame along its length, sending up clouds of oily gray smoke, sharp smelling with a stale uric odor. I added twigs and broken sticks and when the fire was burning strongly I laid on three good-sized logs bracing each other in a tripod arrangement. Smoke vented through the worm and woodpecker holes as the logs heated and panicked ants ran forward and backward, searching for a way down. When the smoke burned away I filled the coffee pot from the water can and added grounds, making a floating pyramid on the surface of the water. Then I replaced the top, set the pot in the ashes hard against the flaming logs, and sat back on my heels before the fire, waiting for the water to boil. If watched pots never boiled the camp fire would never have been invented. When the brown foam rose in the spout I wrapped the handle in my bandana handkerchief and lifted the pot from the fire. I cracked a raw egg on the rim, drained in the albumen to settle the grounds, and reset the pot on the coals. Then I tossed the shell with the yolk inside it under a tree for the birds to find, and when the coffee was ready poured a tin mug full. The egg-white gave it a smooth texture and a faintly sweet, Oriental flavor. I drank most of the pot before John-Wayne was up, scraped the grounds with the congealed whites from the bottom, and set fresh coffee to brew on the fire. He came from the camper wearing only his pants, barefoot, with the new straw hat on the back of his head.

"'Lo Dude," John-Wayne said.

"Good morning. Coffee's about ready."

"I been thinkin."

"What about?"

"We should of gone back there yesterday and took that horse while the old man's away. That little girl couldn't have done nothin about it."

"That isn't the proper way to treat a woman."

"She ain't no woman. Twelve, maybe thirteen years old."

"She'll be a woman some day."

"What difference does that make? A woman is just a woman. There ain't nothin special about it."

"What are you going to all this trouble to please yours for, then? If you'll rustle us up some more wood I can build back the fire and get a bed of coals going for breakfast."

For breakfast we ate eggs fried in grease from what remained of the bacon supply, wiped up with the heel of a loaf of staling sourdough bread.

"I don't want no more coffee to drink," John-Wayne said. "I'm ready to go get my horse now."

"There's nothing to be in a hurry about. Thompson won't be available until noon at the earliest."

"It ain't but forty, fifty miles from Show Low."

"When was the last time your grandfather was up before noon after a night on the town?" I was sorry the moment after I said it, but there didn't seem to be any use apologizing.

While John-Wayne finished dressing I boiled water to wash up with and packed away the cook things. Together we scattered the fire ring, doused the coals with water, and filled in the pit with clay and sand.

"Now what?" John-Wayne asked.

"Now we wait patiently until noon, or a little after."

The sky remained overcast, making it pleasantly cool on the desert. Using my old .44 revolver and tin cans from the trash collector we target-shot until we could no longer bear the recoil and the noise; afterward I taught him the basics of poker and blackjack, sitting at the pullout table in the camper. He caught on fast and I allowed him to beat me in a few simple games, using pieces of sandstone rock for chips. But he kept checking his watch and at ten minutes past noon John-Wayne asked, "Can we go now?"

"All right," I said, sweeping the rock chips into my hand and pushing the table in, "we'll go."

It wasn't ten minutes from where we were camped over to Thompson's. The yellow-and-white pickup truck standing in the yard beside the house hadn't been there the evening before. John-Wayne followed me onto the porch and stood behind me as I pushed the bell. The yard had the neglected look of no woman around and the planter boxes along the porch edge were empty and sun-rotted. I rang again and almost at once a big man with thin gray hair streaked with yellow, a lantern jaw, and a purple face stood sock-footed in the doorway, staring at us across the threshold. The whites of his eyes were inflamed around the faded blue irises and he had a whiskey-breath that could have killed flies at twenty paces.

"Yeah?" the man said.

"Are you Mr. Jake Thompson?"

"That's me."

"I'm looking to buy a horse."

"What kind of horse?"

"No kind in particular. Just a horse."

"Ain't any such thing as just a horse," Thompson said.

"I know it. Whatever the best you have is, I'll buy that one."

He studied me speculatively from his bloodshot eyes.

"I'll be right with you," he said finally, "soon's I get my boots on."

He turned about and went toward the back of the house, leaving the door open behind him. The front room looked as if someone had been raising dogs there. Five minutes later he reappeared, shod and wearing a sweat-stained misshapen Stetson.

"Took me all that time just to find my goll-dang boots," Thompson explained.

We walked down to the corrals together.

"I brought a new bunch in yesterday," Thompson said, " and a few more head this mornin, so you got a better'n-average selection to choose from. I move em through here pretty dang quick, I can tell you."

The horses stood watching together on the side of the corral away from us as we approached. There looked to be six or seven head more than there had been last night. Also there was one less.

"I'll stir em around for you so you can kind of see em in action."

Thompson opened the gate and squeezed through it. He moved carefully, carrying his head as if it pained him.

"That there sorrel," Thompson added, "he's a good horse, now. Not over ten-eleven years old, geldin, long-coupled, not too narrow-based. What'd you say you was wantin to use him for?"

Jake Thompson stood in the corral, nearly hidden by dust and the running horses. His mouth went on opening and shutting but the staggered staccato of the hoofbeats covered his voice. He quit stirring them around finally and walked back toward the gate through the settling dust with his hat pulled over his eyes.

I said, "You had a black bay in here when we stopped last night, fifteen and a half hands high, carries himself like a show horse. I imagine you went ahead already and cut him out of these canners."

"The black bay," Thompson repeated as he pulled the gate shut behind him and secured it. "Now *that* was a horse, goll-dang it."

"Where is he?"

He looked at his hands as if he expected to find blood there, and rubbed them on his pantlegs.

"Gone," he said.

"Gone?"

"Run off with the wild horse herd last night—God damnit!"

"He got loose?"

"He was let loose."

"Who did it?"

"Young girls is crazy in the head when it comes to horses. I mean, they're crazy in the head, period, but *specially* where there's horses concerned."

"Your daughter turned him loose," I said.

"She come down when I was unloadin that bunch I brought from the res yesterday, and the minute she seen that horse it was just love at first sight. Said if I'd hold him out of the lot she'd save up the money to buy him from me. I says, Who's goin to pay for the feed he eats while you're doin it? It's way cheaper for him to be eaten than to eat, I said to her."

"How long has he been gone?"

"I was away overnight in Show Low, pickin up a few more head and playin a little blackjack. A man has to have himself some fun now and then, know what I mean? She broke down and told me about it before I went to bed this mornin. Cass has been actin kind of queerlike since her mama died, year ago last March."

We were nearly to the truck when I asked, "Were you honestly going to let that horse go for dogmeat?"

Thompson looked abashed. "Hell no," he said, "I wouldn't have sold him as a canner. I was goin to pull him over to Flag and sell him off to one of them rich girls from California. Maybe they don't have no more taste than the Injuns do, but they sure as hell have more money. What's this for?"

"It's to encourage you not to be too hard on your daughter," I told him. "What I would have been willing to pay you for the horse—who was stolen, by the way. She's got more taste in horses than a thousand California women, and more heart than a million of any other kind."

Thompson did not speak as we got up in the truck. I drove slowly out of the yard, the empty trailer clattering behind, and the last I saw in the tow mirror he was standing on the turnaround with his feet apart and his wallet out, counting the money.

---

Everywhere in the West you find these old ranchers feeding six or eight times the number of horses they need or really want, because their women insist on it. I rented two fairly good animals from a sheep-and-cattle man in Snowflake for less money than Thompson would have charged me for the hind end of one of his bonemealers, together with the worn-out tack which he threw in at no extra charge. In Holbrook I picked up nylon packs, ponchos, lariats, matches, and topographic maps, and purchased provisions enough for five days—canned goods, dried cereal, and coffee. After a little consideration I went ahead and added a fifth of Jim Beam whiskey. Finally I returned with John-Wayne to the hardware store where I paid cash for the Winchester, a good leather scabbard, and a couple of boxes of .30-30 and .44 Magnum shells. It was the first I gun I had ever bought for a kid and it was worth the money, believe me. I'm not so old I've given up entirely on having a boy of my own someday.

We had the packs loaded and ready by late afternoon, nothing to do but wait on the rancher who was pulling the horses from Snowflake. He had promised to leave after supper, and I was expecting him around seven. It was nine o'clock before he arrived, the sun already down and dusk closing in around the fire we had built at the old campsite within the reassembled fire ring. The horses were a tall white gelding, part Arab, named Quixote and a potbellied bay quarterhorse called Doña Ana. I told the rancher, Baca, to tie up on either side of my single-horse trailer and then come over and drink a cup of coffee with us.

"Good coffee," Baca said. He was a small dark man with pouched, heavy-lidded eyes, a graying mustache, and melancholy face.

"It goes better with a little whiskey."

"Sure," Baca said, brightening a little.

I brought the bottle from the pack and poured a shot into Baca's cup first, my own next. Then I looked at John-Wayne.

"Are you allowed a drink of whiskey now and again at home?"

"My cousin brings a bottle out to Red Lake ever week."

"I won't worry about corrupting you then."

"Where were you fellers figurin on searchin for that horse tomorrow?" Baca asked.

"I thought we'd start by riding east and taking a look into the Little Colorado."

He nodded.

"That's where the water's at, mostly. It's bad country that way. Cold as a witch's tit in winter, hot as the Devil this time of year."

"We're prepared for it."

"And look out for the bruja."

"The what?"

Baca looked into his cup. "Desert witch," he said, and drank the coffee off.

"If you see one, don't follow it."

"It never was any ambition of mine to follow a witch."

The old man shook his head.

"Sometimes," he said, "it's almost more than a feller can do, not to."

# BOOK III
# TORTUGA

We rode before daylight, keeping the horses' noses toward the faint shine on the eastern sky and our collars up against a following breeze, no sound but the steady hoof-falls, early birdsong, and now and again the ring of shoe iron on stone. We had ridden a mile or more when the desert heaved up suddenly from the darkness, pouring gray shadow from the folds and basins of the colorless rock stretching away to the horizon around. The peace and cool of early morning were prolonged for a single instant before the sun squeezed above the horizon in a roar of light from which I flinched instinctively, drawing back in the saddle as I pulled my hat over my eyes.

"God damn that horse," I said.

"It's the girl's fault for lettin him out."

"It wasn't the girl who started all this," I reminded him.

Tors and boulders sent long shadows streaking westward under the sun's oblique rays. The birds ceased singing and the desert lay silent and withdrawn in the scorching summer day. We rode in silence for the most part, watching the horse's ears and halting only when I dismounted on high ground to glass the terrain.

John-Wayne said, "I bet them horses was at Thompson's again last night, eatin off that haystack."

"Baca claims they don't hang around much over here."

"Baca don't know everthin," he observed.

"I know it," I said, putting Quixote forward with my heels to avoid having to argue with him. The horse was well-collected, a natural athlete with good crossover and quick on his feet as a panther. John-Wayne's mare was not as good, being stubborn and basically lazy but careful with her feet and easy in her disposition. On account of her shorter stride she was unable to pace him and after falling behind a hundred yards would break to a lope at her own initiative to catch up with us.

The land was largely purple tuff covered by thin pale grass and broken by volcanic necks and cones, rising in the south toward low pine forests. Round white clouds appeared as the sun rose in the sky, and with the sun the wind got up. What always gets left out of those pictures of the idyllic Western landscape is the Western wind. We moved along at a steady trot, riding out the heights for a look at the country below and dropping down into dry washes among the low broken cliffs where the rock and brush and scrub oak offered shade and shelter from the wind and you could almost always find water if you knew where to look for it. The washes, cutting downhill between eroding banks, were grown over with brush and fragments of polished wood, and the bleached bones of deer and antelope lay strewed around in their sandy courses. Among the tracks of many animals in the wash the wide frogged prints of a shod horse were missing. It was nine o'clock when we came to a circle of green grass in the shade of an alder grove growing against a low cliff and stopped to rest the horses while we sat with our hats off beneath the little trees.

"Are you bored yet?" I asked.

"I hate ridin with all this junk behind."

Besides the packs lying across the croup behind the cantle and fastened forward to the D-rings each of us carried his bedroll tied ahead of the pommel, a lariat, and a gallon canteen hanging on the saddlehorn. The new Winchester rifle in its scabbard was slung muzzle forward on Doña Ana's off side, tucked beneath the saddle skirt.

"Let the horse do the complaining if she wants to," I told him. "She's the one that has to carry your big overgrown carcass."

We bridled the horses, mounted, and rode uphill away from the wash between red parapets of rock to high ground again, where I took a bearing on the Little Colorado to the east. As far as I could see in all directions no living thing stirred except for a pair of hawks circling in a layer of cooler air high above the baking sand and rock. The desert had stiffened into immobility and only the vast sky stretching above it was alive and moving with the white clouds that formed themselves out of nothing while you watched, piling upward in billowing turrets from their darkening bases.

"Nothing," I said, tucking the field glasses under my vest.

"We're goin to have rain this evenin."

"I doubt it. It never rains anymore."

"Those clouds have plenty of rain in them."

"Of course they have rain. We never see any of it, that's all."

"You're goin to see some today," John-Wayne said confidently. "I've lived in the desert my whole life, man. The Indian *knows.*"

We halted again at a little past noon to picket the horses and eat dinner. The water in the canteens was burning hot. We set them to cool in the shade of a stony overhang and ate jerkied beef and crackers while the horses grazed the little grass they could find at the ends of the picket lines. After dinner we lay up under the overhang stretched on the cool sand with the saddles under our heads. When we woke the horses were standing with their eyes shut under a juniper tree and the air was heavy and still.

"How far we ridin today, Dude?"

"We have to make it to the river now. The horses are going to need the water."

"We better get goin then. I don't want to be up on no iron-shod horse in a lightnin storm."

The clouds swelled deep into the blue sky, their shining heads traveling high above the gray undersides, and they had closed up considerably. Now the desert too was moving, crawling with the dark cloud shadow. We crested a ridge broken by outcrops of rock and followed along the ridgeline on a northeasterly heading. The country, tilting away on every side, gradually assumed a dominant pitch sloping vaguely toward the river which appeared in segments, blue, brown, and green, beneath the line of red bluffs ahead eight or ten miles. The wind dried the lathered horses who needed to be pushed now between frequent halts to glass the country around. Once we spied a herd of animals three or four miles out but from their arrangement on the grassy upland I saw even without the glasses that they were beef cattle. Riding on we reached a fence line constructed from ax-cut and ax-trimmed piñon and cottonwood trees supporting four strands of slack barb-wire. I took the wire-cutters from the pack and while John-Wayne held the horse I cut all four of them. He rode ahead and when he was through the hole I made a loop in one end of each of the wires, pulled the straight ends through, and backbraided them until the slack had been taken up and the fence was whole again, tighter and stronger than it had been before.

"It's goin to slow us up a bunch, mendin ever fence we come to," John-Wayne said.

"I know it. But it can't be helped."

The strong wind tipped the horses sideways when we changed direction and came around broadside to it. The clouds had shoved in together to make a single towering formation, dazzling white above and dark as night below, advancing rapidly across the desert, a pillar of the Lord. Scenting the storm the horses grew nervy as we rode forward on a tight rein, squinting under the leading edge of the cloud into the glaring eastern desert. While I fought to keep Quixote under control John-Wayne dashed forward along the ridge, bent low over the mare's neck as he held his hat with one hand. He turned in the saddle suddenly and I saw him shout back to me against the driving wind.

"Horses!" John-Wayne yelled. "Horses ahead out there!"

The herd was out about three miles between the ridge we were following and the river where it made a turn to the south. In sunlight still, ahead of the cloud shadow, they milled nervously, spooked by the storm, looking for somewhere to break to. I slipped down from the horse, handed the reins to John-Wayne, and stepped up to an elevation of rock from where I counted twenty to thirty animals partially obscured by the blowing dust. Behind them a stony column, eroded in the shape of a womanly figure in skirts, rose to a height of a hundred feet or more above the desert floor. Lightning flickered in the lenses, followed by a roll of thunder as I lowered the glasses.

"Let me look," John-Wayne begged.

"What at? Your eagle eye already spied everything there is to see."

We spurred the horses down from the ridge into the broken country below and followed the drainage east, keeping in the shelter of the deepest gullies and arroyos. The hail struck first with a rattling sound, jumping like Mexican beans on the hardpan and then, as it accumulated, bedding in a cover of solid white. Hail popped in the folds of the ponchos and nestled in the horses' manes, and the falling gray sheets showed yellow and pink in vivid flashes of lightning. When the hail turned to rain we rode out of the wash and along the face of a low cliff where we came finally to an apron of red mud rising to a shallow hole in the rock. We tied the horses to a couple of bushes and climbed up to the cave where, surrounded by guano and the nests of cliff swallows, we observed the torrential rain and the chain lightning spreading like livid fractures across the darkened face of the universe while the horses stood with their hindquarters to the wind, their backs humped, and their heads hanging miserably. The desert commenced to rattle and then to roar from gutters, spouts, and veils of foaming pink runoff and a lightning bolt struck directly across the canyon with an instantaneous report and the sharp ozone smell. John-Wayne climbed down in the rain to keep the horses from bolting. He returned streaming water, his black hair pasted to his forehead, carrying the Winchester beneath the poncho. A broad grin spread his wet cheeks wide apart.

"Male rain," he said happily.

"I don't believe it. I guess we're supposed to take it as an omen."

"Plenty of water for the horses now. We don't have to ride as far as the river today."

An inch of hail remained on the ground when the rain quit. We stuffed the ponchos into the packs, wiped the saddle seats dry with our sleeves, and rode off after the storm as it retreated, flashing and booming, ahead of us. Before we had ridden a mile the hail soaked into the ground and a double rainbow arced against the black clouds. The horses left long skidmarks on the downhill slopes, muddying themselves above the knees.

"Where do you guess them horses are at now?"

"Probably around Amarillo, Texas somewhere."

We turned south and rode onto another of the ridges for a look around. The rainbow, slightly faded, held in place to the west, above the woman-shaped column rising wet and shining in the late afternoon sun.

"They was down *there,* under where you see that rock."

"I know it. The white man has eyes as well as you."

We descended the ridge by its southern aspect slowly to allow the horses to keep their hindquarters under them in the mud, and let them drink from the gulley where the water had almost ceased to run. Then we rode on across the gently rolling desert toward the standing rock, feeling the sun striking hot on our cheeks under the wide hats while the horses' flanks steamed in the golden light of early evening. The horses were recovering their footing as the hardpan slowly dried. We put them forward at a trot and arrived after an hour's ride at the grassy swale imprinted with the tracks of the vanished horse herd. I looked over to the woman-form standing above us against the sky.

"Probably they're sheltered up behind that chimney there."

John-Wayne was already off the mare and seated cross-legged on the ground, holding the reins over his shoulder while she ranged behind him, hungrily cropping the bitten-down grass.

"I don't care where they're at, just so's I don't have to go lookin for them tonight."

"Faint heart never won fair lady," I told him. "Get up from your backside now and pull the gear off the horse. We'll make camp here where there's graze still, and enough brush around for a fire."

We laid the packs on the ground, spread the bedrolls, and staked out the horses. John-Wayne scavenged for sagebrush and greasewood while I found rocks for a fire ring and took the cook pans from the packs. When we had a fire going I poured coffee water into one of the pans and set it over the flames. Then, using my camp knife, I removed the lid from a can of hash.

"Only *one* can?" John-Wayne asked, throwing down a load of brush.

"Bring another over if you want it."

I poured oil into the skillet, spread it around with one finger, and spooned the hash in. The meat began to sizzle almost at once and I lifted the pan from the flames and held it a few inches above the fire while the fat melted through into the oil in the bottom of the skillet. When the hash had been warming for about a minute I turned it over with a fork. It was crisp and brown underneath already, and it smelled wonderful. Using the fork I turned it over and over again until the hash was heated through, with bits of crisp in it.

"Quit that now and let's eat," John-Wayne begged finally. "You tryin to kill me, man?"

We ate from the Saltillo plates and cleaned up with thick pieces of bread. When supper was finished we stretched ourselves on the hard ground propped on one elbow with our boots crossed, drinking coffee.

"How do you feel now—better?"

"Feel like I'm goin to live, maybe. Don't know about better."

Overhead the blue sky had the golden glow of evening in it. Shadows spread across the desert and pooled in the hollows, darkening the stone pediment as far as the skirts of the scarlet figure standing in full sunlight above the camp.

"That rock up there looks like a woman," John-Wayne remarked.

"You're at the age where everything reminds you of sex."

The cold came simultaneously with the blue twilight, as if cold itself was a color. We built the fire back with greasewood and the skeletons of the dead cholla lying around and set a fresh pot of coffee to boil. The stars began to show, in the east at first and then overhead, while Venus brightened rapidly in the track of the vanished sun. John-Wayne sat cross-legged on a horse blanket, cradling the Winchester in his arms.

"I ain't seen nothin to shoot at yet," he complained. "Do you miss your woman, Dude?"

"Of course I miss her."

"I miss mine too, you bet."

I went to check the picket lines and give the horses a taste of the little grain I had been able to bring with us in the packs. John-Wayne was already in his bedroll with the rifle beside him and the lariat laid out in a circle around to keep snakes away when I returned to the fire. My socks were damp inside the water-stiffened boots. I pulled them off, turned them inside out, tucked them into the boot-tops as a discouragement for scorpions, and placed the boots together with the revolver next to the sleeping bag. Finally I lay down fully dressed on top of the bag with my head against the saddle seat and the firelight on my face, looking up at the stars.

"Do you believe if you don't drink whiskey and smoke cigarettes you'll have your own planet to live on after you're dead, with all your women around to take care of you?"

"No."

"I have a cousin who's a Mormon, and *he* believes it. That's what I want to have happen to me when *I* die."

"I can't imagine anything worse, myself."

"How come, Dude?"

"Listen," I said, "we'll discuss God, religion, the future, history, women, and the meaning of life some evening when we haven't ridden hard for twelve hours in the heat and rain and two pots of camp coffee can't keep me awake. Go to sleep, now. I'll see you in the morning."

He was asleep and snoring in under a minute and a half and as I lay feeling the hard ground that even after fifty-one years didn't appear ready to receive my old bones yet, I heard a quiet voice within me speaking. "Jeb

Ryder," the voice said, "you may not understand women and you may not understand the world, or even feel at home in it. But one thing you do understand, as well as any man—any Westerner—who ever lived: *Doing this.*"

---

The gray air before sunup felt cool on my exposed face and neck. I lay still for several minutes hearing John-Wayne's snores and the stamp of horses, enjoying the warmth inside the bag. Then I shucked it and went looking for wood to make a fire. Following the storm the afternoon before the desert seemed reborn under a scattering of tiny jeweled flowers. When the fire was burning strongly I walked away from camp a hundred yards to have a look into the wash. John-Wayne was awake when I returned, sitting forward with his hair in his eyes and the bag pulled down as far as his waist.

"How did you sleep?"

"The horses woke me up."

"Don't listen to them, next time."

"I laid awake for hours last night watchin the stars."

"How many shooting stars did you count?"

"A few. Satellites is what I was lookin for."

"I hope the horses didn't wake up with a thirst. There isn't any runoff left in the wash."

We boiled the pot for coffee and ate dried fruit and crackers while we drank it. After breakfast we packed up the camp, rolled and tied the bedrolls, and went to examine the tracks leading away from the swale into the desert. John-Wayne proved to be an excellent tracker, almost as observant as me and with younger eyes. The herd had milled a while before breaking toward the east in the direction of the river. The sun was well above the land line when we took the horses off the picket lines, saddled and loaded them, and rode out with our hats pulled over our eyes and our heads bent, watching the ground.

All that day we tracked the wild horse herd. Several times during the morning and again in the afternoon we lost the main body through following the tracks of stragglers breaking away to the left and right in search of graze or water. A dry hot wind got up and before the sun reached the overhead the desert had begun to die again, the grass blades withering and the bright flowers fading like unheard prayers and curling up in the heat. Between the white-hot sun and the iron-red desert there was only the thin blue sky, hardly enough of it to breathe. Early in the afternoon, following the spoor across tuff, rock shelves, and the desert hardpan, we came to a spring of fouled water surrounded by hoofprints and fresh horse apples and stopped to let the horses drink. John-Wayne swung his right leg over the pack and dropped from the saddle like a bag of dirty laundry.

"Man, my legs have had it."

"You calling it quits already?"

"No way, man."

"My legs are giving me what-for too," I told him. "I feel like Eric after he'd been lying up too long with Enid."

"Say what, Dude?"

"Eric was one of King Arthur's knights. He won the heart of a beautiful woman called Enid in combat, brought her back to court with him, and married her. Eric enjoyed the comforts of married life to the point where he became soft and the other knights were talking about him. So he called for his best armor to be brought and set out on his adventures again."

"Cool, man."

We let the horses stand with the reins over their heads while we walked around on the rocks, stretching the muscles in our legs.

"If we can keep on them they'll take us to water every time."

"After they've mucked around in it to where we can't drink it no more."

"Don't be ungrateful. That pool might look like the Lemonade Springs to you in a couple of days."

John-Wayne stood over the pile of horse apples, regarding it intently. Then he kicked it with the pointed toe of his boot.

"Them horses is just a ball of worms," he said in a disgusted voice.

"Did you know, incidentally, that the urine from a pair of healthy kidneys is sterile?"

"No."

"Well, it's true. You might file the information away for future reference. It could be useful in an emergency."

He gave me a contemptuous look from under the straw hat.

"Navajos would never do a thing like that."

We stayed on the herd the rest of the afternoon without ever sighting it but I felt certain now that the horses were headed for the river. By evening it was in view, slow moving and dull in the shadow of the dark clouds making up above the desert.

"Is it going to storm?" I asked.

"No," John-Wayne said shortly. He did look up to the sky before he spoke.

The river ran low and shrunken in its gravel bed. We made camp beside it in a stand of the big riverine cottonwoods. The trees were green and massy, spreading from broad trunks heavily armored in fluted gray bark. The ground beneath the trees was bare and smooth except for the knobby roots and a scattering of small branches. Salt cedar crowded the river and the mud and gravel bars between the banks. From a cottonwood snag on the opposite bank a pair of ravens watched as we pulled the packs off the horses, ruffling their midnight plumage and shifting their feet on the branch before they spread their wings and departed with harsh, derisive laughter.

We piled the packs and saddles under the trees and led the horses into the river where we stood above our knees in the slow current while they sucked in water and swallowed it with deep groaning sounds. When they had finished drinking we brought them ashore and picketed them. Then we removed our boots and clothes and entered again into the water that felt wonderfully cool and fresh against our skins. John-Wayne made a cup with his hands and dipped them below the surface of the river.

"Don't drink the water," I warned him.

"How come?"

"It's full of giardia."

"What's gee-yar-dee-hah?"

"It's a flagellate protozoan that lives in creeks and rivers and causes acute diarrhea in human beings. It lasts for months and months and the only medicine developed to treat it is probably a carcinogen. You don't want to get infected with giardia, believe me."

"How come it don't make the horses sick?"

"Horses are tougher than people are."

"Except for Navajos. Navajos and horses been drinkin together out of the creek since they come up out of the earth. Nobody never got no gee-hardee-ay, neither."

Lying on my back with my head upstream I let the current carry me, bumping along over the sandy bottom and through the pebbly riffles like a half-submerged log. Through the breaking water I felt the sun hot on my forehead and saw it dazzling red under my closed eyelids. When I was tired of being taken by the current I set my heels hard against the river bottom, stood up in the water, and waded upstream to the cottonwood grove where John-Wayne sat naked on a piece of driftwood.

"I'll race you to the other side and back."

"What for? It ain't very far."

"It's a sprint."

"I can't swim."

"You can't?"

"I told you. I was raised in a desert."

"This is the desert."

"You know what I'm talkin about, man."

"Don't get mad," I said. "I can teach you to swim inside of ten minutes."

I taught him to dogpaddle and started him on the crawl, and then we were both too hungry to swim anymore. We came up dripping from the river and the hot wind dried us before we finished getting our clothes on. When the fire was going and the camp kitchen laid out I brought the bottle of whiskey we had shared only forty-eight hours before with Sr. Baca.

"Have a drink, if you wish," I said. "You've earned it."

I poured a stiff drink for myself and a smaller one for John-Wayne. Seated on a log with the cooling breeze on the backs of our necks, watching the dry thunderheads propel themselves into twilight ahead of the sunset, we drank whiskey while the twittering swallows swooped low above the water picking up insects.

"You know something?"

"What."

"We ought to take the horses before supper and see if we can spot the herd at water along the river." When I saw the look on his face I added, "I'll go, if you'll stay around and keep the fire burning."

I took Ana off the picket line, bridled her, and got up on her fat bare back. Her squeals shivered my backbone and vibrated between my pressing knees as we rode off from camp. But she quieted away from the gelding, quit fighting the bit, and stepped out as briskly almost as a fresh horse until we went easily and fast in the lengthening shadow under the bluff. With the approach of evening the desert came to life again. Birds perched swaying in the salt cedar, lizards scuttled on the hardpan and clung panting against the cooling boulders, and a good-sized rattler slipped from the grass beside the game trail we were following and darted beneath the mare's belly, between her rapidly moving feet. At the first bend we came to I turned in the saddle to look back toward the cottonwoods, green and alive against the purple and rose-colored rock, and the gray drifting smoke from the fire. Beyond the bend the river entered a broad bottom grown up with slim young cottonwoods and before I had ridden a quarter-mile farther I saw the horses, grazing the freshened grass under the trees. Ana saw them too. She put her ears forward and quickened her trot; then, mare-like, she whinnied. It was what I had been counting on her to do. I drew rein and tried to make her stand as I glassed the herd, the long astonished faces staring back at me through the binocular lenses. When she whinnied again I turned her and we rode back at a lope, around the shoulder of cliff at the river bend.

John-Wayne stood a hundred yards from camp in the brush, watching us come up. The mare screamed again, this time for the gelding who paid her no attention as he calmly disengaged his near front hoof from the picket line. John-Wayne seized her by the bridle and held her as I slipped down on the off side.

"You found them!"

"Around the bend and south three-quarters of a mile along the river."

"Is my horse with them?"

"I didn't ride close enough to see. Spook them, and it could be days before we get up on them again."

I slipped the bridle and repicketed the mare who commenced eating calmly again as if the separation had never occurred. The fire, which John-Wayne had built up to a grand blaze, was burning down now to a deep bed of orange and red coals.

"We'll make an early start in the morning," I said, "push them into a box canyon, and cut him out of the herd."

It was dusk when we finished eating and cleaned the cook pans in the river. I sent John-Wayne to bring in the horses and snub them for the night and while he was doing it wetted my whistle from the whiskey bottle before putting it up in the packs. A rind of pale light lay just above the western cliff and overhead the stars were coming out. There was the damp smell of the river and the dry one of cooling rock. I drew the harmonica in its hard leather case from a side pouch of Quixote's pack and carried it back to the fire where, seated on the cottonwood log with one leg crossed on the other, I blew a long C-sharp.

"What's that, man?" John-Wayne asked from the outer darkness.

"Music. Not much going on in camp tonight. I thought I'd be the entertainment."

"You play, Dude?"

"I try," I said.

I played "Turkey In the Straw" to get us both in the mood to shake a leg, and followed it with "Camptown Races." I played "Clementine" and "Red River Valley," which seemed appropriate to the setting. Then I put down the harmonica and sang the words.

> Come and sit by my side if you love me,
> Do not hasten to bid me adieu,
> But remember the Red River Valley,
> And the girl that has loved you so true.

All of them old, old songs but beautiful ones and expressive—especially so down here in the ditch of the Little Colorado, scores of miles beyond the reach of the new America that, in spite of its power and riches, becomes strangely unbelievable in the heart of the ancient American wilderness. Finally I sang "Kathleen Mavourneen," drawing the phrases out romantically and with so much feeling that I almost made myself cry. I stopped singing and then it was as if I was hearing my own performance repeated for my own appreciation, the sweet melancholy pitched words lifted upwards by the draft of the fire and dying out like soft sparks against the velvet night.

"Who's Mavourneen?" John-Wayne wanted to know.

"Nobody. Mavourneen means darling in Gaelic."

Side by side on the log we looked for a long time into the dying glow of the fire.

"I'm tired," John-Wayne said at last.

"Then go to bed."

"I mean—I'm *tired*, man. Like, what exactly are we doin this for, anyway?"

"You're doing it for—for Bette. Because it's her horse."

The breeze got up just enough to make a faint sighing sound in the trees overhead, and then fell again.

"She never ast me. She never even knew there was a horse lost to begin with."

"That's right. She didn't."

"So how come we're doin it then?"

"Because when a man loves a woman he tries to please her. It's a question of love, and of honor."

"You think she'd want to please *me* as bad as all that?"

"I don't know. Probably she wouldn't want to please you in the same way."

"Why not?"

"Because men and women have different ways of pleasing one another."

"That ain't fair."

"It's as fair as the difference between men and women. That's all."

John-Wayne stirred the coals with a stick, sending up a firestorm of orange sparks against the darkness.

"Suppose I bring back this horse and she goes and gets it on anyway with this fat Paiute trainer."

"You'd be proud still to have returned the horse, wouldn't you?"

"No."

"Not even if you thought he might not have cared enough, or maybe had the guts, to do the same thing?"

"No."

"You wouldn't quit loving her just because she decided to go with the trainer?"

"Yes. No. Maybe until I found someone else."

"Fair enough."

"So I get a busted ass and she gets the horse trainer."

"That's what it means sometimes to be a man."

"What kind of a man?"

"Any man. White man, black man, red man, yellow man. Just—a man."

He stood abruptly from the log.

"Then I rather be a Paiute," John-Wayne said.

He walked into the shadows under the cottonwoods to make water while I spread the bedrolls and checked the loads in the revolver. He was away a long time and when he returned at last he set his hat on its crown on the ground, placed the Winchester beside it, and lay down on the bag without saying a word.

"Sleep well anyway," I told him.

He turned on his side away from the firelight to face the darkness.

"Dude?" he asked after a while.

"What is it?"

"Don't never tell no one I said I rather be a Paiute," John-Wayne said.

---

Around dawn I was wakened by a loud noise I recognized by the echo and re-echo as a rifle shot. I rolled over to look for John-Wayne and saw the bag lying unzippered with the top half thrown back. Five minutes later he walked into camp with the Winchester in one hand and a bloody rag in the other.

"Did you mean to scare those horses over into New Mexico, or did you forget to turn your brains on this morning?"

"I killed us a rabbit for breakfast."

"With a thirty-thirty?"

"I was lookin for deer when I saw the rabbit instead. I shot him from fifty—no, seventy-five yards, man. This gun is dead-on."

I took the jack from him and examined it. The head had been blown clean off, leaving the rest of the carcass undamaged.

"You're a good shot even at twenty-five yards, which is the most I'm prepared to give you," I said. "Skin him out and clean him and we'll have fresh meat for breakfast."

"We couldn't have ate a whole deer anyway."

"Not unless we sat here eating a couple of weeks."

"It ain't the Navajo way to waste meat," John-Wayne explained.

We ate the rabbit with the last of the crackers and instant oatmeal reconstituted in boiling water. The rabbit was not very good but it tasted better for not having come out of a can. After breakfast John-Wayne watered the horses in the river while I lined out the equipment I needed. This included a tie rope, sweet grain, and a rosined thirty-foot lariat. We were on our way as the sun rose above the opposite cliff, flooding the canyon of the Little Colorado with a startling golden light.

We rode fast, pushing the horses to an extended trot as far as the bend where we came in sight of the cottonwood bottom and dropped back to a brisk walk. I put John-Wayne forward on the mare and followed at a short distance, watching Quixote's ears as we went. The trees were still in shadow beneath a rise of cliff and I could not see the darkened meadow under the trees very well. John-Wayne turned in the saddle and pointed vigorously ahead almost at the same time the gelding's ears went forward. The animals stood in the river a few yards out from the bank, watching us. They were a uniform dun color in the morning shadow and their wild alertness had a separate, fugitive quality even the wildest of wild horses lack. John-Wayne looked back again, grinning as he dropped the reins on the pommel and placed his hands, fingers spread, above his ears. Before we had on ridden fifty yards the deer faded from the river and into the trees without seeming to move at all.

Following a game trail along the narrow mudshelf between the outside bend of the river and the salt cedar thickets against the canyon wall, we got up on the horse herd a mile below the cottonwood grove. They were across the river in an open meadow bounded on three sides by the meander, grazing downstream with their heads away from us when the mare, who had been going stiff-leggedly with her head raised, pointed her muzzle toward them and whinnied. The herd lifted their noses together and stared sourly, like members of a wedding party confronting a sudden disruption at the back of the church. Tortuga was among them. A hundred pounds thinner, with burrs in his grown-out, tangled mane and tail, he looked contented and completely at home surrounded by his feral cousins.

I put Quixote straight at the river while John-Wayne on Doña Ana crossed downstream. The soft bank caved beneath our weight and we entered the water in a belly-dive, the horse floundering for a footing where the current cut deep into the sandy bottom. We were swimming for some seconds before his front hooves found the submerged edge of the gravel bar and then we heaved up from the river, shedding streams of muddy water.

Below John-Wayne was crossing the riffle end of the pool at a run, leaning forward over the neck as he struck behind himself with the ends of the reins, horse and rider veiled in sheets of spray. I watched them gain the bank, and when they turned downstream across the meadow to flank the herd I rode upriver to get in rear of the horses. The saddle seat was wet between my legs, the soaked shirt stuck to my back, and my water-filled boots squelched as I put the horse into a quick trot. I felt better than a million dollars, I felt young again—almost.

The herd was in motion now along the base of the cliff as we came around, moving hesitantly and even awkwardly in the attempt to watch the two horses and their riders behind and ahead of them, four hundred yards apart. They shuffled as they went in clouds of trailing dust; riding nearer I could smell their fear and observe it in their flared nostrils and rolling eyes. John-Wayne had quit closing on the herd and fallen back to avoid getting ahead and turning them. He was standing in the stirrups now and yelling, pointing along the cliff to a break in the wall a half mile downstream where a side canyon opened into the river bottom. I threw my head up and down to let him know I understood what we were up to and crowded the horses a little, pushing them along. Tortuga traveled with them, not looking around at me and holding his ears back as he drove a small harem of rough-looking mares ahead of him. His whole attitude was that of a horse who, having seen the alternative, is through with civilization for good. The herd moved up to a trot as several of the horses tried to break for the river. I drove them back against the cliff and kept everybody moving along while John-Wayne rode ahead beyond the canyon mouth, drew rein, and sat relaxed in the saddle, watching us come up. When the leader reached the canyon he turned into it, and was followed by the horses running behind him. John-Wayne waited until the last animal had entered the canyon. Then he kicked the mare forward and rode after them at a gallop, erect in the stirrups and screaming like a Comanche, waving his hat.

The herd exploded among the brush and boulders in a storm of dust, squeals, and the clatter of unshod hooves. Yelling and waving our hats we rushed upon them, driving them up canyon across the gullies and cactus flats strewed with the whitened bones of cattle. John-Wayne was asking the mare for all she had and I saw for the first time how superbly he rode, how naturally and effortlessly so that the reins seemed to disappear from his hands and he became one with the horse as the mare kept her hind legs under her going into the washes and her front ones out ahead to take the steep banks on the opposite side. Above the noise and the dust the nervous deer retreated up the terraced sidewalls, skylined themselves briefly above the canyon, and vanished over the rimrock. When the choking dust grew thicker we drew our bandanas over our faces and pulled our hats down to meet them.

We had ridden far enough into the rear of the herd that the animals farther back had begun to turn on us. I was prepared to let them go so long as there weren't too many of them. Ahead the canyon diverged around a rocky prow on which the spread-out herd broke, some running left while the others went right. The soft alluvial soil thinned to hardened clay and the dust clouds began to diminish above the particolored mass of rearing backs and plunging heads.

"There goes my horse!" John-Wayne yelled.

Tortuga was with the band going left into the lesser of the secondary canyons. He was starting to lag and as we closed on him I could hear the strike of iron shoes on rock and his labored breathing. With one hand I untied the lariat from the saddle strings and lifted it free of the pommel. Riding behind me on the right John-Wayne had spotted the small box canyon the horses ahead would be passing in seconds now to the left. Tortuga was behind by thirty yards, badly lathered and nearly winded. John-Wayne ranged alongside on the mare and I knew by the way he squinted ahead of himself he had the same idea I did.

"Go on," I told him. "I'll be right in there behind him."

He heeled the mare to a burst of speed to put her between Tortuga and the herd and turn him while I rode up on his rear. With the horse between us and a little ahead we pushed him toward the box canyon that appeared closer up as a natural corral improved by a low brush fence partly knocked down and rotted by rain and the desert sun. I took the straight end of the lariat in my teeth, shook out the coils, and grasped the rope firmly beneath the running noose. Tortuga was making for the gap in the fence as if it were the old barn door. John-Wayne pulled Ana in so hard she nearly took a seat in the prickly pear and the weeds and as the horse went on through the opening I got up in the stirrups and threw rope, at the precise second that Quixote sidestepped to avoid the mare. The forward part of the loop struck just behind the ears and glanced along the ragged mane before Tortuga wheeled, crashed through the rotten fence, and bolted up-canyon after the horses already disappearing into the narrow defile winding back to the eastern rim of the plateau.

I took in rope, coiled it, and retied the lariat into the saddle strings.

"You missed," John-Wayne said.

The sun was approaching meridian when we returned to camp and the river seemed to have slowed until it was barely moving at all. We pulled the saddles off the sweated horses and picketed them. Then we stripped and climbed down to the river. The water was only slightly cooler than the air and the sun overhead magnified the colored pebbles on the river bottom, drawing them up toward the surface ripples. I swam over to the opposite bank and waited for John-Wayne to follow. When he did not, I swam back again. He sat on a smooth red rock exposed by the low water, looking glum.

"You can dogpaddle over if you want to. There isn't any current to speak of."

"I don't want to paddle. I ain't no dog."

"Well, come out to where it's deeper and I'll show you something new."

"I don't want to know nothin new. I don't care about swimmin."

Across the river a big carp jumped in the pool where I had been swimming. He came out of the water slowly, rolled once in the glistening spray, and fell back into the river with a loud plash, as if he didn't have a care in the world.

"Don't be discouraged," I said.

"We been chasin that sonofabitch for almost two weeks now."

"Two weeks isn't very long. Catching the horse is easy compared with getting the woman, you know. That's always the toughest part."

"It's as tough as that it ain't worth it, man. I rather be a hermit instead."

We left the river and dressed and struck camp while the horses drowsed in the shade of the cottonwoods. It was after three o'clock when we set out downriver in the glaring afternoon light. We rode around the bend, past the meadow where the horses had been, and continued on several miles to a castellated valley carved by the river through the sandstone rock where we made camp in a side canyon. The topo map showed the canyon heading several miles north of Hunt, Arizona. Hunt on the map did not appear to amount to very much but I wasn't looking for a shopping mall to supply us for the next week or ten days. The impression was starting to form in my mind that recovering Jody James's foreign show horse was going to be something more than an overnight job.

We fixed camp and then John-Wayne, taking the Winchester with him, went walking along the river. He returned an hour later without having fired a shot, disconsolate.

"Where's supper?"

"There ain't no deer down here in this part of the canyon. All I saw with this big old snake."

"You should have killed him. My grandfather Ryder thought rattlesnake meat was a real delicacy."

"For the white man maybe. Not for Navajos."

He propped the rifle against a rock, walked over to the packs, and searched them thoroughly.

"What do we have left for supper?"

"Beans."

"Only beans?"

"And a couple cans of deviled ham. And some dried fruit. And stuff."

"I wasn't counting on us eating two cans of corn beef hash every night. Aren't you sorry now you didn't kill that snake?"

We boiled water from the river for coffee and to fill the canteens and ate an early supper of red beans and stale tortillas. It did not take us very long to eat it and when we were finished both of us were hungry all over again. I scoured the plates with sand, rinsed them, and set them on a flat rock for breakfast—if we had any breakfast. Then I produced the whiskey bottle and the tin cups.

"This will cheer us up some."

"There ain't a whole lot of it left."

"There's enough for tonight anyway. I'll buy a bottle in town tomorrow."

I poured the drinks and cut them with the boiled, flat-tasting water.

"Sorry about the floaters," I said.

"What's floaters?"

"In this instance ashes and pieces of charred stick."

He put the end of one finger into the cup and drew out a fragment.

"It's better than swimmers anyway," I offered.

We sat cross-legged, nursing the whiskey while the river purled and sucked between high red banks and the bullbats whished and popped above the silver surface. When the mare nickered hoarsely I swallowed the last of my drink and got up fast from the ground.

"What's the matter, Dude?"

"Quixote slipped his picket line. Let's go."

Ana stood in brush to her belly as she stared with lifted muzzle and forward ears after the gelding. I sent John-Wayne at a run and checked the mare's tether before following more slowly with a tie rope. We flanked the horse before he had gone a quarter mile, and closed on him. He quickened his pace a few strides and then surrendered to us with a resigned look. John-Wayne caught hold of the halter and held him while I came up with the rope.

"You jerk," John-Wayne told the horse.

"He'd have been half-way back to Snowflake by morning if the mare hadn't let us know."

"Maybe he was lookin for the horse herd."

"He doesn't give a damn about the herd. He was looking for green pastures, a bucket of oats, and no work."

John-Wayne remonstrated with Quixote as he led him back to camp.

"You was goin to run off and leave your girlfriend, just like that," he said. "She wouldn't think of goin no place without you."

"And leave us stranded down here in the ditch," I added. "That's horse loyalty for you."

We were nearly to camp when I saw the woman. In the deepening dusk everything about her was vague except the fact of her womanhood. With her long hair falling about her loose clothing she looked like a statue set in a niche in the wall of a stone cathedral. The next thing I saw was the absence of any visible access to the narrow ledge where she stood a hundred feet above the canyon floor.

"Look at that," I said, without intending it.

"Look at what?"

"That woman there on the cliff."

"What woman?"

"Can't you see her?"

I pointed, aware as I did it that she was staring at me without my being able to distinguish her face.

"I don't see no woman. What would a woman be doin way up there?"

"I don't know."

John-Wayne jerked the rope beneath the horse's chin to make him stand.

"I *still* don't see no woman."

"She's gone now," I said.

In camp we restaked the horses and built up the fire with driftwood from the river. The desert chill worked its way down into the canyon as we sat close by the fire to drink what remained of the whiskey.

"That wasn't no woman you saw," John-Wayne said at last.

"What was it then?"

"A skinwalker."

"So you did see it?"

"I didn't see nothin."

"Probably it was a formation in the rock with the light hitting it just right."

"Except it was all smooth rock and there wasn't no light."

He finished the drink and walked away from camp to urinate. I noticed he didn't step outside the circle of light the fire made to do it.

---

For what seemed like days I was at home with Jody in the green valley bordered by red cliffs and overshadowed by the blue mountains, and when I woke at last and reached for my boots I found a scorpion in one of them. I shook him out on the ground and went to have a look at the horses. Flies buzzed in the hot still morning and the air was heavy with the odor of sage and greasewood. John-Wayne lay in the bag facing away from me when I returned to camp, the cowlick at the back of his head standing up in the early light. I found a fragment of loose sandstone and pitched it at him underhand.

"Hey," I said.

"What is it, man?"

"Wake up."

"I am awake."

"Well then, get up."

"I was just layin here, thinkin."

"Thinking about what?"

"It ain't none of your business what."

"Thinking about Bette. I know."

"How do you know?"

"Because I'm thinking about the same thing."

He shed the bag like a snake getting rid of its skin and sat amid the pile of plaid and nylon.

"Did you hear any skinwalkers around last night?" I asked.

"How come you say it like that?

"Like what?"

"You don't believe in skinwalkers."

"I don't not believe in them. I've never seen one. Or heard it."

"I've seen them. Several times."

"What did they look like?"

"First ones I saw looked like men wearin long coats. Other ones looked like big black birds around a campfire."

"What did you do?"

John-Wayne gave me a pitying look.

"I got out of there," he said.

He took his rifle and went looking for a rabbit along the river while I built the fire back from coals and set the coffee pot on. Then I walked out of camp and around the corner of the cliff to the place where I had seen the woman the evening before. In the clear strong light the rock face rose sheer and tall, broken only by a few narrow shelves, the lowest of them seventy-five feet or more above the ground. I stood with my arms folded, looking up at the red sandstone wall rising toward the high blue sky overhead until I had a crick in my neck. The glare and heat of the desert in midsummer can play strange tricks on a man who has had neither food nor water enough in five strenuous days without sufficient rest. In camp again I added the last of the grounds to the pot and brought the water to reboil. John-Wayne returned empty-handed except for the Winchester and in a sullen mood. For breakfast we ate staling fragments of broken-up tortilla, softened in the strong back coffee.

"What sort of grub should we buy in town?" I asked.

"Nothin. I don't care."

"We have to buy something. Unless you're going to do better with that peashooter of yours."

"There ain't no game down here. If there was game, I'd shoot it."

"Well, we need to make a shopping list then. A mental one, that is. We have a good ten miles on horseback to think about it."

The ride up from the river bottom through the side-canyon was gradual and easy for a while until we came to a place where the hardrock formation was worn to a sequence of dry falls and waterspouts separated by benches covered by rubble and grown with juniper, oak, and alder. It took work to get the horses around these, and a couple of times we came near turning back. Once up the going was good in the narrowed defile until, ascending above the rimrock, we had a view of the open country again, the yellow and red plain stretching endlessly away beneath a cobalt sky and the freshened wind bending the lion-colored grasses low. We stopped once to cut fence and repair it, and had ridden on less than a mile when John-Wayne, who had been staring intently across the river, shouted, "Horses!"

The herd was beyond the water gap on a low mesa shelving gradually east from the river, distinct against the prairie in the clairvoyant morning light.

"We'll know where to pick them up when we want them," I said, putting up the glasses.

"If they ain't all the way over in New Mexico by then."

"What do we want in town beside whiskey? You haven't told me."

"Maybe we could buy us a good show horse somewhere," John-Wayne suggested.

Viewed from behind, the billboards along Arizona 180 were one-dimensional blanks against the sky's blue brilliance. We followed inside the fenceline beside the highway for a distance, let ourselves into the right-of-way by the first gate we came to, and rode on into town, taking care to avoid the bottles, cans, and other refuse flung by passing motorists. It's amazing how far sedentary Americans, unused to heavy lifting beyond raising a piece of steak on the end of a fork, can throw an empty beer can from the open window of a car traveling at seventy-five miles an hour. We were a couple of miles still from town when something broad and white and vague looking showed on the skyline.

"What is it, Eagle Eye?"

"Revival tent."

"This isn't the reservation."

"The white man likes revival meetins too."

Men were at work guying the tent as we rode past twenty-five minutes later. The wind boomed the canvas as they stretched the ropes tight with one hand and held their hats on with the other. I raised mine to one of them; he responded by jerking his chin up, not letting go of the hat or the rope. Pickup and flatbed trucks loaded with sound equipment and folding chairs and tables were parked around, and children ran back and forth between the big tent and the cookhouse where the women were placing the cookstoves. Some of the men were white but nearly all the women were Indians. Past the tent we came to the outlying trailer-house ranchettes and arrived at the desert community of Hunt, Arizona, population three-hundred-and-something-odd. We rode into town on the main street and tied up to the two-by-fours supporting the overhang outside the local café where the horses could be out of the sun while we ate dinner.

"You folks with the Overland Centennial Ride?" the waitress asked.

"Centennial of what?"

"Damned if I know, mister."

"Not us," I assured her.

"I guess they ain't comin through 'til the weekend after all," the woman said. "Set anywheres you want to."

The other customer in the café was an oldtimer sitting up on a stool along the short counter. He wore a weatherbeaten hat with a bullet hole through it, a faded-out workshirt, and was taking no chances with his pants, which were held up by rainbow-striped galluses and a tooled leather belt.

We took a table for four by the window and sat reading the menu in the barred light through half-closed venetian blinds.

"They serve breakfast any time of the day. What are you going to have?"

"Everthin."

"That would be the Number Ten, I take it."

"*Three* Number Tens is more like it, man."

"Go ahead, if you wish. It's your stomach."

"Coffee?" the waitress asked.

"Do you make that with river water?"

The woman pursed her mouth like a snapping turtle and glared.

"Don't get smart with me today, mister. I don't need no fresh talk this mornin—not on top of everthin else."

"I wasn't meaning to be smart. Any water you have is fine with us."

She poured the coffee with a trembling hand, spilling it outside the thick porcelain mugs.

"River water," she repeated disgustedly. "Just because we ain't Vegas people think we're some kind of cowtown, or somethin."

John-Wayne asked for change for the jukebox. I took several quarters from my pocket and gave them to him. He was standing over the machine at the back of the restaurant when a young girl came into the café clutching a sheaf of papers against her belly. She offered one of the papers to the old man, who refused it. The girl looked around the café, working the sun dazzle from her eyes, and saw me.

"Will *you* be there?" she asked in a high, hysterical voice. "Are *you* goin to be one of those folks that gets saved tonight?"

"I hadn't planned on it," I said.

The flyer advertised a revival meeting set for seven o'clock that evening and followed by a mutton stew and fry bread supper prepared by the ladies of the Sunrise Baptist Church. The revivalist was the Reverend Duane Small, described in the flyer as one of the greatest living evangelists in the world. John-Wayne came up as I was reading the notice to complain that the available jukebox selections were boring. He stiffened all over like a bird dog when he saw the girl and dropped the hand with the quarters in it against his leg. She had the flyer out of my hand and in his free one without my even seeing her do it.

"I bet *I* can find us some good ones!" the girl exclaimed. "Come on!"

They were away several minutes, bent above the machine with their heads together, before the jukebox began to thump and bang. John-Wayne's eyes were blank and enormous like a cartoon character's when they returned to the table.

"You be there with us-all tonight, you hear?" the girl cried. "Remember, John-Wayne—you promised!"

The screen door slapped behind her; seconds later a form passed quickly across the dimmed glare behind the part-way open blinds.

"Oh man!" John-Wayne breathed.

"Oh man is right. You don't have time for skirt-chasing. You're looking for a horse—remember?"

"Is she a fox, or what?"

"She's a fourteen-year-old vamp if I ever saw one. That's what she is."

"She's all I ever wanted in a girl, man. She's the woman of my dreams!"

"Breakfast is up in the window," I told him.

John-Wayne took up his fork and ate the whole of a twelve-ounce breakfast steak inside of four minutes. He set the fork down, separated the blinds, and peered through them into the street. He drank some coffee, picked up the fork again, and laid it down across the edge of his plate.

"It's a good thing you ordered only the single portion."

"I ain't hungry no more."

"Of course you're hungry. Eat."

He raised the blind half-way in the window but the waitress yelled at him and he lowered it again. He finished the eggs and did some damage to the fried potatoes, while leaving the side-order of toast untouched. When the waitress came with the check I reviewed her arithmetic and pushed it across the table at John-Wayne.

"What's that?"

"Your turn to buy this morning."

"I ain't got no money!"

"That's all right," I told him. "I just wanted to take your mind off women and give you something else to worry about, even if it was only for a couple of seconds."

Hunt is no mecca for mall rats. We bought the supplies we needed from two or three stores along the main street without anyone giving us trouble about the horses, which was enough to convince me that the place was not a hick town after all. In the last establishment we visited I bought two postcards and gave John-Wayne a quarter and one dime.

"There's a pay phone in the back. Call home and see if your grandmother's back from San Diego yet. If she is, tell her what's going on. She won't think to yell at you for calling collect if you don't stay on too long."

While he was using the phone I addressed a card to Jorge Baca, Snowflake, Arizona, and wrote a couple of lines on the back of it telling him his horses were safe and I was expecting to pay him overtime for them.

John-Wayne returned as I was licking the stamp to say he wasn't getting an answer and I handed him the second postcard.

"Go on," I encouraged him when he hesitated, holding the pencil poised. "It's one of those little things in life writing is for."

We mailed the cards from the post office and went outside again, where gathering storm clouds had brushed much of the light from the sky.

"We might as well eat an early supper before we start back," I said. Before we did that I needed to talk to Jody James—her answering machine, anyway.

"I ain't goin back," John-Wayne said.

"You're not?"

"Not tonight, I ain't."

"Forget about the damn girl. We have important work to do."

He shook his head.

"I promised, Dude."

"You did not. Did you really?"

"I promised her."

"Well, *I* didn't."

"You go on ahead, man. I'll meet you on the river after noon tomorrow."

"I'm hungry again already. We can argue it while we're eating supper."

The blinds were still drawn in the café where a few early customers sat at the counter, leaning forward on their elbows to eat. Some of them looked like daytime drinkers pushed out of the bar up the street and told to put something in their bellies before coming back; the rest were the kind of drunk who eats his one square meal a day and then gets down to business for the night. The waitress who had served us earlier was still on shift, and so was her disposition. We found our old table and ordered without any smart talk this time, choosing from among the daily specials listed on a handprinted card attached to the menu with a paper clip. The food was up in minutes, served in large portions on heated plates.

"How's the pork loin?"

"Tastes pretty good to me. What's your meatloaf like?"

"Meatloaf's good too. Better than corn beef hash."

"You don't really have to go to that camp meeting, you know."

"I promised, Dude. You're the one's always talkin about how a man has to keep his promises to a woman."

"Hers wasn't a social invitation. It was a business proposition."

"It don't make no difference what kind of invitation it was. A promise is a promise. Am I right?"

It was hopeless I saw, as virtue always is.

"All right," I said. "We'll both of us go along to camp meeting tonight, and get saved."

---

The crowd looked to be about three-quarters Indian–Navajo mostly, with some Apache and a few Zuni from the smaller pueblos around. We tied the horses to one of the flatbed trucks and took seats inside the tent beside an elderly Navajo couple, the wife grimfaced and small, lost within her billowing clothes, her husband impassive under his new straw hat. The wind through the open flap was fragrant with cooksmoke from the ramada behind the tent as a tall limp-looking white man with a small pot belly tested the public address system. The girl with the flyers hadn't made an appearance yet and I was beginning to feel hopeful that we might have been stood up after all.

The limp man finished flushing the burps and shrieks from the electronic setup. Then he seized a guitar and slung the strap over his shoulder as two other men entered onto the stage behind him. One of the men was an Indian in blue jeans, boots, and a white blouse, with a double strand of turquoise beads around his neck, carrying a banjo in one hand. The other, a fattish, soft-looking white, wore a short-sleeved nylon shirt outside his black polyester pants, like those old-fashioned Main Street barbers who made a profession of brushing talcum powder in your eyes and taking out a piece of your ear with the scissors. As the tent flap was being lowered against the blue dusk the guitarist stepped forward, struck a chord on his instrument, and addressed the crowd.

"Oh God-*duh*! Oh Christ-*tuh*! Do you feel it? Do you have God in you tonight? *I* have God in me tonight—Amen!"

A pretty Indian woman in a green pants suit stood from the audience and raised her arm in salute, while male voices at the rear of the tent began a hoarse, moaning chant. The guitarist struck another chord and invited the people to join him in singing "The Lord Set Me Free." The music rocked along like a country-western song as the audience responded raggedly, looking solemn and stony as a lot of Cabots and Lodges.

"And I want to ask you here tonight—Amen! How many of you feel the presence of God right here in this tent, hallelujah!" the guitarist cried.

He stepped back from the mike and raised his clenched fist above his head.

"Oh God-*duh*! Oh Christ-*tuh*! Who among you people here believe that I have here, in my hand, a twenty-dollar bill?"

The people fell silent suddenly. Two hundred pairs of black eyes fixed themselves on the guitarist with as much enthusiasm as if he was the Kirby Vacuum salesman. The old man next to me touched the brim of his hat with one finger and shifted his feet before stiffening into immobility again.

"Which one of you here tonight in the presence of God—Amen!—will come forward and claim this twenty-dollar bill?"

A shuffle began at the back of the tent and rolled forward like a slow wave. An Indian in sneakers, holding his head down and his arms loose at his sides, came loping down the center aisle. The guitarist asked him if he believed truly in the presence of the twenty-dollar bill, and the Indian responded with an upward jerk of his head.

"This man *believes*!" the guitarist cried. "Oh you people, God is here with us tonight, under this tent—hallelujah!—and this god is a *liberal* God! He will give to you, without thought of return or reward, if only you will take from *Him!*"

He opened the fist suddenly and displayed the bill for us all to see. Then he pressed it into the hand of the Indian, who rubbed it against his leg and pocketed it before loping back up the aisle between the two halves of the silent congregation.

"Be liberal in your minds tonight!" the guitarist begged the crowd. "Be liberal in your minds by giving liberally to God!"

When the ushers began taking up the collection he invited the people to join him in a song. It was a song he had learned in Africa, the guitarist said. He stood aside after he was done singing it, and then the fat man stepped forward and seized the microphone. He was the Reverend Small and he spoke in a booming voice like the voice of God, shaking out the folds and skirts of the big tent. The Reverend was just starting to speak when a blonde child ran in through the tent flap, holding a tambourine. She took a seat up front and began to shake the tambourine vigorously.

John-Wayne grabbed hold of my arm. "It's *her*!" he exclaimed.

"Just because we're holding a revival here in Hunt," the Reverend Small shouted, "doesn't mean the Devil's packed his bags and left for Phoenix! How many of you," he roared, "have said to yourselves, 'I thought I was saved—but I don't feel saved!'? Sometimes, you know, I find myself fighting my fellow Christians along with the Devil! People used to tell me, 'I was once like you, you'll cool off.' But it's been eighteen years, my friends, and I'm still warm! I didn't come all the way from Little Rock, Arkansas to Hunt to give just another sermon! Maybe tomorrow night I might just feel like prophesying. By Saturday night we'll all be climbing the poles!"

The lady in the green suit took a tissue from her purse and dabbed her eyes with it. Around the tent the audience set up a rhythmic clapping, while the girl banged her tambourine harder and shook it above her head.

"Man," John-Wayne said, "ain't she beautiful? I bet you she could make a million bucks a night on TV!"

"In Matthew," the Reverend Small shouted, "Christ tells us that the man who has backslidden is seven times worse off than before he was saved! *I* will not backslide, O Jesus—I *will* not lose what God has given me—I *will* rise steadily, and go forward to claim my reward!"

The Reverend told how he had cast a devil out of his wife after she had returned sick from a trip to Brazil to save souls. The doctors couldn't help her, they'd never seen a sickness before like this sickness, but the Reverend Small told them, "Good—That's all I wanted to know, I'll go and consult with Doctor Jesus!'" He went back to his wife and seized her by the throat where the amoebas the Devil had put there were choking her, and she was cured instantly. "Show me the hands," Small demanded, "of all you people who need God's help!"

They drifted forward in a careless way until more than a dozen people stood before the Reverend Small, adolescents and a few kids mainly, but some adults too, including a couple of aged crones, one of them bent almost double over her cane.

The Reverend Small came down from the platform and asked the congregation to join him in singing "The Blood of Jesus" as his patients gathered around him. Then he placed his hand on their foreheads and blessed them. The old woman with the cane went off with her blessing as if she was holding it under her shawl for safekeeping and sat on the corner of the platform at the feet of the Indian preacher with the banjo. The preacher had finished translating for Small and now he was playing wildly on his instrument, snapping and popping the strings as he gazed across the bent heads of the sick to the singing, clapping, cheering people.

"The Devil's getting jealous now!" Small shouted. "He's getting offended by all the spiritual progress that's going on around here and he wants to see some backsliding pretty quick! 'I shall return!' the Devil says, like General MacArthur. But are we going to run—or are we going to fight?"

Everyone cheered loudly and applauded, and Small told us about his young son who traveled all the way around the world, experienced a revolution in the Philippines, and was taken sick when he got home because the Devil wanted to get even with his father for having converted so many heathen souls to Christ. He pressed back the head of a woman standing before him and laid his hand on her forehead. She fell over backwards and was caught by an usher, who lowered her gently to the ground. Returning to their seats, the healed pushed past the afflicted coming forward to be cured.

"That's not right, that isn't natural: God didn't put that there," Small told a young girl who said she had a heart murmur. "Oh Father God," he prayed, "we call upon you here under this tent to cure this woman—Have the palpitations stopped?" he asked the girl.

John-Wayne knocked my leg with his knee.

"That's my cousin!" he hissed.

"Who is—the girl?"

"Not her, the dude in the wheelchair. There ain't nothin the matter with *that* sonofabitch. He's been in jail all summer for hittin a cop."

John-Wayne's cousin was a handsome young Indian with his hair cut short and graded around the ears and in back in the white man's style. His broad shoulders and massive torso overbalanced the wheelchair, pushed by the accommodating lady in the green suit.

"People that have something wrong with the legs?" Small demanded. "Legs that are immobilized, legs that are paralyzed, legs that don't work right?"

The green woman pressed the chair forward until Small, seeing the cousin, turned quickly and bent over him, holding the microphone away. Then, standing straight again, he began to pray.

"Oh Father God, we ask you here beneath this tent to cure this young man who never walked a single step in nineteen years on Your green earth!"

He bent once more to place his hands on the boy's legs, lifting each one in turn to straighten it. Then he replaced the feet on the footrest of the chair and stepped back, holding the microphone against his chin.

"Young man, I bid you—stand up!"

The crowd applauded as the cousin stood and then returned, looking sheepish, to the back of the tent, followed by the woman pushing the empty wheelchair.

"If it would have been me that was the judge he wouldn't have walked for another nineteen years," John-Wayne said. "When we was kids he used to chase me with a stick until we was both of us ready to drop dead from runnin."

"People having something wrong with the shoulder—the *right* shoulder? Shoulders that don't move right, that don't work? Anybody here with a shoulder like that?"

The old man beside us got a nudge from his wife. He shuffled obediently to the front and stood with his head lowered before the Reverend, who directed him to raise his right arm to the level of his shoulder. The old man obeyed him, bringing the arm up stiffly. Small prayed over him a little and ordered him to lift the arm again. It showed no improvement and when Small asked him how he felt the hosteen didn't answer. Instead he turned away and shuffled back to his seat. Neither he nor the wife looked particularly disappointed.

Small called out a man and woman from the crowd and gave them a financial blessing, prophesying that they would enjoy a great financial benefit very soon.

"And now," he cried, "I want to see everyone in the cookhouse line for mutton stew and fry bread with hot coffee. It's all free, folks!"

"We're getting out of this Hell-hole," I said to John-Wayne.

"But I ain't had a chance to even say hello yet!"

Small was leaving the tent accompanied by the lady in green, the Navajo preacher, and a brittle-looking blonde with streaked hair, about forty years old.

"You're in worse trouble than you know," I said.

"Meanin what, man?"

"That's the Reverend's daughter you've gone and fallen in love with."

"How do you know?"

"I just had a look at her mother," I told him.

He promised to come looking for me in twenty minutes and I went on to the cooktent for a cup of coffee. An old woman across the table jumped up when I sat down and stood facing away from me to finish her supper, tipping the rim of the bowl against her toothless gums as she sucked off the mutton broth. The young man beside me caught my eye and shrugged, smiling. Then he inquired in perfect English if I had enjoyed the revival. It had all been very interesting, I assured him.

The young man felt encouraged. He introduced himself as a member of the Navajo Nation and went on to explain that revivalism had first come to the Navajos thirty-five years earlier. Many were saved, he said, but the movement died out. Now a wave of supernatural influence was sweeping Navajoland. Only the summer before he himself had witnessed a miracle at Window Rock when the preacher cured a woman with one leg several inches shorter than the other one. The young man wore a purple golf shirt and aviator glasses and had his hair carefully styled, like young business and professional people in Phoenix or Salt Lake City. It hurt my eyes to look at him.

I said that I found his country very beautiful.

"Yes," he said with a Chamber of Commerce smile, "we think so."

John-Wayne came over in a hurry and stood behind us, waiting impatiently for the young man to finish outlining the opportunities for tourism development on the reservation.

"We can go now," he said quickly when the Indian paused to catch his breath.

We untied the horses and rode until we were out of hearing of the meeting before dismounting and spreading the bedrolls on the grass. While John-Wayne picketed the horses I rummaged in the half-light for the whiskey bottle among the supplies we had bought, and then both of us took a short drink.

"What happened?" I asked.

"It was bad, man. A real bummer."

"Tell me about it."

"I went lookin for her in the tent, after all the people had gone. It was pretty dark in there, most of the lights were out."

"And?"

"She was back of the stage with her skirt up around her tits, makin it with the dude in the wheelchair. The one her old man cured."

"Your cousin."

"Yeah. My cousin. The cripple."

"It serves Small right. He never guessed that after healing two legs the third one would stand up and hit him in the nose."

"She's just a whore, after all."

"Don't blame the girl," I told him, "blame her parents. Look at the kind of upbringing she's had."

"What's upbringin got to do with it? I'm talkin about morals, man."

"Where are your morals, then? Don't tell me you wouldn't be making it with her yourself this very minute if she'd given you the chance."

"I ain't no jailbird like my cousin. I got good intentions."

"It's your intentions after sex that really matter, not before it. Poor Bette. How do you expect she'd feel if she knew you were trying to two-time her the very first opportunity you had?"

"What Bette don't know won't hurt her."

"And men wonder why the women think they're all jerks."

We placed the saddles for pillows on the ground and lay down on top of the bedrolls. The air was pleasantly cool on the desert after sundown and in the silence around I became aware of the noise drifting across from the infernal glow of the camp meeting. A little civilization goes a long way at times. It felt good to be away from it all, and still better to know we were headed back into the clean, stark wilderness again.

---

In the slanting rays of the early sun the meeting tent shone dazzling white like the New Jerusalem, the Heavenly City. We unzippered our beds to air them and rode into town for breakfast, leaving the horsepacks stretched on the sparse yellow grass. At the café a line of pickup trucks stood parked with their bumpers hanging over the plank walk. We tied up among them and went on inside. The cowboys sat up together along the counter; the Reverend Small, his wife, and daughter occupied a booth against the back wall of the restaurant, next to the jukebox. The girl looked up from her breakfast, glanced indifferently in our direction, and speared another sausage with the end of her fork.

"Come on," I told John-Wayne, taking him from behind above the elbow.

The table beside the window was not popular, it seemed. We sat at it, and the waitress came with the menus under her arm. Either she held a monopoly on the job or no one wanted to fight her for a shift.

"Coffee?" she demanded.

"Yes ma'am," I told her.

"You're the one likes river water."

"Only when I can't get any other kind."

"You'd get it if we had it," the woman said. "I wouldn't charge you extra for it, neither."

"*You* were there!" the Reverend Small shouted across the room. His wife followed his pointing finger with her eyes while the girl studied a piece of the silverware, turning it carefully, over and over, in her hand.

"She acts like she never even seen me before," John-Wayne hissed.

"What are you complaining about? You're a lucky guy, believe me."

The Smalls finished their meal and got up from the table. Mrs. Small and the girl went to pay at the register while the Reverend oiled over to us, rubbing his plump hands.

"You folks plan on being with us again tonight?" he asked.

I said we were leaving town in an hour and he looked disappointed.

"Why folks, you can't do that. Maybe tonight I might just feel like prophesying! Maybe tonight we'll all be climbing the poles!"

"You goin to cure my cousin again?" John-Wayne asked him.

"Do what?"

"You goin to cure the dude in the wheelchair? He's my cousin."

Small kept smiling but he had quit rubbing his hands.

"The poor young man. If his faith fails him again the way it did the first time, I suppose I won't have any alternative."

John-Wayne was about to speak further when I kicked him hard beneath the table.

"It isn't worth it," I said when Small had moved up to join his family. "Let's eat our breakfast and get out of here."

Leaving town we stopped at a service station to water the horses and I called Jody from a payphone on the outside wall between the men's and women's lavatories.

"Hello."

"Hello."

"You're home."

"Actually, I was just getting ready to run out."

"How are you?"

"I'm all right. And you?"

"I'm okay."

"*Where* are you?"

"We're in Hunt, Arizona."

"I'm supposed to know where Hunt, Arizona is?"

"Not very far from Springerville."

"What are you doing all the way down by Springerville?"

"It's a long story, believe me."

"You said a week ago you'd be home in a couple of days. *More* than a week ago."

"I'm sorry. I've been on the desert or I'd have called before now. I sent you a postcard today."

"Have you got Cortez yet?"

"Damnit, no. I threw the other day and missed him when the sonofabitch I was riding went sideways."

"This is getting to be ridiculous, Jeb. Why all this trouble just catching a horse?"

"He's running with a wild herd, so it's hard to get up on him. He seems to be enjoying going native."

"If you don't cut him out of those feral horses soon he'll be ruined."

"I know it. I'm doing the best I can do, I promise you."

"I've missed two shows with him already."

"How are things on the place?"

"Everything's going fine. The second cutting's finished and now we have to take the yearlings off the creek before my lease expires on the thirty-first."

"I'm sorry I can't be there to help."

"That's all right. Dago and I manage beautifully together."

"How is Dago?"

"Dago is Dago. He's always fine."

"All I need now is a little luck."

"I'm worried about Cortez, Jeb. Running with those wild horses is going to break him down."

"He looked pretty healthy when I saw him two days ago. Do you miss me, mavourneen?"

"Of course, I miss you."

"I miss *you,* terribly."

"How long do you guess it will take you to catch him now?"

"A few more days maybe—a week or ten days at the outside. We're going to cross the river and go after them on the east mesa this afternoon."

"You're still riding with Tonto then?"

"Sure. He's a good kid, and a big help to me. I couldn't manage with just the one horse."

"You'll call me as soon as you have him safe?"

"Of course."

"I need to go now," Jody said. "I have a meeting with the BLM in Montpelier at eleven."

"Go, then. And know that I love you. I love you very, very much."

"I love you too. Here comes a kiss."

"I'll see you very soon."

"You'd better," she said.

The shadows had drawn in from the west and gathered around the foundations of the houses and the bases of the electrical poles as we rode out from town about noon. We stopped on the desert to recover and load the packs, crossed the plateau through a universe of sunshine and shadow, cloudscape and the shifting wind, and entered at the head of the canyon winding down to the river. The walls of the canyon rose steadily higher, shutting out the land and sky except for the ragged strip above our heads, and the hoof-falls echoed louder as we descended. When we came to our old camp at last the evening breeze had stilled and the swallows were skimming the silken surface of the river. The horses were tired and very thirsty. We watered them from the bank and grained them lightly, pouring out the oats for them to pick up from the ground.

I built a fire to fry the thick red steaks we had carried from town and buried two big Idaho potatoes in the coals. When supper was ready I uncorked the bottle of red wine I had brought for a surprise and we ate the big bloody steaks, the potatoes in their burst and blackened skins, and a loaf of French bread with the wine. Finally I filled the coffee pot with town water from the canteen and set it on the coals against a flaming stick.

"That's the best supper I ever ate," John-Wayne said.

"I'm glad you enjoyed it. You deserved it. So did I."

We carried the plates and pans to the river to wash up and when we got back to camp the water was boiling in the spout of the Saltillo pot. Seated against the saddles turned up on their pommels we drank the fresh-ground coffee with shots of whiskey and watched the silver river slide smoothly away in the darkening canyon.

"As long as we were in town, we should have thought to find us a shower somewhere," I said out loud.

"Like where, Dude?"

"I don't know."

"We'd of had to go to a motel, or somethin."

"Or something."

"It's easier just to use the river."

"I know it. Everything's easier down here."

Some ants that had been driven by the heat from wormholes in a log of the burning wood raced to the tilted-up end in search of a jumping-off place. Then they ran down to the low end, where they met the tall orange and yellow flames. Curls of smoke rose through the holes where they had emerged from the log's interior.

"She never did tell me her name," John-Wayne said bitterly.

"Miss Small, of course."

"I mean, her *real* name."

"Vera, perhaps."

"Vera?"

"Listen," I told him. "Those people are nothing. In fact, they're worse than nothing. Nothing doesn't take up valuable space. You were lucky not to have anything further to do with them."

"How come you talk like that about your own people?"

"They're not my people."

"They're the white man, ain't they?"

The log was in flames from end to end, the ants shriveling in the heat and dropping into the coals below.

"What's the matter with you, tonight, Dude?" John-Wayne asked.

"I'm getting old," I said. "Or maybe I've had a little too much wine to drink."

---

Early next day we crossed the river, splashing in the current that flowed in one smooth unbroken piece, and rode upstream half a mile to a broad shallow canyon ascending to the eastern plateau where I dismounted and glassed the vast shadowless desert.

"See any horses around, Eagle Eye?"

"See some antelope out about a mile, mile-and-a-half."

"No horses?"

"No."

"We better get started, then."

We rode all morning without sighting the herd. The wind got up finally around ten and by noon it was driving the big heavy-bottomed clouds from west to east across a broken sky. The sun was past the overhead when we spotted them at last, grazing in a grassy swale a few hundred yards behind the upstream bluff.

"You're losing your sight, Eagle Eye. I picked them up before you did."

"No way, Dude. It was me that saw them first. The white man just yelled."

We spent a couple of hours in the approach, using the folded land for cover and playing the wind where we could, and then we lost them. They were spooked now and as soon as we broke from around the two ends of a low hogback they raised their heads from the yellow grass and bolted all together in a thick cloud of traveling dust in which Tortuga, carrying his neck arched and his tail lifted cheerfully, appeared now and again among the running bodies. We got in the rear of them and as I took the rope in my hand and leaned forward over the neck they broke suddenly in all directions across the lava rock, raising separate clouds that closed up rapidly to make a low storm of dust. Sitting our horses two hundred yards apart, we watched as the storm circled around to the west before it was snatched away like a blanket by the wind, and the exposed herd vanished into the prairie swells. Then we turned the horses' heads toward the south and rode down to the bottom to make camp again beside the river.

We camped two nights in that place and rode again the following morning looking for the herd. We had pushed them to the extreme edge of their range and they would be driven no farther toward the head of the Little Colorado. Instead they broke, circled, and doubled back under the pressure, taking flight across the open plain where we could not block them off and corral them. There was an edge to the pursuit now that was like the urgency of the month of September with its shortened days, its cold nights, and with these the feeling of time drawing in, life running down. Already it was August, too hot to ride in the middle of the day. We were out a couple of hours before sunrise, and again from late afternoon until past dark. The hours in between we spent in camp, sitting up in the cliff shade, napping, and trying to cool off in the river. The river hardly amounted to anything anymore, just a braid of shallow currents separating and coming together again around the sand and gravel bars. By staying completely horizontal in the water you could float in it for a little way, but there were few pools deep enough for swimming. The river had the denatured look of boiled water and by early afternoon it felt almost as warm as the air.

After going in swimming we sat naked on the rocks, talking or not talking as it pleased us, and one afternoon we built a raft from cottonwood branches and the straight woody stalks of the salt cedar, using the branches for the flooring and the stalks as a calking between them, everything lashed together by lengths of nylon rope. The raft when we had finished it looked as if it could have navigated the Mississippi River, and if we had had a Mississippi handy, it might have done it. Instead it carried the two of us, stark naked and poling furiously, three or four hundred yards downstream, bumping and scraping on the gravel and mud bottom until it broke up at last against a barrier of the half-submerged volcanic rock. Standing in water a little above our knees, we watched what remained of the raft float away on the sluggish current, revolving slowly and continuing to fragment as it went.

"There's no such thing as an adventure left, is there?"

"That horse is an adventure sure enough, ain't he?"

"No," I said, "that horse is a *job.* Period."

John-Wayne had not changed color at all that I could see but I was becoming very brown and my beard and mustache, reflected in the surface of the river, were sun-bleached. The river kept our bodies clean but our unwashed clothes were filthy. One morning after returning to camp we stripped and carried them to the river where we attempted to wash them as John-Wayne remembered his mother doing when he was a small child. We rubbed them with gravel and the branches of greasewood and spread them to dry on the hot rock, and when they were dried they looked as dirty as they had before, or dirtier, although they did smell better. John-Wayne's new shirt and jeans were holed and the potato-chip hat, streaked with dust and sweat, was acquiring a soft conforming shapelessness as it settled about his head and ears.

The clouds still gathered before noon every day, and by evening they were black, massive anvils, pressing their weight upon the earth. But there had been no rainfall since our first day on the desert and we were learning to ignore the dry distant lightning and the trailing virga. In the welcome cumulus shadow we saddled and rode up from the disappearing river to the plateau to scan for the horse herd. Late in the afternoon on the third or fourth day, riding a quarter-mile apart, we came to a crevasse, very deep and steep-sided, splitting the desert in a long welter of livid rock. I heard John-Wayne shout suddenly and saw him throw up his hands in excitement before he started at a gallop toward me, away from the verge of the crevasse.

"Get back from there, man—get back!" he yelled as he came up.

"Why? What's the matter?"

"The giant crab."

"What giant crab?"

"They live down there in those big cracks for years. All you see is the huge claw coming up to grab a sheep, or an Indian. Get away from the edge, man!"

Obligingly I backed Quixote from the crevasse, slipped the stirrups, and lifted my boots onto the mane to relax my legs.

"I thought perhaps you'd sighted the herd."

"I hope that old crab didn't eat my horse."

"No such luck for either of us," I suggested.

In the evening I was missing Jody James pretty badly. I got the whiskey bottle and also the cigars I had bought in Hunt to keep the whiskey company.

"Did you ever smoke a cigar?" I asked John-Wayne.

"I don't think so."

"Would you like to try one?"

"How bad do they taste?"

"Do you like McDonalds' hamburgers?"

"I love em, man."

"Well, cigars are nothing like as bad as that."

I poured whiskey and lit the cigars from a burning brand that had fallen between the rocks surrounding the fire pit. We stood the saddles on the pommels and sat back to smoke, and contemplate the orange flames.

"Don't blow on it. Just pull, steady but easy."

The sound of waterfowl came from the river, their frightened calls followed by wingbeats and the watery tear of their departure.

"And for God's sake don't inhale. You'll be sick as a dog if you do."

"Tobacco never made me sick."

"Cigars are different. You'll see."

The ducks, still calling, circled around and landed on the river upstream from the camp.

"Booze and tobacco. The white man's curse and the red man's revenge."

"My grandmother says liquor was invented by the white man to destroy the Indian."

"Really it was invented to destroy himself, and have fun doing it. It's what every human invention that's worth a damn has always been for."

"Is that why Columbus invented America?"

"He invented it?"

"That's what Mr. Tom, my teacher in school, says."

"You're eating smoke again."

We set the tin cups carefully behind two rocks while John-Wayne went for more wood and I brought the horses in and snubbed them to a couple of bushes. The ducks were quieting on the river, communicating with each other only at intervals and in calmer voices. Overhead the Milky Way balanced on edge like a silver plate and the wind shifting round filled the camp with the scent of burning sage and greasewood.

"Columbus is probably in Hell for having discovered the New World," I said when we were seated again, resting the cups on our knees.

"You think maybe it wasn't a good idea after all, Dude?"

"I don't."

"How come?"

"Well, just look."

"Look at what?"

"Hunt. Las Vegas. America."

"What about them?"

"You're Dineh. You tell me what about them."

"I don't see nothin wrong with them. They're places, that's all. I think it's good about Columbus."

"Why do you think that?"

"Because if he wouldn't of invented America, I wouldn't be modern."

"No, you wouldn't. But you'd be you."

"I *am* me, man—John-Wayne Bilagody, Tuba City, Arizona, Navajo Nation, U.S.A."

"You're also looking green in the face. Do you know why Columbus came to America in the first place?"

"To steal the Indians for slaves?"

"He came here to find a place to give European civilization a second chance after they'd thrown their first one away. He came because Europeans like him thought they could solve all the problems they'd made for themselves by picking up and moving west three and four thousand miles and starting over in a new world that just happened to belong to somebody else. And do you know what?"

"What?"

"It didn't work. Because the only way they could have solved those problems was by staying home and tackling them right where they were born. All they did in escaping to America was transplant everything that was bad in the European culture to an environment so vast and so rich that it thrived and spread everywhere like a hardy but inferior strain of grass that chokes off every other strain. That's how we Americans came to live the way we're living now."

John-Wayne said feebly, "You ain't supposed to hate your culture, like you do. They tell us that in school, every day."

"I don't hate my culture," I assured him.

At least, I thought while he was away being sick in the bushes, I don't think I hate it. It just doesn't seem like mine anymore.

Riding farther to the southwest we came on a fenceline running north. The fence was three strands of slack barb-wire holding up the weathered sticks they were tacked to, but high and strong enough yet to deter even wild horses. We followed it three or four miles to the river where it hung suspended, dislodged by flooding, a foot above the watercourse before climbing the opposite bank and taking a turn of forty-five degrees from a corner post atop the bluff.

"All we got to do is drive them against the bluff under that corner there and cut him out," John-Wayne suggested.

"You go right ahead, seeing as that's all there is to it. In the meantime I think I'll lie down right here by the river and take a nap."

We spent a couple of hours picking up the herd again and getting in rear of it. The horses were considerably easier to push once you knew where it was you actually wanted to push them to, and they moved along at a steady trot as if the whole maneuver had been entirely their own idea to begin with. Tortuga was pacing them more easily now while the wild stallions in their mild panic ignored him, having more to think about for the time being than the chastity of their mares. By three o'clock we had the river in sight and the fence too, running in on the left to meet it. The horses lifted their noses at the scent of water as we rode in closer yet to encourage them. The leaders balked at the edge of the bluff but when John-Wayne rode up along the fence they plunged over it and were followed by the rest of the herd. I watched until the last straggler had gone over the top before turning the horse and riding downstream to head off a breakout in that direction.

The horses seemed familiar with the corner but they did not appreciate being driven into it. They milled closer as we approached, throwing up their heads and climbing on each others' backs, squealing as their flinty hooves kicked up the red mud that fell in a shower around. Pressed against the hanging fence they searched desperately for a way through or over it, unaware that they could more easily have pushed beneath the bottom wire. The forward part of the herd was against the sheer-looking face of the bluff now, while the hind animals thrashed in the weak current that broke in sprays and sheets of water over them. Tortuga was among these, I saw, his coat darkened with water, nearly unrecognizable, with two mares of a similar size and color.

We rode forward, John-Wayne against the fence and me out in the river, keeping close enough in to the bluff to be able to bolt and cover it. Closing, I loosed the rope from the saddle strings, took the end in my teeth, and unlimbered my throwing arm. The herd was hysterical now, plunging and rearing in the angle. I put Quixote among them and rode straight at the dark soaked horse, standing in the stirrups as Doña Ana pressed in from the other side, John-Wayne yelling and waving his hat the whole time. The loop dropped neatly over the horse's ears and slipped down his neck as I dallied and Quixote braced his feet in the wet sand.

"I got him!" I shouted to John-Wayne.

The horse went up in the air like a marlin and came down snorting in the river, wild-eyed, covered with mud and lather. The herd broke all at once from the angle in a deluge of the watery mud and escaped downstream, except for a few that made a run at the bluff. Hard against the cliff the horses paused. Then, almost on their hind legs, they ran straight up the shaley wall to the top of the bluff where they turned and continued their flight downstream to join the main body of the herd in the river. I watched as two stragglers followed them up and stood in silhouette above the landline beside the corner post, looking down at the river bottom where Quixote and I struggled with the plunging, sunfishing animal at the end of the lariat. One of the horses, slightly taller than the other, held his neck arched and his tail up. Then, putting his ears forward and giving a farewell flag, he bolted upstream through an unstrung section of fence, followed by the second horse running behind him.

"You lassoed the wrong horse," John-Wayne said as I regarded the trembling mare—the slower half of Tortuga's harem—standing spread-leggedly with her head lowered in her rosined collar.

"You can shut up now," I explained, "or take that mustang off the rope. It's your choice. I don't give a good goddamn how you decide."

The going was hard with just the two horses to track in the firm sand of the river bottom and along the dusty verge of the bluff. We kept on them the rest of the afternoon and made camp at twilight below Zion Reservoir.

I was gathering wood for a fire when I saw the woman again. Wearing the same loosefitting robe and her dark hair around her she stood fifty yards upstream against a clump of salt cedar, her face in the half light as indistinct as her figure. Doubled over above an armload of sticks I watched as she raised her hand as if to beckon me, and took a single step backward. I laid the wood carefully on the ground and started toward her among the brush and cactus while she continued to beckon—smiling, it seemed to me—before she was gone, vanished into the bushes. I walked on to the place where she had been standing and went around behind the salt cedar, which was a feathery screen with more cactus and brush behind it. Finally I returned for the wood I had dropped and carried it back to the camp.

We had scrubbed out the cook pans with sand after supper and set the coffee to boil when I said carelessly to John-Wayne, "I saw the woman again this evening."

"In your dreams, Dude. You ain't even been to bed yet." Then he asked in a changed, uncertain voice, "What woman?"

"You know what I'm talking about."

"You saw her again?"

"Standing there by the salt cedar, watching me. I was bringing in wood for the fire."

John-Wayne set his cup down on a rock. He put his collar up around his ears and pulled his hat brim over his eyes. Then he took up the cup again and stood closer to the fire as he stared across the shuddering circle of light into the darkness beyond.

"Baca warned us," he said at last.

"How do you mean?"

"About them witches."

"The bruja?"

"He said, 'If you see one, don't follow it.'"

"I'm following a horse, not a witch."

"Then maybe she's following you."

"Or you. What does an Indian witch want with a white man?"

"Was she an Indian?"

"I couldn't tell. She had black hair."

He requested the flashlight when he went for wood at bedtime and built the fire up to a roaring blaze that lit the canyon from wall to wall and turned the river channel to a braid of liquid fire.

"You know about Bet jo' gie etta hi ee'?" John-Wayne asked from deep inside his bedroll.

"I can't say as I recall ever hearing the name."

"It means Great Vagina. She was a fox who liked gettin it any way she could, you know what I mean? She used to go around lookin for young men and gettin them to do it with her. Then when she got hold of them she'd crush their you-know-what inside her."

"You think that's what I saw tonight?"

"No. Elder Brother used a stick instead and killed her. At Tse et ha' ee—Red Mesa."

"Sleep well, then."

"Goodnight, Dude."

---

For two days we pursued the quarry around Zion Reservoir into Carrizo Wash, following the intermittent spoor in the sandy bottom and over the desert hardpan under the raging eye of the sun; eating the midday meal in the saddle and halting only to rest the horses and let them drink. There was water still in the river but no rainfall, and the heat was enough to make Hell feel at home. Striking Route 666 running from the Mexican border up to Monticello we cut, and carefully mended, fence along both sides of the road.

"Make the splice a good one," I told John-Wayne. "The Devil always demands his due."

"Is it really the Devil's Highway, Dude?"

"It could be. You never know until you come to the end of it."

The third day we lost the trail as completely as if Tortuga and his love had been snatched up to Heaven in a whirlwind. Looking to cut sign we circled into the desert and, finding none, made an early camp. In the morning we rode north from the river across arid desert and came around noon to a high mesa from where John-Wayne spotted a band of sheep and a herder's wagon on the flats below.

"Range maggots," I said before I could think. "I'm sorry," I added when John-Wayne looked daggers at me. "I happen to be a cattleman myself."

The sheep lay resting within a half-mile of the wagons, guarded by the drowsy but attentive dogs. We rode on into camp where two horses stood tied with their eyes shut and their legs locked under them. The horses looked around as we came up and two of the dogs rose and approached to sniff carelessly at us before lying back down again in the shade. I dismounted, handed the reins to John-Wayne, and knocked at the closed door of the herder's wagon. When no one answered, I knocked again.

"He ain't here," John-Wayne said.

"If he isn't here, where is he?"

I knocked once more and tried the door. It gave way, so I went on in.

It was terrifically hot inside the wagon, which smelled of perfumed wax from the burned-down votive candles on the table and unwashed human flesh. The pushed-open windows let some of the hot breeze through but the light was very bad. I waited to let my eyes squeeze the sun glare from them, and looked around. The bunk bed under the window at the end of the trailer was occupied. Two heads lay side by side on the pillow, Hollywood style, with the top sheet drawn over their noses. One of the heads was round and dark, the other gray and long. Sheepherders.

"Get up from there," I ordered, advancing on the bed and throwing back the sheet, "and turn loose of her. You ought to be ashamed to torment a dumb animal that way."

The ewe's forelegs were tightly bound, her rear ones tied more loosely. The herder, a thin, small, but muscular man, wore his unbuttoned shirt above and nothing on below it. I cut the cords with my knife, sunk my fingers into the wool, and pulled the sheep from the bed. She landed in a pile on the floor where she gathered her legs under her and ran, bleating piteously, toward the open door.

"Is she your regular girl?" I asked.

He nodded.

"What's her name?"

The sheepherder stood on one leg to pull on his pants. He was a Basque, with the Basque's coppery skin and the sharp, angular Basque face, like a fine wood carving.

"Rosa. You goin to have me fired?"

"Why? Is she under age?"

"A man gets lonely out here on the desert, all by hisself."

"I know it."

"Jesus, Mary, and Joseph. I'm fifty-seven years old, never been with no whores."

"How about horses?" I asked.

"Horses?"

He looked as if he wanted to punch me.

"Have you had any through here?"

"You mean wild ones?"

"More or less."

"Had two of em come by, day before yesterday. A mare and a geldin, the mare wilder'n hell. She run off. I caught the other with a can of oats."

"Where is he?"

"I sent one of my Meskins out on him this mornin."

"Didn't you notice the brand?"

The herder looked scared all over again.

"Was it yours?"

"Not mine," I said. "It's a long story. Where'd you send your man to?"

"Sent him up the wash for stragglers."

"How far up the wash?"

"However far they straggled to."

"All right."

"You goin after him?"

"You're damn right we are. The horse, not the Mexican. We've been chasing him for three weeks already."

"Only horse I ever seen walked like a turtle."

"A sixty-five hundred dollar turtle, maybe."

"You goin to tell my boss about Rosa?"

"Not if I find that horse, I won't. But it's no way to treat a lady."

We went outside and John-Wayne handed me the reins. I set my foot in the stirrup, swung up, and turned Quixote's nose away from the wagon.

"You boys go ahead and have yourself a good laugh," the herder called after us from the step. "But I tell you one thing. This way, you send your own soul to Hell without takin theirn along with it."

We struck Tortuga's track, clear and sharp from the added weight, right away in the wash. You could tell by the sound the sheep made, a half-mile off still, that no one was with the stragglers. There were three or four dozen of them, spread around in the wash and strung out along the bluff, bleating for one another and all the time wandering farther and farther apart, the iron *clong* of the bells sounding remote and sad. Riding up we sighted their woolly backs above the bushes, starting them nervously in every direction before drawing rein.

"He left them," John-Wayne said.

"And what do you make of that?"

"I think the sonofabitch stoled my horse—again."

"Claro. I think the same thing."

"What do we do now, man?"

"The same thing we've been doing. What else is there for us to do?"

"I'm getting awful sick followin a horse's rear end."

"Faint heart never won fair lady."

"You said that before. How about a sore butt?"

"The poet doesn't mention butts. Be assured, however, there are no assurances in life."

"A guy that abandons sheep wouldn't think nothin of stealin a girl's horse," John-Wayne said bitterly.

The hoof prints paired on each side showed the Mexican riding at fast trot and keeping to the wash which bent southeast toward the border with New Mexico. We pressed ahead, pacing him, and stopped around five to rest the horses before going on again while the sun went from white to yellow to a deep orange color, crisping the sage bushes with light as they stood sharply at attention from the bases of their lengthening shadows on the hardpan. We were just on the verge of sundown when John-Wayne spurred his horse from behind to range alongside me.

"Campfire," he said, pointing.

Ahead the fire was like a small lost piece of the sun fallen off into the desert and abandoned there overnight, to be picked up again in the morning.

"He's ridden far enough for one day. He thinks he's as good as all the way back home in Mexico."

"How far is Mexico?"

"Not more than three hundred miles."

Out on the desert at dusk you feel the sudden chill when the sun goes down before you notice the dimmed light. We rode to within a half mile of the fire before we got down and led, taking the horses through the muffling sand where we could and keeping under cover of the bluff. When we were only a few hundred yards downstream of the Mexican's camp I gestured to John-Wayne to tie up to a large greasewood bush and checked the loads in the revolver. John-Wayne wanted to bring the Winchester along, but I told him to put it up again in the scabbard. Then we resumed our advance together in the wash, moving carefully and keeping our heads down until we could hear the horse browsing among the bushes and the sound of sticks sparking in the flames.

The Mexican sat beside the fire with his back to us. He was eating a sandwich with one hand and balancing a tin cup on his leg with the other, and the flames outlined his head and shoulders in a ruddy light. His bedroll lay stretched on a patch of bare sand against the saddle, between the fire and Tortuga grazing discontentedly on a picket line among the bitter desert shrubs. The horse raised his head in our direction, the firelight blazing in his eyes before he dropped his muzzle again to nibble at the ground.

"Shoot him dead, dude!" John-Wayne hissed.

"Stay down," I told him.

The Mexican looked wide as the broad side of a barn behind the iron sights of the revolver.

"¡Levántate! ¡Los brazos sobre la cabeza!"

The man started as if he had been shot in the back and then he sat unnaturally stiff and straight, like a corpse too stiffened to fall over.

"¡Levántate!" I reminded him.

He was up and running suddenly with a knife in his hand toward the horse. With a single downward slash he cut the line and then he was up behind the withers, holding the short end of the rope in his hand.

"¡Alto!" I shouted at him.

"Shoot him!" John-Wayne yelled.

I fired a shot in the air and we went forward together, dashing across the camp where the fire blazed between two pieces of flat rock set on edge and into the dusk beyond, which echoed now with the uproar of departing hoofs.

"You never even aimed," John-Wayne said disgustedly.

"I'm not about to kill an unarmed man on account of a horse."

We stopped to get our breath back and returned to the camp. The tin cup glinted in the firelight near a half-eaten ham sandwich come apart on the ground where the Mexican had dropped it. The saddleskirts were tucked under to make a pillow, the bridle was dropped on the horn of the saddle, and the saddlebags lay across the foot of the foot of the Mexican's bed. I opened them and found a water bottle, more sandwiches, matches, a folded poncho, cigarettes, and a bottle of tequila, the seal broken but the contents barely touched. I held the bottle to the fire to see the worm lying curled in the bottom of it.

"The poor sonofabitch. He's probably wishing he'd taken his bottle, and left the horse behind."

We brought the horses in full darkness into the camp and checked the rigging by the light of the dying fire.

"He's got twenty-five minutes on us already," John-Wayne said.

"That's all right. He hasn't found out yet he's riding a show-horse, not a cow pony."

"Any good horse can see in the night time, like a cat."

The starshine was just enough to show us the tracks in the dried mud and sand, unswerving except around boulders and the tall greasewood, bunched in a lope for the first half-mile and stretching into a trot after that. I saw where the horse had stopped and the rider dismounted beside him to lead through a rough place in the wash.

"He's a horseman, I'll give him that much. Tortuga's never been ridden with a halter and rope before."

John-Wayne, following behind, did not say anything.

"Is something eating you?" I asked.

"No."

"Yes there is."

"How come you didn't shoot that guy dead when you had the chance?"

"I told you. I won't take a man's life for an animal. Not if I can help it, anyway."

"That ain't the Navajo way."

"I'm not a Navajo either."

"Horse in Navajo means What Men Live By, in the white man's talk."

"In the Old World where the white man came from long ago, we also lived by our horses. We often died by them, too. Chivalry was the name they had for it."

"How come no more, dude?"

"We forgot how to die first, and then how to live. And so, finally, we forgot how to love."

John-Wayne's voice in the darkness was proud.

"That never happened to my people."

"If it didn't happen, don't let it."

"It ain't happened yet," he said.

"And if it does, don't let it happen to *you*."

The constellations crowded down over the eastern horizon as a less familiar sky appeared overhead and the desert night felt chilling when we stopped again to rest.

"If he'd only stop and lay down for just an hour."

"He has no bedroll. No food, or water. Or tequila. He knows he's got to keep moving."

"He's movin all right."

"I didn't know there was ever any Mexican could outwalk an Indian."

"He ain't outwalked me. I just said he was movin, that's all."

The sky paled at the horizon and streaks of color appeared above it. The sun came up all at once the way it does on the desert and soon the day was very hot. The country around looked hillier and brushier and I guessed we had crossed into New Mexico during the night, or were about to cross. The Mexican was remounted now and riding at a trot, the tracks proceeding in a straight swift line up the wash as it became a small canyon cutting down through the hills.

"Our man appears to know exactly where he's going."

"He don't need to know much to find Mexico. Just keep goin south three hundred miles and he can't miss."

We lost him several miles farther on where the canyon floor ascended by wide gravel steps backed by sandstone risers and the sides fell in, burying the greasewood and sagebrush in slides of broken red rock. Here we dismounted to drink the last of the Mexican's water and search for tracks climbing out of the canyon.

"I told you he was a smart one," I said.

"He ain't smart."

"Smart enough to fox a Navajo tracker anyway. I'd call that being pretty damn smart."

"It ain't me he foxed. A Navajo wouldn't never of let him get up off of that rock last night. He wouldn't of missed throwin down at that horse, neither, and we'd all of us be settin at home right this very minute."

"Let's stop now. People who throw stones at one another are likely to end up getting hit in the head."

Late in the afternoon we came to a spring in a swale between grassy hills covered by a forest of low cedar trees. We filled the canteens with the clear cold water and let the horses have their share. Twice they drank the spring dry, turned aside to crop the sweet grass while the pool refilled itself, and drank again. It was a good spring, surrounded by the tracks of birds, coyote, and deer. When the horses had drunk all the water they wanted we led them around behind one of the hills and snubbed them short to a couple of cedars. Then, taking the Winchester with us, we climbed up through the trees to the crest where we lay flat on our bellies above the spring. We had been watching for a quarter of an hour when a forkhorn buck stepped from the trees on his way to water and I told John-Wayne to shoot him. He dropped with his nose in the pool, which had already thickened with blood when we reached it.

"I'm sorry," John-Wayne told the carcass, "but me and the white man has got to eat, and you're it."

He kneeled beside the little buck, dipped the ends of his fingers in the warm blood that flowed from the nose and mouth, and marked his forehead with it. Then he raised the new rifle and kissed it on the breach.

"She's my honey," John-Wayne said proudly. "Don't she shoot good? She's right-on, ain't she?"

We dragged the carcass between us off the spring, rolled it on its back, spread the hind legs, and dressed it. John-Wayne slit the belly skin with the point of his knife and opened the abdominal cavity. He reached inside to cut the esophagus and windpipe, and moved down to separate the diaphragm from the peritoneal sac. His arms were slick and red above the elbow when he had done it. We rolled the deer over, spilling the entrails and the blood on the ground, and John-Wayne cut a stick and forced it into the body cavity, spreading the rib cage wide. Then we skinned out the carcass, laid the hide aside, and began cutting away slabs of the purple meat, taking the backstrap first. We had taken what we could carry and were wrapping the meat in green leaves when the horses turned their heads and put their ears forward. I looked with them and saw a figure just behind the treeline on the hill, watching us from the shadows.

"There she is again," I said, before I could think.

"What?"

"There's a man standing up there in the trees, watching us."

I wiped the blade of the knife on my leg and looked back at the figure across the clear yellow light.

"That ain't no Mexican," John-Wayne said.

"Whatever he is, if he has something to say to us he'll come down from that hill and say it."

He came after we had set the meat aside and were dragging the carcass off the spring and into the bushes beyond. The man was almost a giant, six and a half feet tall and hatless. His hair, falling below his shoulders and pulled back from his face by a headband, was silver gray and so were the long beard and the mustache growing over his mouth, although the lines in his forehead and the deep furrows on either side of his nose were the kind that comes from thought rather than old age. He was dressed in a blue denim shirt rotted by the sun, soiled deerskin pants, and something like moccasins on his enormous feet. A wooden-handled knife hung in a deerskin scabbard on his hip and he carried a scarred and battered looking rifle with the bluing worn off. The dingo dog at his heels gave us a keen look but sat obediently when the man halted within a few yards of us.

"That's a nice little buck you men shot," the Wild Man said. "Just look at the fat on that brisket."

"Are you the game warden?"

"No. Not the game warden."

I dropped the hindquarters of the deer and John-Wayne let the head down respectfully on the grass.

"We've taken all of him we can carry before he spoils. Do you have a use for the rest of the meat?"

"I'll take it. And the hide too, if it's not ruined."

"It ain't ruined," John-Wayne told him, offended.

"How far's your camp? We'll pack him over for you on the horses."

"He isn't all that big, and you already took almost a quarter. I can carry him myself."

The Wild Man dropped on one knee beside the carcass, slung it across his shoulders, and stood again, holding the legs in a tight grip on either side of his neck. Blood and water ran down his denim sides and into the open collar of his shirt.

"I'll bring the hide," John-Wayne offered.

The Wild Man started around the hill with the dog after him, followed by ourselves leading the horses. It did not seem like the polite thing to do to ride. Beyond the hill the ground swept up in a series of hills lifting above the skyline. Toward the top of the rise the pitch became very steep but the Wild Man climbed up carrying the deer on his shoulders without slowing or breaking stride. We clambered after him, forcing the horses back to keep them from running us over, to a promontory of rock overgrown with cedars and falling away on the opposite side into a deep canyon like a bay between two coastal points. The Wild Man stood to wait as we climbed up and then stepped abruptly off into space, the horns of the little buck vanishing after him over the rimrock.

He was a hundred feet below us as we started down the trail to the canyon floor where he did not wait but continued ahead this time with his long stride against the base of the rock wall. We caught up with him at last at the head of the canyon where he had thrown the carcass down in a juniper grove and was boning it out with an old Green River knife, a kind I hadn't seen in years.

"I appreciate the meat," the Wild Man said. "I ask that you stay here tonight and eat supper with me."

"Where is your sheep camp?"

"My camp?" the Wild Man asked.

He turned and pointed to an overhang of rock above a ledge twenty feet up the cliff face where a group of stone houses crowded at the back of a shallow cave.

"That is my home," the Wild Man said. He added, "You can picket your horses down here where the grass is. Tomorrow I will show you a good spring to water at."

We unloaded the horses and suspended the saddles in the trees away from varmints.

"All you need for the night is your bedrolls," the Wild Man said, putting up the knife. "There's no human being within fifty miles to disturb your gear, and if there was, the dogs would get him first."

John-Wayne said when we were picketing the horses, "I ain't climbin up there and sleep in no roo-un."

"Why not?"

"Because I don't want to be haunted. That's why."

We climbed up to the stone village by footholds cut a millennium ago in the convex sandstone, behind the dingo who went as if he were part of a circus act, carrying a leg bone from the deer in his mouth. The nests of bats and swallows hung from the roof of the cave, which was blackened by the carbon of ancient smokes. The Wild Man had a fire going already in a sandy depression in the floor away from the little houses. The smoke rose straight before it met the rocky hood of the cave, rolled under the overhang, and poured around the stony lip arching red against the blue of the evening sky. Using the Green River knife, he was cutting the purple venison into thin long strips.

"Mostly I hunt deer for the hide," the Wild Man said. "Otherwise it's easier to kill a chicken. Easiest of all is to take a few eggs."

Swallows flew into the cave and out of it again and a flock of roosting chickens settled for the night, clucking softly from the shadows. Looking down into the meadow where the horses grazed I saw a cultivated garden planted with corn and squash; past the garden a horse and mule stood inside a brush corral. On the floor of the cave close to where the Wild Man worked a dingo bitch nursed a litter of puppies, mewling and squirming as they groped blindly for the swollen dugs. Small corncobs lay strewn around on the floor of the cave and bags containing fresh ears stood stacked behind the stone houses, together with a supply of firewood.

"Put your beds down anywhere you feel like it. Or sleep inside if you want to."

"Not in one of *them*," John-Wayne said, giving the houses a sideways look.

We found another sandy place at the far end of the cave away from the chickens and spread our bags there.

"That dude is crazy, man," John-Wayne said in a whisper.

"What makes you think he's crazy?"

"White man livin away out here like an Indian? You think that ain't crazy? Even Indians don't live this way no more. Since we got modern, and all."

Sitting cross-legged in the dust the Wild Man continued to cut meat, piling the strips on a clean sandstone slab beside him. The dog, stretched on its belly with the deer bone between its forepaws, paid no attention to the meat.

"I'll salt it down in the morning and smoke it," the Wild Man said. "Except for what we eat tonight."

"Smoke all of it, if you wish. We'll eat from the quarter John-Wayne and I cut this afternoon."

The Wild Man regarded John-Wayne as I spoke.

"You are Dineh?" he inquired.

"Yes," John-Wayne said, looking proud.

"I am Zuni," the Wild Man told him.

"*You*?" John-Wayne was incredulous, and a little indignant. "Indians don't have beards."

"By marriage," the Wild Man said. "That's always been good enough for me."

He looked around himself, reached for two of the little cobs lying at the edge of the circle of light the fire made, and examined them briefly. Then he handed both cobs to John-Wayne.

"One of these is seven hundred years old, the other maybe fifteen. Or maybe both are eight hundred years old—or twenty. Can you say which, young man?"

John-Wayne studied the cobs.

"No," he said finally in a reluctant voice.

"I can't either," the Wild Man told him, taking the cobs back, "and it doesn't matter anyway."

He rose, wiped the knife on his sleeve, and replaced it in the scabbard.

"I am chief, mayor, shaman, elder, and warrior in my own pueblo," he said. "I am its people, its history, and its legends. I am its spirit, and its memory. I am the preserver and caretaker of a destroyed and vanished civilization. Without me there is nothing here but rock, water, and the eternal wind. That is why I can never leave this place."

The Wild Man put the meat up in the granary he had converted to a smoke house. Then he brought out from another of the buildings a metate and pestle and with these a canvas bag.

"We will have coffee to drink before we eat supper," the Wild Man said. "The beans are very old, but it is a long time since I had visitors to the pueblo."

He ground the beans in the bowl of the metate, filled an ironware pot from the water jar he brought from the back of the cave, and added the grounds to the pot. He laid more cedar sticks on the fire and shoved the pot among the flames.

"A Zuni herder left me these beans, I no longer recall when."

"You have lived here for a long time?"

"A long time, yes. Since before my wife died. My wife was a wonderful woman."

"The pueblo is part of the Zuni reservation?"

"No. This is government land. Some day they will find my pueblo, bulldoze a road in, and build a visitors' center and a parking lot for cars where your horses are grazing now. By then I hope I will be dead. There are more pueblos in these canyons than any but the Zuni know."

When the water boiled he took the pot from the fire, broke a hen's egg, and drained the albumen in among the seething grounds. He replaced the lid and set the pot in the fire again. Then he flung the egg shell with the yolk inside it over the cliff edge.

"It's hard to keep things tidy up here with so many chickens around," the Wild Man said.

The coffee tasted the way the corncobs might have if they had been boiled for ten minutes. We still had plenty of coffee in the packs below, but I did not wish to seem rude. We would have fresh coffee to drink in the morning, anyway.

"A good thing about coffee," the Wild Man said. "It stays fresh forever almost, thank God."

"How often do you have to go for supplies?"

"I don't go. I help the herders out a little in summer and they give me something extra."

When the fire had burned to coals he brought two pans and some ground cornmeal. He mixed egg yolks into the meal, patted it into cakes, and set the cakes to cook. The final light faded from the sky as the stars appeared in the cave opening, glittering with their ancient sight. The Wild Man turned the cakes and set the larger pan with the venison strips on the coals beside them.

"This is the best I've eaten for months," he said. "A man has no ambition, cooking for himself."

We ate from battered plates, using our knives and fingers. The corn cakes had grit in them but the venison, basted with eggs and a little of the meal, were tender and sweet. The Wild Man cut the last strip in two and hurled one piece to the dog who had watched politely from a distance as we ate our supper, the other to the nursing bitch. Then he rubbed the plates with sand, built the fire back with an armload of juniper, and pounded a handful more of the coffee beans. The flames blazed up brightly as the boughs caught, filling the cave with a strong perfume.

"We're looking for a Mexican on a black bay horse," I said.

"A stolen horse?"

"Yes."

"Your horse?"

"My horse," John-Wayne told him.

"I have seen no one in this canyon since early spring," the Wild Man said. "Except you."

"He seemed to be familiar with the country."

"Zuni and their herders know it well. Few others ever come here. It is no easy country to know."

"This fellow worked for a sheep man in Arizona."

"They hire Mexicans when they can find no one else. These are bad times for our people. For yours, they are terrible."

The coffee tasted worse than the first pot, the Wild Man having neglected to add egg white. The resulting bitter flavor gave me a thought.

"I need to go for something from the packs," I said.

The Wild Man nodded. He drew a flaming stick from the fire and gave it to me.

"Take this and be careful going down. The steps are difficult to find in the dark."

Holding the torch above my head I climbed down the rock face below the cave blazing out from the darkness where John-Wayne and the Wild Man faced each other across the fire. The footholds were spaced erratically, causing me to slip at the bottom and drop the last couple of feet to the ground. I took the whiskey bottle from the horsepacks and buttoned it safely inside my shirt. I was about to close the flaps when I remembered the harmonica, and brought that too. Then I climbed up again to the cave where the two Indians, man and boy, sat motionless, silent as their shadows projected on the backwall by the yellow flames.

The Wild Man's eyes had a shine brighter than firelight when I drew the bottle from inside my shirt. He said nothing but gathered the three cups, returned their contents to the coffee pot, and handed the cups back. Then he sat on the cave floor again and waited, holding his eyes fixed on the whiskey bottle.

I unscrewed the cap and poured a couple of fingers of whiskey all around.

"Do you care for water with your whiskey? It will go a little farther that way. At least, it will last a little longer."

The Wild Man hooked his finger around the handle, raised the cup, and traced a series of small circles, swirling the liquid around as he considered.

"No," he said at last, "good whiskey is like a marriage. An ounce of pure joy beats six of the adulterated kind."

We drank each other's health in measured sips. Without having to be asked, John-Wayne brought wood from the pile and threw it on the fire. The flames blazed high again, sucking oxygen with a roaring sound and waking the chickens who responded with sleepy clucks from their roost in the shadows at the back of the cave.

"Perhaps you are curious to know why I have not asked for news of the outside world," the Wild Man said. "The reason, if you are interested, it that it *is* outside, not of the pueblo only but of life itself. It is like a spirit that has detached itself from the body and is able neither to operate on its own or to reattach itself to the body it once rejected. The outside world with its automobiles, its airplanes, its space ships, its telephones and television, its modern highways and its great cities is no longer inside itself, and so it is no longer real, and therefore it is no longer of interest to me. The people who are content to use all these things interest me least of all."

He raised his cup high above the flames and drank the whiskey off.

"This is good, though."

"Have some more."

John-Wayne finished quickly, not to be left out, and I refilled the cups.

"Do you smoke?" the Wild Man asked.

"I take a cigar every now and then."

"Long as my grandmother don't catch me," John-Wayne said.

Our host drew another brand from the fire and passed it to him.

"Young man, inside the house you will find a wooden box to the left of the door. Would you get it and bring it out to us, please?"

John-Wayne drew back as if the man had struck at him.

"I ain't goin in there!"

"Do you mind telling me why not?"

"I don't want to be haunted!"

John-Wayne's voice was desperate. Tears appeared at the corners of his eyes.

"Are you afraid?"

John-Wayne said nothing.

"What are you afraid of?"

Still he did not speak.

"Are you afraid of your ancestors? Of your own people? Of your heritage? Of the past?"

John-Wayne put his hands up to his face.

"Of yourself?"

Behind his hands the kid was crying. I started to speak, but did not.

"Never be afraid of the past. We cannot be certain that the future will happen, but the past is forever. It is all that we have and everything we are, the only thing we can really know, ourselves included. And do not fear the dead especially. Or the unborn still to come. The Navajos dispossessed the Old Ones, and the white man the Navajos, and the other Indian peoples. Now he is dispossessing himself. And who is to blame?" the Wild Man asked. "All of them are to blame," he answered himself. "All we can say is that, if life goes on and the future arrives in time, there will be others. Go on then and bring the box, and we will smoke cigarettes together and finish what is left of the whiskey."

The cigarettes were made from something cured and dried in a cornhusk wrapper, bitter tasting. I smoked mine politely but John-Wayne, humiliated and full of resentment, made a face.

"You do not care for my cigarettes," the Wild Man observed, smiling. "They are made from the cured heads of the thistles growing around here. They are not the best I have ever tasted but what is important is I don't have to go to Gallup or Springerville to buy them."

We smoked in silence for a while before I remembered the harmonica. The Wild Man, seeing the instrument, set down his cup and stared.

"You are a musician?" he asked.

"No. I play the harmonica in cow camp, usually when I've had one drink too many."

"A few of the herders play also. Except for them I have had no music to listen to in many years."

"What would you like to hear?"

"Anything you play will be a pleasure for me. Music is the only thing the wilderness cannot give a man."

I played "Barbara Allen," "Yankee Doodle," and "Oh, you buffalo gals," repeating every other verse or so a cappella, like a kind of chorus—which sounded awkward and *was*, of course.

I'm Captain Jinks of the Horse Marines,
I feed my horse on corn and beans,
And I often go beyond my means,
For I'm Captain Jinks of the Horse Marines,
I'm Captain in the army!

The Wild Man tapped his knee with his finger, the whiskey beside him forgotten, the cigarette cold between his lips. I gave him "Oh Susannah!" next, and after that "The Irish Washerwoman":

Do-si ladies, do-si-do,
Come down heavy on your
Heel and toe!

—and before I could finish the Wild Man was on his feet, dancing. I finished out the song and as John-Wayne sat applauding I swung into another.

Old Dan Tucker was a fine old man,
He washed his face in the frying pan,
He combed his hair with a wagon wheel,
And died of a toothache in his heel!

John-Wayne threw his cigarette down on the stone floor and jigged beside him, copying the old man's steps. You never forget the music, which always seems new and fresh, but the dancing was something I hadn't seen or even thought about since my grandfather's day, going into town on Saturday night. I was nearly out of breath and my lips felt sore and swollen as if I had been blowing up inner tubes, but the old fellow was tireless so I gave him more: "The Devil's Hornpipe," "Money Musk," "Arkansas Traveler," and several more I don't remember now. Finally the Wild Man quit dancing, reached for his cup, and drained it.

"By God!" the Wild Man said. "I haven't heard music like that since I was a boy growing up in Kansas City."

I poured him more to drink and when I had my breath back and my lips had returned to their normal shape I played "Jeannie With the Light Brown Hair," "Old Man River," and, finally, "Kathleen Mavourneen," thinking he might be familiar with the melody even if he had never heard the words.

It may be for years, and it may be forever,
Oh why art thou silent, oh voice of my heart?
It may be for years, and it may be forever,
Oh why art thou silent, Kathleen Mavourneen?

The Wild Man wept as I was finishing.

"You know the song," I said.

He wiped his eyes on his sleeve and shook his head.

"Not the song," the old man said. "But the feeling I know very well. Give me a little more of the whiskey and I will tell you about it.

"I met my wife," the Wild Man began, "at a dance at Black Rock, New Mexico, many, many years ago. A Zuni I met on the track crew invited me to go with him. The dance was at his uncle's house. Although there were many people there, I was the only white man. Only a few of the people wanted to talk to me and the railroad man was embarrassed. He had been living away from the tribe for a long time, working in the white man's world, and he had begun to forget how things were with his people. Among the few who welcomed me was a beautiful girl with shining hair, a glowing skin, and lustrous eyes. All that afternoon while the ceremony lasted Dark Flower was beside me, and when it was over we left the uncle's house together. There was another girl waiting at home for me in Kansas City, but I did not believe that one girl had anything in particular to do with the other.

"I took Dark Flower to Gallup with me that evening and we became lovers in my room at Mrs. Broadbent's rooming house on Route 66 overlooking the Santa Fe tracks. After that night Dark Flower did not wish to return to her family at Black Rock. Instead she wanted to be married in the white man's church in Gallup. There were several Christian churches in town and she did not care which one of them I chose to marry us. Dark Flower's father was dead but she had a brother named Winter Elk to look after her. Winter Elk was violently opposed to his sister's involvement with a white man, and one night he surprised us outside the bungalow I had rented in Gallup and offered to fight me. As you see, I am a big man, twenty years old then and doing hard labor ten hours a day. I accepted his offer and knocked him down with the first blow. He thought I would kill him and when he was able to stand up at last he promised not to oppose his sister's choice of a husband if we would come to Black Rock and be married in a Zuni ceremony.

"It was late in August by that time and the track work was to be finished at the end of September. I agreed to the marriage with Dark Flower because I was going home to Kansas City soon and an Indian wedding was no real marriage. I loved Dark Flower but it is supposed to be possible for a man to love several women at once and of course I was not considering her own love in all of this. We were married in a ceremony at her parents' house, when I received my Indian name which means Man in the Moon. We lived for another month in Gallup before the railroad paid me my last wages and I told her that I must return to Kansas City to see my family. Dark Flower begged to be allowed to come with me but I explained to her that just as she had needed to persuade her family to accept a white husband, in the same way I had to prepare my family to accept her. I gave a month's rent on the bungalow while I was away and took a train east to Kansas City where my fiancée had been waiting with growing impatience and alarm on account of my increasingly infrequent letters. We were married two weeks before Christmas and moved into a small frame house near the river where the barges passed day and night, sounding their deep tragic horns that haunted me even in my sleep.

"My American wife and I had not been married very long before our marriage was in serious trouble. She had a job with an automobile sales agency and she was used to going out every evening, spending money and having a good time. Beyond that, I believe that she suspected me. Women have an intuition that men lack, almost a sixth sense that tells them, often, more even than they want to know. She had guessed that I had been unfaithful to her in Gallup but she went ahead with the marriage anyway, perhaps to show the other woman what.

"After we were married she went on living her old life, going out at night with friends while I worked late at the office where the company was grooming me for a management position. I did not care for office work and when I left it life at home was even worse. My wife was not a true wife to me and I was not a proper husband to her. Both of us were busy apart and had no time for one another, not even to make a child together. At night she did not sleep well from having drunk too much and smoked too many cigarettes in the bars and I could not sleep from worry about the office and the noise of the barge horns. At last my wife managed to conceive. As soon as we understood for certain that a child was on the way we stopped being excited about having a child. In the third month of her pregnancy she miscarried, and a month after that she told me she wanted a divorce and moved in with a man she had just finished selling a new Cadillac convertible to.

"I quit my job with the railroad, left Kansas City, and drove seventeen hours to Gallup without stopping except to fill the gas tank and change a flat tire. After a few hours' sleep at Mrs. Broadbent's I drove on to Black Rock where no one recognized me wearing city clothes and a business haircut. Dark Flower was living in the pinyon and juniper forest ten miles from town, alone except for the child she had given birth to. She lived in disgrace, having been disavowed by her brother and by the rest of her family. When I asked her forgiveness she did not speak a word but went to bring my son from the cradle and lay him carefully in my arms.

"We lived alone in the forest after that, cut away from the white man's world and treated as pariahs by our own people. We raised sheep and a few goats, many chickens, and we grew a little Indian corn. Dark Flower became pregnant once again but the child, a daughter, was stillborn and after that she was unable to conceive anymore. Our son, who we called Dawn

Boy, became a great breaker and trainer of horses before he was ten years old. Late in spring each year we took the sheep from Black Rock south to the high country for the summer. During many summers we lived in these canyons and, for most of July, here in this pueblo, while the sheep grazed below and on the pastures around. It was here, finally, that I lost my wife and son, after they fell sick of a virus that infects people living among mice and rodents, which our pueblo of course has many of. My wife became ill in the morning and died before sundown the following day. My son, who helped me to care for her when she was dying, grew sick hours before her death and died in agony himself before another day had passed. Since that day, many years ago, my wife has never left this place. My son, however, comes and goes. The young are restless spirits, after all."

We finished the whiskey in silence and turned in, the Wild Man entering his stone house while John-Wayne and I got inside the bedrolls. He fell asleep immediately, snoring beside me as I watched the glow of the dying fire fade across the stony ceiling until the only light was from the stars spread across the cave mouth where a cold wind blew—thinking how it was, after all, a nice place to bring a woman.

---

The Wild Man smoked meat in the granary while we loaded the packs on the horses. Seeing we were ready to ride, he climbed down from the pueblo with pemmican for the saddlebags.

"You will need the strength that comes from eating meat, the boy especially."

"How far east does the wash head up?"

"I do not know. I have never ridden farther than twenty miles myself. But it is three or four times as far over to Datil."

We told him goodbye, and started. Riding up the trail from the bottom we could see the smoke fanning from under the arched roof of the cave, through the slanting rays of the early sun. The smoke showed blue against the forest green at the verge of the plateau as we rode across the rimrock, then vanished from sight behind the intervening ridge.

"Some day that smoke is going to get him the attention of someone he'd rather not be noticed by," I said.

"What do you think they're goin to do with him when they find him?"

"Stick him in jail for camping on federal property without a permit. Fine him. Send him to a mental hospital for the rest of his days."

"Why can't they just let people live the way they want to anymore?"

"What kind of question is that for an Indian to ask?"

"Who should know better than the white man?"

"The white man," I said. "He knows least about it of them all."

We circled out from the spring for a couple of hours in the hope of cutting sign. Finding none, we continued in the wash on a southeasterly heading. The horses went without enthusiasm, stumbling and dispirited in spite of being well fed and rested. The sun swung up toward the center of the sky stretching above the green wilderness shimmering with heat, and the cold sweet-tasting water from the Wild Man's spring turned hot and brackish in the canteens. We stopped a little past noon to rest the horses and eat some of the pemmican in the shade of an ancient juniper tree holding by partially exposed roots to the caving bank of the wash. As we dismounted, a buzzing noise from beneath the tree caused the horses to shy. The big rattler lay coiled among the thick roots, his seeing tongue flicking ahead of his blind yellow eyes.

"You underfoot again," I said to the snake.

We ran him off with a stick and sat down in his place where the roots made a cradling bench against the clay wall.

"Trust a snake to find the best place to lay up for the day. Whoever is always at exactly the right place at exactly the right time, he's the one you don't ever want to trust."

"How come you didn't just shoot him, man?"

"I figure there's room enough in New Mexico yet for the three of us, anyway."

"Four."

"How four?"

"You, me, him, and the dude back there in the cave. Do you think he ever had to eat snake when he was hungry?"

"Probably he's done it many times."

"Least *we* ain't never had to eat snake, in the desert."

"Yet."

"*I* wouldn't eat it—ever. Not if I was dyin, even."

"You'd eat it all right if you were dying—and call it manna from Heaven, too."

"I would not. Navajos ain't allowed to even *look* at a snake. I told you that already once."

The visit to the pueblo seemed to have enervated rather than refreshed us. We rode at a distance from one another for the rest of the afternoon, not wanting to talk and feeling out of sorts, and made an early camp. The next morning we started before sunup and rode all day in the diminishing wash without seeing any sign beyond the tracks of deer, elk, and a few half-wild cattle. Discouraged and tired we called an early halt again and I was helping John-Wayne carry wood for the fire when I became aware of feeling unwell. My head hurt, the glands in my neck were swollen, and the muscles in my legs and the small of my back ached. I built a fire while John-Wayne finished bringing the wood and sat by it in the warm evening shadows that felt chill through my denim shirt. John-Wayne staked the horses for me and browned the meat the Wild Man had given us along with his corn cakes. The whiskey was gone and the bottle too; the old fellow had asked for it to place cut flowers in. I ate as much of the meat and cakes as I could manage, got inside the bag, and lay there shivering with my cheek against the polished saddle seat while John-Wayne sat cross-legged beside the fire, his soft, boyish features carved by the firelight like the stern immobile face at the top of a totem pole.

In the morning I was very sick. So far as I know no one but me and a couple of unkillable Navajos full of cheap whiskey ever survived hantavirus. I forced myself to eat a little of the Wild Man's pemmican and drank most of the water remaining from the spring before my stomach contracted like a squeezed pig's bladder and I tossed everything up. John-Wayne saddled and loaded my horse for me and helped me to mount, placing his arm under my thigh and lifting. I got up in the saddle at last and before we had ridden ten or twelve miles I was so weak that he had to dismount again and tie my legs loosely in the stirrups.

"Don't die, Dude!" John-Wayne pleaded. "Cops would say the Indian killed the white man and left him out on the desert to rot."

I promised to write him a note to show the authorities, telling how I had fallen sick and died from a fever spread by an ancient race of rats the size of human beings, before the violent motion of the horse, the burning heat alternating with the racking chill swallowed me like Jonah's whale into a black pit of misery. Slumped forward over the horse's neck I found I could dream, and that way escape. At times I was at home with Jody James in the green valley cutting between red cliffs below the high blue mountains, playing the harmonica and making love. Others I was with Lydia again up in Montana, listening to the screenwriter who was not a stick, out of sight somewhere, talking, talking, talking. The dreams were like a raft beneath me, rising and falling on the ocean tide, a yellow ocean stretching away as far as the horizon and dotted with white flowers. As I dreamed the dots grew larger, swimming on the heaving waters which drained away suddenly from the empty desert covered by an array of round white figures standing high on skinny legs above the ground. Alien and huge, these monsters from another world brooded over the wilderness, preparing the invasion. Sitting straight in the saddle I felt my mind clear suddenly and knew we must attack at once. I put my heels hard to the horse and we were ahead a few lengths already before I thought to give a call behind me.

"Charge!" I yelled as I drew my revolver and waved it above my head.

"Where you goin, Dude?"

"Attack the enemy!" I shouted, plunging forward down the rocky slope. "Pour it into them!"

"You crazy, man, or somethin?"

John-Wayne was alongside us now, running neck and neck as he leaned from the stirrups to take Quixote's head.

"Keep your hands off my horse," I yelled, "and follow me!"

The pale circles ahead swelled larger and larger and they grew human features as we ran, noses eyes and mouths taking shape on the concave surfaces until the faces mirrored each other all around, exact replicas of the same perfect countenance—a final apparition whatever it was we had been pursuing for weeks across the desert. I got a shot off before John-Wayne seized the reins behind the bit and worked the horse down to a trot, and finally to a fast walk.

"The *bruja*!" I shouted as he took the reins from my hands and swung them forward over the neck and head. "Don't you see? Are you blind? It's her!"

"You're sick, man," John-Wayne said. "You really are. I think that maybe you are going to die."

"No," I told him, letting the hammer down with my thumb and holstering the revolver, "I think that I'm already dead."

# BOOK IV
# CIVILIZATION

This is me—John-Wayne Bilagody, Tuba City, Navajo Nation, U.S.A. I'm tellin the story here on account of the Dude's been sick and you want to know what happened between when he attacked them big saucers—the VLA, short for Very Large and Airy—on the Plains of San Augustin and when he got out of jail—but that ain't no way to tell a story, he would say. He's been real careful up to now to tell it right but there's things he left out, anyway. The Dude's smart, bein the white man and all, but he's nuts too, even before he got haunted by that dead kid in the pueblo and begun to sweat and shiver and talk about the Night of the Lonely Heart, though with his hair and beard growed out he looked like Buffalo Bill to me. I like the way he makes the story move along real good and tries to make the scenery and stuff less borin, but to tell you the truth it ain't as good as the stories he tells when we're settin by the campfire—not them borin ones about the nights and ladies and dragon snakes and that, but how the girl rustler almost shot him to death up in Montana and all the movie stars he was married to. If I was married to a movie star I wouldn't be ridin around in no desert lookin for a horse that didn't even belong to me when I could be settin home with her, you bet. What I'm sayin is this story don't make no sense, somehow, but it's his story, it ain't mine, and I'm here to fill in kind of until we get to the really *good* part, which is about me and him and—but he's goin to tell you all about her, soon's he gets out of jail.

So it was all I could do to keep him from chargin them saucers, thinkin they was space monsters or witches—or somethin. The horse was goin full out and the Dude was hangin onto the mane with one hand and his gun in the other, flappin his legs in the stirrups where I tied them that mornin. I rode alongside on Ana and grabbed the bridle, which is when he yelled at me and fired the gun in the air. We got slowed down to a walk finally and then he didn't seem to notice the saucers no more. They was set on wheels and rolled around on train tracks in the desert and in and out of these big hangars, like. It was all good sheep country around here but somebody probly was makin just as good money with them saucers, I don't know. We rode all afternoon except to stop a couple times for him to be sick, and the second time I seen a truck and trailer off in some trees and a white man cuttin firewood. "You see that guy over there?" I says. "That's some dude cuttin up firewood for the winter, it ain't no space man or heehaw," but he didn't pay me no attention. The white man wanted to take him to the hospital but the Dude said no, he wanted to die a clean death outside. The man's trailer was half fulled up with firewood already but we put the horses in with the wood and got up in the cab which was one of them crew kinds—four doors and a back seat. We laid the Dude acrosst it and rolled the window down so his boots stuck out and he didn't have to lay there in no fecal position and then we started, driven' slow so the wood didn't fall on the horses and kill them.

The Dude moaned and kicked all the way to Reserve and when he talked about lonely hearts and mavooreen, that kind of stuff, I sang kareeokey, *loud,* for the white man—to keep him entertained. And then a really awesome thing happened. We got to the ranch finally and this woman comes out of the house and looks in the truck and she goes, "Jeb Ryder, what is the matter with you?"—and it's like they've known each other for years and years. Like if you're white you know everbody, I guess.

The woman's name was Mrs. Quantrill. She was married to Mr. Quantrill who was this rancher, and also one of them lawyer men makes his money tellin cops and judges and that kind of people what to say, as well as bein a politician—just in case he run out of things to do. Eons of Mr. Quantrill's family had lived in Reserve and they all knew the Dude and his folks, who had mostly died or moved away since then. Mrs. Quantrill was short and pretty with dark hair goin gray, a little, and she wore glasses. Mr. Quantrill looked tall but he wasn't, on account of bein skinny. He had black hair like an Indian's, except for bein wiry instead of smooth, and his face looked red hot, like a pumpkin that's got a lighted candle inside of it. Ever five minutes or so he would mention his Cherokee blood, and when he wasn't tellin you about how the Iroquois Indians invented democracy, he would badmouth the feral goverment in Warshinton, Dee Cee; in between he talked about the Kelts, who invented the stirrup along with minin and trees. Mr. Quantrill hated the army in Warshinton for runnin his people out of Missippi into New Mexico, and tryin to tell them how to run their lives after that. He was explainin all about it while we carried the Dude into the house and laid him down on a bed in the bedroom and took his clothes off after Mrs. Quantrill had left. "We *are* going to win," Mr. Quantrill said. "Maybe not in my lifetime, but some day. There's no doubt in my mind about it: We're going to *win.*" Then he closed the bedroom door with a bang. "You ready for supper, young man? We'll burn a couple of thick, bloody steaks, or some other politically incorrect thing."

The Quantrills' ranch was the most beautiful thing I ever seen, except maybe the Heaven Room my cousin who's a Mormon sent me on a post card from Salt Lake City. It had big old cottonwoods growin down along the river with hay fields on either side of it and a lot of white-painted buildins with the sun glarin on the tin roofs like they was burnin up and meltin in the heat. The hills come all the way down to the river and pushed it around into blue glittery loops and back of the hills was the mountains, summery green and dark except for the cliffs which turned red in the evenin with the sun goin down over in Arizona somewheres. At night the javelina come down from the hills, gruntin and groanin like pigs do while they rooted around in Mrs. Quantrill's rose bushes, and Mr. Quantrill would have to get up and shoot off his shotgun out the bedroom window. Then in the mornin she'd yell at him that the bushes looked like Sherman had been marchin through them. We never did get to meet Sherman, probly because Mrs. Quantrill didn't seem to want him around, much. The Quantrills' house had *three* showers in it, so that when you wanted to take one you always got to do it right away without havin to wait for the water to be hot again afterward—unless the twins, Jack Jr. and Jesse, was usin them. It was good to sleep in a soft bed again and eat food that didn't have no floaters or swimmers in it and had been cooked by a woman, and watch *Seinfeld* reruns on TV. Mr. Quantrill he always treated me good and so did Mrs. Quantrill, until she begun to be schoolteacherish, like white women get. They called the doctor in to have a look at the Dude and the doctor, he said it wasn't no hamster virus at all but the ordinary kind and there wasn't nothin he could do for it but rest up and drink lots of liquids on account of he was dehydrogenated. I tried to tell him how the old man's kid's chindi made him sick but Mrs. Quantrill told me to stop talkin superstitious rot, so I shut up then. A couple days after that the Dude was up and around, tryin to call his woman on the phone in Utah and settin out in Mr. Quantrill's law office in back of the heavy equipment shed where the tractors and that was. The office had a rolltop desk with a wooden swivel chair in front of it, an armchair for people to set in when one of the dogs wasn't asleep there, and a pellet stove for when it was cold. Also there was lots of books, enough to make a real liberry with. I asked Mr. Quantrill had he read all them books and he said no, just the ones big enough to get the judge's attention when you pitched them at his head in court. The office smelled of Mr. Quantrill's pipe and the dog baskets around the pellet stove where the pointer dogs come in in the afternoon to lay down when it got too hot for them outside.

Mornins, the Dude slept in and I was allowed to too, a little, before Mrs. Quantrill would start bangin around or runnin the vacuum cleaner outside of my room until I come out to shower finally and she'd say, "I *hope* I didn't wake you, John-Wayne, but do you have any idea what time it is?" After breakfast she sent me down to the barns to help the Meskin bottle-feed the bum lambs he was takin care of and water the calves, and then in the afternoons I hepped with the hayin or cut out cattle with Bert Loomis, Mr. Quantrill's ranch foreman that rescued us at Datil, and Jesse and Jack Jr., who was gettin ready to go back to the university at Silver City. The twins had black hair and black eyes like their dad and was skinny like him, but tall and muscular too, always laughin and havin jokes. In the evenin after supper while Mrs. Quantrill read schoolteacher magazines in the kitchen me, the Dude, and Mr. Quantrill—the twins too, if they wasn't out drivin around with their girlfriends—would target shoot in the big field back of the house to be ready for the government when the Bad Time comes, or make bullets and reload shells in Mr. Quantrill's office and set around afterward talkin and drinkin whiskey—me included, though I had to swear not to tell Mrs. Quantrill about it—while Mr. Quantrill and the Dude told stories. Some of the stories was excitin ones, like about the mountain lion that stalked Mr. Quantrill in the Florida Mountains when he was bow huntin for deer, and some of them—about Susan Toxic Schock, the entirementalist from Tucson, Arizona—was funny, but mostly the conversation was really borin, all about politics and stuff. Most nights it ended up with Mr. Quantrill makin himself so mad he could hardly talk and the twins laughin at him and mussin his hair.

"Maybe you *will* win—legally," the Dude told Mr. Quantrill. "But it could be legally will be too late to do the actual winners any good."

Mr. Quantrill swung his cowboy boots up onto the top of his rolltop desk and tilted back in the swivel chair. Then he took the pipe from his mouth and knocked it out into the spittoon next to where he was settin.

"I had a lady journalist down here from Albuquerque last spring," Mr. Quantrill said. "And you know what she said to me? She said, 'It's transplants like me from back East that are going to take New Mexico away from rednecks like you and make it part of the United States—finally.' And you know what I said to her? I said, 'Lady, you'd better be real careful who you call a redneck, because there's some of us consider that to be a compliment, and it only encourages them." Mr. Quantrill quit talkin to strike a match on his boot, relit the pipe, and blew on it. He went through a bunch of tobacco ever day just by gettin mad and blowin on that pipe instead of suckin at it, like you're supposed to do. Right then the telephone rang and he picked it up.

"Jack Quantrill here," Mr. Quantrill said, like he wanted them to make somethin of it. He pressed the phone against his ear until it turned white and his face got redder and redder so that, with them black eyes, he *looked* Indian–Cherokee Indian, not Dineh, of course.

"Yes, ma'am," Mr. Quantrill said; "no, ma'am… I am *not* trying to intimidate you. I am telling you what we intend to do here in Catron County, New Mexico, and I am even telling you how we are going to go about doing it. Forewarned is forearmed, isn't that so?… No ma'am, that is not a threat. It is simply by way of letting you know that what goes in New York City and Washington, D.C. does not necessarily go here in New Mexico. We have our own custom and culture out here, and we are going to make you people in the East respect it, and respect us. Catron County is ranching and timber country, and we don't propose to sacrifice it to the Sierra Club and the spotted owl…. No ma'am… Yes ma'am… Yes, you may quote me on that. Quote me all you want to, just be sure you get it right… Yes ma'am. Goodnight, ma'am."

"I get calls like that all the time," Mr. Quantrill said, puttin up the phone. "Some woman newspaper reporter in New York, never been west of Chicago or east of L.A.—she accused me of trying to 'intimidate' her! They call from New York, Boston, Washington—so sensitive, you know, thinking they're talking to a Western badman: picturing me in a black hat and a couple of six-shooters on my cartridge belt. And I sound like a redneck to them. One of them kept using the word, complaining about the 'rednecks' in southwestern New Mexico. I waited for her to shut up for just one second and then I asked, 'When you say "redneck" you mean someone who is rural, ignorant, violent, and white, don't you?' 'Yes,' she said. 'Well, we're all of us natives here either white Indians or red white men, and we'd surely appreciate Easterners like you remembering that fact,' I told her." Mr. Quantrill whirled the chair around to look out through the window to the full moon shinin on the valley. "Let's go outside and do something useful, like irrigate the orchard," he said. "I never wanted to be a lawyer, anyway."

The Dude was really bummed about that horse, wanted to get it back just as quick as we could so he could go home to his woman again. He talked to her a lot on the phone, and once he let me call Bette too but she had gone out somewheres—with the fat Paiute, probly. There's a song goes somethin like "If I ain't with the one I love, I love the one I'm with," so I didn't let it bug me too much. Like my grandma says, what don't happen wasn't never meant to happen. Ever other person you meet's goin to be a woman, and if it hadn't been for him bein a Paiute I wouldn't of minded—much. So except for school gettin ready to start, I was ready let him have that horse when we found him without no argument about it and tell that horse goodbye forever. But the Dude, he wasn't ready to give up yet. "A promise is a promise," he says, "especially to a woman." So just as soon as he was feelin good again and Baca's horses was rested up, he wanted to leave even before the barbecue dance Mrs. Quantrill was havin at the ranch, until she sweet-talked him into stayin—I know; I seen her do it.

There was striped tents on the lawn between the house and the river and Mr. Quantrill dug pits and built fires down in them and stuck a cabrito, which is a kind of goat stuffed with peppers and tomatoes and onions and that, in each one of the holes and covered them up with dirt and cooked them that way for a whole day and a half before diggin them up again and servin them for supper, along with everthin else they had to eat. There was another tent for the musicians to be under while they played and a dance floor covered with sawdust and a metal fence around it with kerryseen lanterns hung on the posts, and a little ways away this big metal cactus, painted green with colored lights in it, to light up all the people that was dancing—kickin around in the sawdust. Then between the big tent and the dance floor they had like an outhouse and a dude inside in a white shirt and black bow tie servin drinks—any kind of drink you wanted and it was all FREE—through a little window. There was about a thousand people there and it was the best dance I ever seen in my whole life, except for there wasn't nobody for me to dance with. The twins had their girlfriends and everbody was dancin to western swing but me and the Dude, settin together at one of the tables around the dance floor, drinkin. The man in the black tie give me a whiskey when I ast him without battin an eye, but the Dude told me to say it was Coke if Mrs. Quantrill come along and seen us.

"There's plenty of girls your age here tonight," he says to me. "Why don't you grab one and get out there on the dance floor?"

"White girls don't want to dance with no Indian," I told him.

"Don't be ridiculous. Being Indian gives you an edge these days. That preacher's daughter would have been more than happy to dance with you. Not to mention anything you might have wanted to do with her."

"How come *you* ain't dancin?" I ast him.

"Because dancing makes me feel stupid. That's why."

"How come, man?"

"I don't know, it just does. It always did."

"It's your custom and culture, ain't it?"

"Not really. Don't tell Quantrill I said that."

"You want another drink?" I ast him.

"If you're buying."

"Everthin's free, man."

"I know it."

I brought the drinks over and we set in the shadows outside the circle of colored light, drinkin and watchin the dancin. The twins's girls was both of them, like, these incredible foxes. Jack Jr.'s had curly yellow hair and big bazzooms, and when they slow-danced it was like she was tryin to climb on top of him. Jesse's girl was a redhead, with a long waist and long redhead legs that just seemed to go up and up, twinklin in the darkness under her skirt. I watched til I couldn't stand it no more, and pretty soon this white lady comes over and asts the Dude would he like to dance. She was a blonde lady, skinny with a thin face, kind of old with no tits, and he tells her no thanks, he don't never dance.

"You never dance?" the lady asked, lookin like he just told her he never had to go to the toilet. "Nope," the Dude said, not like himself.

"Really? You're kidding. Or is it just me?"

"It isn't something I enjoy doing."

"You don't enjoy being out on the floor, feeling the beat go through you from head to toe—like it's your own blood pounding?"

"It doesn't mean anything to me."

"You're going to break a lot of hearts tonight then," the lady said. "All the girls want to know who the handsome stranger is. They're waiting for you to ask them for a dance."

"I'm sorry," the Dude says. "Tell them I'll be happy to send a round of drinks over, instead."

It was embarassin, him bein that unpolite and all. I waited until she was gone before I told him.

"You hurt that lady's feelins," I said.

"Women aren't supposed to ask, men are. I've spent my life avoiding invitations to dance. I'm getting sick and tired of it."

He set drinkin bourbon and watchin the dance from a faraway place inside of himself, while I thought how he was crazy not to want to pick up on all the great lookin white chicks around. "You know," he says after a while, "I wouldn't have a goddamn thing to say to any one of them."

"You don't have to say nothin, man—just dance."

He wasn't drunk, but drinkin didn't seem to have nothin to do with that empty place inside of him I'd never seen before and couldn't get to. Maybe it's on account of white women bein skinny inside, if you know what I mean, or maybe it's just the way he is. We went to bed soon after, without him havin broke any hearts—me neither, but I'd of liked to try and give it a shot, anyway.

It was a couple days after the barbecue dance Mrs. Quantrill come down to the barns where I was bottle-feedin lambs while the Meskin went around a couple of cow ponies, resettin shoes. She took off her glasses to talk to me and I knew I was in trouble, then.

"John-Wayne," Mrs. Quantrill began, "when does the new school semester begin for you in Tuba City?"

I said I thought it started around the beginnin of the month, but I didn't know for sure.

"Well," she says, " *My* school commences the week before Labor Day. That's next week. I think you need to be sure about something as important as school. Don't you agree?"

I didn't, but it wasn't what she was wantin to hear, I knew. So I didn't say nothin.

"Well? Don't you?"

"Yes, ma'am," I says.

"What class will you be in this year?"

"I don't know. Whatever class they put me in, I guess."

"Where did you finish last spring?"

"I didn't finish. We had to feed the sheep on account of there's a drought, and Shorty—he's my cousin—and me got into the horse business to make money to help pay for it. Then my grandfather got drunk and drove his truck over his foot and—"

"He drove his truck over his *own* foot?"

"Well, he was drunk, and he got out to open a gate when the gear popped and—"

"So you lost a whole semester? How many points do you need to certify?"

I didn't know what she was talkin about when she said points and it wasn't none of her bidniss anyway. There was this old white teacher in our school when I was fourteen reminded me of her—wouldn't let us wear no cowboy boots or hats, give us black marks for talkin Navajo in class. She was at least ninety-nine or a hunnerd years old when she died of a heart attack shapernin the junior prom. Mrs. Quantrill wasn't that old though, yet.

"I don't know," I said.

"Give me that bottle," she says, "and I'll finish feeding. I have a few questions to ask you, young man."

I set on a milkin stool while she ast me about math and algebra and history and English and science—most of my answers was wrong, accordin to her—until finally she says, "Tell me, now, John-Wayne; how many years, exactly, have you been going to school?"

I thought quick and says, "Since I was about two."

"How old are you now?"

"Sixteen and a half, ma'am."

"I place you in about the fifth week of the second semester of the fourth grade—at best. How did that happen, then?"

"I don't know, ma'am."

"What's your favorite subject in school, John-Wayne?"

I thought how white people are hung up on love and stayin healthy, and that, and says, "Sex ed, ma'am."

"Don't get smart with me, young man. What do you want to be when you grow up?"

The answer come to me right off then.

"Want to be a teacher, in high school."

"And what subject would you like to teach?"

When you can't please white folks one way, you turn it around and give them the other end and they're happy, then.

"Sex ed—ma'am."

We was gettin ready for bed that night when the Dude, he says to me, "You're goin back to Tuba City on the bus tomorrow."

"How come, man?" I ast him.

"School starts the week before Labor Day. That's how come."

"Please, Dude!" I cried.

"Don't try and argue it with me. You're going, and that's that."

"What about my horse?"

"I'll get up with the horse, sooner or later."

"How about my honor?"

"What?"

He'd been jawin at me for weeks and weeks about honor and promises and stuff, and now he didn't remember hisself.

"My promise, my honor—to, you know, a lady."

"Education for boys is as important as honor is to grown men."

"You mean it's okay for me break my promise to Bette?"

"You're not breaking your promise, you're entrusting it to me. That's all."

"But Bette ain't your woman."

"That's all right. She doesn't have to be."

I had to try hard to keep from cryin then.

"I don't *want* to go to school!"

"Of course you don't. I never did, either."

"They don't teach us nothin but AIDS and puttin condoms on squashes."

"They must teach you *something* more than that."

"Not that I remember, except you ought to wear real shoes, not cowboy boots. Last year the English teacher decorrected my homework."

"How do you mean, she decorrected it?"

"Changed all the right answers to wrong ones—that's how. Bette's mom looked at my paper and showed me where."

"How long does tribal law say you have to stay in school?"

"Til I'm sixteen. I'm sixteen and a half right now."

"Don't you want to go to college and get a good job?"

"My grandfather says college is for the white man. Says all it does for *him* is make him worse than what he was already."

I got my handkerchief out of my back pocket and blew my nose in it. The Dude was thinkin—I seen it in his eyes. "You can't get that horse back without me along to hep you, anyways."

"You think not, do you?"

"You're eyes ain't good enough, for one. Who'd find firewood while you cook supper? Who'd tie you in the stirrups and keep you from fightin TV saucers when you get sick? Without me to talk to, you'd be twice as crazy as you are already."

The Dude turned away and put his hand up to his face. Then he looked around again and I seen everthin was goin to be OK.

"So you think I'm crazy. Is that so, John-Wayne?"

"All the white men are crazy—that's what my grandfather says."

"Well, we certainly don't want to make him eat crow, do we? I guess you're as civilized already as you need to be. I'll tell Quantrill to tell Mrs. Quantrill to mind her own schoolyard, and we'll get started after that horse again. I'm getting tired of hot water and sleeping between sheets, anyway."

For a while we was five red lights makin a circle in the darkness. Then the moon rose all of a sudden out of the mountains and you could see faces, sort of, behind the cigars, settin out by the horse paddocks in them log chairs the white man keeps on his lawn to scare company away. Around, the fence posts and rails crossed shadows on the grass and the valley was silver as far as the foothills, like the river had rose up and flooded it. (It's awesome what-all you notice when you have to tell about it afterward.) It was after supper and we was talkin politics—Mr. Quantrill and the Dude, was, anyway; the twins and me just drawed on our cigars while Jack Jr. passed a bottle of his own between the three of us. The trouble with politics is you have to be arguin it all the time, while my idea is like: Don't argue with the enemy unless you need to argue with him. Then, you just kill him. "When General Lee handed his sword to Grant at Appomattox," Mr. Quantrill was sayin, "he surrendered the old American Republic along with it. But the Civil War never ended. It's lasted already for one hundred and thirty-eight years, and we're still fighting today, right here this very minute. The Confederacy had the Constitution on its side, and it ought to have had time, but they were defending their rights on the field of battle. We're using the *law* to prevail, and this time, we're going to *win*—without force, or violence, or civil disobedience—in a court of *law.*"

The radio phone rang and he reached down and felt around for it in the grass underneath his chair.

"Jack Quantrill here," he said into the phone. "...Yes, sir....What?... Well, I'm sitting here in my back yard, frying up a mess of Mexican spotted owls and overseeing my indentured environmentalists hoe beans....No, I don't advocate lynch law, I'm an attorney and an officer of the court, sworn to uphold the Constitution of the United States...."

The twins caught my eye and we stood up together and walked back to the house where I seen Mrs. Quantrill through the kitchen window, readin her schoolteacher magazines.

"I ain't goin in the kitchen," I said.

"Why not?" Jesse asked.

"My boots are dirty."

"We weren't intending going in the house at all," Jack Jr. said. "You're welcome to come along to town with us if you like, John-Wayne."

The headlights showed the white trunks of the pine trees risin up into the night and the straight black shadows layin acrosst the silver grass. Jack Jr. let the truck out on the straightaways and hugged the yellow line in the curves. She was a 1988 Ford 250 with a four-sixty engine and the muffler cut out, which was why she didn't sound like no Stealth bomber.

"If you rather have stayed to hear about R. E. Lee, you should have said so," Jack Jr. says to me.

"Who's Harry Lee?" I ast him.

"*General* Lee was the greatest American there ever was. It's just we hear about him all the time, when we're at home."

"If the U.S. military hadn't licked our ancestors," Jesse explained, "Jack Jr. and me would be officers in the Marine Corps now, instead of at the university."

I was goin to ask what made General Lee so great before I thought how it was the probly the same thing made General Custer and Kit Carson great, so I didn't need to ast them anythin then. The white man's history ain't all that hard to understand, once you understand what it's about which is killin people, mainly, like the Paiutes.' The cell phone rang on top of the dashboard and Jesse lifted it out of its cradle and answered it.

"Yeah Dad," he said. "We're going in for a few beers....I don't know, we're not to town yet, just coming up on the new bridge....Sure thing, we'll let you know if we hear anything.... 'Bye, Dad."

"Something going on in town tonight," Jesse said, puttin up the phone. "Dad got a tip as we were leaving."

"What about?" Jack Jr. ast him.

"The guy didn't say. Just ast if he believed in lynch law like all the other vigilantes, and hung up."

We cruised on into town and stopped at a place had a beer sign in the window and music comin out the open door.

"Lot of people around, anyway," Jack Jr. said. "Could be there really *is* something up."

Inside the bar was crowded. We went on in and set down at a table in back where the people was just leavin. The twins jammed their hats over their ears and spread their knees wide under the table.

"How old are you, John-Wayne?" Jack Jr. ast.

"Sixteen and a half."

"Tammy won't serve him," Jesse said, lookin over at the waitress standin with her tray at the service bar. "They suspended her back in June for not checking IDs."

"Alls I wants a Coke anyways," I told him.

The girl come over with the tray and served the people at the table next to us. Jack Jr. turned around in his chair and pulled at her sleeve.

"Can we get some service here?" he ast her, grinnin to show he didn't mean it.

"Hi there!" the girl told him. She was short and kind of wax colored with a pushed-in face like she slept on it, not too bright-lookin. "Hello Jack—hello Jesse! How you-guys doin tonight?"

"We're good. 'S'up in the 'hood?"

"I heard a demonstration like or somethin, I don't know for sure. What you-guys havin this evenin?"

"Pitcher of beer and three glasses," Jack Jr. said.

"How old is *he*?" the girl ast, pointin her pencil at me.

"Old enough," Jack Jr. told her. "He's French."

"I need to see some ID," the girl said.

"I told you," Jack Jr. said: "He's French. He doesn't need to show any ID."

"He looks Indian to me. What does bein French have to do with it, anyways?"

"In France they drink beer or wine with every meal, every day from the time they're six months old, maybe a year. It's their custom and culture over there, like guns are here. They don't have to carry ID and it's against the law to ask for it while they're in the U.S., a violation of their civil rights. All John-Wayne has to do is drop thirty-five cents into that phone there and you're in trouble with the EPA, Tammy—big time."

The girl looked scared, and then she looked confused.

"He's awful young lookin," she said.

Then she smiled at me.

"I didn't know French guys was cute like that," she said, and went back to the service bar with her tray under her arm.

"I bet John-Wayne could score if Mr. Ryder was to stay around for just a couple more days," Jesse said to Jack Jr.

Jack Jr. shook his head. "Mr. Ryder's in a big hurry to find that horse and take it back to his lady friend."

"It ain't *his* girlfriend's," I explained. "It's mine that *really* owns him."

The twins looked puzzled.

Jesse ast, "You have a girlfriend owns a ranch up in Utah?"

"She don't live in Utah, she lives in Arizona. Bette Atcitty, Tuba City, Navajo Nation, Turtle Clan. I'm Coyote Clan, so we can get married soon's I bring her horse back and the Paiute that's in love with her has to bend over and kiss his ass goodbye. You ought to see her, man: She's a fox, a real cool chick."

"Who's this Jody James person up in Utah then?" Jesse wanted to know.

"That's the Dude's woman, man."

They looked puzzled all over again, and then Jack Jr. shrugged.

"So long as you guys have it figured out between you," he said.

The girl come with the pitcher, finally, and set it down along with three frosty mugs.

"Can he *speak* French?" she ast Jack Jr., and I was thinkin what I was goin to do then when he says right off to her, like maybe she's the dumbest thing he ever seen, "Sure, he speaks French—*when he's had enough to drink!*"

The beer went down easy and it tasted wonderful while it was cold. After that it wasn't so good no more, flat with kind of a disappointin taste like a good dream is after you wake up from it, and all the time I was thinkin what was that business they were talkin about the Dude's woman before I realized it must have been when he was sick and didn't know what he was sayin hisself. We finished the pitcher and Jack Jr. had already ast the girl for another one when suddenly the people around us began gettin up and leavin all together. Jesse put a couple quarters down on the table and looked at Jack Jr.

"Ready?" he ast.

"Let's go," Jack Jr. said, pushin back in his chair.

Outside it felt fresh and cool after the bar but still there was people everwhere and traffic, all movin down the main street to the center of town and pushin in from the side ones. Pretty soon we heard shoutin ahead and seen the people in the street lit up by the lights overhead between the rows of buildins and the orange flames of a bonfire.

"Team rally," Jesse said.

"Can't be. Football squad's in Vegas on the ninety-nine dollar special."

It wasn't the happy sound of folks cheerin for the home team but a kind of roar, deep and scary to listen to, and some of the people was carryin torches. We pushed through—Jack Jr. first, Jesse next with me behind him—to the edge of the crowd and stood watchin the fire blazin up and next to it four big birdlike things feathered all over and spotted, with pointy ears like an owl's, hoppin and staggerin, tryin to stand while two men worked at pushin a pole between their legs.

"Tie em by the feet!" somebody shouted. "Tie em and hang em upside down underneath!"

A breeze comin down from the mountains brought the smoke around in our direction, smellin of hot tar and burned feathers.

"Tar and feathers is too good for greenies!" somebody else shouted. "Go ahead and hang em—hang em by the *neck*!"

"Hang em!" several people yelled together.

"Hoo! Hoooooo! To-wit to-woo!" everone hooted.

The pole rammed between the legs of the first bird and the mob roared again, louder this time and mean-sounding.

"You guys wait here," Jesse told Jack Jr. "I'll call dad on the cell phone." He turned and started pushing his way back through the crowd.

"Hang em!"

"Burn em at the stake!"

"Draw em and quarter em!"

"Remember Brave Heart!"

"Hoooo! Hoooooooo!"

"Go ahead and roast the sonsabitches!"

"Look up there!" I told Jack Jr.

Mr. Quantrill was standin on one of them worker platforms against the side of the courthouse. He was holdin his hat by the brim with one hand and had a long-barrel pistol in the other, and he looked mad. As we watched he raised the pistol above his head. There was a crash and a streak of blue fire in the dark, and then the crowd was silent all at once, like when the home-room teacher walks in on a food fight.

"You fools!" Mr. Quantrill told the people, still holdin the gun above his head. "You damn fools. I taught you better than this."

He looked down and around at the crowd like it was pond scum it made him feel dirty just to think of gettin in with.

"I taught *you*"—pointin out the guy with his chin—"and *you*, and *you*, and *you,* and *you.* I taught *you,* Billy Haynesworth, and *you,* Will Catron. I educated *you* in the way of our Celtic ancestors, and the ancestors of some of us who invented democracy in longhouses before Europeans ever set foot in North America. I am learning this evening that I was wrong," Mr. Quantrill went on. "I am learning that in the seven and a half years I have worked with you and other counties of the Western United States to effect lawful constitutional change within the struggle against an oppressive, centralizing government, I have been deluding myself. You are not—as I understand it now—educable. Maybe you are not even civilizable, unlike the red man who devised the constitutional system on which the governments of the thirteen original colonies were developed. You are barbarians—throwbacks to the days before the Gauls invaded Europe from the steppes of Asia and created the Celtic civilizations of eastern and western Europe, and in Italy. I have wasted my time with you, I see, and I am embarassed—deeply embarassed. And I am ashamed. *Ashamed!*"

Mr. Quantrill lowered the revolver and held it against his leg while he stood there on the platform, starin down at the people. They had all four of them Big Birds on the pole now, and the crowd give a shout as ten or twelve men heaved it up onto their shoulders. It was a speech like George Warshinton would have made, but I could see it wasn't goin to have no more effect on the crowd than if it had been by Bob Dole that Mr. Quantrill hates so much. Now and then one of the Birds would moan or cry out, and I could tell one of them was women, at least.

"You can't understand—*can* you?" Mr. Quantrill went on in that voice sounded like he drunk a barrel of vinegar and had the taste of it still in his mouth. "You can't comprehend that this isn't how you win—it's how you *lose.* It's how *they* make *you* wrong, and put themselves in the right: how *they* take *your* legitimacy in exchange for *their* illegitimacy. It's how *they* steal *your* birthright, and claim it for themselves. Our enemies know they don't need to defeat you, when you've gone ahead and defeated yourselves, first!"

"To-wit, to-woo!" a voice hooted. "Death to the tree-huggers!"

A dude with a mutton gut and a black hat on, standin on the sidewalk beside the platform, hooked his thumbs into his suspenders and faced around to the people.

"Don't listen to Quantrill," the fat man said in a high, sharp voice like a back-up horn. "Quantrill's gone over to the other side—could be he's been with em all along. Whichever, it don't matter now. Go ahead and ride em out on a rail, boys, ride em all the way to Mexico—anywheres they won't want to come back here from anytime soon!"

That touched them off, then. The mob give a snarl like an animal and moved in on the bonfire and the Big Birds above it on the shoulders of the men. There was some sheriffs deputies around but they didn't do a thing to stop it—not that I could see, anyways. Men, and women too, was snatchin sticks out of the fire as they ran past it until the fire caved in, rainin down sparks out of the night sky onto the people. I heard Mr. Quantrill's pistol fire once more—I guessed it was his, but there was plenty other men had guns along with them, too—and then a woman screamed for hep. It was the female bird had got free of whatever they had put in her mouth to keep her from yellin, and the next thing I knowed the Dude was there alongside her, takin her from the pole onto his shoulders like he was liftin her down off a runaway horse. Him and Mr. Quantrill must of rode into town from the ranch together, though it was none of his business that I could see—cept for anytime a woman drops a handkerchief, the Dude, he's there to pick it up and give it back to her. He disappeared in the crowd suddenly as the snarl turned to shoutin again, and I figured he was a dead man then. They started off like a mixed-up army, confused but movin all in the same direction down the main street with the three big owls and the smokin torches at the head of it. I looked around for Jack Jr., and didn't see him nowheres. People in front of me kept stoppin while the ones in back was runnin in behind until I thought I was goin to get trompled to death. The night air when I could get any of it tasted cool and lovely but the hot breath of the mob was all around, mixed with the pine smoke and the tar.

We was almost out of town when there was the sound of sirens and I saw lights flashin ahead. Everbody stopped, and then the people in front started tryin to push back. The lights spoked around and around and more shoutin come from up front in addition to the noise the sirens made, and all at once the crowd—thousands and thousand of people—was goin backward, pushed by the ones ahead. It broke suddenly and started to come apart in all directions like a band of scared sheep, down the main street and up the side ones, people throwin down their torches and runnin away into the night, chased by state troopers in helmets hittin at em with clubs. I took one look at them cops dressed like space men, and then I turned around and run myself. It just seemed like there was no point in John-Wayne Bilagody gettin mixed up in the white man's bidniss tonight—not even if I happened to be really French.

I felt bad about how if it had been the Dude in my place *he* wouldn't of run away and left *me*; later I decided it was the right thing to do after all, because it wouldn't of done neither one of us no good for me to get arrested and have to go to jail along with him. Mr. Quantrill did everthin he could to hep except be our lawyer, on account of he was politically compermised, he said. So instead of him we had Mr. Castellanos from Silver City, where they took the Dude along with all them other folks they arrested that night that wouldn't go into the jail at Reserve after it was fulled up, to repersent us.

Mr. Castellanos was thin and stoop shouldered, about thirty-five years old. He had blue eyes, kind of a yellowish face, and kinky brown hair, and wore a big metal button on his coat said CESAR 'EDDIE' CASTELLANOS FOR SCHOOLBOARD DISTRICT # 5. Me and Mr. Quantrill lived with him for two days in his house off in the sandhills south of Silver City while we waited for the Dude to be arranged. The house had a beautiful view of the big copper mine at Tyrone and you could hear the big trucks runnin all day and all night and hear the blastin, which was awesome. Mr. Castellanos said he designed and built that house, all by himself. It was in two parts that wasn't even connected to each other, one single-level like a shoe box, the other like a shoe box standin on end that he called the Tower, with two floors. Both parts was made of cinderblock covered over with chickenwire and plaster painted like adobe. The floors of the house didn't come together with the walls too good, and the kitchen wall pushed out a ways to make room for the tub that was too big for the bathroom on the other side. There wasn't no room in the kitchen for a stove, so Mr. Castellanos cooked all his meals on a hot-plate, or an electric spider. The lower floor of the Tower was a music room, he called it, fulled with woofers and recordin stuff that was what was left of the rock band Mr. Castellanos had when he was young, and it had a ladder bolted to the wall goin straight up through a trap door to his office. There was windows at both ends of the office but no cover for the trap door, so you had to be careful walking around in it among the law books and papers and stuff to keep from fallin through into the music room below.

Mr. Castellanos was one of them politicians like Mr. Quantrill, always talkin and arguin about the govermint the way the white man does, like it's what makes him happy or sad—the govermint is, I mean. After gettin himself elected to school board member, Mr. Castellanos said he was goin to be governor of the state of New Mexico and, after that, president of the Hispanic Republic of New Mexico, all before he was sixty years old. The Hispanic Republic of New Mexico wasn't a real thing yet, but someone named Mr. Valdez was goin to begin by startin what he called cads in the local govermint, beginnin with the school board distrits, and after that the cads was goin to infillate the county govermints. Then the rayon-keeskas would call in the gorilla bands they had been trainin in Mexico, march on the Round House in Santa Fe, declare the Hispanic People's Republic of New Mexico, and chase out all the gringos, startin with the rich movie stars and Oprah Singers in Santa Fe. When Mr. Castellanos wasn't workin at politics he was writin a novel about his family in Old Spain and New Mexico that he showed me. The novel was written in diffrint color ink dependin on who in the book was talkin just then, and Mr. Castellanos said it was all about murder and love and incest and theft and empire and disposition, with scenes from the Eskorail in Spain to the Val Verde Hotel in Socorro. The book was already a couple thousand pages long but Mr. Castellanos said he had a lot to put into it, still.

Mr. Castellanos talked about his book and the Hispanic Republic of New Mexico while the three of us set out in foldin chairs in the sand in front of the house, drinkin beer and waitin for the dynamitin to start again. Mr. Quantrill kept interruptin him to tell him what it was he wanted him to say to the judge, and the next day we had to go up to Silver City to the courthouse where the Dude was goin to be arranged. Mr. Castellanos drove. At the courthouse Mr. Quantrill said to let him off at the steps in front before he went lookin for a place to park the truck at.

We had went around the block three times already when Mr. Castellanos said, "Those bastards." He said it in a quiet voice—you know, like he really meant it.

"Who?"

"The state cops."

"What did they do?"

"What did they *do*? They brought those people down here from Reserve in stock trailers—*stock trailers!*—after they were arrested. Full of flies and bull shit."

"Probly that was all they could find to bring em with—in the middle of the night, and everthin."

Mr. Castellanos flicked the ash at the end of his cigarette onto his lap.

"It's because to the U.S. government Hispanic people are only spics."

"Most of them they arrested was the white man."

Mr. Castellanos made a noise like he swallowed the cigarette.

"They never knew it until they had all of em sorted out down here," he said. "It's inhumane, and probably illegal as well."

Mr. Castellanos slapped the top of the steerin wheel suddenly with his hand.

"You know, that gives me an idea," he said. "That was a parking space back there, wasn't it?"

Mr. Quantrill was waitin for us inside the courthouse and the three of us went on into the big room where the TV people get to video the judge and all the lawyers fightin together, and set up front in the best seats where we could see everthin that was goin on. More people kept comin into the room and settin down behind us and pretty soon the judge—Justice of the Peace, he was called—come in through a little door up front and everbody stood up. Then he set down and everone did the same, like they been practicin to do it.

The judge was this little old skinny dude with slicked-back hair and a purple mole looked like a worm comin out of his face, and he had on red suspenders and a belt holdin his pants up. His voice was raspy and weak soundin and behind it you could hear him breathin, like my Uncle Gus that's dyin of emfesteema over at Coyote Canyon. The cops brought the prisoners in one by one through the side door opposite the one the judge come through. They was men mostly but some women too, and almost all of them had been arrested in what the judge called the riot. Some had their lawyers with them and others was alone. The judge called most of the people by their first names like he knowed them, even if they was criminals and had handcuffs on. One after the other they told the judge, "Not guilty, Your Honor," and stood while he mumbled over them like it was a purification ceremony, or somethin. Then he made them sign a bunch of papers and when they was through doin it they could leave, after the cop took the handcuffs off. There was eleven or twelve of them arranged before it was the Dude's turn. He come in through the little door with the cop who was yawnin, like he did this ever day, and stood very straight in front of the judge with his hands in front of him. Maybe it was just them cuffs, but the way he looked—rough, with his clothes tore and bloody, face dirty, hair and beard all messed up and his eyes red—I was ashamed for him. If it was me that was the judge I'd of stuck him back in jail and throwed away the key. Of course *I* knowed he was a good person really, but the judge, *he* didn't. Mr. Quantrill was settin very straight too, with his arms folded acrosst his chest. He looked hard at Mr. Castellanos and Mr. Castellanos stood up then and went on to the front to where the judge and them was waitin.

The judge says, "Mr. Jeb Stuart Ryder, you are charged with one count each of disturbin the peace, incitement to riot, sexual harrassment, and resistin arrest. How do you plead?"

"He pleads innocent on all counts, Your Honor," Mr. Castellanos told him.

The judge hooked his thumbs into his suspenders and leaned forward across the table.

"Stranger in town, are you?" he ast.

"Not exactly, Your Honor," the Dude says.

The judge read from a piece of paper in front of him.

"Complaint has a Monticello, Utah address. You from Utah, Mr. Ryder?"

"It's where I'm living now. I grew up on a ranch near Lordsburg."

"How come you left there?"

"I didn't leave. The ranch picked up and left me."

"That must have been some dust storm. So you come all the way down here on vacation to get drunk, grab onto women—make whoopee?"

"No, your Honor. And I'm not on vacation. I'm a range detective, looking for a stolen horse."

"Because we got enough trouble right here in Grant and Reserve Counties as it is."

"I can see that, Your Honor."

"Without no agent provokers comin in and stirrin up more."

"Your honor, I didn't mean to provoke anyone. All I intended was helping a lady in distress."

"They wasn't no ladies, them gals. You think someone here in Reserve stoled your horse?"

"Not an Elk or a Rotarian—somebody *from* here. Just another Mexican illegal on his way home."

Mr. Castellanos says, real polite, "Your Honor, may I have a word in private with my client, please?"

The judge said it was okay with him and Mr. Castellanos led the Dude aside a ways and they whispered together for almost a minute. Then the Dude nodded and Mr. Castellanos faced around to the judge again.

"Your Honor," he says, sharp and impatient-like this time, "the Court can dismiss all charges against Mr. Ryder—right here this afternoon—or it can invite a lawsuit against the state of New Mexico, charging criminal violation of my client's civil rights."

"So he *is* one of them environmentalist activists, after all?"

"Of course, he isn't an environmentalist—or an activist."

The judged look puzzled.

"Just what is it you think you're aimin at, Eddie?"

Mr. Castellanos went around behind the table, bent over, and put his face down beside the judge's. The judge cupped his hand around his ear and closed his eyes while Mr. Castellanos talked into it. He talked for about a minute before the judge took his hand away, and then Mr. Castellanos come back around the table and stood with the Dude and the sleepy cop, watchin him.

"Case dismissed," the judge said finally. "Next case," he told the cop.

We left the courthouse together and all four of us—me, the Dude, Mr. Quantrill, and Mr. Castellanos—went to dinner at the Spanish Kitchen where Mr. Castellanos said they had the best menudo in the world. Menudo is, like, soup the Hispanic people make from the linin of a sheep's stomach. You can't eat better than sheep, but the stomach ain't the best part. We set down at a table up front by the window and Mr. Castellanos lit a cigarette, pushed back in his chair to cross his legs, and swallowed the smoke down deep in his lungs. He looked proud of himself, like the People's Republic of New Mexico had begun and he had just been elected president of it.

"I don't want to know what you said to the old fart," Mr. Quantrill told him. "Whatever it was, it must have been a good idea. But what was that civil rights bullshit about?"

Mr. Castellanos smiled.

"You can still treat a man like a horse or a mule in this country," he said, "but it can be expensive if they catch you doing it. Especially if it's a black, or an Indian, or a Hispanic man—or an Anglo willing to make a test case of it, like Mr. Ryder was. Clyde Adams would just as soon load a few stock trailers full of white environmentalists as he would spics, anyway."

When dinner was over we went in the bar and set up on these saddles they have for bar stools there. The Dude bought drinks for everone, and pretty soon Mr. Castellanos had to go run for schoolboard member somewhere. When he was gone the Dude ordered another round. He waited until the girl had brought the drinks and gone away again before he says, straight-faced and casual like, lookin at me over the whiskey glass, "Well, J-W, I found the man that stole our horse."

He never called me J-W before.

"Which one?" I ast him, after I saw it was me he was talkin to.

"The Mexican."

"You spent the last forty-eight hours in the Grant County Jail," Mr. Quantrill reminded him. "Does time fly so fast in there you've forgotten already?"

"That's how I found him. We were cell mates—Sr. Gutiérrez—and I. The state cops arrested him in the same sweep they picked me up in."

The Dude was grinnin now to split his face, but he still looked terrible—especially the chin beard, like an old billy goat's.

"You're certain it's the same fellow?" Mr.Quantrill ast him.

"I'm certain, all right. He is, too. Jaime Gutiérrez, Casas Grandes, Mexico."

"You mean, he admitted it?"

The Dude just pulled at his beard and kept on grinning.' He winked at me.

"Gutiérrez is still in jail?"

"And enjoying a private room with a view, since everyone else got sprung. He's a common criminal after all—not one of us politicals."

Mr. Quantrill smiled.

"In that case, I'm no longer compromised," he said.

So that's how we got back on tract finally after the hamster virus and the saucers and Mrs. Quantrill and the riot and all, and with the Dude out of jail I don't have to work at keepin the story goin no more. We're comin to the best part now, and I ain't up to it. They never taught us in school and it's hard enough anyway just livin your life without tryin to tell about it, too.

# BOOK V
# REVOLUCIÓN

There is enough betrayal in the world without wanting to pass some of it along even to a Mexican horse thief and scofflaw. So I felt bad about Gutiérrez. I paid Quantrill's fee for handling the DWI defense—no bail—and left money earmarked for the unpaid speeding tickets going back a couple of years to when Gutiérrez was still able to afford a car, since his former boss over in Arizona wasn't going to fix the horse part—as promised by Quantrill, not quite pretending to be the rancher's agent. On the other hand there wasn't really going to be anything to fix, contrary to Quantrill's assertion that the penalty for horse theft in the American West is still hanging. It scared Gutiérrez plenty, though—enough to persuade him to give us the name we wanted, and along with the name a note addressed to its owner. He was mestizo, about twenty-five years old with raggy hair that hadn't shown under his straw hat pointing fiercely from his head, gorgon-like (they'd taken his big-handled pocket comb away from him in prison), but his brown eyes had been gentle-looking, and soft with fright. I was sorry for him, but it's the price they pay for coming over into a foreign country without learning something—not even a little—about its culture and customs beforehand.

The name was Orsino, Albert Orsino. Gutiérrez had talked to him in a bar in Reserve and sold him the horse for three hundred dollars the same evening. He thought Orsino lived on a secluded ranch in the foothills of the mountains west of town and that was all he thought, though he said he'd sold him horses on several earlier occasions. I didn't ask if they were stolen or not, mainly because I didn't care. The three hundred dollars, in addition to what he'd had in his pocket when they booked him, had paid his bar tab the week before the lynching (Judge Adams and the local police were calling it a riot, of course), and during that time he never laid eyes on

Albert Orsino again. The mountains of the Gila wilderness take in a lot of territory but they aren't the Front Range, either; no development to speak of along the edges and not a whole lot of earth muffins running around in them. Anyone living in the vicinity would certainly be familiar with a hare-lipped boy with a speech impediment living off on his own and trading horses—if that was what he did—for a living. Militia types like to think that, way out here out in the Wild West, they're living where nobody—the government boys included—can find them. In fact, they'd probably be a lot less findable in Simi Valley or Denver, where your neighbor is just the faceless guy whose paper you pinch from in front of his door while he's sleeping in with his girlfriend on Sunday morning.

John-Wayne and I rode back to Reserve with Quantrill for the horses. At the ranch, we spent a day and a half lining out gear while I put off calling Jody James for almost twenty-four hours before I finally went ahead and did it. It was one-thirty in the afternoon and she was just taking a roast from the oven for dinner, she said.

"Hello."

"Hello. Who is this?"

"You know damn well who."

"The voice is familiar, but I can't remember the name."

"What's eating you this afternoon?"

"I don't know."

"You don't know much, do you?"

"Maybe I don't. But I'm not lost, as the farmer said to the city tourist."

"I was lost, once. But now I'm found."

"Where *are* you, Jeb? You sound like you're calling from the moon."

"We're still in Reserve, actually. I just got out of jail."

"What did they have you in for? Horse theft?"

"Sexual harrassment. Among other things."

"How lovely. You were enjoying yourself at the time, I imagine."

"Not especially. The lady had been rolled in tar first, then covered all over with chicken feathers. Kind of a sticky proposition, believe me."

"What time is it in Reserve?"

"One thirty-five in the p.m.—same as Monticello. Why?"

"You and your friend Quantrill ought to be ashamed of yourselves, drinking before dinner time."

"I'm sober as a judge. So is he."

"The J.P. here in Monticello was arrested for DWI the other night. He's LDS, naturally, so it's a scandal. A silent one, of course."

"What else is going on at home?"

"Mrs. Twitchell who manages the grocery store in Moab is preggers. She went before the judge last week asking him to order a DNA test to identify the father. The judge thought that was fair and asked for the name of the romantic party. The list she gave him had sixty-five names on it."

"Don't tell me. Dago O'Grady was one of them."

"Of course he wasn't."

"I've got a lead on Tortuga," I told her.

"His name is Cortez," Jody reminded me. "A lead *rope*, I assume you mean?"

"I wish."

"That's all right," she consoled me. "I'd probably have heart stoppage if you did."

"The Mexican sold him to a harelip for three hundred dollars. The harelip lives somewhere down around Glenwood. We're on our way there this afternoon."

"I'm glad to hear it," she said ironically. "Should I go ahead and enter him in the Labor Day show?"

"I'd hold off showing for a while if I were you. He's going to take a little grooming, first."

"Maybe what I need to do is just go out and buy another horse."

"Don't give up on us just yet. We've only been at this six weeks."

"I'm not giving up on anything—yet. I want a lover, Jeb."

"You have a lover, my darling."

"I want a lover *with me*."

"I'll be with you again in just a little while. I promise."

"When have I heard *that* before?" she asked, and hung up the phone.

The café outside Glenwood had a view of the bridge across the San Francisco River and massive cottonwoods shadowing the slow-moving water. The trees were white with dust from the road except where the yellow was coming in the foliage. I left Quantrill's old ranch truck and trailer shaded up so Baca's horses would stay cool while we ate. In the restaurant two men faced each other across a table with the toes of their boots drawn under the chairs, drinking coffee. Otherwise the place was empty. John-Wayne and I ordered hamburgers with green chili and sat listening to the men having a conversation while we waited for the food to come up. They were elderly types with grey sideburns streaking down from under their hats, discussing the problem one of them had with a pod of javelina rooting up his vegetable garden. The guy offering advice was in favor of shooting the pigs. The one asking for it was not so sure. His neighbors, who'd moved recently from New Jersey, were environmentalists who he was afraid would call the game warden if they heard shooting in the middle of the night. I interrupted them finally to ask if they knew someone named Albert Orsino. The gardener shook his head morosely, and was corrected by the pig shooter.

"Yeah, you know him," the shooter said.

"Who is he?"

"He's the guy been hangin out at Geiger's place this summer."

"Him, you mean? He's crazy in the head."

"No he ain't. He's slow, that's all what's wrong with him. Just a little bit slow."

"Slow my ass. He was any slower, he'd lay down on hisself at night gettin up in the mornin.'"

"The trouble with you is you're prejudiced against crazy people."

"The hell I'm prejudiced. I ain't got nothin against crazy people. They just don't make good sense is all."

When I interrupted again to ask where Geiger's place was the shooter directed me across the bridge, five miles back in the foothills against the national forest boundary. The ranch, he said, had not been worked in twenty years; previous to Orsino moving in, a hippie environmentalist cult had camped out in the abandoned house. I thanked him for his time, and then the waitress came with the food. We ate fast, paid up, and left while they were debating whether Albert Orsino took drugs or was born that way. I waved at them as I went through the door, but they never saw me.

The creosote planking thumped under the tires as we drove across the bridge over the river. A hundred yards beyond the blacktop ended and the washboard dirt began, climbing up from the river bottom through the thinned grass around the yucca and alligator juniper into the hills covered by dark juniper forest. A fence made of crooked juniper posts supported by three strands of rusted barb wire ran on one side of the road, and on that side the range was badly bitten down and eroded. Nearly four miles on, the hills were steeper and more thickly wooded, and then we came to a hollow between two ridges and a windmill standing above a water tank at the bottom of it. From farther back in the hills and higher up a single-storey adobe ranch house with one end fallen in and the wooden porch sagging, partly screened by the advancing forest, overlooked the well through glassless windows.

"It looks like a house a crazy guy would live in," John-Wayne said. "He's probly got a ski mask on and a knife in his hand, watchin us from the window."

"You've been watching too many video movies at Quantrills.'"

"Except for videos I wouldn't never of met you, man."

Across the hollow a chained gate with no padlock closed off the road beside a hand lettered wooden sign nailed to a post. EARTH SANCTUARY the sign read. SACRED GROUND. KEEP OUT. BEWARE OF CATS. John-Wayne got out, unwrapped the chain, and swung the gate open. He swung it shut again behind the truck and trailer and climbed back in the cab after rewrapping the chain carefully and fitting a link sideways into the metal slot to hold it. The road curved uphill between boulders to the bench where the house stood on worn bare ground, with off to the side some barns and a corral enclosing a wooden lean-to where four horses stood dozing in the shade. One of the horses was a flea-bitten white, another a light roan color. The last two were more or less nondescript bays with black points, looking as if they'd come out of the same sire. As we drove into the yard a couple of blue ticks stood up on the porch where they'd been napping and pointed toward us ahead of their cold blue eyes. Down in the bottom the windmill and tank looked far away and very small. When we were still a hundred feet from the house I stopped the truck and switched off the engine. In the stillness of late afternoon the only sound was the buzz of flies and the occasional demented cackle of half a dozen half-wild guinea hens, the descendants probably of old man Geiger's domestic flock. The house was built of old adobe bricks handmade from clay reinforced with straw. We sat on in the truck, watching the house, and after a while someone pushed out through the torn screen door at the good end of the building, stepped over the dogs, and came walking toward us across the dirt yard carrying his head down and his hands in the front pockets of his denim pants. He was halfway to the truck already when the dogs caught up and ranged beside him with their tails in the air.

Albert Orsino was a very young man, sallow and delicate looking, his figure boyish and undeveloped. His black hair falling straight behind him was fastened with a rubber band between the shoulder blades. His chest was thin, and when he raised his face I was aware of the eyes even before I saw the hare lip exposing a quarter-inch of red gum above the long brown teeth. Orsino's eyes were bright as an animal's, full of a soft animal sadness but also the cheerfulness that human beings, alone among the animals, possess. The lack of facial hair showed a bad complexion, and the loose underlip bared more gum and the few teeth remaining in it. Besides the jeans, Orsino had on a faded U.S. Army camouflage shirt with the sleeves cut out of it at the shoulder holes. He wore farmer's boots, plain-toed, and a string of turquoise beads around his neck.

"Hi!" Albert Orsino said, smiling widely, in a high voice that whistled a little through the hair lip.

"Are you Albert Orsino?" I asked him.

"Do I look like someone by the name of Albert Orsino?"

"I don't know. I never met anyone named Albert Orsino before."

"There's only one Albert Orsino I know of."

"Are you him?"

"Look around you and tell me if you see another one."

"So you *are* Albert Orsino?"

"I don't know. Albert Orsino ain't nothin but a name, anyways."

"He's crazy, man," John-Wayne said. "You're nuts," he told Albert Orsino.

"No," I corrected him, "he's only a philosopher. This *is* his place, isn't it?" I asked the hare-lip.

"I guess so. It ain't much of a one, is it?" Albert Orsino laughed.

"He's got a nice view anyway," I suggested.

"Yes. A view of the mountains. Where the men are."

"What men?"

"Albert Orsino's."

"Is that where Albert Orsino is?"

"Who wants to know?"

"A friend of Jaime Gutiérrez."

Albert Orsino, who'd been grinning broadly during our exchange, now assumed a mysterious look.

"Come with me," he said at last, "and I'll show you where Albert Orsino lives."

We followed him into the house, accompanied by the dogs who came in through the screen door with us. It had been two rooms, the kitchen where Albert Orsino lived and beyond the connecting door another, same-sized room, with the roof and end-wall fallen in on weeds growing up through the floor. A mattress covered by an Indian blanket had been pushed against the wall on one side of the kitchen, faced by a wood stove on the other, and at the center of the room there were a battered wooden table and four folding aluminum chairs. Stuff stood piled on the table and all but one of the chairs, and more stuff was packed in cardboard boxes around. Another blanket pinned over the south-facing window shaded Albert Orsino's bed where a beat-up acoustic guitar lay face down on its strings. The room was very dirty and smelled terrible. A couple of large-caliber rifles were stacked in a corner. John-Wayne looked around and made a face.

"It is very hot inside here today," Albert Orsino apologized. "Does anybody want a beer?"

"Sounds good to me," I told him. "You too, J-W?"

He took two cans of beer from a box on top of the table and handed each of us one. Then he took another for himself. The aluminum felt cool in my fingers but the contents were warm as the water from a shut-down steam boiler.

"Warm beer won't make you drunk," Albert Orsino said. "It tastes too bad," he explained.

We drank the beer in gulps and gave the empty cans back to Orsino, who threw them into another box beside the door.

"That Gutiérrez sure can drink beer," Albert Orsino remarked admiringly.

"He drank a little too much of it in Reserve the other night and got himself some unwanted attention from the local constabulary. So now he's living rent-free in a modern, air-conditioned American house in Silver City with three square meals a day, also at tax payers' expense. In the old country they'd be sticking him with the food bill. On the other hand, he could've slipped the jailer the mordida and had all the beer and tequila he wanted as well."

"Gutiérrez is in jail?"

"It happens to drunks now and then. Especially drunks who make their drinking money selling stolen horses."

Orsino smiled uneasily.

"Probably it is not Gutiérrez, after all."

"Whoever he is, he's sold you a bunch of horses recently. Including one he admits stealing from a sheep rancher over in Arizona a couple of weeks ago."

Albert Orsino raised one finger as if to scratch his upper lip, then placed the end of it squarely into the rabbitty gap.

"You're a horse trader, aren't you?"

"I don't trade stoled horses."

"Not intentionally, maybe. In this case your quality control system seems to have slipped a little."

Orsino looked nervous.

"Could be he's over there in that big corral," he offered.

"He could be, but he isn't. We're looking for a black bay stallion, Peruvian Paso breed, height fifteen hands. Worth about five thousand dollars. A real aristocrat. You're not holding anything that can hold a candle to him with those field hands outside."

"That's because I ain't got him, Mister."

"You do remember the horse?"

Orsino said nothing.

"Of course you remember him—an expensive horse like that. And you can't just throw a stallion in with the mares and geldings you're holding."

"How do I know you're a friend of Jaime Gutiérrez?" Orsino asked.

"How do I know you're really Albert Orsino?"

The kid looked at me, and grinned. "Everyone just calls me The Mouse," he said happily.

---

The note from Gutiérrez admitting the horse to be stolen property did the trick. Albert Orsino did not want any trouble with the law. His clients in the mountains were in need of horses and he had already supplied them with four good ones, Tortuga among them. It was too late in the day to leave on so long a ride, but he planned an early start in the morning. For now Orsino wished us to make ourselves comfortable and at home—Mi casa es su casa, and so forth. He showed us a separate pen to put the horses in, threw them a few flakes of hay, and added oats to the feeder, while politely refusing my offer to help with the chores. It would hurt the feelings of his animals very much, he explained, to be cared for by anyone except himself. At times as he talked he had trouble finding the right words, and when this happened he would lapse into gestures and a kind of crude sign language. Later I noticed, watching him at work around the barns, that his coordination was bad. John-Wayne and I carried two of the folding chairs onto the porch and sat outside to enjoy the freshened air. The sun was low above the western ridge, its long rays picking out the spires of the black pine trees, edging them in a fringe of golden light. From the corrals the impatient stamp of feeding horses drifted over, and the mad squawk and flap, alternating with anxious chirrups, of the guineas. A pair of crows flew overhead, circled, and settled with harsh cries in the top of the tallest tree. Round white clouds turned gold in the paling sky and the air that had held the fullness of the summer's heat all day was abruptly honed, as evening approached, to the sharp edge of fall.

"The guy is totally out of his gourd," John-Wayne remarked in an insulted voice.

"He happens to be a textbook case of fetal alcohol syndrome, for one thing. Besides that, it's how he has his fun. How sane do you think you'd be, living way off here alone all by yourself?"

"I'd be stone crazy, man."

"Actually, it isn't being out of the world that drives a man nuts. It's being in it does that."

"What about girls, Dude?"

"It's possible for a man to live without women and still maintain his sanity."

"How about hot showers?"

"That's tougher, I agree."

"The worst thing about him is the way he stinks."

"Plenty of good men, and women, have stunk. Some of the early Christian prophets lived their entire lives in the wilderness. Many of them lived to be very old men. How do you imagine they smelled when it came their time to die?"

"How come they wanted to go off like that and live in the wilderness?"

"Probably because they couldn't stand chaos anymore."

"So he ain't really crazy, then?"

"I'd say he makes pretty good sense, myself."

"A guy like him couldn't get a girl even if he wanted one," John-Wayne said contemptuously.

Orsino returned, grinning, from the corrals. His clothes were dusty from the hay, and bits of timothy grass stuck in his long hair. He went indoors and came out again after a minute carrying three cans of beer. I told John-Wayne to bring another chair from the kitchen but Orsino said he didn't need any chair. He sat cross-legged on the sun-rotted flooring as the three of us watched the tree shadows draw themselves out longer and longer on the ground and the light in the hollow below deepen into dusk, drinking warm beer.

"How far into the mountains will we be riding tomorrow?" I inquired.

"Far enough that nobody will find us. And then farther."

"They're outfitters—these clients of yours?"

"Not outfitters, no."

Albert Orsino had not quit grinning since he finished the chores. He sat with the beer between his knees, twisting his fingers together and separating them, watching with pleasure as the fingers unwound. Then he would take a drink of beer and laugh out loud to himself. He seemed to be looking forward quite a lot to something.

"Would you care to ride into town with us for a hamburger?" I offered.

"In town there are always people. I have plenty here for supper when you are hungry."

The sun lurched behind the ridge and instantly a million distinct shadows merged in a single dark expanse, solid and universal as the coming night, while at the same moment a chill wind came down from the darkening mountains. That was when I noticed Orsino studying the treeline in a way that made me nervous. Obviously, he was expecting somebody.

"It will get cold now," Orsino said. "Come inside and I will build a fire. After that, we can eat."

He lit the kerosene lantern suspended from a hook screwed into the water-stained ceiling above the table and laid a fire in the stove, taking wood from the pile of split cedar on the warped pine floor beside it. When the fire was burning well he closed the drafts at the back and sides of the stove and opened the frontal door a way. The hot yellow flames licked out, putting fresh carbon streaks on the cast iron face, and the stuffy leftover warmth of the cabin began to be replaced by a warming comfortable one. Orsino cleared the boxes from the table and invited us to take seats around it while he fixed supper. He filled the tea kettle from the water bucket and set it to boil on the stove top. From a crate against the wall he took a cracker box and two tins of deviled ham, and from the cupboard a white plastic bag. When the water boiled he pinched instant coffee into three cups and poured the water after it. Finally he placed the cups and three plates on the table and the ham spread, crackers, and the plastic bag at the center of it. We spread the paste on the crackers, passing the single knife between us, and then Orsino opened the bag.

"Eat some dessert," he offered. He was keeping an careful eye on the window beside the door while he ate.

Inside the bag were pieces of jerkied meat, blackened, gnarled, and edged with bristle.

Orsino leaned forward across the table, his mouth slightly open in anticipation as I selected the smallest piece and placed it on the end of my tongue.

"You got to really chaw down on it," he advised eagerly.

I wanted to be polite but it was like eating a fragment of asphalt with the roadkill left on it. I raised my eyebrows in an expression that was meant to be inquisitive but was probably just agonized.

"Javelina," Albert Orsino explained proudly.

We all heard the tap at the window, discreet and soft as the touch of a large moth.

Orsino stood up as I pushed back from the table and sat clear of it with my hands on my knees, wishing I'd carried the pistol in from the truck. John-Wayne's eyes were wide and his breathing appeared to have quit. I gave him a look and he started to breathe again. He did not turn about in the chair.

Albert Orsino crossed quickly to the door and opened it. He put his head through and looked to the right first, where the window was, then left. Then he stepped outside, pulling the door most of the way shut behind him. What seemed like a very long time went by before the door swung in and Orsino entered, followed by a girl. She was a very young girl, certainly not over fifteen, and she was very, very pretty, a sunbrowned will-o'-the-wisp with enormous green eyes and black hair falling below her waist. When she hesitated at the door Orsino reached behind himself to take her by the hand and draw her gently into the room.

"They only come here about a horse," he assured her. "It's all right. Don't be afraid."

John-Wayne had turned in his seat to stare at the girl as if she had stepped before him out of a fairy tale. It seemed like quite a logical conclusion to draw from the instant appearance of a lovely female child wearing a cotton shift with holes cut in it for her head and arms and absolutely nothing else, including shoes.

"This here's Doe," Albert Orsino introduced us. "She can't tell you herself what her name is on account of she can't talk. She can't hear neither, so it don't make no difference what you say about her." He added, "I talk to her like she understands me because it makes her feel good watchin my lips move."

I said, "Hello, Doe."

The girl was still staring at Albert Orsino. Very gently, he took her chin in his hand and turned her face toward mine.

"Tell her again," he said to me.

"Hello, Doe," I repeated, and gave her an encouraging smile. I felt self-conscious doing it, as if I was addressing a deer peering out from behind a fringe of forest leaves. She dropped her eyes immediately and Albert put his arm protectively about her. He squeezed her thin shoulders.

"She's shy," Albert explained. "Like me," he added, grinning.

He led the girl over to the mattress where she settled herself cross-legged and chewed on a strand of her luxuriant hair while he brought her a beer. Then he sat beside her with his legs straight out in front of him on the Indian blanket. She took his right hand in her left one and gazed at him, not removing her eyes from his face as she drank. The light from the single lantern burning above the table illuminated the center of the room while leaving the lovers in shadow. With his free hand Albert reached into the darkness behind them and lifted the guitar from the pillow. He said, "The only thing I am sorry for her about is my music."

Albert let go the girl's hand and stood with his feet apart and his shoulders back, holding the guitar against his stomach to play. He struck a few chords, and began. It was wild music, a rapid succession of chords on the guitar accompanied by a series of shouts and hoarse cries in the voice, and to the extent it had any form or coherence at all it was a kind of untrained flamenco sung by an even wilder Camarón—a passionate singing full of defiance and lamentation, brave and joyful and at the same time achingly sad and tragic, with all the suffering of unredeemed nature in it as well as the agony of man. At one level it was just a dreadful inhuman cacophony, a travesty of body and mind and spirit, at another the raw authentic expression of human experience and human love. Albert Orsino's screams shook the collapsing house, threatening to bring it down about our ears and push him into an epileptic fit. Through it all the girl continued to sit quite still on the mattress, her hands folded decorously in her lap until her lover finished abruptly and set the guitar against the wall. Then, in what was almost a single movement, she raised her arms straight up, pulled the shift off over her head, and lay back on the bed in the altogether, her slim white body ending in tanned limbs glimmering in the half light.

"Man-oh-*man*!" John-Wayne exclaimed afterward in a whisper as we were crossing the turnaround toward the truck.

"You might as well forget you ever saw that. It doesn't have anything to do with you."

"I though he said she was shy."

"It isn't that she's shy or not shy, she's simply innocent. Completely, utterly innocent."

"Man, I wish I had somebody innocent like that with me."

"Just forget it. Where do you want to lay the bedrolls?"

We made our beds on the soft needles beneath the pine trees where the road came up from the bottom. Lying on our backs we could see the stars through the black branches of the trees and the shine on the sky where the moon was getting ready to rise. The lantern was out in the house now, the only light showing from it the brightness of the night reflected in the single remaining window pane. In the darkness the house appeared secret and self-contained, mysterious—disturbing in a way that made me feel strangely restless.

"Dude."

"What?"

"How does a person get so innocent?"

"You don't 'get' innocent. You begin that way."

"Were you ever innocent like that?"

"No."

"Was *I* that way once?"

"You weren't, either."

"You ever know anyone that was?"

"Not like that. She's the only one."

I rolled on my side in the bag and tried fitting my hip to a small depression in the ground. It seemed impossible to get comfortable this evening. The pine needles under my nose had an acrid smell like dry tinder.

"What you guess they're doin in there now?"

"I told you twice already. Don't think about it."

I rolled onto my back again and shut my eyes. By regulating my breathing to a slower rate I could draw the first shallow waves of sleep in, lifting my body as though it were a raft on rising water.

"Dude."

"What is it?"

"You think she's happy, bein innocent like that?"

The boundless and amazing ignorance—*not* innocence—of the young.

"My bet is she's the only truly happy person either one of us has ever met in his entire life," I told him. "Now, go to sleep."

The stars had changed position during the night but they were still bright overhead and the eastern sky was almost colorless, a thin green wash behind the black mountains before dawn. I fell asleep again and when I woke for the second time frost had formed on the outside of the bag and smoke was rising from the broken house chimney. I shook John-Wayne awake and we sat up together and shucked the bags as far as our waists. Shivering with cold, we stared at one another in the bleak morning light.

"You first," I said.

"No, you."

"Chickenheart."

"Winter's comin, man."

"Winter, my eye. It isn't even Labor Day yet."

"We need to find that horse pretty quick now."

"You'd better get out of bed, then."

"I don't know where my pants are at."

"Try under the bag."

John-Wayne felt beneath himself, tugged, and retrieved the pants.

"It's your head that's supposed to need a pillow, not your ass."

He looked behind me and grinned.

"The white man's pants are wet."

"No they're not."

I reached around behind me and felt.

"Shit."

John-Wayne jerked the bag the rest of the way down and swung out his long brown legs. They were the longest legs on any kid I ever saw. He was into the pants in a second, drawing the end of the belt through the buckle as he went toward the house.

"Better hurry before you catch nimonia, Dude."

The girl was gone already from the cabin. Moving back into the woods at first light like a wild animal, she would have been what had wakened me briefly just before the dawn. Albert Orsino's kitchen was smokey in spite of the natural ventilation system, and it was very warm. While I stood close against the stove to steam my pants dry, Albert fried bacon and eggs on top of it. The guinea eggs were small and delicate looking and bits of straw and bird dung stuck to the shells. On account of their size Albert had carried in a dozen of them from the barns to feed the three of us. He had pushed the coffee pot to the back of the stove, and he and John-Wayne were drinking coffee with condensed milk in it from cracked china mugs. John-Wayne held his mug with both hands for the warmth. He and Albert had been laughing together when I came in and I wondered what the joke was. There was no third mug but Albert scrounged around until he found an empty tin can which he poured full of coffee and gave to me. I had to wrap my handkerchief around the can to hold it, and each time I took a drink of coffee the hot tin burned my lip. The coffee tasted wonderful anyway.

"Eat good," Albert said. He had fried about a pound and a half of the bacon, to go with the eggs. "We got a long way to ride today."

"How long is long?" I asked him.

"Twenty, twenty-five mile."

"Where exactly is it that you're taking us?"

"Into the mountains." Albert grinned. "You'll see."

We ate from flimsy tin pans, the kind they sell commercially made pies in, using bent forks and spoons and the single knife we passed between us, and when we'd finished eating Albert slopped water into the pans and refilled the coffee pot, which he replaced on the front of the stove after adding wood to the maw.

"You guys bring your saddles with you?"

"In the truck."

"Because I only got the one leather one. The other two's made of wood."

I pointed to John-Wayne.

"Give him one of the wooden ones. He needs to learn to ride vaquero."

"Not me. I ain't no Meskin greaser with a iron ass."

Albert Orsino faced around to John-Wayne. He looked older suddenly, less innocent, and a lot meaner.

"Don't talk like that where we're goin," he said.

"Or what?" John-Wayne asked belligerently.

"Or you'll wish you hadn't," Albert told him shortly.

He took the pot from the stove, poured what was left of the coffee into a canteen, and set the canteen on the floor to cool.

"We'll get the horses ready now," he said.

The horses stood with their heads over the top rail of the corral, watching the house. They looked down their long noses at us and nickered as we came up. Albert threw them a flake of hay apiece and grained them. He gave them plenty of grain and they ate all of it. Albert's horses were strongly muscled and, though their hooves were freshly trimmed, the shoes had worn thin already in front.

"How often do you need to shoe?" I asked.

"Ever two weeks. Three at the most."

"As often as that?"

"Mountains wear them shoes down, fast as I can put em on almost."

"You do your own shoeing then."

"Sure." Albert grinned. "You don't have to be no genius to shoe a horse and it helps if you're a little runt, like me. I've had horses' feet between my knees since I was eleven-twelve years old."

"So that's his problem," John-Wayne mumbled.

"Say what?"

"How many times you been kicked in the head?"

"How many times you had your ass whipped?"

"Cut it out, both of you," I said. "Save it until there's some woman around to show off for."

We rigged out the pack horses in their pads and crossbucks and loaded them with the supplies Albert had been holding in the shed behind the ranch house. He was not due to resupply his clients for almost a week yet, he said, but it was no use making the extra trip. When everything was in place and the string stood quietly waiting on the pack line, John-Wayne and I brought Baca's tack from the truck, saddled, and fitted the straight bits to the horses' mouths.

"I'd as soon put one of them things in my old granma's teeth as I would a good horse's," Albert remarked to no one in particular as he carefully placed a snaffle bit for the tall roan he'd just saddled with a high, stiff looking piece of weather-blackened Spanish leather.

"Back home, we only use snaffles on greenbroke colts."

John-Wayne slung the Winchester in its already battered scabbard beneath the saddle skirts, I belted on the holstered revolver, and we were ready to ride then. Before we did, Albert went back to the house and returned carrying a gallon canteen of water and a bag of candy bars. The smoke was still rising up straight from the chimney as we rode away, and the first rays of the sun striking the single pane of glass was like a silent small explosion behind us on the verge of the hill.

We went in file between small rises of ground—Albert on the roan leading the pack string behind him, followed by me on Quixote and John-Wayne and Doña Ana bringing up the rear—and then spread out crossing the sandy bench above the wide bottom. Across the river pale headlights passed now and again along the grey highway curving against the dark foothills of the mountain range. We forded the river, scrambled up the opposite bank, and crossed the highway midway between two wide curves, the iron shoes ringing sharply on the asphalt. When we were across Albert paused for us to regroup in file before we started again up a narrow sandy canyon scattered with volcanic rock and cutting down through gravel hills covered by the feathery green mesquite. Albert's horses moved out briskly, setting their feet with care and taking shortcuts across the bends in the trail, which they seemed completely familiar with. For an hour we rode in the shadow of the looming mountains ahead, before the sun climbed above them and the day began to be very warm. Then the trail entered a split in the mountain side and it was dark again and chilly, almost cold. We were nearly beyond the reach of the desert now, the yucca and Spanish bayonet confined in the open spaces between the alligator juniper and piñon pine on the steep-pitched south-facing wall of the gorge, high above the alder and cottonwood clumps standing green against the reddish-purple rock along the watercourse. It was the real Southwest again, not like Utah, and I felt glad to be back in it as we rode in silence except for the occasional ring of metal on stone and the whine of the circling horseflies. When my mouth felt dry I lifted the canteen from the saddle horn and took a long drink, washing the water around in my mouth for nearly a minute before swallowing. In spite of the chill that persisted in the bottom of the canyon, the water was already warm.

The sun went on climbing until it was high enough to look down into the bottom of the canyon where snakes, tired after a night out hunting, lay warming themselves before returning to their dens: rattlers three or four feet long and big around as my thigh at the middle. Unalarmed by the shock of approaching hooves, they waited coiled in the trail ahead of us. After the first three or four encounters Albert dismounted and gathered a handful of stones to throw ahead of himself as he rode but the pebbles made hardly any impression on the snakes, which oiled off slowly a short way from the trail to watch with unblinking yellow eyes and flicking tongues as we passed by. One of them, a big old fellow with a rattle the length of a cob of Indian corn and weaving his bulging triangular head from side to side, caught my eye as I rode past.

"Good morning, grandfather," I told him. "I didn't expect you to move as far away as southern New Mexico, but thanks anyway for taking my advice to heart. It's nice down here in the Gila, isn't it? Warmer, and a whole lot more peaceful. You'll like it here. A good place to grow old and die, full of years and lizards."

"Say what, Dude?" John-Wayne inquired behind me.

"Nothing," I said. "I was just talking to the snake."

We climbed up through the piney forest closing on both sides and topped out after a couple of hours on a plateau above the headwall of the canyon, with a view to the south of the blocky central mass of the Mogollon Mountains. Ahead of us Albert drew rein and the pack string came to a jolting stop in an open park where the young trees were growing back from a burn among the blackened snags and the wildflowers. John-Wayne and I rode out from behind the string and drew rein alongside Albert, who sat shading his eyes as he looked away to the dark mountains scarred with falls of the sheer red lava rock.

"See that mountain there?"

Albert pointed.

"Is that where we're headed?"

"No. Do you know what the name of that mountain is?"

"It's called Whitewater Baldy," I said. Years ago we used to hunt elk back there every November, my father, grandfather, and I.

"No it ain't."

"What is it then?"

"Mount Albert."

"Who's Albert?"

"Albert Orsino."

"It's on the map?"

"Not on the map; in my heart. The heart of Albert Orsino who named him. His secret name."

From where we sat the horses I saw that the headwall backed a second canyon draining in roughly the opposite direction to the southeast. This canyon was steeper than the one we'd ascended by, heavily wooded in places and almost sheer rock in others. Away down the canyon the gorge widened to a narrow green valley where a creek, glinting silver in the piney haze, meandered between pitched blue forests. When we had breathed the horses sufficiently we put them forward again on the descending trail with an up-canyon wind smelling of pine needles and the heated earth in our faces. This time I rode ahead of the string, followed by John-Wayne and Albert Orsino behind him.

"Are you Indian?" I heard John-Wayne ask Albert.

"One-half of me's Apache. The other half is just Meskin."

"I'm full Dineh," John-Wayne told him proudly.

"I wouldn't want to be full anythin,'" Albert said.

"Why not?"

"Because you're stronger with the strength of two men than you are with just the one."

"But a halfbreed ain't two men, he's one man—just like anybody else."

"What kind of horse is stronger, a blooded one or a mesteño that's all horses mixed together?"

"The mustang mostly, but I'm talkin about people—"

"People and horses is the same thing. You run them together and before you know it you got somethin else. The same and different, both together."

"Maybe it ain't nothin to you, but *I* like to know just exactly what's in a horse—or a person."

"What for? You never know what he's goin to do next, anyway."

"Well, I'm glad *I'm* pure—not no halfbreed Indian. I'm glad *I* know who *my* people are, and where they're goin. I'm glad *I* know who *I* am."

"Does it tell you what they're goin to be next and where it is you're goin to?" Albert asked him.

It was cool along the trail after it went into the forest and now there were no more snakes in our path. I made Quixote step out a way into the trees to let the boys go by with the packstring, while they finished their argument and I checked the loads in the revolver to make sure I was carrying one under the hammer, a thing I generally don't do when on horseback. The horses' hooves drummed on the forest floor with a hollow sound and off in the stillness of the woods flies droned. I didn't believe Albert Orsino meant us any harm, but he was only a kid. What I did think was, he wasn't taking us to visit any Boy Scout camp practicing their survival skills in the heart of the southwestern wilderness. A man never knew, nowadays, what he was going to meet up with in the mountains. I locked the cylinder, holstered the gun again, and kicked Quixote into a trot. We caught up with the string a few hundred yards ahead where they'd halted to water at a seep beside the trail, the boys sitting their horses with their stirrups slipped, looking relaxed.

"Here comes the One Who Talks With Snakes," I heard John-Wayne say to Albert in a voice that was meant to be overheard, and the two of them looked at each other then and laughed. In any group of three males there has to be an odd man out always, and it was natural in the circumstances for that man to be me. I didn't give a damn one way or another so long as the two of them had decided to be friends, finally.

They jerked their horses' heads away from the spring and started forward again along the trail together ahead of the pack string, while I moved

Quixote onto the seep. Long before he'd finished drinking the whole kit and kaboodle was out of sight around a bend in the trail.

The forest ended where the trail leveled at the edge of the park and we rode on in the open along the creek, past young cottonwoods overhanging the clear water and the tangled black-eyed daisies bobbing and weaving on the banks. Snags caught the current in the bends where gravel bars pushed out from the opposite shore and the lush grass at the stream's edge was alive with small green frogs that dove with a plopping sound for deeper water as we went by. A light wind riffling the runs turned over the slender leaves of the willows, exposing the pale undersides, and jays balanced in their swaying branches. A small gray bird, nondescript, appearing suddenly from nowhere, lighted on a rock a few yards ahead of the horses. It flew on as we approached to a farther rock from where it watched as we ride up, and then on again, closing the distance each time until its takeoff point was almost under Quixote's feet as we advanced, spread out once more across the open park, the horses' tails streaming out behind them in the wind. The wind felt cool on my face and neck, the sun on the backs of my ungloved hands warm and pleasant. White small clouds floating overhead looked friendly, but in the distance, above the mountain peaks, the afternoon storms were already building.

"Can I have one of them candy bars?" John-Wayne asked Albert.

"How much farther are we going, anyway?" I inquired.

Albert Orsino smiled knowingly.

"A ways."

"Let's take a break here, then, where there's water and graze for the horses."

We picketed them on the grass and sat on our saddle blankets by the creek with the sack of candy bars between us. When Albert got down on all fours to drink John-Wayne stopped him.

"Don't drink the creek water, dude. You'll get gee-yardy."

"What's gee-yardy?"

"You shit and shit all day for months and months, and the medicine you got to take gives you cancer."

"What kind of cancer?"

"I don't know. Just cancer is all."

"I been drinking out of creeks since I was old enough to fall into one."

"Well, you'll get gee-yardy then."

Albert got off his hands and knees and stood looking down at the creek. I lifted the canteen from the blanket and offered it to him.

"Drink all you want to. We always ride with plenty of water."

Reluctantly he accepted the canteen and drank from it, making a face after the first swallow.

"How come horses and cows don't get gee-yardy?"

"Because cattle are what put it there in the first place," I told him.

"What about the deer and elk and all?"

"They're tough," I said. "Like cows and horses. They've got strong stomachs."

Albert handed the canteen back. He turned around, got on his hands and knees again, and drank, long and deep, from the dark clear stream. Then he stood and faced us, wiping the water from his dripping face with his sleeve.

"I could be ate by a bear or hit by lightnin'," he said contemptuously. "I ain't worried about no gee-yardy nor no cancer."

The horses stood dozing in the sun with their eyes closed and their knees locked comfortably beneath them while they switched at flies with their tails. We ate some of the candy bars and lay on our backs on the soft grass with the sun glaring red behind our eyelids. Then we saddled up and continued on in the meadow, riding abreast through the crooked cholla and the headed stalks of mullen below rocky terraces where mesquite, juniper, and the brown blades of Spanish bayonet grew.

The creek bent right at the tail of the meadow and plunged down through a forested gorge. We crossed to the right bank before it entered the trees and followed a steeply ascending trail into the timber. The trail was slippery with pine needles except for patches of bare ground imprinted with the track of elk, and exposed tree roots lifted it from one step to the next like stair risers. The trees were mostly Ponderosa pine, with oak growing in clumps between them. The horses breasted the mountainside gamely, lifting their feet high and setting them carefully while we leaned forward over the necks and wrapped our hands in the manes to help them up. Sweating, they drew the horseflies which buzzed and circled before settling on the damp flanks just out of reach of the switching tails. The air had moistened as afternoon progressed and it was humid now within the shadowed forest. In silence except for the knock of hooves on the ground, the creak of saddle leather, and the horses' labored breathing, we climbed upward through the piney woods toward the endlessly receding sky behind the farthest line of the trees until, unbelievably, the crest of the ridge appeared ahead. Coming up through the trees we jumped an elk herd bedded just below the treeline. They broke from the forest edge and over the ridgeline where, a couple of minutes later, we rode straight into them as if they'd been domestic cattle, too shocked and astonished to run. Almost certainly, they'd never seen human beings or horses before. The herd stood, frozen, for several seconds and then scattered in all directions, leaving behind the powerful scent of elk and two calves not long out of spots and too young yet to fear. Mewing, the two of them followed after the horses as we rode across an open saddle toward the farther ridge. When they tired at last and lay down at the forest edge John-Wayne dismounted and approached them on foot. Turning in the saddle to brace the flat of his hand on the roan's croup, Albert called back to him.

"Get up on your horse, now. We got a ways to go yet."

Lying in the shade of the trees the calves watched over their shoulders as John-Wayne walked up on them carefully with his hand outstretched. They watched him from the dark wet globes of their eyes, deep as the wilderness and softer, as if they possessed a secret that the wilderness itself could never know.

"Don't touch them!" Albert called to him in a sharp voice.

John-Wayne froze three feet away from the elk, still holding his hand out. Then he turned and walked slowly back to the horse. He gathered the hanging reins with one hand on the horn, swung his leg over, and caught up with us at a trot.

"I wasn't goin to touch them," he said defensively. "I just wanted them to smell of me, that's all."

"Why would they want to smell you?" Albert asked him.

"The white man says humans stink to animals. Stink worse'n anythin in the world. White men and Navajos both, he thinks."

"You gave them a noseful then," I said.

But John-Wayne was proud. "I ain't had no shower since Silver City," he said, "and them elks didn't even bother to get up and move."

All that afternoon we rode the steeply pitched hills and ridges, heavily wooded in places and open in others, cut by draws and lava canyons, some of them deep enough that hawks and eagles hunting down there floated far below the horses' feet on columns of light and shadow that played on their patterned wings. Albert proceeded now along no trail I was able to make out. The wind got up and blew hard out of the west as the afternoon sun worked down below my hatbrim, burning one side of my face, then the other. Emerging from trees into one of the small high parks we saw only mountains—forested slopes, ridges, and headlands in shades of green and a deeper blue circling around, as if the vast and arid southwestern desert beyond had been completely displaced or never been at all. The wind stayed warm but the clouds were darkening and closing together over parts of the sky as they pushed higher into it, blotting the sunlight and shadowing the swimming confusion of the ranges. The horses humped along uncomplaining but we stopped often now to let them blow, sitting the heaving barrels with our feet hoisted onto the necks until they had their wind back and we started forward again.

We were climbing through a rocky chute onto an outlying shoulder of mountain when all of us heard a sudden noise like cannon fire from the opposite side of the ridge. Albert turned in the saddle to look back at John-Wayne. John-Wayne glanced across his shoulder at me, and I looked forward to the two of them. A storm cell was building quickly to the south over where Silver City would be, and another bulging up due west above the Arizona line. The sky where it touched the ridge ahead of us was a clear blue shading to ultraviolet overhead. Albert shrugged and kicked his horse forward. We followed and had ridden only a hundred yards when the sound came again behind the ridge, a deep concussion followed by a protracted grumbling. This time Albert did not look back but pressed his horse and the pack string behind him to a trot to the summit where they stood in long silhouette against the sky, Albert holding his hat against the wind up there. Quixote and Ana ascended at a lope to the head of the chute where we stood flanking the roan on either side, the three of us staring downhill at the storm as it advanced rapidly toward us. It was a small, compact storm, no more than a ball of light and dark mist swelling like rising bread and propelled rapidly by its own winds against the mountain slope.

"There ain't but a couple miles more left to go," Albert said. "We can make it down and acrosst to them trees before it catches us. If we run for it."

"Let's run then," I said. "We're twelve pair of iron feet just waiting to be a shortcut for some lightning bolt in a hurry."

We put the horses forward at a run, diagonally across the curving sidehill that formed a shallow bowl in the side of the mountain. The cloud swept on, spreading out as it came and driving skirmishers ahead of itself, vaporous columns vaguely human in shape that drifted like wraiths without moving themselves except as the storm winds changed them, pulling them apart and reforming them again. One of the ghosts looked familiar: tall, featureless, unmistakably feminine in form, it moved ahead of the rest, treading down the sky in our direction—my direction, headed directly toward me. Right then there was a flash of lightning, and the cloud spoke again in a great crash that seemed to shake the surrounding mountains and disconcert the orange ball of the sun going down behind them.

Light and warmth failed in the same instant and I felt the hairs on my neck and the backs of my hands prickle with the encompassing electrical charge. Gusts of cold air chilled my face and stiffened my horse's sweated coat. Made nervous by the wind and lightning the horses ran stiff-leggedly, dodging and crowhopping, the pack string flopping on the leadline like fish on a stringer.

The bowl reverberated like a drum with a crash of thunder, echoed by the surrounding mountains. The rain hit first, soaking globes of warm water the size of a thumbnail, and then came the hail—pebble-sized, rock-hard pellets that bit like shrapnel and closed out the view the way a northern blizzard does. The hail ricocheted from the saddles and lodged in the horse's manes as they tossed their heads, and we rode on through grey mists that brightened every few seconds with the electrical flashes. With the closest strikes the sound came simultaneously with the glare, and a strong smell of ozone. Albert Orsino was invisible and the last horse on the string an indistinct silhouette ahead, but I was aware that he was attempting to take his bearing by the pitch of the mountain slope. We had slowed to a trot on account of the poor visibility and bad footing and it seemed to me that our course was too much uphill, away from the trees along the drainage farther down in the basin. The storm raged without letup, as if it had expanded to fill the entire state of New Mexico. There had been no time to take the oilskins from the pack. My coat and pants were wetted through and the soaked horse shivered in spasms between my legs. I reined him in, stepped off, and began to lead on foot over the muddy ground until, discovering I was unable to keep up in this way with the riders ahead, I remounted and rode on. The lightning bolts kept coming, but I no longer payed them any attention: like a soldier in the midst of battle I was unconcerned about the immediate danger, my mind fixed solely on the peace and silence that must follow in the end. The hail changed to snow, then rain, then back to snow again, a soft wet snow that whited the horses and their riders until they were almost indistinguishable from the storm swirling around them.

We had traveled in this way for better than half an hour when a darkness deeper than the storm showed ahead and a skirmish line of trees rushed at us suddenly from the whirling snow. We rode through them and into the woods beyond, dismounted stiffly, and tied up. Albert built a small fire in the duff of the still dry forest floor and I used the last of the water in the canteen to make coffee. While we were drinking it the storm cleared away as quickly as it had arrived and a double rainbow appeared above the wet green mountains. Carrying the steaming cup in his hand Albert walked forward to the forest edge and stood with his back to us, gazing across the open basin. When he returned to the fire the cup was no longer steaming and Albert's narrow, disfigured face had an apprehensive look.

"Is there something the matter?" I asked him.

He drank off the coffee and turned the cup over above the piney matting on the ground.

"We come too far already. I got confused in the storm."

"Well, let's ride back and find wherever it is we're supposed to be."

Albert gave no sign of having heard me. Instead he said, "Come, and I'll show you where I want you and him to ride to tonight."

I followed among the pines to the treeline and stood behind his shoulder as he pointed below to a clearing in the trees we had missed by keeping too high on the inside of the bowl. The park was twenty-five to thirty acres in size, about a mile out and five hundred vertical feet down.

"There's water in the drainage, and pasture there in the clearin. Make camp overnight and I'll bring that horse down to you in the mornin, early. Follow the draw down and stay inside the trees where you can. Go now."

Albert spoke fast, his voice pitched high and a little shaky.

"You want us to go now? It's going to be dark in an hour."

"Go right now," Albert said. He was being very decided about it.

I shrugged.

"Okay," I told him. "But you better come through with the horse, my friend. First thing in the morning, like you said."

John-Wayne was eating a candy bar when I got back to the fire.

"Get up on your horse again," I told him. "The two of us are camping down in the drainage tonight, on account of Albert says so. I'm agreeing to take him at his word—this once. We'll build a proper fire and dry out when we get below."

Albert was still standing there at the forest edge as we rode out, and he still looked scared. The tired horses balked at first and then they began to whinny and sidestep, looking back at Albert's horses in the trees. Albert flung up his hand in a gesture at us to quiet them. Then he turned suddenly and ran back into woods to calm the pack string. All six horses were screaming now, deep shuddering shrieks that rose from the belly and trumpeted through the mouth and the flared red nostrils, traveling nearly the full length of the animal. The horses went on calling to one another after we had dropped off the top of the bowl and started down through the trees into the drainage.

It was cold in the trees, and almost dark. The horses stepped inattentively, looking uphill over their shoulders and whinnying while we fought to pull their heads around, sliding on the pine-needle steep. We made more noise than the soundtrack of a Grade B Western, and each time one of the horses screamed he was answered by Albert's string, sounding farther and farther away on the hillside above. In spite of his warning to be silent, it was not apparent to me what for. Approaching the bottom we spied daylight beyond the dark trees where the red sun reflected from the cliff wall ahead. John-Wayne's horse whinnied again, and this time it had its nose pointed downhill.

Five men sitting their horses in the gulley watched as we rode out from the trees. They wore camouflage fatigues, and red cloth masks hanging below their chins with eyeholes cut in them under the bills of their camouflage caps. Their saddles were of an antiquated Spanish style and the bridles mostly rope with long braided leather reins attached to them. The leather scabbards hung empty beneath the skirts, but that was no reassurance as the rifles that belonged in them were all leveled in our direction.

"Well done, amigos," the leader said in a heavily accented voice. "Now, will you please come with us?"

Two men rode ahead of us and three behind. The sun went down and in the darkness there were only the stars the storm had swept clear overhead and the sudden cold. The walls of the gorge, rising on either side of the column, echoed the clop of the horses' hooves and now and then the strike of metal on rock, accompanied by sharp small sparks.

No one spoke to us while we went except once when John-Wayne whispered to me as we rode abreast and one of the men behind hissed at him in Spanish to shut up. They had taken the packs from the horses and tied them to their own saddles, and they had not missed the revolver I wore inside my coat after requisitioning the Winchester. The canyon walls diminished as we climbed until the gorge became an arroyo and the arroyo leveled and widened to a bench backed by an amphitheater of terraced rock grown up with low trees and barely illuminated by the rising moon.

"¿Quién vive?" a low voice called from the darkness ahead.

"Nosotros, nomás."

"Avancen, pues."

We rode on by the sentry, also in camouflage with a rifle on his shoulder. The moon took him sideways as he turned slowly to watch us pass and I glimpsed the unmasked face and hanging dark mustaches under the military style cap. When we had gone a couple hundred yards more the riders behind moved up to surround us as a film came between us and the stars, patterned and wavy on the night breeze, and I caught a faint odor of woodsmoke before the red lights of the campfires appeared from the darkness. Quixote raised his head and released a long whinnying bellylaugh. He was answered immediately by another horse, close by on the right as we rode, and then I heard the stamp of corraled horses and smelled the strong scent of horse. We rode closer and I saw men grouped around the fires, which were enclosed on three sides by flat rocks set on edge and covered by another to form a sort of oven visible only at the open end. The men quit talking at our approach, and watched.

"¿Qué tienen ahí, compadres?"

"Un par de espías, claramente."

So they had taken us for spies—gumshoeing for Earth First! or maybe the BATF. I didn't really blame them. Anything can happen up here in the mountains nowadays. Anything at all.

The men at the nearest fires walked up and stood by the horsemen with their hands in their pockets to study us. They looked like Mexican Indians, dark, short men in dirty uniforms that copied the pattern in the camouflage netting stretched on poles overhead. The men studied us coldly, without real interest, and then one fellow spat suddenly on the ground. He stepped forward and took hold of Quixote's reins beneath the chin strap.

"¿Qué vas a hacer con ellos?" he demanded.

"Pues, ¿qué te parece que voy a hacer?"

The man spat again and scraped dirt over the spittle with the edge of his boot sole.

"Apúrense, pues." He turned and walked back to the fire, followed by the other men.

Our captor spoke briefly with the man on horseback beside him. He did not lift the lower part of the mask to speak and in the firelight the hanging point of red cloth was visible, moving in and out with his breathing. He looked from one to the next of the men who'd ridden up from behind and I saw for the first time that only the leader and his lieutenant rode horses, the others being mounted on tall mules.

"¡Vamos!" he told them.

We rode on past more fires and more men around them holding tin cups and talking; they all fell silent as we went by. There appeared to be somewhere between seventy-five and a hundred men in the camp. Beyond the fires was a twenty-five-man U.S. Army tent and, off by itself, an eight-by-twelve sidewall one staked down between two pine trees. Light showed from behind the tent flap and smoke rose from the guyed chimney rising through the canvas roof. The leader dismounted in front of the tent and motioned to us to do the same. We did it, while his lieutenant covered us with an AK-47. Then the men on muleback took the horses by the reins and rode back in the darkness the way we had come. The leader spoke in a low voice to his second, who lifted the flap and disappeared inside the tent. For nearly a minute the masked man, John-Wayne, and myself stood facing one another with the short, ugly-looking barrel of the rifle between us. Then the lieutenant emerged from the tent and stepped aside, holding back the flap as he gestured with his gun for us to enter.

A woodstove braced by pine wedges on the bare scraped ground kept the tent warm—too warm for the mountains, even in late summer—and a butane lantern suspended from a crosspole filled it with harsh, hissing light. Beneath the lantern was a table made of rough-hewn pine boards placed across two stumps with some maps and other papers on it and a couple of folding stools—the three-dollar kind that go over backward when you forget to balance with your feet for two seconds when you're eating supper from your lap—set around the table. Off in the corner was a double-wide cot bed with two sleeping bags on it and a woolen army blanket thrown over the bags, neatly folded down and smoothed. At the foot of the cot a wine bottle with freshly gathered wildflowers stuck in it stood on a small leather trunk. Someone had stretched another blanket across the opposite corner to make a curtain, and even before I saw the tin wash basin filled with tubes and small bottles I had a feeling about that tent. John-Wayne's face in the lamplight was sweating and pale, almost white. I gave him a short wink, which he did not acknowledge. There was no sound in the tent except the settling noise of the fire and the low breathing of the man behind the red cloth mask.

Then the curtain bellied slightly and a figure emerged from behind it. It was a straight, tallish figure, dressed in overlarge fatigues that looked too small for it in certain noticeable places and with small feet and hands that were pulling the last of a handful of dark copper-red hair out of the collar of the olive drab jacket at the nape. I felt shocked and embarrassed at the same moment, as if I had absentmindedly walked in on the ladies' powder room instead of the gentlemen's urinal.

"Mayor Carmen," the man with the gun announced.

"Buenas tardes," I heard myself mumbling.

"Good evening," she replied, as coolly as if we were being introduced in the lobby of the Metropolitan Opera House in New York City.

"Oh," I said. "You speak English."

Her hazel eyes were wide in a face constructed delicately around a straight nose and fine, high cheekbones, with a high forehead, even chin, a full red mouth that was not over-full, a double row of small white teeth, and a profile that belonged on a Grecian urn in some high, Mediterranean seaside castle. The end of her nose was shiny with sunburn, contrasting with her lightly powdered cheeks, and the long lashes curling above her eyes were carefully blackened. Of course she had a mirror behind that curtain. Women are wonderful. And where us men are concerned, they have to just happen—always.

"If course" she said, "I speak English."

"You're not American?"

"My mother is an Englishwoman. I was born in Madrid."

The leader addressed her from behind me.. He spoke very fast in a language that was not Spanish this time but sounded like some sort of dialect. Major Carmen replied in the same way and then I heard the snap of steel as he set the safety catch and the scrape of the tent flap falling behind him.

"I'm Navajo," John-Wayne told her. "Fullblood, not halfbreed. John-Wayne Bilagody, Tuba City, Arizona."

His voice was high and disconnected sounding, as if he did not really know what it was he was saying.

"You are not Navajo," Major Carmen said, looking at me.

"Just plain old Yankee, I'm sorry to say."

"But you do speak Spanish?"

"Muy poco. I'm a New Mexico boy, originally."

"Do you have a familiarity with Old Mexico?"

"Some. Not a lot."

"Does that mean you have friends there?"

"Not anymore. Not for years."

"What are you doing *here*," she demanded, "in these mountains?"

"Seeing America first. It's still my country, after all. More precisely, I'm looking for a horse."

"What happened to this horse?"

"Someone stole it."

"Do you know who?"

"I've lost count at this point, but it seems to me like everyone and his grandmother between Cortez, Colorado and Silver City, New Mexico."

The major smiled—in spite of herself, it seemed to me.

"He must be quite a valuable horse," she suggested.

"He's valuable to people who value Peruvian Pasos, me not included necessarily."

John-Wayne said, "He belongs to Bette Atcitty in Tuba City. She's my girlfriend," he added modestly.

The lamplight, putting small lines at the corners of her eyes, made her out to be around thirty, the perfect age for a woman. Her hair had wonderful lights in it, and it smelled of shampoo.

"Please, describe this horse for me," Major Carmen said.

I described Tortuga closely except for Shorty's brand, which struck me as being not relevant at the moment.

"And the brand?"

I identified it for her—hesitating a little in the description, but she didn't seem to notice.

"That's Juárez," she said positively when I'd finished.

"What is?"

"I named him Juárez—after the great mestizo revolutionary, of course."

"Of course. You have the horse here in camp with you?"

"Humberto brought you past him in the corral," Major Carmen said.

The canvas scraped again and I knew Humberto had his head through it when the woman, looking past me, nodded.

"Un momento, por favor, ¿vale? Todavía no hemos terminado de hablar."

I noticed that she used Spanish this time and wondered if it was because she wished me to understand.

"It isn't a question of money with us at this point," I told her. "Name your price and I'll pay it. Within reason, of course."

"It isn't a question of money with us, either," Major Carmen said.

"And who is 'us', if you don't mind me asking?"

"That *is* the question, I'm afraid. Humberto!" she called.

I heard the safety come off as he came inside the tent again. The two of them spoke once more in that dialect I didn't recognize before Humberto gave an order through the tent flap and the second entered behind him, holding his rifle at the ready.

"We will talk again in the morning."

The woman looked straight at me as she said it, and I knew right then both of us were goners already. "The two of you must be very hungry. Humberto will see to it that you are given supper." Then, as the men took hold of us by the arm, "¿Cómo se llama Ud.?—What is your name?" she asked.

"Jeb Stuart Ryder. Monticello, Utah."

"I am Carmen Dominguín de Córdoba Herbert— a great admirer of your namesake. You know General Lee wept at receiving news of his death."

"He better have," I said.

Major Carmen held out her hand. "Buenas noches," she told me, and smiled. It was a smile to make a Mormon apostle kick his eighth and newest wife out of bed.

The camp looked emptier than it had an hour before. The fires had been banked and most of the men were gone from around them. With the dimmed light the camouflage netting had darkened and the stars shone in from beyond it, thinly veiled. The commandos hurried us along briskly between them to a clump of pines where they invited us to lie on the ground while they tied our ankles and bound us together at the waist. Then, while Humberto stood guarding us and smoking a cigarette from under his mask, his lieutenant disappeared in the direction of the big tent. He returned after several minutes with two Saltillo plates and two tin mugs which he set down before us on the pine needles as if he was putting food out for the dogs. It was some kind of stew with corn meal, boiled to a fiberless mess and stone cold, like the coffee, with under the mess a stale flour taco. The men stood smoking in the darker shadow of the trees while we ate, lifting the tail of the masks from their chins and blowing the smoke from under them. When we had finished eating they tied our wrists, secured us by a rope tether to a tree, and went away without saying goodnight. "¡Buenas noches!" I called after them, but nobody answered.

Bound together on the ground like loosely joined Siamese twins, John-Wayne and I looked at one another. There wasn't anything else to look at.

"Who are these dudes, man?"

"I don't know. Some kind of Hispanic militia from Albuquerque, maybe."

"What's a militia?"

"Middle-aged men playing revolutionary war games with each other in the wilderness."

"Do they let women in the militias?"

"They do in this one, apparently."

"She's a good-lookin woman. Ain't she?"

"Very good-looking."

"You think she's married to this Humberto guy?"

"Not married. She doesn't wear a wedding ring."

"Do revolutionaries get married?"

I thought about it, and didn't answer him.

"You suppose her and him are, like—?"

"For God's sake, how should I know? Don't ask so many goddamn questions."

The kid was silent for a while. Then he said, "They can't be that bad—to have a woman with them, I mean."

For a second time in the course of the conversation I found I had nothing to say to him.

"What you think they're goin to do with us, Dude?"

"Turn us loose in the morning, probably, and tell us to get lost and not come back unless we want to put on camouflage suits and play games with them."

"Get lost—with the horse?"

"Definitely, not with the horse. The woman seems to have taken quite a liking to Tortuga. Women always do."

"What time is it?"

"Almost ten-thirty."

"I'm tired."

"Then go to sleep."

"I can't—without you."

"I can't either. *With* you."

We lay side by side on the hard ground, feeling the cold work its way up through the pine needles and into our bones.

"We'd have more room between us if you didn't lie on your back."

"It hurts my hip, layin on my side."

"How long did you say it's been since you had a bath?"

"You don't smell like no prom queen yourself, man."

We shifted onto our sides and then on our backs again like a pair of crippled performance artists, trying to get comfortable on the pine needles. Once we both rolled away from each other at the same time and the rope caught us and snatched us together again.

"Dude."

"What?"

"I miss Bette—my girl."

"Of course you miss her."

"Why don't we just let them have that fuckin horse if they want him so bad, and go home. He don't look like no show horse no more anyway—just an old cow pony's been rode hard and put up wet."

"You know why."

"But you *said* they ain't goin to let us take the horse with us."

John-Wayne's voice broke suddenly and he began to cry. I saw the tears shining on his upturned face in the moonlight.

"We're going to come back here tomorrow night after dark and take him from that corral," I said.

Somehow, in the darkness, it didn't sound like my voice saying it. Somehow I knew that what I actually wanted was to come back, in the darkness, and take *her*.

---

We rolled about like a couple of chained logs all night until the camp began to stir before dawn, men going about in the darkness gathering wood and lighting fires. There was the rip of dead branches being torn away, the clink of tin pans and pots, and from the corrals the stamp and whinny of horses. John-Wayne and I sat shoulder to shoulder, hugging our knees as a fan of sunlight spread behind the cliff and beads of moisture glistened in the grass ends. The sun was just up when two men on horseback brought Albert Orsino into camp, looking scared and small as he rode between what looked like Humberto on a big buckskin and the lieutenant riding a handsome gray I recognized from the night before. Apparently horses were a status symbol for these people. Both Humberto and the lieutenant were masked again this morning. The men rode on through camp to Major Carmen's tent, where all three dismounted and went inside.

"They wanted him, too," I said.

"What they goin to do with him, do you think?"

"I don't know."

It was a long time before someone came with coffee. The man who brought it also was masked, the lower part of the cloth hanging below his chin like a red trunk. His cold impersonal eyes through the holes had all the humanity of a jailer serving a pair of condemned men their last meal. He did not reply to my greeting and went off as soon as he'd finished untying our hands. We drank the coffee fast before it lost its heat to the metal cups and sat staring at the bottoms when we were through.

"How do you say elephant in Spanish?" John-Wayne asked.

"Elefante. Why?"

It was much longer before the man came again with breakfast. John-Wayne made a downward gesture from his chin as if he was stroking a beard.

"Elefante," he told the commando in a grave voice, and laughed.

The man stiffened as the eyes lost their coldness, which became something less pleasant. He snatched up the cups and went off with them without asking if we wanted more of the coffee.

"You don't have the sense God gave an honest politician," I told John-Wayne when he had gone. "The bottomless cup of coffee wasn't what I would call an honored tradition up here in the first place."

Breakfast was the same overcooked mush and stale tortilla with scrambled eggs over them, the kind that comes as a powder and you add water and powdered milk to it.

For a couple of hours after breakfast they were too busy to pay us any further attention. We could hear the grunt and gasp of men being exercised and the bark of orders given. Afterward the camp fell eerily silent, as if it had been abandoned quietly. Then I caught sight of figures moving about and crouching on the rocky terraces above, nearly invisible in their camouflage and distinguishable only when they moved among the scrub. These weekend warriors were dead serious about something—only God knew what.

The sun got up above the cliff and then it was warm in the amphitheater and very humid, away from the upslope wind. Bareheaded, unable to reach our hats, we sat exposed to the sun until, feeling faint with the heat, we moved back into the shadow of the pine trees again like monkeys on a leash, and fell asleep. The sun was at the overhead when we awoke, and Humberto and the lieutenant were picking at the cords that bound our ankles.

"Get up," Humberto said. "You have Spanish, yes? ¡Levántate!"

"Si, Sr. Elefante," John-Wayne said in a respectful voice.

The lieutenant struck him across the face with the back of his right hand. John-Wayne's eyes watered as four livid welts came up beside his cheekbone.

"You didn't have to do that," I told the man. "He's just a kid."

"He doesn't speak any English," Humberto growled as he untied the cord between us. "Vámonos ya."

They hurried us, hobbling, between them across the prickly pear and lava rock scattered in the rain-freshened grass toward the tent, where a horse stood tied in the trees behind. It was a black bay gelding, somewhat ganted but well brushed out under the fancy Spanish saddle and blanket. Facing away at a three-quarter angle the horse looked vaguely familiar, but it was not until he turned his head to look at us that I recognized Tortuga under the vaquero rigging. Horses are like people, you don't always see them for who they are in an unfamiliar outfit.

"It's my horse!" John-Wayne shouted, as the lieutenant took a stronger grip on his arm.

Tortuga-Córtez showed no surprise at seeing us. He watched impassively as we approached the tent, and turned his face away again to the woods. The commandos halted abruptly and Humberto went in under the rolled canvas flap, letting it down behind him. He stayed inside the tent for a long while and when he came out he was swearing under his breath and his face had an ugly look.

"Pasen," Humberto ordered in a low, angry voice. He did not look at me as we passed and dropped the flap hard after us.

Major Carmen stood across the table with a tin cup in her hand. She was out of fatigues this morning and into a pair of riding britches and an open-necked cotton shirt that were not too big for her anywhere and fitted her exactly in every place you could hope to see them fit.

"Buenos días," I said, clawing the hair out of my eyes with my fingers.

"Good morning," Major Carmen told me. "Coffee?" she asked.

"Yes ma'am," John-Wayne said.

"Please," I requested.

We stood while she took the pot, poured coffee, and set the cups down on the table before us.

"Sit down," Major Carmen invited.

We sat cautiously on the treacherous stools while she seated herself on one of the upended saw logs standing around.

"I imagine Juárez was overjoyed to see you again," Major Carmen suggested.

"That could be over-stating it a bit."

"Does he appear to be in good condition to you?"

"To me, he looks like a horse that should have broken down a thousand miles ago. I doubt his owner would recognize him, either."

"You should have seen him when I got him," she said. "I've done my best, but you can't bring a horse back overnight."

"You've had him how long now?"

"Two weeks, perhaps. It's hard to keep track of the time up here."

"And how did you happen to acquire him in the first place?"

"I bought him. The same way his owner did—unless he owned the mare, too."

"I'm glad to hear it. The last few owners never bothered with the purchase part."

The woman's cheeks flushed and her lovely eyes flamed out at me.

"Did you imagine I was a horse thief?"

"It crossed my mind. I've known several in my life. But that's all it did. Albert Orsino told me he sold the horse for five hundred dollars. I had no reason to disbelieve him. And I heard you confirm his story, just now."

"Albert Orsino brought you here," she said. "Being a simple boy, he brought you too far. And now what am I going to do with you?"

"I'll make up the five hundred," I said, "plus five hundred more on top of that. Then we take the horse and get out of your hair."

"Humberto wants me to kill you," Major Carmen said calmly.

I laughed.

"Well, if you want a mock execution John-Wayne and I will be happy to play along."

Then I saw she actually meant it.

"I mean, he wants me to have you killed," she explained.

"Killing people is one of those fantasies every normal militia man has."

She gave me a long, scornful look, dripping with Spanish pride and disdain.

"You talk like a child. Americans are children, American men especially with their role-playing, their made-up reality—their 'militias'. But *we* are not children, *we* do not play games, *we* have no militias, so-called. Instead, we have the revolución, not just Saturdays and Sundays in summertime but three hundred and sixty-five days a year, summer and winter, good weather and bad, twenty-four hours a day, whether we are actually fighting or not. Permanent revolución, revolución that never sleeps, that only waits, to kill and be killed; not just something for the magazine journalists to write about but for the government, and those who own the government, to fear. We are no militia, we are the brigada—the kernel of a new civilization that will end by making the whole world new. If we appear to you like a fantasy, it is because you yourself are living in a fantasy world. Look here!"

She undid a cuff button with a snap of her fingers and shot the sleeve of the cotton shirt up a shapely white arm, as far almost as the shoulder.

"Feel!"

She made a muscle and extended her arm across the table. I felt of the raised biceps. They were hard and warm. And smooth as satin.

"Do I feel like a fantasy to you now?"

"Perhaps you could have a talk with Humberto—alone—and persuade him not to shoot us, after all."

"I could," Major Carmen agreed. "But why should I need to bother? I am the commander of the brigada, not Humberto. I am the one who is in control here."

Then, just for a moment, she did seem like a fantasy to me.

"If I had even the slightest reason to suspect that you were agents of the Mexican or United States governments, I would have had you shot last night. However, you identified my horse. Also your Spanish is atrocious. Even the U.S. government is not stupid enough to try and use someone as obvious as you—with a Navajo boy for cover, no less. And Albert says you ride too well to be government men. So—I believe you, Yanqui."

"Thanks. Does that mean you're not going to shoot us—have us shot?"

"It means I have no reason as of now to have you shot."

"Well, we don't plan on thinking up any new ones."

"I'm glad," Major Carmen said, "because you're going to have plenty of time for a while now in which to think. Will you drink a fresh pot of coffee with me if I put one over the fire?"

---

Carmen Dominguín de Córdoba's daddy was an oil man living on a big ranch in the pampas of Argentina where he bred fighting bulls for the corrida. Her mother, a member of the lesser English aristocracy with a law degree from the University of Madrid, had divorced her husband and returned to Madrid to live. There was also a former husband in Buenos Aires, a celebrated matador she had been divorced from after a five-year marriage that produced no children though it had started as a passionate love affair in defiance of her father, who had brought her up to make a fine match in Buenos Aires where she was already a famous society beauty. After only a week in the brigada's camp—most of it spent in the Major's tent—there seemed like very little I didn't know about Carmen Dominguín, with the exception of her precise age (I'd dropped my estimate from thirty to twenty-eight, then raised it as high as thirty-two, based on the latest hints as they became available) and what it was she saw, or had ever seen, in Humberto Cárdenas besides, of course, the brutally insensitive good looks women often go for.

They had met in Chiapas, where together they witnessed a massacre of Indian villagers by a paramilitary group paid, equipped, and sicced on by the Partido Revolucionario Institucional. Humberto himself was from Hermosillo in the State of Sonora and most of the brigada also were natives of the Republic's northern provinces. They had been camped here in the wilderness of the Gila since July, when soldiers of the Republican Army cooperating with the Federales surprised them after a sabotage job in rough country east of Agua Prieta and chased them north across the border. On the American side they met Albert Orsino, a Mexican native equally at home in the States where he lived on and off in abandoned ranch buildings on the money he made as a coyote bringing Mexican illegals into the country, and who offered to hide them out in the wilds of New Mexico for a couple of months before guiding them down to the border again. From the New Mexico bootheel, Albert had brought them north through the rugged mountains on the Arizona-New Mexico line, losing horses as they went but without encountering a human soul. There was not a lot for the men to do in camp beyond physical training, guard duty, running a supply line from the valley towns, and soccer games under the camouflage net among the rocks and bushes, using an improvised soccer ball made from a piece of inner tube. After nearly eight weeks in the mountains they were bored, restless, dirty, and mean, but with Carmen determined to wait a couple weeks more before beginning the trek back to Mexico, and because the brigada was essentially her private army, financed indirectly by South American oil and Ford Motor Company stock, they had a choice between pushups, soccer, grumbling—and nada. Since John-Wayne, Albert, and I weren't going anywhere until they moved, we had the same.

They took the ropes off the second day and after that we slept with Albert Orsino in one of the cheaply made, leaky backpack tents the men used to stay dry in during the monsoon season. It was only a two-man tent but the three of us made do, piled together on top of one another like rattlesnakes in a winter den. For several days more we were closely watched while a sentry stood duty at the horse corral—and then we were in like Flynn, except for having a guard set on us at night. Waking in the dark with John-Wayne's arm flung across my chest, I could just make out the fellow through the open door of the tent, innocently snoring as he sat with the small of his back against a pine tree, face forward on his drawn-up knees. Carmen was as bored as the rest of the brigada—more so, really, on account of her intelligence and having gone months with no one to talk to besides Humberto. He was fortyish, tall for a Mexican and well built with dark skin tanned copper by the sun, even features that would probably be a little too smooth under a recent growth of mossy beard that showed more gray than the black glossy hair curling down over his collar behind, round eyes whose dark brown pupils bled into the surrounding whites, and a red mouth guarded by flashing white teeth. Around camp he wore a denim jacket in place of the camouflage one, a black beret, and a red bandana handkerchief knotted about his neck. Although an obvious Spaniard with little or no Indian blood, Humberto was largely uneducated, his vocabulary limited to a relatively small number of words of the kind that in English would be characterized as Anglo-Saxon.

Humberto loathed me, and although this naturally made for complications I almost loved him for it. Because Carmen and I were in love from the moment we laid eyes on each other and of course it showed as love always does, having a kind of invisible presence and even, perhaps, a barely perceptible scent. John-Wayne for one was aware of it, and so was the lieutenant, Gabriel. Humberto hated our hanging around the wall tent with her most of the day, and he never missed a chance to show us how much when Carmen's back was turned. Then his dark eyes went bloodshot with suppressed rage, the left eyelid twitched, and the point of his red tongue protruded between his white teeth. He would have killed me in an instant—and not for la revolución either. He hated John-Wayne too, partly perhaps on account of the old Mexican-Navajo enmity but also because he was the kind of lover to be jealous of anything male, from a geriatric in diapers to a sixteen-year-old kid. One morning after Carmen had returned from her morning ride horseback around the camp and John-Wayne and I were sitting with her over coffee while she recounted the story of a two-week cattle drive on the pampas for us, Humberto came into the tent and walked back to the cot bed without saying a word. He kneeled down, reached beneath the bed, and drew out a fully loaded clip to replace the half empty one he extracted from the handle of his side arm. Our eyes met as he inserted the fresh clip into the pistol and pushed the other under the cot. Then he rose, holstered the weapon, and went out of the tent, still without speaking as Carmen, ignoring him, continued her account of a shoot-out with German and Italian rustlers along the trail.

It took her only a few days to make a pet of John-Wayne, teasing him about his girlfriend until he blushed and fidgeted. Naturally, he took her attention the way any sixteen-year-old kid would—meaning the wrong one—which was okay and didn't hurt anyone's feelings except Humberto's. Of course, that was all right with me, too.

"I really am going to miss that horse," Carmen said. She, John-Wayne, and I sat outside the tent watching the monsoon clouds pile up over Arizona while Tortuga, picketed from the tree where she had tied him, grazed at the end of his line, carefully lifting his feet free of the rope as he moved around. In the week we had been in camp he'd filled out some more and his coat was shiny from Carmen's vigorous brushings. "He's such a gorgeous animal, and so docile for a stallion. He doesn't seem to care much who's riding him."

"He's gorgeous as long as he's standing still, anyway."

"You're just not accustomed to Pasos. We always had them around when I was a girl in Argentina. Mother helped to improve the breed before she moved to Europe and I helped her show them, when I had the time."

"There's plenty of room for improvement still, if you ask me."

"Pasos are a woman thing. You wouldn't understand."

"I'm beginning to get the picture anyway," I said.

She was wearing the riding britches again, which made me uncomfortable, and had her hair pulled off her forehead and combed down behind. The direct sun that is so unflattering to most women's complexions only made hers more radiant.

"A beautiful horse deserves a beautiful woman," Carmen said. "Is Juárez's owner beautiful?" she asked.

"Not quite beautiful perhaps," I began, "but—"

It was John-Wayne she was speaking too, of course.

He turned red and squirmed on the upended log. Then he giggled and gave her a dumb, apologetic smile.

"Well, is she? She's your lady, after all."

"I…I don't know."

"Is she beautiful to you?"

"I don't remember."

"Don't remember?"

"I ain't seen her in two months," John-Wayne explained.

Carmen watched him with a serious expression. When she smiled her face was like a burst of flamenco music, but when she was quiet it was more beautiful still, smooth as a millpond and with depth beneath the smoothness.

"She ain't beautiful like you," John-Wayne got out, and turned red from self-astonishment, as if he'd inadvertently sassed the teacher.

"How old are you, John-Wayne?" Carmen asked him.

"Sixteen—ma'am."

"I told you before, you don't have to ma'am me. Young as you are, you're probably expecting some sort of reward from her for bringing her horse home. Aren't you?"

He hung fire.

"Well—aren't you?"

"I guess."

"What kind of reward do you expect?"

"I don't know. A little one."

"What's your idea of little?"

Purple in the face, he was unable to answer her. Carmen laughed.

"Men are all the same," she said. "It makes no difference if they're sixteen or sixty-six. They all want that same little thing, and most of the time they get it, too. That's why they so rarely get anything more—even when they deserve it. Do you love this girl, John-Wayne?"

"I guess. Far as I can tell."

"That's a good answer. I wish most men were as honest. So remember when you bring the horse home at last to the beautiful lady: Don't sell yourself short. Or her either."

"No ma'am. I ain't goin to."

"Didn't I just get through asking you not to call me ma'am? This is almost the twenty-first century and I'm not the type, anyway."

The agreement between us called for John-Wayne and me to accompany the brigada, led by Albert, as far as the border, where they would free us and turn over the horse—for nothing. It was all wasted caution on their part, and time on ours, but the alternative being summary execution we guessed we could stand it, having wasted most of a whole summer already. One way or another I was a prisoner of love and she for her part had reasons of her own, as I understood it, for keeping me around.

It was peaceful in the mountains where the daily monsoons grew the grasses tall and lush for the horses, mules, and burros, taken from the corral and picketed around the perimeter of the camp each morning and evening, to graze on. There was plenty of game in the area, and after Albert and I shot a big cow elk and packed the quarters into camp the men smoked and dried the meat to carry with us on the trip into Mexico. Once it was made clear to them that we were part of the camp their hostile attitude fell away and they accepted us—to the extent anyway that any Mexican mestizo ever accepts having a tall blue-eyed, red-faced yanqui around. One way or another we got along, which is really all that matters between human beings. I taught the men to play horseshoes after collecting the dropped ones scattered around the camp and played the few Mexican songs I knew on the harmonica for them as we sat drinking coffee after sundown. We were careful about lights after dark, which explained the stones around and over the separate camp fires, and gunfire was prohibited except in emergencies. So was shouting and calling out in a carrying voice. Some nights though, following supper, a few men with guitars and one with a banjo strummed their instruments gently while the guerillas, seated cross-legged on the ground around the hooded fires, swayed in time to the music. Mainly they played the sad, soft songs out of Old Mexico, or corrido—the protest ballads of modern Mexico—or, other times, Indian melodies. Carmen and Humberto, who always ate with the men, stayed to listen, and John-Wayne and I did too, after we were invited to take our meals with the brigada. Once, in a surge of good feeling, I gave them "Kathleen Mavourneen" a cappella after having played the melody through first, which failed somehow to convey the green isle of Erin effectively to these sons of Montezuma.

Among the musicians one man—dark and thin with a narrow gypsy face and a bladed nose—played excellent flamenco guitar. Flamenco is no good played and sung guardedly, at something like the decibel level of a noisy lullaby, but he did a fine job even so of conveying the metallic clash and the controlled vocal scream that is flamenco. The men—seated bolt upright in the wavering half-light of the fires like galvanized demons—loved it, while Carmen at the start became instantly rigid as if holding herself still while she stared across the flames at the gypsy. The gitano seemed to be addressing her directly, his thin mouth gaping between gleaming eyes piercing out above the nose that hooked forward like an eagle's beak to grab her.

"¡He, Carmen!" someone cried in a hushed voice.

"¡Bravo, Carmen!"

"¡Ándale, Carmen!"

The brigada, gathered around the big fire, went on calling out to her until she jumped up at last from beside Humberto. Laughing and running her hands through her hair, Carmen struck a pose suddenly before the flames. She held it for a long moment, her arms raised above her head, her profile cutting straight across the firelight, her eyes shut. Then she opened them wide, and began to dance.

Carmen began in a sequence of slow formal poses, a straight aristocratic figure vaguely backlit by the flames, surrounded by wild men and the wilder wilderness beyond them. The gypsy adapted himself to her tempo as she accelerated it, breaking out from those Cleopatra stances into flaunting abandoned movements, a proud queen joining in the bacchanal. Acquiring momentum, she created somehow an illusion of swirling skirts and the clack and clatter of castenets in the fingers of her flying hands.

"¡Ándale, Carmen!" the men shouted again.

Someone standing at the edge of the circle that had closed up around her and the fire tossed a bouquet of asters in her direction. The flowers landed near her feet and she bent and swept them up in one long unbroken musical gesture and thrust one stem through her hair behind the right ear, as the men shouted out once more. The whole camp was in an uproar when the gypsy player switched from falsetto to full voice. His voice sounded ragged and torn the way that all flamenco singers sound and that seems to be the inevitable result flamenco singing has on the human voice until you hear the young singers, and they sound that way too. I guess you can't wail and grunt and sob and snarl and yodel your way through a big song and sound like Pavarotti while you're doing it. The louder the gypsy sang the louder he played and the faster Carmen danced, until it was like a whole guitar orchestra chasing after a single dancer who whirled always just out of reach, leading the camp on to madness and beautiful destruction. She plucked the aster from behind her ear and the brigada cheered as she placed the stem between her teeth. Carmen was perspiring in the humid night; wisps of hair were plastered against her forehead and sweat ran down her throat and under the collar of her blouse. Humberto watched her with fixed eyes and slightly parted lips—obscenely, as if she was a creature of his own imagination, held in existence by his will alone. Carmen was a spinning top that can only spin faster and faster and never stop—when suddenly the gypsy's guitar ceased in a crash of silence, and Carmen with it. Panting and radiant, she swept the cheering audience with her glorious eyes, then tossed the stem to John-Wayne who went white in the face as he stared at the flower lying almost in his lap. Laughing and whistling, the men applauded him lustily.

"¡Órale, muchacho, agárralo, agárralo!" they shouted.

Redfaced now, he took the stalk up and held the blossom with both hands before his nose. Humberto smiled along with the rest of the men, but it wasn't the kind of smile you get rich selling Fords with.

"I'm glad it wasn't me she accidentally threw flowers to," I told John-Wayne when Carmen and Humberto had retired to their tent and the men were damping the fires for the night.

"It wasn't no accident. It's me she's in love with." John-Wayne gazed adoringly upon the aster stalk. The stem was broken in a couple of places but the long lavender petals surrounding the yellow eyes like lashes were fresh and lovely still. "You're too old for her, Dude."

"Isn't it the truth," I said.

"What about your lady back home, anyways?" John-Wayne wanted to know.

"What about her?"

"Don't you love her no more?"

"Of course I love her."

"You can't love two women at the same time. Least, that's what you're always tellin me."

"And who am I supposed to be in love with now?"

"You know who, man."

"Well" I said. "Yes. I suppose I do know."

"That ain't what you would call shiverous, is it?"

"It may not be up to the ideal, exactly. Look who's talking, by the way."

"It's different with me, I'm sowin my wild oaks still. You're an old man already."

"Do you imagine that's a real difference?" I asked.

"With you, they're goin to get cut down most of the time," John-Wayne said.

I let him have the last word, then. Nobody grown up ever got anywhere trying to argue anything with the smug, unconquerable arrogance of condescending youth.

A day or two short of a week after Carmen danced a plane flew over the camp. The brigada was at breakfast around the fires flaming pale in the early morning light when we heard it come droning in over the green mountains and watched it pass overhead on a straight unswerving course. It was a small single-engine job with an over-swept wing, glinting dark against the high yellow sky. We were still listening to the sound of it boring away to the southeast when Humberto came from corrals, walking fast in the direction of the sidewall tent.

"Che must have got up with a bad conscience this morning," I said in a low voice to John-Wayne. I had begun calling him Che—behind his back, of course—for Che Guevara, the Bolivian revolutionary hero who Humberto had shaken hands with as a kid and idolized ever since.

"How come, Dude?"

"He thinks that plane's looking for him."

"He's crazy, man. It's just an airplane."

"Nothing is just anything to a paranoid. We'll know in a few minutes, though."

It took a little longer than a few minutes for Humberto to get over to our tent but he got, finally. He seemed nervous and apprehensive, but more than anything he looked mad. For the first time in two weeks he carried an assault rifle as well as the pistol he always wore in a shoulder holster under his armpit.

"Ven conmigo," Humberto told me roughly. To John-Wayne he added, "Sólo él, pues tú, ¡quédate aquí!"

He took me at one of those forced marches of his to the tent, grasping my arm above the elbow as we went along. Nearing the tent he let go the arm and we went through the open flap affably together, like Stonewall Jackson and Pete Longstreet having a strategy meeting. Carmen sat on the edge of the cot bed with a cup of tea in one hand as she smoothed the map spread across her knees with the other.

"Buenos días," she said, not looking up from the map. It was one of those big folding ones, in several colors and drawn to a large scale, the Forest Service prints up for hunters, backpackers, and the general tourist trade.

"Buenos días," I told her.

"Coffee?" she asked.

"Certainly."

"Does it feel to you a little chilly this morning, or is it just me?"

"It's just you," I said.

Humberto, not liking the familiar tone, glared.

"You don't think it's getting to be winter up here?" she persisted.

I laughed.

"Not for another two months, at least. Maybe three."

"Here in the mountains there's so little to do but drink coffee. It sets everyone's nerves on edge. Humberto, give Jeb the rest of the pot and start a fresh one going, por favor."

Humberto emptied the coffee pot into a tin cup and thrust it at me as if he would have preferred to fling it in my face. He refilled the pot with water from a collapsible bladder and placed it on the little stove, which was putting out an almost intolerable heat. It gets pretty cold down in Argentina from what I've heard, so it must have been a couple of years in Mexico City had thinned her blood some.

"Did you see the plane go over an hour ago?" Carmen inquired in a casual tone.

"Sure."

"What was it?"

"Hard to tell with the sun coming up. It looked like it could have been a Cessna, or maybe a Maule, to me."

"I mean—*whose* was it?"

"I wouldn't have any idea."

Humberto said something in that guttural dialect I hadn't made a stab at trying to understand yet.

"Could they possibly have been friends of yours?"

It was what I had been expecting since I first heard that airplane.

"Not even possibly," I told her, innocent looking as a schoolgirl at her quinceañera.

"Humberto thinks the opposite. Why were they flying low like that?"

"He wasn't particularly low. We're pretty high up here, you know. It takes a powerful engine to climb very far above these mountains."

That was what I told her, but all the time I was thinking fast. In Mexico where only the government, drug smugglers, and bandidos are armed, nobody hunts big game except rich Americanos from Chicago and Dallas.

"Oh," I said, "it was probably the game warden taking a count of the elk populations back here."

It was an honest guess and, for all I know, an accurate one, too. They never could have imagined, naturally, that with the coming of fall the wilderness Albert Orsino had chosen as the summer refuge for their little guerilla band would be invaded by an army of a few thousand hunters, raising elaborate camps that would have gratified bear-hunting Russian princes and stag-hunting German noblemen, fanning out, on foot and on horseback, across thirty-three million acres of rugged, pristine country and all of them armed to the teeth with high-caliber rifles and powered by alcoholic stimulants. It's the Western way, but it had taken Humberto to concentrate my mind for me and focus it—briefly—on something else besides a woman.

---

It took the brigada two days to pack itself up and move out. The hushed activity began long before dawn and continued until nearly midnight, filling the camp with the stamp of horses, the huff of collapsing canvas, and the chink of cook things being gathered in and stowed. The camouflage netting came down late in the second day, and after that you could smell the nervousness in camp. The men walked about gazing up at the sky as if they expected it to fill with bomber squadrons flying overhead. But this wasn't the Spanish Civil War and the only thing there was to see was now and again a hawk or eagle spiraling in slow circles, and beyond it a thin stratospheric haze from forest fires burning away to the west in California or Nevada. With the monsoons about finished for the year, the fire season stood waiting in the wings to burn up what hadn't been washed away yet.

I didn't see much of Carmen except when she rode past on Tortuga, who looked as if he might be enjoying himself. The rest of the time she spent poring over maps with Albert. John-Wayne and I tried to help in striking camp, but there wasn't a lot we could do to be useful. The brigada had their system down pat and our attempts only interfered with their system. We were still asleep when the lieutenant came for us on the third morning and marched us across camp to the corral where the animals stood tied in the red light from the fires while the men loaded the packs onto them. Among the brigada only Carmen, Humberto, and the two or three other brass rode, the rankers being mounted on donkeys, mules, and burros. From the number of animals rigged with crossbucks to which the pantries, tents, and rolled camo netting had been secured with diamond hitches, I guessed there was going to be a number of footsloggers as well and it was an easy conclusion that we would be among them when I noticed Quixote and Doña Ana saddled and tied behind the other horses. The cooks were already washing up the breakfast pots and stowing them but we were given what was left of the maize porridge, along with cold tortillas and a cup each of cold scorched coffee. When we were done eating we gave the bowls back and sat on a couple of lava rocks, waiting for something to happen.

At a little past dawn Carmen rode up on Tortuga. She was dressed in woolen army pants that were going to be too hot for comfort in about an hour and a khaki sweater with a camouflage poncho over it, and she looked very beautiful up there astride the prancing horse, handling him with complete possession while the dawn breeze lifted his tail and riffled the black mane. Her cheeks were flushed above the arch of bone, her eyes were bright, and her dark hair was falling out from under the black beret she wore pulled down over her little ears.

"That's one fine-looking horse you have there, Señora," I told her.

Carmen smiled.

"Thank you. I'm enjoying him. For now, anyway."

"How far are we going today?"

She looked coy.

"That's Albert's decision. Not mine."

"I take it John-Wayne and I are hoofing it?"

Carmen frowned.

"What gave you that idea?"

"Our horses are tied along with the others over there."

"Humberto thought you should walk. I informed him you could be trusted with your own horses."

"Thanks."

"Thank *you* for being model prisoners of war," she answered crisply, and trotted off.

Humberto rode up twenty minutes later on the buckskin, leading Quixote and Ana with ropes. Both were outfitted with our tack and carried heavy canvas packs belonging to the brigada behind the cantle.

"¡A caballo, vamos!" Humberto ordered in a poisonous voice, speaking from the side of his face. "She wishes you to ride with us."

The brigada was already in motion as we rode forward with him along the line. It looked less like an army than an Outward Bound expedition and I had a hard time, as we passed along the column of short, dark, mostly beardless men, remembering that these ragtag little foreigners meant business—the woman most of all. Humberto would have shot you for looking crossways at him, or watching an airplane fly overhead, or just for no reason at all, but he was not serious the way the woman was. He meant meanness, while she had no meanness or hatred in her at all—only resolve. That did not make her any less dangerous, of course—it made her more so, whether as the Eva Perón of Mexico or the leader of a dirty little revolutionary brigade in the sun-stricken, snake-ridden deserts of Chihuahua and Sonora. Every beautiful, brilliant, and competent woman is dangerous, but Carmen Dominguín's dangerousness had another element to it, and that was the male element added to the female one. The quality of her character was recognized by her men and also by Humberto, who I believe was actually afraid of her—and not just for her sexual power and social position. If it is true that the highest type of human being combines essential characteristics of both sexes in a single personality...well, that would explain Carmen, all by itself.

She rode at the head of the brigada behind Albert who ranged in advance, carrying the poncho neatly rolled and tied in the saddle strings and the automatic rifle slung under her left leg. Tortuga paddled along at his rolling platypus gait, sleeker and fitter-looking from the two weeks we'd spent in camp and plainly self-aware where his superior equine status was concerned. From our first acquaintance I'd noticed his responsiveness to feminine beauty mounted between his withers and kidneys, and how it caused him to show off like a circus horse. Humberto rode beside her, more or less, while John-Wayne and I kept right behind. The column had advanced a couple of hundred yards already when Carmen looked back at us, smiling.

"Of course, you were entitled to your horses," she said. "We regard you more as reluctant guests than prisoners of war, anyway."

"Thanks. I'm glad to hear it."

"Don't thank me. Thank Humberto."

"Thanks a lot," I said.

Humberto did not reply, or even nod.

"There were two gentlemen in particular who didn't want to see you take those horses," Carmen added. I supposed she referred to a couple of the out-of-luck footsloggers bringing up the rear.

The shadow line drew higher on the mountainside as the morning sunlight advanced downslope ahead of the brigada descending by the long draw cutting down to the bowl where we'd become disoriented by the hailstorm. It was one of those clear September mornings that seem to exist outside of the seasonal cycle and even the weather itself; an escape into an eternity of soft blue cloudless skies, even temperatures, and no wind to push a haze that was compounded again today with the brown smoke that was too high for us to scent yet. Slouched lazily in the saddle as we rode, John-Wayne was smiling—smugly, it seemed to me.

"What do you have to be so pleased about this morning?"

He looked up and away from the horse's neck, grinning so that his eyes nearly disappeared behind his thinned cheeks.

"All the guys back home are in school this mornin—right this very minute."

The column halted twenty minutes later at the top of the bowl, from where we looked west across the jumbled blue-green blocks and bergs standing against a pale sky.

"What lovely country," Carmen said. "Like Mexico—and then, not at all like Mexico."

"It *was* Mexico, not so very long ago," I reminded her.

"Did you imagine I'd forgotten that?" she asked, drily.

"Mexico or not Mexico, what's the difference?" Albert wanted to know. "The mountains don't care. The desert don't care, neither."

All that day he led us on a southwesterly course through the mountains, following one drainage downhill into another among the great white-barked sycamore trees and the green live oaks and the alder. Albert rode on the tail of his spine, loose-hipped in the saddle, looking half asleep with his hat pulled forward over his half-shut eyes except for his forward chin and his slowly turning head as he surveyed the country ahead. He appeared completely relaxed and at the same time totally alert, like a wild animal at home in its own territory. The sky remained blue overhead behind the pinkish smoke, and by noon the wind was still not up. The men traveled so quietly that, riding near the head of the column, I could hear the whining flies and the chink of snaffle bits as the horses tossed their heads to chase them. Carmen rode wonderfully, pliant and supple in the saddle, moving with the horse and smiling all around herself and at the sky, liking what she saw of the wilderness. As the day warmed she had removed her sweater to go bare-armed through the sunshine and shadow. Her arms were brown and smooth, shapely with developed muscle. Once, looking back, she caught my eye and smiled gayly, giving me something to think about on the long miles down the dark green piñon and juniper canyons.

Late in the afternoon, with the mountains behind us, we came to a bench in the foothills above the valley of the Gila River where Albert called a halt in a juniper forest above a wash. We had made better than twenty-five miles that day, he said. At his command the brigada dismounted from their animals, threw down their packs, slung their rifles in the trees, and stretched themselves on the firm, warm ground. Carmen allowed them to lie there for a quarter of an hour before she ordered the burros and mules to be watered and cared for and the pantries unloaded. It was much warmer now on account of the lower elevation, making the tents and bedrolls unnecessary. The wash, bedded with gravel and brush, appeared dry but when Albert set a couple of men to digging into the clay and gravel bottom they hit water running in a subterranean channel three or four feet down. The foragers brought in wood and soon we had a fire burning in the camp. Overhead, the smoke that had been accumulating in the sky since noon had thickened to a greasy pall, darkening the sun and smearing the blue evening sky already coming in the east behind the mountains. The acrid smell was pervasive, almost blotting the pungent one from the single cookfire.

"How far off is the fire?" Carmen asked Albert.

"I don't know. A long way. Far enough."

"It looks as if it were burning just behind that ridge over there."

"It wouldn't be worth while us tryin to run, if it was."

He went off with John-Wayne to bring in more wood. The boys, who hadn't spoken much to one another during the two weeks in camp in the mountains, had renewed their friendship on the long ride out this afternoon. I was seated on a rock, trying to look busy, when Carmen came up holding a lariat coiled in her hand.

"Come along with me while I picket my—I mean, our—horse," she invited.

We walked together to the corrals the men were busy throwing together, stretching lengths of wire and rope between the shaggy trees. Tortuga stood snubbed with the other horses, dozing in the afternoon sun. He opened his eyes as Carmen approached but he did not look at her, and he did not appear to notice me at all. She untied him, and the three of us walked uphill to a grassy knoll screened by alligator juniper, out of sight from the busy camp.

"Unlike his namesake, Juárez is an aristocrat," Carmen said. "He deserves to be by himself at the end of the day. He doesn't have anything to say to the equine hoi polloi."

"So he isn't a revolutionary after all?"

"He's essentially a philosopher, I think—like Albert."

"Are you a revolutionary—essentially?"

"No," she said, "essentially, I'm a woman."

Carmen ran the straight end of the lariat around the base of a juniper tree, through the loop, and tied it into the halter ring under the horse's chin while I held his head. I let go when she finished and Tortuga stepped forward on the rope and thrust his nose into a clump of bunch grass.

"Albert tells me it's a week's ride down to the border. Only one week from tonight and you'll have your horse back."

"If he was mine to give, he'd be yours already."

Carmen shook her head.

"No," she said. "There are plenty of Peruvian Pasos down south. Besides, you're committed to fulfilling a promise. You mustn't give up now, when success is within reach at last. It isn't really John-Wayne's love the horse belongs to. Is it?"

"No," I told her. "It's not."

We'd been climbing slowly as we talked through ripened grasses to the crest of the knoll from where we had a view of the big cottonwoods down on the Gila, the lights of Cliff and Buckhorn coming on now in the river valley, and beyond the valley the grassy hills rolling up to the mountains standing flat against the smoke darkened horizon. The afternoon wind had died away and a pleasant breeze sprang up, lifting the hair from her damp forehead.

"So much fire worries me," Carmen said. "If we become cut off from Mexico and the authorities catch us on American soil, Mexico City will claim we're operating with the support of the U.S. government. It would be very bad propaganda for the revolutionary parties."

"I wouldn't worry if I were you. The entire West is on fire every year now, and no one seems to think much about it."

Standing elbow to elbow in the tall grass, we watched the flaming sun plunge suddenly through shelves of smoke.

"Is she very beautiful?" Carmen asked.

"Is who beautiful?"

"Your friend. Juárez's owner."

"Jody's a good-looking woman. She's beautiful to me."

Carmen laughed.

"My experience is that men are always looking to move on to the next thing. They'd rather not stay with what they have and try to make something of it. Somehow, I feel you're not that sort of man. Because you really are a romantic at heart. Aren't you, Jeb Ryder?"

"I don't know if romantic's the word. I do know that, to me, life without a woman you can love is like spending three-score and ten years sealed in a space capsule, flying between someplace that didn't exist when you left it and another that isn't going to exist when you get there."

Carmen gave me a closer look.

"Do you know you have a rather large speck in your left eye? Let me remove it for you. Just hold still."

She took a folded bandana from her shirt pocket and placed a steadying hand on my shoulder as if I was a boy of ten.

"And try not to blink."

I took her in my arms and kissed her then. Her body in the grip of my digging fingers felt soft and muscular, firm and yielding at the same time as our backs arched in and our bellies pressed together. Our mouths joined and her strong little tongue ran in as far as my back teeth. She withdrew suddenly, placed her hands palm-forward on my chest, and pushed me hard away.

"We ought not to have done that," Carmen said. "In convent school, the nuns used to teach us you're tempted from the moment you make up your mind to talk to a man."

"I'm sorry," I told her. "I wouldn't want to tempt a lady. Would I?"

"You didn't tempt me, I tempted you. I meant to—fatally perhaps, unless both of us are very, very careful."

For a long moment we looked at each other in the sultry light.

"Well," Carmen said. "I suppose we should getting on down to camp."

---

By sunup next day we'd ridden for two hours already across the valley of the Gila and into the steep grassy hills beyond the paved highway between Glenwood and Silver City. Looking back I saw the black headwall of the split, eroded mountains with the sun rising behind them, the river winding between cottonwood trees and the peaceful ranches spread out around it—old adobe houses surrounded by windbreaks of more trees, the barns with their gently sloping tin roofs, and windmills on iron tripods standing above cattle grazing in the meadows. The hills ahead showed red under the thin grass cover between splashes of acid green manzanita, the darker clumps of live oak and juniper, and the soap yucca whose stalks the men hacked off with their machetes as they rode past, tossing the rattling globes—all that was left of the milky white flowers—at one another. The soft soil was precarious underfoot as we humped across the steeps on the diagonal and dropped over the top of the frontal ridge into the swale beyond where, out of sight of civilization, Albert called a halt to rest the animals beside a well-made section of new fence. Humberto turned in the saddle with his hand gripping the cantle to look back at me.

"¿Vas a reparar esta cerca también?" he asked, sneering.

"Claro."

Mending fencelines Albert had been compelled to cut on our march across private land was an issue between Humberto and me. He resented the time it took to make a casual repair job, but I insisted on taking it anyway. Although Carmen acted as though it was nothing more than wrangling between blood brothers, our quarrel obviously made her plenty nervous.

"¡Abajo los hacendados ricos!" Humberto declared. Down with the rich ranchers.

"In your country, perhaps," I told him in English; "not in mine."

Albert snipped the wire and the brigada started forward again. I sat Quixote by the fence, and when the last man was through I made the repair job. It was good work, and I was getting pretty quick at it too. When all three strands were tight and strong I put the horse forward at a lope toward the head of the column where Carmen, looking back across her shoulder at me, smiled slightly and shook her head.

"Imagine it's your daddy's hacienda," I suggested.

She faced jauntily ahead once more and set her right hand on her thigh.

"The only thing I care to imagine is getting my men back to Mexico safely."

All that day we rode toward the dark line of the western mountains, losing sight of them as we dropped into the swales between the parallel ridges and finding them again as we topped out on the ridgelines. By afternoon we had reached hilly but more rolling country, lush and green from the monsoons and blowy with the feathered mesquite and the black-eyed daisies growing in bunches, where the wind blew cool from under banked, wet-looking clouds lying above the mountains. Farther on were clumps and stands of alligator juniper laden with clusters of the blue waxen berries, and more oak growing in copses on the hillsides. John-Wayne had moved up to ride with Albert, the two of them appearing like Indian scouts in silhouette against the sky before dropping down into the cloud-shadowed greenery again. Away off I spied white ranch houses shaded by green cottonwoods beside yellow meadows and what I guessed was the hamlet of Mule Creek, New Mexico half concealed by a grove of trees. We made camp just inside the pine forest where the mountains began in steep hills cut by canyons carving through a whitish soil of clay and limestone, and Albert and John-Wayne took out a hunting party in search of camp meat. The men had the pack animals hobbled and a fire started when a single shot sounded from deeper in the woods above the camp. Forty minutes later John-Wayne and Albert returned on foot ahead of the two guerillas leading a mule with a big buck mule deer slung across its back. From the Great White Hunter expression on his face and the blood mark between and just above the eyes, I knew right off who the shooter had been. Albert must have lent him his own rifle to use.

"Am I a shot, or ain't I?" John-Wayne demanded as they came up. "When I shoot a gun I *shoot*—I don't miss, man. *Pow!*—his dick is in the dirt."

"You'll be in the dirt in about half a second," I told him, "if Albert and I have to listen to any more of the white-boy talk."

Boys will be boys, it doesn't matter if they were raised in Salt Lake City, Utah, or Tuba City, Arizona. Human beings, the male sex in particular, love cause and effect—making things happen—and the more violence and firepower they use to do it, the better.

---

The copper colored sun was already above the land line, climbing behind a haze of brown smoke when I woke the next morning. I lay on my side watching the men on the grub line rub their reddened eyes as they shuffled toward the fire holding the tin plates against their legs, and sat up in the bag. John-Wayne was a shapeless rag bundle half under a scrub oak tree, snorting and jerking like a hog digging for acorns. I threw handfuls of the ones I found around at his head until the snoring quit and he rolled over in the sand.

"Wake up. We overslept."

John-Wayne raised himself on one elbow and rubbed his face with his sleeve.

"Dang smoke hurts my eyes."

"I don't see how. You've had them shut for the past nine hours."

He took the arm away and stared at his feet sticking up under the blanket. His grimed face was framed by a mane of greasy uncut hair falling over the torn sun-faded T-shirt with the rubberized applique WE ARE THE OVERLORDS coming away from it in pieces. Pink dust caked his earlobes and traced his forehead wrinkles and the smile lines beside his eyes, and his hands were blackened like a miner's with dirt and charcoal. A sunburned Indian is as rare as a frostbit Eskimo, but the broad end of John-Wayne's nose and the skin over the high cheekbones was red and peeling.

"You look godawful," I told him.

"You're sort of skanky yourself, Dude."

"Like something they pulled out of a hole in the earth."

"Like what Indian dogs have been eatin on for a month."

"It's what love does to a man, remember."

"I give up countin how many days since I had me a hot shower."

John-Wayne lay back down on the ground and drew the blanket over his eyes.

"Get up, now," I said, "before we miss breakfast and have to travel all day on empty stomachs."

Carmen was bringing Tortuga up when we went for the horses. I did not call out to her over the heavy pack across my shoulder and she looked away with a self-conscious expression as she passed by leading the horse. John-Wayne and I saddled up and secured the packs and sat in the shade of a spreading alligator juniper that was not as old as Methuselah maybe but could probably have given us a tip about how to survive a second Flood, while Humberto rode hollering around camp and the brigada prepared to hump itself. We were getting a late start and I knew from their voices and the looks they gave him that Carmen and Humberto blamed Albert for the delay. Albert sat his horse at the edge of the forest looking away to the mountains as if they were where his strength came from, oblivious to the commotion around him in a way that drove Carmen wild. In the rush to break camp she'd neglected to brush her hair out and even to wash her face, which was streaked with sweat and rigid with exasperation. A couple of times I heard her bark at Humberto—once in front of the men, at which he gave her a killing look. The smoke seemed to be working on her to the point where she was not really herself anymore.

It was rough going all that day in the mountains where the canyons were deep, steep-sided, and grown up with bristlecone, junipers, and oaks on the southern aspects and Ponderosa pine on the northern ones. The forest floor beneath the tall trees was brown and springy with the fallen needles, and looking downhill through deep shade between red-barked trunks you glimpsed well-watered creeks meandering in grassy bottoms where a few lonely cattle grazed. Across canyon, through the dark pine branches, splashes of sunlight glared on the rocks and bushes and the blades of Spanish bayonet thrusting between them. Albert would follow the ridgeline for a way, then drop down into a bottom and continue along the fork until he found a way up to the next ridge over. Plenty of elk and deer sign around meant there would be no need of rustling a beeve for supper. We pushed hard all afternoon and into early evening—well past the usual halting time—before Albert drew rein abruptly and turned in the saddle, pointing ahead of himself. He slipped down from the horse like a cat and we dismounted after him in a hurry as he drew his rifle from the scabbard and walked quickly back to where we sat our horses.

"Puercos," Albert said in a whisper.

"¿Puercos?" Humberto repeated, as if he were speaking to a crazy man. He was a city boy from Hermosillo, a revolutionary theorist who thought wild pigs grew on farms, if not at the local Piggly Wiggly.

"Puercos salvajes," Albert told him. "Valen más que frijoles y tortillas rancias." Better than beans and stale tortillas.

*"¡No!"* Carmen ordered him. She was looking at Humberto. "Haríamos demasiado ruido."

"There isn't anyone within fifty miles to hear it," I said.

She turned on me then, contemptuously.

"You're not the one guiding this party."

"It's the guide who wants to shoot the pigs," I told her.

Humberto handed the reins of his horse to Carmen. He walked back to the head of the column and spoke briefly with the lieutenant before he and two of the men dismounted and came forward with him, lifting their rifles off their shoulders.

"¿Dónde están los puercos?" Humberto asked Albert.

Alberto pointed once more toward a gravel wash cutting down through a shallow canyon three or four hundred yards out. Juniper grew thickly on either side of the wash and the steeply eroded banks were bordered with agave and yucca.

"Allí están—en ese arroyo. ¡Muchos puercos, señor! ¡Bastan para una fiesta grande!"

Humberto, observing the wash through fieldglasses, said he didn't see any pigs.

"O sí, señor, muchos puercos - ¡muchos! Detrás de esos palos ahí abajo."

Humberto, not knowing if he should take this business of wild pigs seriously or not, looked harassed. He tucked the fieldglasses inside his shirt and turned to Carmen, who sat looking down on him from the horse.

"Okay," she said.

Humberto shrugged and gestured vaguely in the direction of the wash. "Está bien," he told the men. "¡Vamos!"

John-Wayne put up his eyebrows at me. They still had our guns, of course.

"Come along," I said. "A real hunter appreciates the hunt even when he isn't allowed to shoot."

We walked with Albert while he explained how he'd spotted javelina moving down from the head of the wash through the trees. They were a big pod, thirty or forty animals strung out in a line a hundred yards long or more, going for water. Because javelina have very good hearing and a keen sense of smell while being nearly blind, his plan was to keep downwind of them, ambush them in a flanking movement, and pick off enough pigs to supply the brigada with a roast pork dinner.

"The meat tastes okay if you soak it in sody water before you cook it," Albert said. "Course, we ain't got no sody water with us."

We climbed down to the arroyo holding to tree branches to keep from sliding in the loose sand and gravel, the guerillas cradling their automatics in their arms. After Humberto spoke to his lieutenant, the man relieved the other two of their pistols and handed them to John-Wayne and me. Then Albert organized the line according to plan and started us forward, going twenty feet apart, toward the wash.

The bank undercut the trees along the arroyo, exposing their roots and tipping them over above the watershed. Where no trees grew there was squawberry and sarvisberry, thick enough in places to obstruct gunfire, to screen us. Getting into position I nearly stepped on a baby rattlesnake, only six inches long with a single button on his tail and dangerous as sin without the warning rattle and enough experience to know to control the venom charge. The light was bright in the canyon but within the trees the air felt cool, musty with the smell of the shagged juniper bark and only bird calls and the scratch of squirrels' claws along the tree branches to violate the silent stillness. I checked the safety on the pistol and settled forward on my knees in the dust to wait, and after what seemed like a long time I heard a rustling sound down in the wash. The sound was followed by a small cloud of white dust carried on a down-canyon breeze and right after the cloud the lead boar, coming at a determined trot and holding his snout low.

He was a big boar, massive forequarters tapering to the wasp waist and the narrow hind ones, his pig eyes darting sideways from the short yellow tusks, his brindled coat shagged stiff as the quills on a porcupine. His movements were intent but not hurried, alert but without suspicion, and the small heart-shaped prints appeared straight and unswerving behind him in the sand, despite the quick sideways movements of his head. He was followed almost immediately by two more boars trotting abreast of one another and after them others of the pod, scattered more widely across the wash. I sat back on my heels and watched them through an opening in the squawberry bushes. An entire pig army seemed to pass in review in front of me before I heard Albert's pistol fire away to the left down the wash where the lead animal would have arrived by now, followed instantly by a terrific crash of gunfire all along the line.

I set the pistol sights on the first pig to appear in the hole in the brush and dropped it, and the one behind it too. Down in the wash pigs were running and dashing about, trying to escape from the arroyo into the forest. They leaped and fell back, leaped again, and crashed into the steep banks, bringing down falls of gravel and clay on their backs and shoulders. I fired again and missed, fired another time and did not miss. The gravel bed was spotted with crimson and littered with twitching gray-black bodies. Lead slugs passing clean through the pigs and striking the opposite bank raised puffs of dust that drifted and mixed with the clouds kicked up by racing hooves and the madly hurtling bodies. The pigs never had a chance, and when we quit shooting at last and climbed down into the wash we had killed seventeen of them and wounded eight more. The steel barrel of the pistol was scorching to the touch. I checked the clip which had four shells remaining in it and handed it back to the lieutenant, who accepted it without looking at me and returned it to its owner. Gathering the carcasses I all at once felt terrible, as if a tragedy had occurred. The pigs hadn't been doing anyone any harm, and they were no good to eat anyway.

John-Wayne stood in the wash amid the carnage admiring the shiny automatic pistol he'd been issued.

"I shot three of them pigs," he said proudly when he saw me.

"Good for you."

"How many did *you* shoot, Dude?"

"I don't know," I told him. I still had that empty, desperate feeling of looking straight down to the bottom of the universe, finding nothing there worth living for, and being hardly able to bear it.

"I'm goin to get me an automatic pistol like this one they loaned me."

"Where are you expecting to get it from? You don't find goodhearted Mexican revolutionaries giving them away. Unless you sign up for their revolución, of course."

"And lay out on the hard ground ever night and eat pigs and beans for supper? It ain't our war anyway, man."

"No," I said, "it surely isn't."

The little pigs were heavy even after we'd field dressed them. Albert poked around until he found a tanque half a mile from the arroyo, the sand around it beaten down by hundreds of heart-shaped hooves. We made camp under an overhang of sandstone cliff a few hundred yards away and soon the smokes of the camp fires were ascending against the sheer rock face, curling out around the rocky lip and rising toward the smokey sky above it. The atmosphere was less heavy than at sunrise, while dark streaks of smoke down Mexico way showed how the wind had shifted south during the afternoon.

"Have the fires reached as far as the Sierra Madre, do you think?" Carmen asked. She was holding the gutted corpse of a small pig by the heels and her camouflaged pants were wet and stained with the bloodied water.

"Not a chance of it. That smoke's at least twenty thousand feet high. It's traveled hundreds of miles down here, from the northwest. It is isn't anything we have to worry about, believe me."

Often when I thought I was alone I would find Carmen suddenly at my side, or close by. She had grown quieter and more thoughtful in the few weeks we had known each other, and she looked thinner. Although she had the social confidence as well as the bravery not to be intimidated by anything merely human, Mother Nature certainly was capable of putting the fear of God in her. Smuggling scores of heavily armed guerillas across the international border was no fireman's picnic, of course, but I believed I detected that some deeper, more personal concern was eating her besides. No one was going to shoot me for hoping, anyway. Right now, we were standing downhill from camp where I'd been skinning out pig carcasses while she washed them with water from the tanque and John-Wayne carried the meat up to Albert for spitting over the fires.

"Maybe they dropped an atom bomb on California," Carmen suggested.

I shook my head, trying to dislodge the vision of the massacred pigs from it.

"It isn't going to be as simple as that. The world will just burn a little bit further, year after year, without anybody ever really noticing."

"You could be a revolutionary yourself, with a little training," she said.

"No I couldn't."

"He who is not with us is against us. That makes you the enemy, then."

"Actually I'm a revolutionary party of one—fighting against myself, mostly."

"And where," Carmen asked," do you expect that to get you?"

"Not very far, I suppose."

"Come with us into Mexico and help burn Mexico City. We can take care of Phoenix later, if you wish."

"Not me. I'm looking for a stolen horse."

"You already found him," she reminded me.

Of course, the javelina meat was inedible. We ate it anyway, the guerillas tearing meat from the roasted carcasses with their teeth and fingers. The fires played a red light against the backdrop of cliff where human shadows, magnified, moved like giants emerged from the earth, mute except for the rip and tear of the half-burned, half-raw flesh of wild swine. Watching their feast was like being present at the creation of a new world, terrible and glorious at the same time.

"It ain't McDonald's," John-Wayne said as he stuck a blackened pork crisp in his mouth, "but it's better than beans."

"You're crazy. Beans done any way are always better than anything McDonald's has to offer."

"That's 'cause McDonald's don't do beans."

I watched as Carmen took a spare rib in her hands and gnawed on it. Her hair was a crow's nest and she looked as wild, dirty, and unkempt as the rest of us. Daddy on his bull ranch in Argentina wouldn't know his little girl now. In addition to her other accomplishments she'd studied ballet for several years in Buenos Aires, I remembered her telling me. Inert except for his hands fumbling between his mouth and the tin plate balanced on his closed-up knees, Humberto was a hairy uncouth shape beside her in the half light.

The first man to know the pigs' revenge was struck down within the hour. Moaning and holding his belly, he staggered from the firelight in a doubled-up position and was violently sick a little way off from camp. By bedtime we had more men on the sick-list, clutching their guts with one hand and loosening their belts with the other as they ran for the privacy of darkness. The worst cases were stomach cramp, keeping the camp awake for hours after we'd rolled ourselves in our blankets on the ground.

"How's the gut?" I asked John-Wayne as we were getting ready to turn in.

"No problemo, Dude. Navajos can eat roadkill, if we have to. 'Course, only a Paiute would *do* somethin totally gross like that."

"You've had plenty of practice anyway, eating at McDonald's."

"Don't mention McDonald's no more. Okay Dude? It makes me homesick just thinkin about it."

"It makes me just plain sick."

"Goodnight Dude."

"Goodnight J-W."

"Brrrrrup."

---

I slept badly on account of the cries of the sick men, people coming and going, and the pain that probed my own guts like a knife, starting around midnight. Later, when the crisis became acute, I fought free of the bedroll and relieved myself behind a large boulder. Finally I returned to camp, lay down, and fell asleep with my face turned up to the waxing moon. Dreaming, I heard the rustle of ghostly pigs in camp, their low inquiring grunts and the tear of tubers torn from the earth. Or perhaps it wasn't a dream. I slept until dawn when I woke all at once and lay still on the hard ground with my knees drawn up to my belly, listening for the sound that had wakened me to come again. Instead there was a generalized commotion and the sound of hushed voices from across the camp.

"What was that?" John-Wayne asked from a few feet away.

"Somebody screamed."

"You mean a girl did?"

"It was a man, of course." (Wasn't it?) "I'm going to find out what's up," I told him.

John-Wayne lay back and pulled the blanket over his head again. "You can tell me all about it later, man."

Four or five men stood around a sleeping bag lying off by itself near a pile of stone rubble fallen from the cliff overhead. There was a man lying inside the bag, and the man was Albert Orsino. His face was whiter than any white man's and rigid as a corpse's. But corpses no longer know fear. Albert looked as if he had wakened from a nightmare only to find it was real and he was face to face with the Devil himself.

"¿Qué pasa?" I inquired.

The men around the bag looked at me and then at Albert again. No one said anything.

"¿Mareado también?"

"Es una culebra," one of the men said in a low voice. A rattlesnake, of course; the mountains were crawling with them.

"¿Y ha sido mordido?"

"Que yo sepa, todavía no."

"¿No?"

"La culebra está en el saco con él," the man explained. In the bag with him. It's every outdoorsman's nightmare.

Albert had wakened some minutes before to find the snake stretched alongside him for warmth. Now he lay petrified, unable to move—or do anything.

"Pobrecito," another of the men added piously.

Albert's left arm was across his chest, the other against his body inside the bag. Albert shut his eyes and sweat sprang on his forehead. He moved the straightened arm just a little, starting at the shoulder.

"¡No te muevas!" the first man told him sharply.

Albert's eyes opened and rolled wildly in his head. His mouth lost its terrible rigidity and began to quiver.

"¡No te muevas!" the men urged together.

Albert gave a series of terrific kicks inside the bag, dragging himself backward at the same time on his free elbow. He was halfway clear when he let out another piercing scream, rolled over onto his stomach, and crawled from the bag on both elbows.

"Ahora sí que le mordió," the first man announced gravely.

While two of the guerillas attended to the wound the others lifted the bag at the closed end and shook the snake out. He was a big evil-looking diamondback, almost as long as Albert and thick as my upper arm at the middle. The men crushed his head with rocks, lifted the body between them, and threw it into a shallow wash a couple of hundred yards from the camp.

Albert was bit in the calf of his right leg. A fang had punctured the big vein and there was nothing to do but make him as comfortable as we could and watch him die. It took him about ten minutes to do it. The poison reached his brain before he had time to swell very badly, but his face became horribly discolored and for the last five minutes he was out of his mind, rolling convulsively on the ground and screaming like someone possessed by a demon. His screams brought John-Wayne running, wearing only his T-shirt and jockey shorts, in time to watch his friend in the final agonies.

We buried Albert in his sleeping bag in a grave three feet deep, with stones piled above it to keep the coyotes from digging the corpse up (maybe) and a rude cross made of sticks bound together stuck into the top of the pile. One of the Indian brigadistas produced a Roman Catholic missal and Carmen read a few prayers over the grave. Just before the shovel men filled it in, John-Wayne pulled a turquoise good-luck charm from his pocket and placed it inside the bag beneath the folded hands. His face was pale and his eyes were shocked and angry, which I guess is how you feel when you're sixteen years old and a thing like this happens. The men looked very serious and Carmen was obviously shaken. She had put on lipstick and brushed her hair—I noticed it had grown out some since we met—for the funeral and her eyes were swollen and red, though there was hardly any smoke in the air this morning. The lieutenant explained to me that Albert's death was the first casualty the brigada had suffered since it was recruited fourteen months before.

We were finishing a silent breakfast an hour later when Carmen walked over, followed by Humberto. Earlier, I'd noticed them having a discussion off by themselves without being particularly curious to know what it was they were discussing. Carmen's hair was a mess again from running her hands through it every minute or so and Humberto was stroking his beard, which I had learned to recognize as a bad sign. She, as usual, went right to the point and did almost all the talking. It was her operation, after all.

"You claim to know something about this part of the country," Carmen told me. "How familiar are you with it—exactly?"

"Well," I said, "I'm not lost."

"Is that meant to be an answer?" she snapped.

"Look," I told her, "if two hundred people—maybe—can claim a working knowledge of southwestern New Mexico based on a lifetime's personal experience, then I'm somewhere in the top one hundred. I'm not the guy to play Buffalo Bill and Kit Carson, but you want the truth and I'm giving it to you."

"Can you find the way down to Mexico from this dreadful—this God-forsaken place?"

"Have you ever been to New York City?" I asked her.

"With my father, several times. Why?"

"Us old wilderness hands and desert rats are like New York cabbies, we can take you anywhere in the West you want to go, by any route you choose. Just say the word and—presto!—you're there."

"The last time I visited New York the driver wore a turban and got lost somewhere between Kennedy Airport and the Waldorf Hotel. The fare would have bought dinner for two at La Grenouille."

"Sure," I told her, "but your man was from Afghanistan. The natives will sometimes turn the meter off to help a lady in distress. They don't charge extra for the gab, either."

Humberto was frowning at me and Carmen never smiled, not even with her eyes.

"Then from here to the border, you're the driver. If you don't have your medallion paid up, we don't want to know about it. Humberto—be sure their weapons are returned to them before we break camp this morning."

It was nearly noon when the brigada got started for Mexico again under a high gray sky without any smoke in it, but instead a hint of fall. John-Wayne and I rode ahead together, followed by Carmen and Humberto with the lieutenant keeping a little behind them at the head of the column. The day was cool and the men's canteens were filled with the warm flat water from the depleted tanque. I took them south through the Stein's Peak mountains for seven hours until the shortened September light caught up with us and Humberto called a halt among the volcanic cones and snags of rock like rusted metal rising around. The only water source was a narrow wash with a couple of inches of scummy green water in it for the animals to drink, but the men had taken advantage of the cooler weather to conserve their supply and we were carrying enough for another day's march yet. This was worn-down country with a dangerous beauty of its own that I, for one, was not in a mood to appreciate this evening. The men, having traveled in silence all afternoon, seemed disgruntled and depressed by Albert Orsino's death. There were beans and tortillas at the end of the chow line and the carnival atmosphere of the evening before had been replaced by a sullen, resentful torpor.

"It's goin to rain tonight," John-Wayne observed.

"So what if it does? You won't melt. And you'll smell a hell of a lot better afterward."

"If I have to eat any more of them beans I'll toot myself to death."

Carmen came up with Tortuga's bridle on her arm. She looked tired and unhappy, as if she too had not recovered from the loss of Albert.

"Such awful country this is," she said. "I'm sure Albert didn't bring us this way in July."

"There isn't any alternative except across the open flats between here and the Burro Mountains," I told her. "The Stein's Peak Range was the route that Apache raiders took between the Sierra Madre and the Fort Apache and San Carlos reservations in Arizona. They killed Judge McComas and his family on the Lordsburg Road on a raid out of these mountains, and a few men at the copper mine in Clifton. For hundreds of years it's been a naturally defended highway for outlaws of all kinds."

"And just look what happened to the Apaches," she said retorted.

I was fed up with her suddenly, and decided to let her have it. "I don't know," I said. "As late as nineteen or twenty years ago the Sierra Madre Apaches were living free still in Mexico, supplied by humanitarian drug smugglers and benevolent left-wing guerillas who gave them AK-47s and even machine guns to shoot up the Federales with."

We spread our bedrolls under the thickest juniper tree we could find and John-Wayne, for the first time since the Little Colorado, circled his with the lariat.

"The snakes will be out afterward if it does rain," John-Wayne said. "I bet you one of them gorillas is a witchcrafter. I bet you *he* made that snake come to Albert last night," he added darkly.

No one paid us attention as we joined the supper line moving up to the fire where the cooks ladled beans from the bunged and carboned pots.

The tortillas, toasted on flat rocks half buried in the coals, were scorched and the coffee, though scalding hot, was thin and nearly tasteless. Humberto sat with his back against a small boulder and his legs stretched out, chasing beans with his fork and looking morose. We carried our half-filled plates over and joined him. Humberto said Carmen had gone to bed already with a headache and no supper. He did not look at me as he spoke and his manner was less friendly even than usual. We ate in embarrassed silence and afterward I took John-Wayne with me to have a look at the horses before it was full dark. All of them were asleep except for Tortuga who Carmen had tied at a distance from the others to a juniper tree where he stood patiently stripping bark with his teeth. We checked the tie ropes and walked on past the animals, feeling the ground push steeply up toward a dark volcanic neck rising above the camp.

"Let's climb up there, Dude," John-Wayne said suddenly.

"Up there? It's too steep."

"We can climb as far as we can get—then stop."

"It's too dark already."

"Too dark for the white man maybe. Navajos can see in the dark, good as cats or horses."

"Navajos are full of beans. You go first."

For a hundred yards or so it was fairly easy going over grass and pancake pear bedded in the loose gravel. Where the pitch steepened abruptly we stopped to get our breath, turning away from the slope to look behind us. Below the fires of the camp burned out of the darkness, illuminating the tiny grouped figures of the guerillas and beyond these, at the edge of the circle of light, a canvas sidewall tent. We faced about again and climbed higher until the footing became too bad and the handholds above our heads felt precarious.

"Lights!" John-Wayne exclaimed, between loud intakes of breath.

I looked around and there it was—civilization. The city seemed to float in space, embedded in layers of night like darkness separating the waters in the Bible. Even at that distance the colors were perceptible through the dry desert atmosphere: warm yellows, hot reds, cool blues and greens twinkling like jewels and glimmering like coals, or a constellation of bright stars and habitable planets sighted across eons of black emptiness.

"Lordsburg," I said.

"How far?" John-Wayne gasped.

"Thirty miles, perhaps. Maybe forty."

"Beautiful, man!" he breathed.

Holding there to the cliffside we stared across invisible foothills and the playa beyond them toward the distant city glinting and winking beyond our reach. It was just honkey-tonk of course—motels, bars, fast-food restaurants, shopping malls, filling stations, and railroad yards—but still it *was* beautiful, somehow.

"I want to go home," John-Wayne said in a breaking voice.

"Soon," I promised him. In the wavering firelight Carmen's tent appeared to breathe gently in and out. "Let's get on down to camp, now."

Stones jumped from underfoot and went rattling down over the talus, singly and in small avalanches, as we descended. We reached the grassy pedestal at last and began working our way across it toward camp. When a snake buzzed at us from somewhere off in the darkness John-Wayne picked up a rock chip and tossed it in the direction of the sound.

"Oh!" he exclaimed.

I saw the thing almost at the same time: a triangular outline like a dress on a clothes-hanger, filmy and vague as a patch of moonlight—only there wasn't any moon. The shape had nothing particularly human about it, yet both of us instantly recognized its humanity, somehow. Hanging there in the darkness close above the ground it was about ten yards off when it appeared, drifting closer as we watched to within ten or twelve feet, semi-transparent and energetic as ectoplasm. John-Wayne gave a long yell and threw himself face-down on the grass.

"Get away, Albert," he moaned. "Please don't haunt me, man—don't, *please.*"

I looked up to the sky where the clouds had shoved away to the east, leaving a faint starshine on the western horizon. When I looked back again, the apparition had vanished.

"The stars are out," I told John-Wayne. "It was only a trick of the light. Get up off your face so we can climb on down and go to bed."

"How come you come back to haunt me?" he blubbered. "What I ever done to you? Ain't I always been your friend, long's you known me? I'm sorry for sayin you was crazy—honest I am."

I seized him by both arms and jerked him up onto his feet.

"Look," I said, "it's gone. Open your eyes now and look. Whatever it was it isn't there anymore. It's time we were down there in camp, asleep."

"It was Albert," John-Wayne said. "He was tryin to tell us somethin, man."

"What do you guess it was he was trying to tell us?"

"He was tellin us we're goin to die."

"Everyone's going to die, sooner or later."

"I *told* you one of them gorillas was a witchcrafter," John-Wayne said.

In camp the fires burnt low and the men were shaking out and spreading their blankets for the night except for a small group sitting up with Humberto around the remains of the cookfire. Arguing in low voices and gesturing broadly in the air they did not notice as we approached out of the shadows until one of the men, catching sight of us, nudged the man beside him and all of them fell silent, watching us. In the sallow light of the dying fire Humberto looked tired—sick almost. He barely acknowledged my goodnight as we passed, hunched forward on a rock and holding his palms pressed together between his open knees. No one else spoke to us, and the murmur of conversation did not begin again until we were almost out of hearing. Getting inside the bedroll I heard voices raised in anger, and after that a sudden hush in which the night seemed very still.

"Goodnight," I told John-Wayne.

"Goodnight, Dude."

There was no wind and even the crickets were strangely silent, as if it was getting ready to storm. I opened my eyes expecting to see clouds again and saw only stars, misty and bright overhead.

"Dude."

"What is it?"

"What do you guess they was arguin about over there around the fire?"

"I don't know. I think they just want to get on home to Mexico as soon as possible."

"I thought the Mexes all wanted to be up here."

"A lot of them do. Those are the runners. These ones of ours are fighters. They're smart enough to understand there's nothing for them in the U.S. of A., anyway."

I turned on my side and dug the soft soil with my hip bone, which felt as if it had developed a callus an inch thick on it. Lying with one eye open,

I watched the desert bushes fade into darkness together with the distant light of the dying fire.

"Dude."

"I'm sleeping."

"What *really* happens to people when they die?"

"They go to Heaven if they've been good. Otherwise they go straight to Hell. That's what the preacher man on TV says, anyway."

"Albert ain't in Heaven. He ain't in Hell, neither. He's *here.*"

"Maybe here *is* where Hell is," I suggested.

"How come he's hangin around in it, then? He never done nothin bad to no one that *I* know of."

"Maybe because it wasn't Albert you think you saw in the first place," I said.

I wasn't having any part of John-Wayne's haunt, one because it didn't happen and two because the bruja did. That seemed like a lot of ghosts for a single summer unless you were willing to agree that the world was made for the dead as it much as it was for the living, and I didn't feel quite ready to believe that, yet.

---

The clouds had moved in again by morning, hanging low above the desert and wetting our faces with a fine mist. The cookfire waved like a red flag against the gray light as three or four men converged on it slowly, dragging dead juniper branches and the woody skeletons of cholla through the brush.

"Sleep okay?"

"Okay except for being haunted."

"All that's haunting you is an empty belly. Let's go see if they're serving breakfast yet."

In the desert everything, people included, takes its life from the sky—its clarity, depth, and color. Nothing else is vibrantly alive like the desert on a bright day, and nothing so dead on a flat one: the only time the desert really *is* a desert, meaning you feel lost and alone and *deserted* there. Carmen knelt by the fire, boiling beans, as we came up. With her gaunted cheeks she looked thinner than ever but her face, flushed with heat and the fire's ruddy glow, was radiant. Behind her in the brush Humberto and the lieutenant were striking the tent. His shoulders and back were rigid and he moved stiffly, like a man hugging his anger to himself like a bag of gold. Around camp the men were rolling blankets and stuffing their knapsacks before getting on line with their plates, cups, and spoons. Except for not walking into or over us, they acted as if we were specters, invisible men in their midst. Once as we shuffled forward I spoke pleasantly to the man behind me in line. He stared through me and away without responding and I did not try him again. We approached the fire and held our plates out to Carmen, who was ladling the half-softened beans with a spoon. Looking down on her auburn curls nested within one another as she knelt on the ground beside the cookpot, I felt a nearly irresistible urge to place my hand on the crown of her bent head. Instead I pushed John-Wayne along, and we went off and sat away from the others to eat our breakfast.

"What's goin on with everbody this mornin?" he asked.

"I don't know."

"It's like in the movies when the Indians are gettin ready to attack."

"We *are* the Indians, and there isn't anybody around to attack us."

"Them ain't Indians," he said, "they're just Meskins."

We cleaned the plates with brush and sand and went to bring the horses from their pickets. No one had saddled yet, so the brigada was going to be off to a late start again this morning. With the flat of our hands we brushed the dust and burrs from Ana's and Quixote's backs and were setting the blankets when shouts came from the brushy sidehill below the camp where ten or twelve of the men were running toward us, waving their arms and shouting.

"What do *them* guys want?" John-Wayne demanded.

"They want us to stop, I'm guessing. 'Alto' doesn't mean 'Meet me with your skis in Salt Lake City.'"

"What for? We ain't goin no place without them."

They formed a circle around us and closed in, grabbing at the horses' heads and pulling the blankets down. They forced our arms behind our backs and held us while two of them tied the animals to a couple of small bushes. Then they rushed us along between them through the dust, up to the rise from where the rest of the brigada silently watched as we were led into camp.

Humberto stood with his back to what remained of the fire, holding a tin cup. He drank it off and wiped his mouth on his sleeve. Finally he dropped the cup on the ground, stepped forward, and spoke a few words to the men, who promptly let go their hold on us. I looked for Carmen and spotted her a hundred yards away leading Tortuga by a rope and carrying the bridle on her arm.

"We weren't attempting to run on you," I explained. "Just readying the horses for an early start."

Humberto grunted like a Juárez cop being offered a too small mordida in exchange for no speeding ticket.

"Better for us all," he said, "if you'd run a long time ago—y buena suerte."

"¿Qué pasa?"

"The men won't move."

"Why not?"

Carmen dropped the lead rope and pushed in among them, still with the bridle in her hand. Unsecured, Tortuga stood with his four feet solidly planted and his eyelids drooping. Her movements, like her face, were tense and angry.

"¡Basta ya!" she told the men. "¡Corre prisa! Que ya vamos retrasados."

They looked at the ground and moved their feet around in the sand, but otherwise they did not stir.

"Enhorabuena," Carmen said. "Que Cada quien haga lo que le dé la gana."

She reminded them that they were still in enemy country with little food and a day's supply of water where, if captured, they would be imprisoned and given over to the Mexican authorities at whose hands they faced certain torture and execution. She was nearly through speaking when I realized she'd been using Spanish rather than dialect—as she always did when she wanted me to understand her.

"Aquello es lo que desean Vds.—¿Verdad?"

The men went on scraping the dust into ridges with the sides of their boots. They still looked sullen but the resolve had gone out of their faces and they stood a little limply now, as if their spines had gone soft.

"¡Dénse prisa!" Carmen ordered. "Ya vamos retradísimos—Pues, ¡a la!"

"What was that all about?" I asked as the men, dispersing, went for their packs and to bring in the horses.

"It was about you, of course," Carmen said.

"But why?"

"The Indians as you know are very superstitious." With John-Wayne standing almost at her elbow, she spoke with complete unselfconsciousness. "Some of them believe you are a witch—have the evil eye, or some such medieval nonsense. They think you sent the snake to kill Albert, and that instead of taking us back to Mexico you're leading us into a trap to be rounded up and killed. So this morning they refused to go on."

"What good did they expect a sitdown strike in the middle of the damned desert was going to do for them?"

"Absolutely none—if it didn't persuade me to order the two of you shot before we got started again today."

"But you talked them out of it."

"I didn't talk them out of anything," Carmen explained. "I told them.... Ahora, ¿nos vamos?"

"Nos vamos," I agreed.

John-Wayne rode with me well in advance of the column, and a hundred yards ahead of Carmen and Humberto. The sun burned the mists away even before we started and the day became very warm. When a gust of wind lifted my hat from my head and I had to dismount to retrieve it, I picked a handful of broomgrass and thatched the broken crown from the inside before remounting.

"First they stoled my horse and now they want to shoot us," John-Wayne complained. "We ain't done nothin bad to them, that I can think of."

"They say no good deed goes unpunished. But we never did them much of a favor either, did we?"

"'Cept for showin them the easy way back to Mexico."

"That could turn out to be our revenge yet—you know?"

"I'd just like to know what sonsabitches called me a witchcrafter," John-Wayne said.

The desert, like a woman, is constantly in motion, always becoming something else before you've had a chance to get used to what it was before. After the cool morning it began to be very hot, the fired blue sky pressing down from above, molding the heat to our bodies. In the canyons and arroyos there was no trace of water except for the carved banks, cave-ins, and the matted brush left by runoff from the summer rains. It was maddening to think of so much water only a few weeks ago—all that aliveness poured out and gone to waste overnight for want of something to hold it and somebody around to make use of it. Nature is almost never a friend to man. Most of the time it merely tolerates him, while for the rest it's just a tease or an enemy ready with insults, followed up by the fast sucker punch. The men straggled forward, the most exhausted of them falling out of the line and dropping in a seated position on the sand where they remained until the tail of the column, in passing, took them by the hand and pulled them onto their feet. The horses were badly lathered between the legs. They went with their heads down, lifting their feet mechanically, the back hooves catching up and striking the front ones with a sharp ugly sound. Baca would be unimpressed when he saw his animals again. I did not want to think what Jody was going to be, but the fact was I thought less and less of Jody James at all as the days went by. I still loved her, of course, but more dutifully than romantically, the way a man thinks about his life's work rather than the woman he adores. Hoofbeats sounded behind, and then Carmen rode up beside us.

"How are you?" she asked.

"Okay so far, thanks."

"I'm sorry about this morning."

"Me too. But we could both be a lot sorrier."

"Be careful with Humberto," Carmen said.

"Is he the one behind the insanity?"

"It's worse than insanity, it's Mexican superstition, and he knows how to play on it. So does everyone in Mexico above the level of a peasant, including the priests of course—and revolutionists like Humberto. ¡Dáte por advertido!"

She reined the horse around sharply and left us to ride back to the column.

"Is she more of a fox than the other one?" John-Wayne asked as we rode with our stirrups almost touching.

"What did you say?"

"I said—Is she more of a fox than the other one?"

"Is who more of a fox than who?"

"Miss Carmen. More of a fox than the Mormon chick in Utah."

"Are you crazy? Jody's no Mormon. She can hold her whiskey as well as any man I ever knew."

The sky was still flat blue overhead but a darker haze showed in the west behind the mountains. John-Wayne unslung the canteen from the saddle horn and took a short drink, washing the water around in his mouth before he finally swallowed it. His cheeks had grown so thin that the water only restored them to their former roundness.

I said, "You'd do better to drink more water, less often."

"I guess I know what I'm doin.' *I'm* the one was raised on a desert."

"This desert happens to be where *I* was raised, but you suit yourself. It looks like we might have rain before nightfall, anyway."

He said nothing further but moved out ahead a little, riding in a sullen silence that traveled with him like a cloud. I was going to call him on his bad mood when he reined Ana back to ask, "You think he don't notice—don't you?"

"I think who doesn't notice?"

"Humberto—who else?"

"What doesn't Humberto notice?"

"Look, Dude," John-Wayne said. "If *I* can feel it, man, you know damn well who else can. He's been feelin it for weeks, and it's only two and a half days left to Mexico now."

I dropped the reins over the horn and rode on, looking at him.

"Lancelot and them other Table Nights was supposed to be willin to sacrifice their lives for their *own* woman, wasn't they? Not for somebody else's."

I thought about that for a minute.

"Point taken," I told him finally. "I was hoping hard it didn't show—too hard, I guess, like a woman wearing a new slip she bought off the discount rack that doesn't fit right. J-W, you're getting to be a man."

"What happens," he asked, "after we get to Mexico?"

"I wish to Heaven I knew," I said.

We'd ridden for a couple of hours more when John-Wayne drew rein suddenly.

"Look there!" he said, pointing.

"What at?"

"Mountains, man—big ones!"

The mountains were a long way off still and only the blue tips of the familiar peaks rose behind the brown and red swells of the nearer hills.

"Mexico!" John-Wayne shouted.

"Those are the Chiricahuas in southeastern Arizona. We're getting closer, though."

"Anyway, I saw them first."

"There isn't really any competition, you know. I'm getting to be an old man."

"You ain't old, you got white man's eyes is what's wrong with you. How far over to them Chimichangas, Dude?"

"I don't know for sure. Day and a half, maybe."

"And then we're in Mexico?"

"Then we have to go around the mountains."

His face fell.

"Mexico's on the other side of them," I encouraged him. "Why don't you ride back and give Miss Carmen the good news?"

Five minutes later Carmen, coming at a lope and followed by John-Wayne, caught up again.

"You're not going to have a horse in the morning if you don't ease up on him," I told her. "Worse still, I won't, either."

"Where are the mountains John-Wayne told me about?" she asked, a little breathlessly.

"Away beyond those hills over there. You can't see them from where we're riding now."

"I remember seeing big mountains with snow on them the morning after we crossed from Mexico. They would have to be the ones, wouldn't they?"

"They would if that's how Albert took you."

"This is wonderful," Carmen said. "I feel as if you've brought us almost home, now."

The horses breasted the rise ahead and we came in sight again of the spired blue summit of the Chiricahuas pointing high above the mangled desert ranges.

"They *are* the same mountains!" Carmen cried.

I looked away to the purple and black clouds piling above the western horizon. There was water in those clouds, but you couldn't count on getting any of it on the desert.

"How are the men doing?" I asked.

All the pleasure went out of her face, and she looked worried now.

"Badly. The water's almost gone and this heat is killing, like the fires of the Inquisition."

"Go back," I said, "and tell them if they can hold out another couple of hours—two and a half at the outside—I can put us on water, tonight."

It was a gamble, but one I had a good chance of winning, I thought. Twenty-five years, which do so much to change a man, alters the desert not at all—so far anyway as the man can tell. Twenty-three years ago, to be exact, my dad and I had tried running cattle out here before selling out to a rancher down on Animas Creek who, knowing this particular section of the range like his wife's mood swings, had been watching us make fools of ourselves for ten and a half months, laughing into his steak dinner every afternoon as he hovered like a vulture waiting to pick our carcasses. It could be rough country when the weather didn't cooperate, scattered with the bones of plenty of operations before ours—some of them, I recalled, in the vicinity of where I was guiding a bunch of ragged, hungry, dehydrating revolutionaries on their way to lay siege to Mexico City. Fifteen minutes after I had these thoughts, the first whiteface appeared, staring broadly from the shade of a juniper tree.

John-Wayne saw it too and let out a yip before I silenced him.

"Don't move them," I cautioned, "they're on their way to water. We'll just stand here a while and let them show us where."

The cow backed away as I looked around and saw Carmen and Humberto ride up. Then she turned and trotted heavily downhill, udders and belly swinging, followed by her calf. Humberto took his rifle off his shoulder and raised it.

"Don't shoot," I warned him. "We need water worse than we need meat. She knows where to find it."

Carmen said, "I always thought cattle were stupid."

"And you were raised on a cattle ranch?"

"I mean common cattle, of course—not fighting bulls."

"Cows are *not* stupid," I told her, "they're very intelligent animals. Cows have a complex and highly developed social organization, cooperative to the point almost of being socialistic. When a mother has to go to water she can park her calf with another cow, who babysits it for her until she returns. Cows understand cow-ponies and are willing to work with them if the rider knows cattle and how to handle a cow-smart horse. If you think that cow there is dumb—go after her. You'll see how quick she can hide herself, and her calf too, in country that looks—but isn't—as flat as the back of your hand."

From the side of her face Carmen was smiling at me in a way I was very glad Humberto could not see.

"I'm sorry," she said, "I didn't mean to defame the better part of a whole species. Thank you for enlightening me on the intellect of cows."

More cows emerged from cover along the sidehill as the men came up and stretched themselves on the ground to take advantage of the unexpected halt. Those who still had water in their canteens shared with those who did not. They put their heads all the way back and tilted the canteens upside down to let the final drops run into their wide-open mouths, like baby birds taking worms.

"Can you tell where it is they're going?" Carmen asked.

I glassed the desert and found a streak of green following what looked to be a dry runnel cutting downhill to a grassy swale between two ridges where clots of manure lay scattered along a dirt trail curving around the end of the farther hill.

"I see a good cow track," I told her. "It isn't headed toward the Cattleman's Saloon."

"Prob'ly it ain't no more than just an ole stockpond," John-Wayne offered. "Full of mud and cowshit—more piss than water."

We got the men on their feet and started downhill into the bottom, watched closely by cattle scattered at intervals among the little trees. I was expecting a stock pond, so what we actually discovered around the hill beyond the patch of yellow grass made me as proud as if I'd used a magic spell to put it there myself: a waterwell operated by a pinwheel working off the solar panel and propane tank beside it, drawing clear water from deep in the ground into a galvanized iron stock tank. The area surrounding the well was trodden down and holed by the dried-out tracks of cattle, some of which lay around chewing the cud in the late afternoon sun. The cows rolled their eyeballs and humped their hindquarters in the air as the men, cheering loudly, rushed the tank. They threw down the packs and rifles and plunged their faces into the sun-heated water, heaping it on their heads with cupped hands and spitting and blowing between long, heaving drinks.

Some, removing their soaked shirts, splashed water over their naked skins, where it evaporated almost instantly in the desert heat. Whooping like Indians they scooped water in their palms and flung it at one another until Carmen, to stop the waste, made them quit. The cows watched the ruckus from a safe distance with bland disapproving faces. When the brigada had drunk its fill we led the pawing, snorting horses to the tank, jerking their heads from the water finally so as not to founder them. John-Wayne caught my eye as we stood with Ana and Quixote. He winked.

"We got lucky in the nick of time, Dude," he said.

"I guess. Lucky in exactly the same way Custer and his people didn't."

Carmen came up on foot, leading Tortuga by the reins. The horse's muzzle was wet above the nostrils and water dripped from his sparse chin hairs. He looked relieved but something less than grateful, as if finding a gas-operated water-well in the middle of a howling desert was nothing to get excited about. But Carmen was smiling delightedly.

"Well done, both of you," she said. "You have saved the revolution!"

"If only we had somethin to eat…," John-Wayne began.

"Humberto's going to shoot a cow," Carmen told him.

"No he's not," I told her.

Humberto stood at the edge of the oasis of dried crazed mud with a rifle in his hand, staring uphill at the whiteface cattle we'd run off the well. The gun was an old forty-five seventy belonging to one of the men, not one of the Russian-made automatics that were standard issue for the brigada.

"Take my horse," I told John-Wayne.

Humberto had the rifle up and pointed at the largest, heaviest animal when I reached him. I put my hand on the barrel and pushed it down and away.

"What is it you think you're doing?" I asked him. "That cow just happens to be some rancher's valuable property."

He stared at me, hatefully.

"Some fat petit-bourgeois pig's, you mean."

"We have a government in Washington feels the same way," I told him. "That, however, is not the point. The point is, it's his cow."

Humberto brought the rifle up fast and fired from a distance of twenty-five yards. The cow gave a lurch and settled forward on her knees as if life had suddenly become too much for her to bear. Humberto lowered the gun and gave me a look.

"Now it belongs to the revolution," he said.

They butchered the cow where she lay on the hillside and Humberto sent another party up the opposite slope to fell juniper trees and carry the wood down for a fire. The men skinned the carcass out and boned it, hacking purple slabs of meat from the gleaming white frame and bringing them by armloads into camp, where a pyre of gray trunks and twisting branches with the greenery left on them rose within a circle of roughly fitted sandstone rocks. The wood ignited instantly when they touched it off in sheets of ragged orange flame shooting up through clouds of grayish-yellow smoke, rank and uric as a panhandler's drawers. The fire roared toward the sky as the trees settled into each other and collapsed at last in an upward shower of red sparks. The men raked the burning coals smooth with long sticks and set flat rocks among them just inside the fire ring, and then the cooks laid the meat on the rocks and turned it with forks as the mind-altering odor of frying beefsteak roiled in the air. Around the camp the guerillas were taking their horses to drink again, piling their saddles and packs, and searching out the smoothest and flattest ground to spread their blankets on. The men who had removed their shirts wetted them once more before they pulled them on, wanting to enjoy the feel of soaked cotton against their skins. Already Humberto had the sidewall of the big tent up, and the low sun striking through the canvas revealed Carmen's figure in silhouette as she moved about inside of it.

Latinos are a different people, changeable in their moods almost as women. These men who'd been prepared to murder us a bare twelve hours before and had behaved all day as if I was reenacting the Bataan Death March for them were having a fiesta now: joking and laughing, flashing white teeth as they sat or lay stretched out on the ground in the even heat of the small lake of fire burning at the heart of the rapidly cooling desert. The cooks turning the meat leaned back from the coals from time to time, laid down their forks and sharpened sticks, and went to soak themselves at the trough before returning to work beside the fire, shielding their faces behind their raised arms. The meat spat and smoked, the fat bubbled, and everything tasted wonderful, good enough to make a believer out of a Hindu, or even a tofu-eating Californian. Whatever the vegetarians tell you, there isn't anything in this world like beef for dinner—stolen beef especially, maybe. I ate and ate and it was enough to loosen up even an Anglo stick like me, while the men sitting around grinned and jabbered at us in that unfathomable lingo of theirs, and John-Wayne and I nodded and stroked our chins to show we understood perfectly and laughed from time to time—above all, we kept on grinning.

It isn't Miss Manners to use plates, knives, and forks at a barbecue, even if you happen to have them on hand, which we didn't. The thick slabs of meat bordered by a belt of fat thicker than you might expect to find on an animal that has spent the last seven months of its life wandering in the mesquite-and-yucca wilderness were rich and greasy in our fingers, and running with blood. You ate your steak, and instead of a second course there was another hunk of red meat, crisped and blackened on the outside, waiting within reach on the fire. I don't believe I ever appreciated beef so much: beef for the soup and salad course, beef for the main course, beef for dessert; beef for the wine selection, beef for the supper rolls, beef for after-dinner coffee, beef for the napkins, beef for the fingerbowls, beef for the final glass of cognac, beef for the big Havanna cigar. In my experience, Mexicans won't eat beef without it being pounded and shredded and stuffed into tamales, or ground and rolled inside tortillas. These men absolutely gorged themselves on beefsteaks, and when they'd eaten a thirty-six or forty-eight-ounce chunk tossed the gristle into the fire, or backwards across their shoulder like King Henry the Eighth, and went for another piece. And these were small men, not above five-foot-five or -six for the most part. The Plains Indians couldn't have done better justice to a fresh-killed buffalo, and if someone had proposed the best for last, eating towards one another along the entire length of the small intestine the way the Shoshone (if I recall rightly) used to do, I'd probably have gone ahead and taken them up on it.

We finished off the entire cow. The men built the fire back to a roaring blaze and the musicians among them brought out their simple instruments. Tonight, instead of traditional Mexican ballads, they played—and sang—the broken haunting songs of Meso-America, not centuries but millennia old, composed for wooden flutes carved from the jungle trees or meant maybe to be sung alone, echoing out of ancient Mayan nights and lovely to listen to, in an eerie sort of way. They were young men, and though they'd walked and ridden all day under the brutal sun and stretched their bellies to bursting with red meat, only a few of them fell asleep, tipping suddenly over backward and lying with their distended paunches turned up to the stars. The rest, defying the normal digestive processes, rose from the ground to dance in the orange light of the fire—singly at first, then pairing off in couples which eventually became trios and quartets of howling, stamping males dancing with their arms thrown about each other's necks. Seated on one of the collapsible stools Carmen watched the dance intently, leaning forward on one elbow with her chin in her hand. The bonfire picked out the red lights in her hair and profiled her clean, straight features ending in the strong, determined chin. Backlit by the flames, she was a wild romantic creature, dangerous and unknowable beyond the capacity every beautiful woman has for mystery and danger, and I wondered, not for the first time, how far Humberto comprehended the true nature of this tiger he was riding.

We had difficulty, stumbling around in the darkness among the packs and blankets, finding our own bedrolls fifty yards from the blazing fire and the circle of leaping, half-naked bodies surrounding it.

"They'll sleep like babes in the wood tonight," I told John-Wayne.

"Not if they don't never shut up and go to bed, they won't."

"They'll be turning in any time now. Like zombies discovering suddenly they're really dead."

"*Don't* man," he begged.

It was barely an hour later by the stars when I awoke. Some of the men were still awake around the fire, but these were no longer dancing. Instead they sat cross-legged on the ground or lounged with their hands thrust into the deep pockets of their fatigues and their caps pulled over their eyes. At the center of the group Carmen and Humberto stood facing one another at a distance of eight or ten feet. Straight as a queen and holding her shoulders back, she addressed him in a strong carrying voice that did not waver. She used the Spanish language, every word coming sharp and clear in a way that penetrated my fogged brain and concentrated it the same way a hanging might have done. Even so, I didn't need to recognize every word to understand she was reading Humberto the riot act—not in a shrewish, brow-beating way but precisely, almost surgically and a little sarcastically. She was talking about superstition as the mark of peasants and reactionaries alike. Those who believed in old wives' tales such as the evil eye, Carmen was saying, had no business fighting for the revolution. Her voice as she spoke became scornful with the intent to debase and humiliate; the men, embarrassed, shifted their weight and stared at the ground as Humberto advanced on her a step.

"¡Hazte para atrás!" Carmen commanded them. Her arm went up fast and there was a semiautomatic pistol at the end of it.

Humberto stopped and looked at her for a moment without speaking. Then he unbuckled the shoulder holster from under his arm and dropped it and the weapon it held contemptuously in the dirt. But he did not take the next step forward.

When Carmen spoke again her voice dripped with the sarcastic sweetness women know how to use against men, infuriating them first and driving them finally to stark raving madness. She told Humberto how, except for being a revolutionary, she would despise him for threatening a poor, weak, defenseless female. Instead, as a daughter of the revolution, she invited him to throw chivalry to the dogs where it belonged and deal with her as he would with any man. Take up your gun, Carmen urged him sweetly, and challenge me. There is no issue between us but two people wishing only to have their horse returned to them and be allowed to depart in peace. The men, though keeping a close silence, continued to shuffle uneasily, looking from the ground to the sky and back again, and I could see the revolutionary-woman speech wasn't going over very well. As for me, it made my blood run cold as an IRS man's to listen to her.

Humberto stood there, taking it. He did not reply to Carmen's mockery but commenced to move on her again, holding his hand out for the gun. Humberto stepped very carefully with the exaggerated slowness of a man walking up on a wild animal. Carmen held her ground without flinching but I saw the gun waver slightly in her hand as Humberto advanced. The two of them faced each other now across six feet of firelight, the distance nearly bridged by the combined reach of their extended arms. Humberto took another step forward and waggled his fingers for the gun.

"Dámela, por favor," he directed in a detached, almost dreamy voice. And she gave it to him.

"Gracias," Humberto told her in his normal voice, and smiled. The smile spread as he lowered his arm—then crumpled to an agonized grimace as Carmen kicked high with her right foot and knocked the pistol from his hand, sending it spinning away over the heads of the men into the desert.

In that split second I felt sorry for the fellow, the unsuspecting victim of hundreds of hours of her childhood spent practicing on a ballerina's rail. And when Carmen set both hands on her hips, put her chin up and her head back, and laughed at him, I should have felt even sorrier—but I didn't.

John-Wayne, waking, had seen everything. I put a finger against my mouth and we pressed the bedrolls into two loose bundles and slipped silently out of camp and up into the junipers growing along the sidehill above it.

"Amazing, isn't she."

"She's somethin else, man. Like she's not entirely human. More like a skinwalker, if it wasn't for bein so good lookin.'"

"Can't skinwalkers be beautiful?"

"I guess so. Sometimes. Bet jo' gie etta hi ee' was beautiful—you know, Great Vagina, the one who would get men to lay with her and crunch their you-know-whats when they was inside."

"Miss Carmen did a lot worse than that to Humberto tonight. Guess who's going to take the heat for it, though."

We unrolled our beds on the ground inside a clump of trees. How many nights now? How many days? It no longer mattered, I thought. Time is only a civilized concept, not a human one.

"Dude."

"What?"

"It's goin to storm."

"No it's not."

"There ain't no stars out now."

"There were a little while ago."

I looked up through the shaggy branches of the junipers and this time I didn't see any stars.

"It smells like stormin," John-Wayne whispered.

"If it storms, might be we'll get a little bit wet. Until then I'm going to sleep." I turned over onto the calloused side and drew the cover up to my face.

The dog howled and went on howling from outside, wanting to be let in. It was Jody's dog and this was Jody's house, I knew, although it looked different. The dog howled while I waited for Jody to come out from wherever she was and let it in. The howling grew louder and longer and still she did not come. I got up from bed and walked through the house, taking the gun with me. The dog howled once more as I kicked the back door open with my foot. Then I was awake and hearing the coyote.

He was on the sidehill beyond the camp, calling to his friends and relatives to join him on what little remained of the cow carcass. The clouds had pulled apart in places and in the starshine coming from behind them I made out the white bones gleaming faintly across the darkness. Down in camp the circle of red coals rippled like water beneath layers of heat and ash. The wind had come up, and except for the coyote the only sound was the sough of it in the branches that closed above our heads. I let myself down with my elbow and lay flat again on the ground, listening to the coyote's intermittent howls and the answering barks and whoops coming from the hills beyond the camp. A flash of lightning lit the clouds and pulled the desert landscape forward all around, white and stark as if it had been carved from prehistoric bone.

Skirmishes of wind advanced ahead of the storm, whipping the trees madly before passing on and leaving them limp and exhausted. I smelled dust and ozone on the air, but not the sharp expectant scent of rain. Lightning came again—the dry soundless desert heat lightning—as I listened for the coyote. But he was quiet now, and after a time I fell asleep once more.

When I woke again the storm was all around us. The stars were gone and the little light the hills gave back was blotted by the flying dust, mixed with bits of grass and with juniper needles. As I reached to draw the cover farther over my head John-Wayne stirred beside me.

"Dude."

"What."

"It's stormin."

"Never mind. It isn't going to rain."

"Somethin's happenin," he said.

They came at us from beyond the trees like the dark spirits of the storm itself. John-Wayne was already on his feet with his knife out but I was caught half-wrapped in the covers, struggling to free myself and find my revolver at the same time. One of the figures leaped at me with his arm raised for a downward strike, and as I rolled away I heard the scrape of a knife blade penetrating the ground. Then I was on my feet with my own knife open and my back against a tree and John-Wayne beside me, the two of us circling the trunk as we faced the three attackers keeping pace with us, slightly crouched to spring. In the nearly complete darkness they were no more than vague outlines above the waist, black on what was only a slightly paler darkness. The wind roared in the little copse and when it came hard again at our backs I quit circling the tree and reached for John-Wayne's arm to make him stop too. The figures halted with us and we stood facing one another, two flesh-and-blood men confronting three faceless demons of the desert. Then they jumped us, and I heard John-Wayne grunt as the knife went in. It was like fighting those silhouettes cops practice on, come alive from their cardboard backing. Going for the chest area I felt the point of the knife strike bone, withdrew it, and struck again lower down, upward from the abdomen. The demon gave a very earthly gasp and I turned to help John-Wayne, who had the other two on top of him now. This time I heard the *chunk* and *chunk* again of a blade burying itself to the guard in flesh and muscle as he fought free of them, and then the terrible triumphant war cry of the Navajo warriors rising above the din of the wind storm at the same moment that I felt a hard shock and a stab of pain to my left leg.

"You hurt?" I asked him as he stood gasping beside me.

"Not me, Dude. You?"

"The sonofabitch got my leg, a little. My God, John-Wayne. I hope you never come at me with a knife."

"No way, man. You're my brother. I think I killed mine."

"Is he down?"

"Layin over there beside that rock."

"What's that you have in your hand?"

I squeezed, and felt something soft and pliant between my fingers. Soft like wool, loose and still warm like an article of clothing. Humberto's black beret. I'm not a pious man, so what happened next came as a surprise even to me.

"May God have mercy on his soul," I said. "Hell is too good for him. So it's no sin on my part to hope it's where he is."

Drumrolls of thunder came all that night and in the morning the lieutenant was gone from camp and with him half the brigada, more or less, and their animals. We buried Humberto where he fell on the hillside and loaded the mules and burros that were left, abandoning supplies in order to mount all our men, some of whom went doubled up on the mules.

John-Wayne rode out a few miles before breakfast on the defectors' track and returned to report that they appeared to be headed west into the Peloncillo Mountains over in Arizona.

"Are you certain you're going to be able to ride with that leg?" Carmen asked.

"If John-Wayne will tie the other one in the stirrup I should be able to manage to stay up there."

"That, or you could ride double."

"Behind John-Wayne?"

"Behind me. He'll have your horse to pony, remember."

"I wouldn't want to put you to the inconvenience."

"My convenience is nothing compared to getting the men home safely," she said. "Also, I'm going to change your dressing before we start."

The knife cut was to the thigh, causing a heavy blood flow and slicing through some muscle while missing the artery and the big tendons. The wound had bled again during the night and I felt weak and tired, with no revolutionary spirit to speak of. Carmen was drawn and also tired but she was taking Humberto's death well, considering, and I guessed the defection of the lieutenant's men was actually a relief to her. What really kept her going, I suppose, was the sustained daily pressure of what was both a harrowing ordeal and a thrilling adventure at the same time. As for me, after a thousand miles and more in the saddle the freedom and exhilaration I'd felt that first night out from Holbrook on the ride over to the Little Colorado had increased, rather than the opposite. I was, I mean to say, still enjoying myself.

When we were ready to ride John-Wayne boosted me as gently as he could manage onto Tortuga's croup before Carmen stepped up to the saddle ahead of me. The effort hurt like hell and the wound bled a little under the bandage, but after we'd gone a mile or so I learned to position the leg away from the hard jolting cantle ahead of my knees that I reached to grip with both hands. The day was fine, almost cool and with the clean feel of fall in the air.

I'd posted John-Wayne out ahead of the column with orders to halt and wait on us when he required direction. He rode like an Indian warrior in a painting by Russell or Remington, the rifle butt braced on his right thigh and the barrel angled, glinting, across his chest as he ponied Quixote on a rope. The men had instructions to ride in file behind, but they kept moving up where the trail allowed for it to form a protective flank as we traveled southward. We were out of the hills now and headed across a wide dipping plain, spiked with yucca and sotol standing up from the mesquite and creosote bush, sweeping away to the vermilion snags of the Peloncillos and—far to the south still—the blue Chiricahuas with an early storm building above them. Mostly I was able to steady myself from the cantle, but at a trot or coming out of the basins and arroyos I was compelled to embrace Carmen around the waist with both arms. Her shirt, damp with sweat, stuck to her back in patches and beads of perspiration slid down her neck and beneath her collar. Her hair, strong smelling and sweet as sagebrush after a rain, was only inches ahead of my nose as we rode, so close that I could almost feel the tickle of it.

"Are you doing all right back there?" Carmen asked, after we'd topped a rise of steep ground the horse had elected to take at a scrambling run that forced me to get a particularly strong hold.

"I'm fine," I told her. It was a lie and at the same the truth, and nothing but the truth.

"It's so much easier on them to give them their head on the uphill."

"It's the right thing to do, always. He's the one doing the work."

She drew rein while, over the crown of her head, I surveyed the country around, folds of red and tan ground showing in the open spaces between the low greenery.

"You can let go my waist now," Carmen reminded me.

"Sorry."

I disengaged my arms and held them against my sides.

"You needn't to be," she said. "Why do you suppose they chose to go west, into Arizona?"

"Probably to avoid taking the same route we're on."

"*Is* there another route?"

"Dozens, as a matter of fact. All of them long, hard, roundabout, and through the mountains. It could be they aren't planning on returning to Mexico right away."

"They're going there," she said decidedly. "We'll hear from them again before they get there, too."

The men had ridden up beside us and sat their horses now on loosened reins to let them crop the thin grass growing in clumps against the rocks.

"What is that line of trees off there?" Carmen wanted to know.

"That's the Gila River," I said.

"Again?"

"In this country, friendly old rivers like the Gila can be tough to shake. It's what makes them friends in the first place."

"It's almost as if it's trying to follow us," she said.

Between us and the river were windmills and cattle and fence lines running at right angles to one another. We watered the animals from the ranchers' tanks, paying for the privilege by repairing the fences we cut, and came around noon to the river where fieldstone houses stood abandoned under massive cottonwood trees amid lush fields of cotton, corn, and chili peppers that spiced the air with their sharp heat. The Gila here was no more than a narrow channel flowing listlessly against the near bank of the river. We crossed upstream of an iron bridge in cooling sprays of muddy water and dashed on over the gravel bed to the south bank, across acres of alfalfa in purple flower, and up through gravel hills to the tableland from where we could hear the crickets and cicadas shrilling from the riverine greenery below.

South of the river the land was flat as a sick horn player for some miles, nothing but the sour green creosote stretching away and a few bloomed yucca stalks coming to pieces above it. We rode on toward the Peloncillos, an escarpment of naked rock roughening into crags and bladed points as it crossed over from Arizona on a southeasterly heading into New Mexico, before after some miles the plain tilted downward like a ouija board and there began to be grass and mesquite among the yucca, and more fences and windmills in the middle distance. Rufus cattle stared from groves of mesquite as we watered the horses from the iron stock tanks, and stood bawling after us as we rode away. The ranches were poor ones mostly, trailer houses surrounded by windbreaks of immature trees and acres of the red dust, but after these many years I envied them the view stretching all the way from Tadpole Ridge north of Silver City to the Pyramid Mountains south of Lordsburg. Where the angle of sight ran through belts of creosote and mesquite the desert looked green and lush while, viewed at a steeper angle from higher up, it appeared yellow and broken, a panorama of alternate bands of tan and green verging through gravel fans to the upswept blue of the sheer mountains floating on heat waves above the plain. If you didn't trouble to look too closely but squinted just a little, the country hadn't changed at all in the same half century that took both sets of grandparents, my mother and dad, my brother and two sisters, and the ranch itself. Quite an achievement for Mother Nature, Uncle Sam, and Corporate Agribusiness in cahoots together, except for one major oversight on their part. They forgot to take me too.

"Do you see that group of triangle-shaped hills out there?" I asked Carmen.

"What are they?"

"The Pyramid Mountains. I was raised on a ranch a few miles this side of them, near Cotton City in the Animas Valley."

She gazed away at the mountains and then around us.

"Does it look like this?"

"Pretty much."

"I can see you love it, but it's too damn remote for me. How did you manage to avoid growing up to be a—how do you Americans say?—redneck?"

"I didn't," I told her. "This is what a redneck looks like."

In spite of all the fence repair we made good time down to the Peloncillos before the storm hit like a pink fog rolling in from the sea. The wind got up ahead of the advancing ground-blizzard and then it was screaming all around us, biting our skins like sandpaper and choking our lungs with the parching red dust that blotted the desert and the sky above it except for the pale sun sailing high behind the dust clouds. I called a halt against a broken hogback of rock and we went into camp immediately, taking shelter where we could find it and raising the canvas tent for everyone to crowd into while the storm lasted. To keep morale up I had the men build fires in protected places in the rock. The coffee was gone but we were carrying plenty of water from the wells we'd passed, and as Mormon Tea grew thick in the area we gathered the thin, jointed, yellow-green stems and boiled them. It was the first time in years I'd thought to do it, or needed to, but the flavor was just enough to make the saline water palatable. We were out of meat again but there were beans and rice left, though the last tortillas had long since dried up and been pulverized to flour in the horse packs. The storm blew until nearly ten o'clock that night, long after the brigadistas had curled up in pockets in the rock with their blankets to try and catch some sleep. Carmen had invited John-Wayne and me to share the sidewall tent with her. We placed our bedrolls just inside the flap and stepped outside at the appropriate moment to take a leak, while she made her toilette. Standing in the half dark with a shaggy sotol plant between us we made water together against the low cliff face and watched the dust clouds darken the emerging stars.

"It looks like making up its mind to clear, finally," I said.

"I'm goin to take my bedroll and sleep outside."

"Why would you want to do a thing like that?"

"'Cause I want to—that's why."

"Don't tell me you're shy about sleeping inside with Miss Carmen." I stopped then. "Oh," I said, "I see. Is *that* why?"

"I don't want to be no nuisance to nobody," he said, with dignity.

"That *is* the reason, then. Where did you get an idea such as that? Carmen is an honest-to-goodness lady, and Jody James and I are practically engaged."

He shrugged and turned away from the rock wall to button up.

"Everbody's engaged anymore," John-Wayne. "It don't seem to make much of a difference, one way or the other."

At sunrise the sky was clear and the air felt a lot chillier behind the front that had passed through the evening before. My leg wound had begun to heel but the weather change made it ache like a cowboy's lonesome heart. We got the men started early and around the middle of the afternoon I saw, over Carmen's shoulder in the middle distance, broken lines of bright alien shapes crossing a narrow valley between two gravel hills, at an unnatural speed and in opposite directions.

"I see cars moving out there beyond those hills," Carmen said.

"Interstate 10. The timing's about perfect. We can make it over there by evening, cross the highway after dark, and lay up in the hills beyond overnight."

She sat the horse, viewing the prospect ahead and gauging the expanse of desert between the highway and the ridge on which we paused.

"My God, I'm tired," Carmen said, in a low voice so as not to be overheard by the men.

I touched her side secretly with my hand.

"'¡Ánimo!" I told her. "Two or three days more of this and it will all be over for you at last."

"No it won't," she said. "It will all be starting all over again."

John-Wayne rode up at a trot, trailed by Quixote—under saddle and looking like the fallen hero's steed, minus only the empty boots reversed in the stirrups—along the ridgeline.

"Out there's the interstate!" he bellowed, pointing.

"We sighted it already," I told him. "The red man's eagle eye doesn't work so well in the world the white man made. That's a compliment, by the way."

The highway with its double row of moving steel objects appeared and reappeared before us all that afternoon, a mechanical mirage shunting one way and the other across the desert. As the sun lowered they began to flash and glow in strung-out lines like traveling campfires. Pointed shadows lengthened and spread in dark pools to fill the desert hollows, and wheeling spokes of light shot from the sun as it bit down into the black horizon like a circular saw into a log. A cluster of jeweled lights sprang out suddenly along the interstate.

"What town is that?" Carmen asked.

"It ain't a town, it's a truck stop," John-Wayne explained. "The lights just come on all at once, like they always do."

"But they will see us!"

"Don't worry," I said. "A brigade of mounted Mexican revolutionaries armed with assault rifles wouldn't even be noticed at an American truck stop."

"But these people are not our friends—they're enemies of the revolution!"

"In Mexico they are, maybe. Americans don't know such a thing as revolution exists anymore."

"Then your people are not paying attention!" she cried.

"Claro. That's why they wouldn't see us. Not if we tied the horses at the diesel pumps, stacked arms, and marched inside to use the showers."

It was dusk when we arrived at a pass between twin cones of vulcanized rock overlooking a valley crossed at the far end by the four highway lanes over graded fill and the two lines of the Santa Fe railroad running beside it. Between the tracks and the highway a group of antique, false-fronted, frame houses—Stein's Ghost Town, a well-known strip of tourist flypaper—stood, looking temporarily deserted. An old wagon road ran from the town up to the pass. Three vehicles were parked halfway along it, off in the prickly pear cactus where a large Mexican family was having a picnic. They had a cookfire going and we watched from behind a pile of boulders a quarter-mile distant as they fixed their supper over a scarf of orange flame waving beneath the tilted column of blue smoke. The highway traffic ran with its lights on now, schooling like fish with empty and lightless intervals between them. Carmen made the brigada dismount a few hundred yards below the pass, and John-Wayne helped me off the horse when she'd stepped down from Tortuga. After that we all sat around on rocks holding the reins in under the drooling horses' chins, waiting for full dark to come. We didn't want the Mexicans up here searching out a fire, but there was still a little pemmican left in the bags and we had that for our supper, together with the flat, stale-tasting water. Afterward Carmen helped me on foot up to the pass for a look into the valley below. The leg throbbed painfully and once I thought I was going to pass out, but before I'd hobbled as high as the saddle the stiffness began to work out of it and the pain let up a bit.

"See," Carmen said pointing, "the first star."

"That isn't a star," I said. "It's the planet Venus."

"The evening planet, then. Will you make a wish on it?"

"I didn't know wishing on the first star was a Spanish custom."

"As far as I know it's multicultural, the custom of people around the world. 'Star light, star bright, first star I see tonight.' My mother taught me when I was a little girl."

"Sure. Didn't you tell me your mother's English?"

"Stop arguing with me, Jeb, and make a wish."

"What is it I'm supposed to wish for?"

"That's up to you, of course."

"I've lived the life of my choice. I've never wanted anything else."

"In this life it is necessary at times to be a little bit greedy," Carmen said. "All right, then. *I'll* make a wish."

For several seconds she was quiet.

"Did you make the wish?"

"I made it."

Downslope the Mexicans' fire fanned about on a quartering breeze, lighting the grouped figures and winking red in the taillights of the standing pickup trucks. The door of one of the trucks hung open and we heard corrido music playing on the radio above the happy laughter and the relaxed, half-drunken talk. Beyond the ghost town the highway was already invisible, illuminated occasionally by a lonely car or two or a convoy of night-riding semis like apparitions from another world.

"What do you think?" Carmen asked.

"I think it's time," I said.

She helped me down again to where the men stood with their horses now, tightening their girths and securing the packs.

"¡Vámonos!" Carmen orderd them.

"You goin to ride your own horse?" John-Wayne asked.

"Not if I have any choice in the matter," I promised him. "But I don't."

He heaved me up onto Quixote where I sat for some seconds, blind with pain. John-Wayne handed me the reins, and when the worst of the agony was past and the men were getting mounted I took the wire-cutters from the saddle bags and passed them down to him.

"You'll do the honors this evening. Take the wire between three T-posts and pull it outward, toward the highway."

"You want me to put it back afterwards?"

"Hell no. If the tourists get out on the highway, it's the Chamber of Commerce's lookout."

Keeping together in the dark we rode up to the pass and halted there. A long finger of white light pointed across the valley and there was another sound now behind the Mexican's party, a kind of throbbing whine ahead of a lengthy rumble dragging out of the desert night as if it was being drawn from the bowels of the earth itself. I raised my hand and looked at Carmen, and then around to the men.

"Tren," I said.

I used to love these long Western trains. This one was traveling on the westbound track between El Paso and Tucson, a freight a mile or a mile-and-a-half in length pulled by eight diesel locomotives grinding toward the Arizona state line ahead of their monotonous string of shipping containers and autoracks, ending in a final car equipped with a red light attached to the rear coupling as a miserable excuse for a caboose; you could make out the individual units dimly in the faint starshine. I let the last car vanish behind the dim silhouette of Mr. Stein's bit of historical fakery before giving the high sign.

"¡Adelante!" I called, putting Quixote forward.

The brigada made quite an uproar on the hillside, knocking loose small rocks and crashing through brush in the dark, but the Mexicans were having a good enough time, and had drunk enough beer and tequila, that they heard us only after we'd joined them in the bottom and kicked the animals into a lope.

I've been hearing since I was a boy how horses—and mules, and burros—can see in the dark, without ever having any evidence of it until now. I couldn't see a thing myself, except ahead the ghost town standing against the blacker sky and on the right somewhere the Mexican's campfire, blazing out of the night like a fallen sun burning off by itself in some dark corner of the universe. Thundering hooves raised clouds of choking invisible dust as the horses, running close together like a wild herd, swept down through the little valley. I heard screams and shouts coming from around the fire and saw, looking sideways as we dashed past, what looked to be three or four large Mexican families fleeing into the darkness—the men turning to drag the women after them and the women bending as they ran to help the children along, some covering their faces with their arms and yelling, others wailing in terror.

"¡Salve María!" they cried—mistaking us apparently for Stein's Ghosts—"¡Dios me guarde!"…"¡Aparecidos! ¡Fantasmas!" "¡Salve María, O!"… "¡Dios me guarde!"—while the truck radio blared corrido throughout the commotion.

The mules were closed up to the point where I could make out ghostly rumps and flanks around us and the dark demonic riders above them, bent over their animals' necks. All it was going to take was for one of them to stumble or go down and the rest of the cavalry would go down with it. We breasted the roadbed, clattered across the railroad tracks, and sprinted for the highway ahead. Three semi-tractor trailers, following in tandem like elephants holding each other's tails, passed on a blast of wind, their fanned headlights picking out the topmost strand of fence running parallel to the road halfway up the embankment. In the lights of the third truck I saw John-Wayne slip down from his still-moving horse and rush the fence, the wire cutters ready in his hand.

He had the four strands separated in seconds, dragged the stiff barbwire aside, and bent it back against the intact fence, leaving the space between three posts open for us.

"Good man," I told him. "Now the fence on the other side. You have two minutes exactly, and then we're coming over."

"Is your leg all right?" Carmen asked.

"Now that you mention it, it hurts like hell."

It galled me, a little, that she *had* asked. I'd forgotten the pain completely until now, and there wasn't a thing she could do for it anyway. I kicked free of the off stirrup and let the leg hang against the saddle skirt, without the pressure. If you need two legs to ride a horse it ought to be a wooden one on rockers and painted blue with pink spots, anyhow.

"Dude," John-Wayne called in a low voice from the top of the embankment.

"What is it?"

"There's a semi stopped the other side of the road."

I kicked Quixote forward and joined him up on the highway. Across the median a semi stood parked on the shoulder of the eastbound lane a hundred yards away with its running lights on and the engine idling, between a set of cautionary triangles. The driver, at work on his knees beside the rig in the light of an electric torch, appeared to be checking a tire. Eastward, headlights burned three or four miles out on the playas of the Animas Valley. To the west, where the highway rose along a gentle incline, no lights showed beyond what I remembered as the summit of a low hill. I decided then I didn't care about the trucker, one way or the other.

"He's got problems of his own to worry about," I said to John-Wayne. "Ride on over there now and get that fence cut, fast as you can make it."

I watched him as he worked, illuminated by the truck lights, and when he had the section pulled back I waved Carmen up and trotted forward across the lanes. At the sound of hooves on the tarmac the driver straightened up and looked around, his blond ponytail switching the yoke of his striped cowboy shirt.

The brigada surged up onto the highway and crossed in the glaring headlights where they appeared like a small army of homeless people mounted on broken-down sharecroppers' mules. I sat Quixote in the median while they rode down the opposite bank toward John-Wayne standing aside with the four barb-wire strands gathered in his hand, and then turned the horse to follow after them. The oncoming lights had closed the distance from the east by a couple of miles, and a large billboard filled with the face of a man in a cowboy hat smoking a cigarette from the center of his mouth stood angled beside the road and almost beyond the reach of the parked semi's twin beams. I looked over and saw the driver, illumined by the cab light, climb lithely up to the seat in a way I wasn't really accustomed to seeing truck drivers move. Across the highway the last mule was going through the fence while John-Wayne, from the other side, appeared to watch me. I turned the horse away from him again and rode over at a trot to the truck.

The girl was perched sideways behind the wheel with her knees through the open door of the cab, wiping her hands with squares of damp tissue she pulled through a hole in the top of a plastic container. Framed by wings of the pale blonde hair, her face looked small and wistful except for the eyes, which were gray with a sly determined humor behind them. Very slender, with small breasts and narrow hips connected by a willowy torso, she had a cowgirl's build to go with the showy rodeo clothes.

"Good evening," I told her, touching the brim of what was left of my hat with my gloved forefinger. Between her position on the truck seat and mine on horseback, our eyes were about on a level with each other's.

"Hel-*lo*!" the girl said in a voice that, like her eyes, was sad and cheerful both, at the same time.

"Something I can do to help?"

"Thanks. I just got through changing a tire."

She rubbed with a wet-wipe at a streak of grease along one side of her hand, crumpled the towel in a ball, and pulled another one from the container she held gripped between her slender knees.

"Was it a blow-out?"

"Just a flat. My retreads are in good shape."

"What company do you drive for?"

"Me Myself & I—Incorporated! It's my own truck. I got it paid off finally six months ago."

The traffic from the west passed on the other side of the median in a rush of colored lights and trailing the sound of staggered horns.

"Good for you."

Backlit by the lights of cars coming up the other side of it, the western hill showed for the first time against the night.

"I didn't know you could herd cows in the dark," the girl said.

"You can't. Unless, of course, you have to."

"All those cowboys. I'm impressed! Where are the cows?

"We're looking for them."

"I always wanted to be a cowgirl. A real one," she added modestly, adjusting the silver concho belt at her middle.

"You ought to go ahead and do it, then."

"Well.... There isn't a whole lot of future in cowboying, is there?"

"No future at all. If it's future you're interested in, you're better off doing anything but."

"There's no future in what I do, either. All I got in this whole world is this lousy truck."

Light fanned behind the hill before the beams poked over, tilting at the sky and then dropping as the car came onto the downslope.

"Well," I said, "I'm sorry I came along too late to help you out."

"Thanks. It wasn't ever anything more than just a dream, anyway."

I rode around in front of the clattering engine and down the bank to the fence where John-Wayne still held the ends of the wires in one hand and his horse with the other.

"Come on, man!" he hissed.

"I'm coming."

"What the hell you did think you was doin?"

"Nothing. I asked the driver if she needed help."

"The driver's a woman?"

"Oh yes, she's a woman."

"How come you thought she needed help?"

"Wrestling truck tires around is a big job for a little girl."

"If it was too big of a one she wouldn't be doin it, would she? We could of put both them fences back in the time it took you not to help. Now some rancher's goin to lose his cows or get em stoled or killed on the highway—whichever—just on account of us." The car I'd watched top the hill less than a minute before flashed past on the highway as the girl's truck roared suddenly out of idle.

"Where did everbody ride to?" I asked John-Wayne.

"Off there a ways."

He tilted his head vaguely and rode away in the darkness without looking back. I watched the truck pull slowly off the shoulder into the outside lane, then turned the horse and rode after him. The upward shift of gears sounded long after it had disappeared behind the low hills south of the highway.

We rode for another hour or more and made camp by an irrigation ditch at the edge of a dark field having the smell of sun-cured alfalfa on it. The men jerked the packs down from the animals and watered and hobbled them, and in a few minutes the only sounds were their exhausted snores and the tear of mule teeth pulling at the grass. Beside me John-Wayne lay spread-eagled on his back, his face turned up to the stars.

Off in the darkness something pale moved: Carmen, walking slowly among the still prone figures like a field general inspecting his fallen troops after a battle. I threw off the blanket, rose quietly, and went to her. She took firm hold of my hand and we walked off a little way in the stubble field together beneath the faint stars. We did not walk far on account of my leg, and everyone but us being asleep anyway.

"So," I said, "what is it I'm supposed to do with you now?"

"You mean," she asked, "I have to tell you, Jeb?"

She fell sideways as she spoke as if in a swoon and I caught her in my arms and held her bent backward over my supporting arm, kissing her repeatedly on the mouth. Then I lifted her to her feet and we went on kissing, drawing apart for breath before coming together again to explore each other further. Finally she pushed away firmly and held me from her at arm's length. In the starshine I saw reflected in her eyes I could see her smiling with a mouth still wet from our kisses.

"I love you," I told her. "I love you very, very much. More than I ever loved two wives and I hate to think how many mistresses, put together."

"Do you really?"

She spoke in a light, amused, almost ironic voice.

"Absolutely, on my honor. I love you."

"That's the fastest-working star I ever wished on then," Carmen said.

---

"I don't want your scorpions all over me."

"Ain't no scorpions. Only dust."

"Or your dust either."

"What difference is a little more dust goin to make? You already got the desert all over and inside of you. You ain't never goin to get rid of the desert, man. You *are* the desert."

"Just so it isn't all over breakfast."

John-Wayne stopped shaking out the blanket. He laughed.

"When was the last time you saw anythin looked like breakfast?"

Objects appeared out of the gathering light as the world floated free of the darkness and spread itself everywhere. A mile away across the gray alfalfa field a two-storey ranch house in pink stucco glowed from the surrounding shade trees like the sun emerging from behind dark clouds. Light showed in the window at the back of the house and pale headlights swung on the turnaround and advanced slowly along the fence line of an adjacent field.

"I hope he doesn't spot us and drive on over here to see what we're up to," Carmen said.

"All that would happen is he'd offer us coffee from his thermos and chew the fat awhile about cattle prices, coyotes, and the spotted owl. His enemies don't live in Mexico City. The biggest of them all is himself, anyway."

"Look at the mountains this morning," she admired. "What did you tell me they're called, Jeb?"

"The Chiricahuas. For the Chiricahua Apache, of course."

Behind sharp red hills the mountains were gray except for the peaks, shining in the rays of the early white high-hitting sun, and the golden vapor clouds above the peaks being pulled apart by the dawn winds.

Carmen breathed in the morning air deeply.

"I feel Mexico already," she said. "I can smell it."

"That's not Mexico. It's the rancher's manure pile."

It was just a wisecrack, not anything I meant, and Carmen seemed to know it. Anyhow, she ignored me.

"But we're going to clean all that up," she said.

We were all of us excited to be approaching Mexico at last, even the mules who surged ahead over the hilly and broken desert as untiringly as if they were powered remotely by the sun swinging slowly across the white-hot sky.

"What's the first thing you're goin to do when we get to Mexico, Dude?" John-Wayne asked.

"Call Jody and let her know I've got her horse safe and sound."

"I didn't know they had phones in Mexico."

"Of course they have telephones in Mexico. Mexico is a modern country—almost as modern as New Mexico."

"How about showers? They got showers in Mexico, too?"

"Claro, señor."

"So when we get to Mexico I'm goin to spend the whole of a whole day in the shower. Goin to live in it, sleep in it, eat in it. Goin to spend the night as well as the day there—maybe two days."

"And when you come out you'll be shriveled up like a dried prune."

"I'll be clean though," he said. "I'll be the cleanest person in Mexico and New Mexico, both. I'll be the cleanest I ever was since I was borned."

The mountains moved slowly to meet us as we rode, rising taller through shades of blue that deepened each time you looked ahead to them. The wind got up shortly after noon, stirring the heat around without lessening it any and raising wind spouts lifting the pink dust a mile or more into the blue sky. Underfoot was the same mesquite and cholla and prickly pear and creosote bush, the bushes in full yellow flower that tickled your nose and made the hawes of your eyes burn. The animals kept a good pace as we rode spread out across the desert, each man taking his own way around the rocks, torrs, and arroyos, diverging from the central group of riders and angling back by degrees, a isolated double figure regularly resolving itself from the desert spaces. John-Wayne rode sometimes on my right, sometimes on my left, occasionally behind, keeping a distance of a hundred yards or more, while Carmen ranged ahead on Tortuga without breaking stride or slackening speed. Watching the one woman, hour after hour, I found myself thinking of the other, taking advantage of the opportunity to reflect on the events that had occurred since I left home so many weeks ago now—a chain of interlocking experiences and adventures that seemed to be happening not to me but to some other man, in some other time. I thought about Jody, what a fine woman she was, how intelligent and loyal and beautiful, and how fortunate I was to have found her and to have won favor in her eyes. And then I thought about the brave, brilliant, and resourceful lady riding up there ahead as if she were a dream—what about her? Not much, of course. Really, nothing. We were intellectual equals speaking the same language, vigorous adults thrown together in the wilderness for a period of weeks with no other company than ourselves, each of us with a defined particular mission to accomplish, a duty to perform. Duty, said General Lee, is the most beautiful word in the English language. And nothing had happened at all between us, really. A kiss in time saves nine. And I missed Jody terribly. I honestly did. I would call her the first chance I got once I had everyone safely across the border, and to hell with the rotten Mexican telephone system. In Mexico, we could buy an old truck and trailer for a few hundred pesos and John-Wayne and I would be on our way with the horse by the end of the week or in three or four days, whatever it took to get started. And Carmen and I would never see one another again. It's amazing how simple life can be when you make up your mind to have it that way.

John-Wayne nudged his horse left to close up the gap between us, and we rode together for some time, saying little and with our hats pulled over his eyes to keep the afternoon sun out of them.

"You'll be seeing Bette again in just a few days now," I said at last. "Aren't you excited?"

"Yeah."

"Have you been thinking what you're going to tell her when you do see her?"

"Nope."

"Well—what do you think you *might* say to her?"

He considered.

"Probly just, like, 'Long time no see.' Somethin like that."

"You young people are such romantic souls."

He shrugged.

"Maybe she's found her another boyfriend already."

"I doubt it," I said, and quit before he got around to the subject of the horse. I hadn't figured out what to say to him about that, yet.

Looking ahead I saw Carmen and Tortuga take a brushy hill at a lope. When I looked again, expecting to see them out of sight beyond it, they were stopped for what seemed like the first time in hours, poised in silhouette against the mountains and the yellow sky behind them.

"She sees somethin,'" John-Wayne said.

"I guess she does. I wish she'd do her looking from below the skyline, though."

Apparently the same thought occurred to her, since she vanished abruptly from the hilltop. We rode over and found her standing beside the horse in the close cover of a tangled mesquite copse. Carmen watched us as we came over the hill. Then she turned and pointed with her field glasses across the plain.

"We already seen it," John-Wayne told her.

At a distance of a couple of miles the incandescent point of reflected sunlight might have been a ranch truck making fence. Through the glasses, it showed distinctly as an enclosed utility vehicle painted pale green and following a grassy two-track in a northwesterly direction across the desert.

"La migra," I said quietly.

"Not when we're nearly there!"

"They're cutting sign between the highway and the mountains. I'd be doing the same thing exactly if I had their job."

"What are we going to *do,* Jeb?"

For the first time since I'd known her, Carmen appeared at a loss. Poking Uncle Sam in the eye is a different game entirely from thumbing your nose and heaving dead cats at the Mexican government.

"We'll figure something. They're only human beings after all, you know, not genies or poltergeists."

"Do you imagine they've spotted us already?"

The men had caught up with us by now. Some of them were off their mules already, while others sat with their legs over the pommels or across the animals' necks. Dismounted or astride, they'd dropped the reins to allow their mounts to forage what they could find from the mostly bare ground between the mesquite trees.

"It's their job to have seen us," I said. "I'm supposing they have."

I explained to Carmen how I wanted her, using the ridge we'd just crossed for cover, to take the men around behind the western hills lying between the plain and the greater mountains to a butte standing out from the mountain pediment at the end of a forested promontory of rock. They were to ride as hard as they could without raising dust and conceal themselves and their animals while they waited for us to find them again. I made her try to visualize how the butte might appear to someone approaching it up close, from the northeast. Then I had the men remount and held her stirrup for her while I called John-Wayne over to me.

"John-Wayne is going with you?" Carmen asked anxiously. "I was hoping you'd let me take him."

"I'm sorry. I need a straight man for the job, and John-Wayne's a one-hundred-percent American, unlike me. Stay oriented by the landmarks and you'll do just fine."

We left them and started downhill toward the flat-looking, seemingly unbroken plain that would be neither flat nor unbroken when we finally reached it. Twice I looked back at the rougher country, full of cover, we were leaving; spying nothing, I did not look again. We rode without speaking, the afternoon sun burning our faces under the hat brims, straight toward the green vehicle creeping at intervals in the direction of the mountains. It would move a few hundred yards and stop, and then the men inside would climb out and pace a pair of circles on the desert floor before returning to the truck and continuing farther in the grassy road. Observing their progress, I adjusted our own speed and direction so as to make our encounter appear entirely casual and accidental. The wind out on the plain was stronger than in the hills, and scouring with its burden of red sand.

"You know what huaraches look like?"

"What's war-rotchees?"

"Mexican shoes made from old car tires."

"They think it makes them go faster, or somethin?"

"They're just very poor, many of them. Anyway, if you see any tracks that look to you like a car walking, let me know. We'll show the Patrol something they can really get their teeth into."

"How come Meskins are so poor?"

"I don't know. Because they haven't any money."

"Navajos don't have no money neither. But they don't wear no war-rotchees."

"What goes in one place doesn't necessarily go in another."

"*Car-tires*," John-Wayne said in disgust, wrinkling his nose.

The agents had obviously been aware of us for some time now. They stopped more often and paid less attention to the ground, and once I caught a wink of light from the business end of a spotting scope. They drove slower as if to let us catch up, braked finally, and stepped out of the truck. The one with the scope put it away on the seat and then the pair of them stood together beside the open passenger door. The older agent was Mexican-American, the younger one a white fellow.

"Don't say a word unless they speak to you directly," I warned John-Wayne while we were still out of hearing.

The men stood very still with their hands hanging near their service pistols, cautiously watching as we rode up to them.

"Afternoon," I told them.

The young officer touched the bill of his cap to us. The older one did not do anything.

"It's a warm day to be chasing aliens out on the desert."

"It's a warm day to be chased, too."

"Are you an American citizen?" the Hispanic agent asked.

"Am I an American citizen." I paused, considering. "The Duke of Wellington was approached once on the steps of Parliament by a man wanting to know if he was Mr. Smith. 'My good man,' the Duke told him, 'if you can believe that, you can believe anything.' What would *you* say I am?"

He missed the reference but flushed a dull resentful red anyway.

"What is your destination this afternoon?" the other officer inquired.

"Mexico."

"And what is the purpose of your visit there?"

"Buy a lot of beer and tequila. Get drunk. Get laid. Buy stuff to take home to the little woman so she won't suspect anything, just like every other red-blooded Americano. We're tourists," I added, helpfully.

"Why aren't you driving?" his partner wanted to know.

"You don't want to have an auto accident in Mexico," I explained. "It's safer just taking a horse."

He was looking at John-Wayne now.

"You are you an American citizen also?" he asked.

John-Wayne was insulted.

"'Course I'm American! I'm a full-blooded Navajo Indian—John-Wayne Bilagody, Tuba City, Arizona, U.S.A.!"

"You are traveling alone," the Hispanic continued. "Just the two of you together—is that correct?"

"Yes," I said.

"Who were the other riders you were riding with?"

So they *had* seen us, then.

"We weren't with them. Not for long, anyway. They came pretty close to riding us down."

"Who is they?"

"An endurance-riding club out of Silver City. All of them on A-rabs. Most ridiculous looking thing I've seen since the Deming duck races."

"Where were they going?"

"You don't think a lot of snobs from Silver would give the time of day to folks like us, do you?"

The Hispanic looked disapprovingly at our ragged clothes. His partner nodded.

"Well, you boys have a good day," he said cautiously. "Watch out for bandits on the border. And don't get too drunk down there in sunny Mexico, or you'll end up in one of their jails for a month—or two, or three."

"We'll be careful."

"So long then."

"Adiós."

Putting the horses forward at a trot we rode off from the patrol, two men alone with their guns and spotting scopes and night vision in the vastness of the desert, windswept and smoking with dust, on which the whole world was trying to evade them on its way into the United States in search of freedom, hypertension, and MacNuggets. We did not look back before we'd ridden a couple of miles and crossed over a low ridge— and then we *did* look. Seeing nothing, we slowed the horses to a walk to breathe them and get our own breath back.

"Awesome, man," John-Wayne said. "You're the best liar I ever heard."

"I wasn't exactly given a choice, was I?"

"I won't never believe a word you say to me after this."

"I don't like having to lie. And in this case, we're helping smuggle aliens out of the country, not into it."

"They broke the law by comin here in the first place, didn't they?"

"I guess they did. They didn't really want to."

"What do you mean, they didn't want to?"

"Well," I said, "they *had* to."

"If it was me I'd of told those policemen all about them Meskins so's they could round em up and send em back where they belong, and you and me could of gone home with the horse tomorrow."

"That wouldn't have been the honorable thing to do."

"Lyin ain't the honorable thing, neither."

"Well, well," I said, "so you're learning. But the one big thing you need to learn, after you've got all the rules and regulations down, is that life isn't the way we would have it, sometimes."

We rode down and across the arroyo between parallel ridges and up and over the second of them, from where the mountains showed black and sheer and massive ahead—towering, like a whole world waiting to fall on us.

"What it is," John-Wayne said at last, "is, you'd do anythin for her."

"Yes," I agreed, "I *would* do anything for her. But not *only* her."

The butte we were riding for was visible from the next ridge where it appeared as a foothill to the cordillera, dark and indistinct in the shadow of the building storm, behind it. We turned the horses' heads and kicked them up to a steady trot with the cool wind leading the storm in our faces, and the scent of rain. Riding apart we spoke only occasionally, when the increasing roughness of the country forced us to ride closer together.

"Where do you guess the lootenant and them guys are at?" John-Wayne asked.

"I don't guess. I'm not even thinking about them."

"Maybe them cops back there will find em and shoot em all dead."

"That's unlikely. They missed them coming across in June, remember."

"I guess them guys are kind of dumb, huh?"

"Not really," I said. "They just have an awful lot of work they're supposed to do, saving Western civilization and getting the Washington politicians reelected at the same time."

The closer up we rode on the butte the deeper it seemed to recede into the vague mountainous terrain beneath the black overhang of storm. I was beginning to despair of rejoining Carmen and the men when John-Wayne, drawing rein sharply on a rise of broken ground, pointed ahead.

"See something, J-W?"

"Out there!"

"Where?"

"There! Can't you see it?"

"I don't see anything."

"It wasn't the red man had to invent eye glasses."

"What is it that you see?"

"See somethin looks like trees, 'ceptin they move more like horses."

"Can you see people riding the horses?"

"I think so. If I look real hard and use my imagination."

I was still fumbling at the straps on the saddlebags for the field glasses when I made out what he was pointing at: a line of dark shapes moving almost imperceptibly among juniper trees wide-spaced across a grassy shoulder of the foothills.

"What I don't want is for us to ride over there and find it's the lieutenant."

"It's what your binoculars are for, man."

"They're too far out to be certain even using binoculars."

"Why don't we just keep ridin then, 'til we're close enough to see what is we're lookin at?"

"Aren't we lucky having two good heads between us. Otherwise we'd be standing out all night on this knoll."

"*I* wouldn't," John-Wayne said. "It's fixin to rain hard around here, pretty quick."

Dust led the storm, a whirling red cloud bending the bushes flat and cartwheeling the tumbleweed, obliterating the desert and the mountains from sight, scouring my eyes and tightening my throat like a drawstring. Behind it the rain advanced, overtaking the dust and turning it to mud in midair before pounding the mud into the earth again. Lightning flashed in sheets across the blackness, thunder knocked and crashed, the wind shrieked, and water torrented in the arroyos and cut fresh channels in the desert where no channel was before. Blinded and confused we put the horses forward, keeping to the high ground and kicking them ahead to leap the racing water where it crossed our path. Water pooled in hollows and basins in the desert floor and the clay beneath the hardpan turned slick as grease. Trying to dodge a water course Quixote slipped and went down on his knees, nearly unseating me and covering us both with the red mud as he floundered to get his feet under him. Ahead John-Wayne's and Ana's doubled form was dark and indistinct through the mists. The near fall had caused my leg to bleed again and the injured muscle burned like hot wires bundled beneath the skin.

"Where are we going?" I shouted as we came up behind them.

"I don't know, man! You're the leader—remember?"

"Might as well keep on the way we're going, then."

We slogged along through what seemed like an eternity of storm, nothing but rain and thunder, the rush of water all around, and the sucking sound the horses' feet made coming out of the mud until at last they struck something like turf underfoot and I saw the expired flower stalks of yucca looming ahead through the grayness. The ground rose steeply into Spanish Bayonet and mesquite and then we came to a forest of juniper trees growing far apart. John-Wayne looked around at me with lifted eyebrows under his dripping, shapeless hat, and I nodded to him. There wasn't anywhere else to go but on.

The trees stood taller ahead, set closer in larger and larger copses, some of them offering cover enough for several horses and their riders. The rain subsided to a drizzle as the storm went booming away on a slow vortex of wind and the vapor clouds rose perpendicularly from the slope like ascending spirits. Ahead on the hillside something moved, repositioning itself inside a clump of trees.

"Horses," John-Wayne said in a low voice.

"Yep."

"Maybe it's just cowboys. Or a sheepherder."

"And maybe it's not," I said.

He tugged the rifle free of the soaked scabbard and laid it across his thighs as we approached the trees, and I unfastened the holster guard at my hip. All we could see were the water-slick rear ends of the animals and a patch of rain-streaked flank. In color they were nondescript, anybody's horses—or mules, if we were lucky. Quixote and Ana paced the wet grass noiselessly, the only sound the click of metal between the horses' teeth and the squeak of wet leather when we shifted our weight in the saddle.

"So la migra didn't get you, after all," a soft voice from somewhere said. "What would they have done with you if they *had* arrested you—put you in a van and shipped you back Mexico? The oficiales wouldn't have had you, so they'd have put you in another van and deported you to the States again. You'd have been men without a country, both of you, for the rest of your lives."

She stood against the trunk of a rain-blackened alligator juniper, concealed almost entirely by branches and the camouflage parka, only her sweet sunburned face with its fringe of auburn hair peering at us from within the camouflage hood.

"You fool," I told her, "we might have shot you."

I stepped down painfully from the horse, limped over to the tree, and reached among the wet fragrant greenery to hug her. John-Wayne saw the whole thing but I no longer cared what he saw, or knew, or thought. It had nothing to do with him, anyhow.

"So you found the place," I said. "What do you think you need me as a guide for?"

"*Is* this the place? I wasn't sure. I went just as far as I could go in this storm, and stopped."

The men emerged slowly from the trees around as we talked, stuffing their playing cards and dice into their packs. They unloaded and unsaddled the mules and burros, picketed them, and began foraging for dry wood in the depths of the tallest, thickest stands of trees. The mists cleared off from the foothills as light broke through the shadows, and the columned face of the mountains glowed under a double rainbow.

We built a big fire at the center of a grassy space between the trees and stood up close to it to let our clothes dry, steaming. One of the briagada had shot a number of sitting ducks off a conservation pond dammed among the foothills, and we had a supper of hot roast duck to look forward to. It's amazing how well you can live off the land if you only have faith in it, even on the desert.

When we'd eaten the men sat by the fire boiling water for Mormon tea and playing cards, while John-Wayne wandered off into the darkness by himself. I noticed he'd said little to anyone during the evening, and barely spoken to me at all. Without anyone noticing Carmen and I found a dry place within some trees to sit in, beyond the reach of the firelight.

"Well Major," I asked her, "how goes the war?"

"It goes very well, thank you. I was terribly afraid for you this afternoon."

"There was no reason for anyone to be afraid. I'm a taxpaying citizen of the United States of America. I pay those men's wages. They work for me."

"Doesn't your country have a law against harboring enemies of the United States?"

"Are you the enemy?"

"I don't know. I suppose not."

"You and I aren't enemies."

"Yes, we are. We're sweet enemies."

"Sweet enemies?"

"From *Don Quixote*," she said. "The greatest novel ever written in the Spanish language—or any."

"My grandfather used to read aloud to us from *Don Quixote* when I was a boy. I don't remember the part about the sweet enemies, though."

"Did you enjoy it?"

"Pretty well. It didn't make as much of an impression as some other things I've read."

"Read it again," Carmen said. "A great work like that must be read a second time at least, in middle life if possible."

"I'm sure it should. I don't have a whole lot of time free for reading these days."

"Tomorrow night we'll be in Mexico, and then we'll have time. A little time, anyway."

"What will you do with the men?"

"I've promised them four weeks' furlough to visit their families and bring in new recruits."

"Will that be easy?"

"No. It will be very hard."

"What if you don't find enough men?"

"I will get the men." She emphasized the "will" slightly.

"You're a woman who's used to getting what she wants, when she wants it, aren't you?"

She shook her head.

"No. I'm used to taking it!"

"You're a very strong woman, did you know it?"

Again she shook her head.

"I'm not strong, I'm stubborn. But perhaps it amounts to the same thing, in the end."

"It's what gives all women a certain strength. But you have it more than most. You're the strongest woman I ever met, and I've met some strong ones, believe me."

"Is that a compliment?"

"Definitely, it's a compliment."

"Then I hope it isn't only that. Because tomorrow I need true strength, the strength any woman ever had—not the complimentary kind."

Already some of the men had gone in search of their blankets, but the greater number sat on around the fire. They'd put up the cards and dice and were talking quietly among themselves with intervals of silence in between, like the rural peasants and villagers they were. The low flames reddened their dark faces and accentuated the harsh Aztec and Mayan features half-concealed by the glossy black hair grown out to shoulder length and beyond. Except in speaking the faces were immobile and nearly expressionless, from fatigue now as well as three millennia of conquest and bloodshed.

"They're really only boys," Carmen said. "If I had the milk of human kindness in my veins I'd send them all home to their mothers to finish weaning them and set them to work on the eijidos."

"They've marched well though."

"Yes," she said, "they have. I'm very proud of my boys—of my young men."

Unobserved still by the men we rose and walked off a little way, deeper into the trees. I placed my arm about her waist and Carmen laid her head against my shoulder.

"I'm taking us through by the pass east of Douglas, Arizona. The Border Patrol will be busy miles away, down on the desert where the drug smugglers come across."

"I'm not afraid of la migra," Carmen said bravely.

"You were afraid this afternoon."

"I refuse to be afraid of more than a single thing at a time—the biggest thing."

"If it's the lieutenant you mean, I don't think there's anything to worry about this late in the game."

"That one always strikes from behind, like a cuguar."

"All the same I wouldn't worry."

"Old lovers are like the past, always running to overtake you—even when they happen to be dead men."

"Why not let go of the past now," I said, "and take hold of the future for a few minutes."

The smell of her wet hair eclipsed the juniper fragrance as she clung to me, pressing her face to my chest as she worked my back with her fingernails.

"Oh darling," Carmen said, "as much as I love you now, I'll love you so much more when we're together at last—at home in Mexico."

"Dios te salve, María, llena eres de gracia, el Señor es contigo; bendita eres entre todas las mujeres, y bendito es el fruto de tu vientre Jesús...Dios te salve, María, llena eres de gracia, el Señor es contigo; bendita eres entre todas las mujeres, y bendito es el fruto de tu vientre Jesús... Dios te salve, María, llena eres de gracia..."

Well before daylight the men, led by a lean, longhaired, haggard-looking fellow of about thirty named Héctor, were on their knees praying around the rekindled fire. In its light their faces were still and impassive, only the eyes expressing the anticipation, the joy and excitement they felt after a night lying out in damp blankets on the soaked ground. It would rain again this afternoon perhaps, or tomorrow, and it would rain also in Mexico where worse things would happen besides, but on this morning they were going home and so they were happy, full of gratitude and praise to all their saints, the greatest of them in particular. When the men had been praying for some time a woman's voice added itself to the chant, rising clear and sweet above the rest like the voice of the Mother of God Herself, and I lay on my back in the blue early light that looked colder than it felt and listened in surprise since Carmen, who loathed religious superstition, privately despised the daily religious rituals observed by her Mexican-Indian troops, though she never expressed her feelings in their presence.

No one was interested in breakfast that morning. The men worked fast to load the animals and we started soon after sunup, riding in broken country with the mountains running close in from the west. The air felt oppressive after the storm and the sky above the mountains and the eastern desert was heavy with the grey saturated clouds. The brigada traveled this morning behind a collective mask, daring and at the same time cautious, as if they were expecting some enemy to try, in a last-ditch effort, to snatch victory from them just at the moment when it was within their reach. John-Wayne, who seemed to have got over his snit, dropped back frequently to joke with the riders while I ranged ahead across the green foothills with the confidence of Coronado approaching his Gran Quivira. The kid was, I realized, more than a little jealous: He'd obviously only been pretending to sleep when, after kissing Carmen goodnight, I got in my bedroll the evening before. Adolescents make life so damn hard for themselves.

The fields and pastures drew eastward from the mountains as we rode, the forest crept down toward the plains, and the ground grew rocky and increasingly steep underfoot. Attempting to follow the drainages uphill we were twice entrapped by box canyons forcing us to backtrack and attempt another way up to the pass. There were cattle scattered in these draws and canyons, and here and there a windmill with its pinwheel jammed stood above the tops of the trees. Riding up a long draw carpeted with late summer flowers freshened by the monsoon rains we came on a water-well with a rusted tank standing half-filled beside it and behind these a cabin built of pine logs with the bark on and roofed with tarpaper tearing away in strips from the underlying planks. To the right of it was a stables as big as the house itself, collapsing inward on a pile of moldering straw and manure where the inhabitants would have put up the horses that were the only means into this roadless and isolated place—some rancher's summer camp, visited infrequently if at all anymore by vaqueros, sheepherders, and hunters caught out in an early winter storm. The windows of the house remained intact but the front door was pushed partly inward. We rode up to the trough and dismounted around it, taking care to fill our canteens before we gave the horses and mules their chance. Across the clearing a cow watched us from under a juniper tree, her face a pale death's head against the dark green foliage.

"This is an unlucky place," Carmen said. "Let's not stay long around here."

"No place with water in the desert is unlucky," I told her.

The horses, having drunk to satisfy their thirst, dished the surface of the stale water with their muzzles, slobbering.

"There's a haunt around here somewheres," John-Wayne said nervously. "Let's get goin now, man."

"You and your damn haunts," I told him. "Maybe it's a witchcrafter in that house, trying to put a spell on us and turn us into skinwalkers. Or would it be giant crabs today?"

I shouldn't have let him have it like that but the end of the line was in plain sight and we were both more or less out of patience with each other by now.

"Witchcrafter just run out of there," he said.

"What are you talking about?"

"Old Man Coyote come through the door while you was talkin.' Only it wasn't no real coyote, if you know what I mean."

"I'm going to have a look in there," I told him.

John-Wayne shrugged hopelessly and stared away as if all was lost.

"*Man-o-man-o-man-o-man-o-man-o-man-o-man-o-man-o-man-o-man!*" he exclaimed.

I threw him the reins to hold and walked on to the house. Blankets hung behind the windows and inside it was very dark. There was also a bad smell of the kind you encounter only a few times in your life if you're lucky, and that you don't have to be told about after the first one. I pulled my handkerchief from my back pocket and tied it behind over my nose and mouth. Then I pushed the door all the way back with the side of my arm to let the light in, and as much fresh air as would enter there.

The bodies lay carefully arranged in a half-circle on the wooden floor like trout on a bank, the white bone gleaming through rags of disintegrating clothing and at the fleshless wrists and ankles, which were tied with wire. All nine corpses lay face down and all had been shot in the base of the skull—once—by some small-caliber weapon. They had been five men, a woman, and three children. The men had on jeans and cowboy shirts, the woman jeans and a floral blouse. The children wore nothing that was recognizable. Two of the men were sockfooted while the rest wore huaraches, the blunt toes turned outward on the rough planks. The ones who remained booted wore old pairs, scuffed and cracked, that the killers found not worth stealing. Among the mess on the floor only the huaraches remained intact, dull black and rubbery, incorruptible. I backed out of that house and into daylight, where the sun had burned through the clouds at last and Carmen sat her horse, watching me.

"Go back," I told her. "I'll have the men take care of this."

"Is there someone dead?"

"Nine people. Three of them children."

"What do you want us to do?"

"Bury them, of course."

"There isn't time!"

And I'd thought to spare her feelings. All women are tough and the really tough ones, like her, are merely inhuman.

"For Christ's sake, Carmen."

"But—nine people? We'll be digging until Domesday."

"We can't just ride away and leave them."

"How not? 'Let the dead bury the dead.'"

There was a cave in the wall of lava rock across the little canyon. It was a squarish hole, black as though it went a long way back into the cliff, seven feet high and about three wide. I walked over and took a look inside. The rock walls converged about six feet back and there was stony rubble on the floor, but it would do all right for the purpose I had in mind for it—a morgue for all eternity.

John-Wayne rode off down canyon a way, out of sight of the burial, and Carmen and I sat our horses while the men carried the corpses out and stacked them head first in the stone mortuary. Already they were half mummified, releasing little stench when brought out from the poisonous house into the fresh air.

"Poor bastards," I said. "The coyotes must have done them in."

"There was only one coyote," she reminded me. "And I thought you said they were shot."

"They were shot, and robbed. By their coyotes."

"I don't understand."

She was Argentinian, not Mexican, of course. I kept forgetting that.

"Coyotes charge Mexican nationals hundreds or thousands of dollars to bring them across the border illegally. Once in the United States they often rob and abandon their clients—or worse."

"And these coyotes, as you call them, are themselves Mexican nationals?"

"Claro."

"But that's terrible. Their own people!"

"Your—I mean, the Mexican government—makes something of a business of that."

"But that is the government. This is el pueblo—*the people*!"

"That's all the government is, any government. El pueblo—in power."

Carmen looked distressed.

"If I believed that, I'd give it all up, go home to Argentina, and show horses for the rest of my life."

The last bodies to go into the tomb were the children, the men driving them headfirst in among the adults. They went with difficulty, and when the burial party had finished they gathered rocks fallen from the cliff and filled in the opening of the cave to keep the coyotes out. Before we left I called Héctor over and had him recite a couple of decades of the rosary for the repose of the souls of the dead. I felt a little silly asking him, but it wasn't my religion, after all.

"What a good Catholic you would have made," Carmen said, "if it weren't for the sin of scrupulosity."

"What's scroopilosophy?" John-Wayne wanted to know.

"It means trying too hard to be good. A thing Catholics are supposed to believe in—or rather, not believe in."

"I'm Catholic, sort of, and I ain't never heard of it."

"Maybe because no one figured it was anything you'd ever have much call to worry about," I told him.

"My granma always said to try and be as good as you can be, but don't worry too much about it if you ain't."

"That was her way of telling you not to be like Sr. Ryder," Carmen told him. "Scrupulous."

"I'm not scrupulous," I said. "I just believe in a code of behavior that no one else seems to believe in anymore."

"You *are* oldfashioned."

"Meaning religious?"

"No," she said, "it doesn't have anything to do with religion, I think."

"Anyone with religion knows it's bad luck to move dead people around," John-Wayne put in.

Carmen turned on him. Her eyes were enormous, the tip of her sunburned nose white, and her mouth red and full of teeth.

"People who talk of bad luck carry bad luck. Don't you bring your bad luck around me."

John-Wayne looked away from her at the ground.

"Sorry," he said. "I didn't know you was superstitious too."

Neither did I, I thought.

We crossed Highway 80 between Rodeo and Douglas and, riding higher, entered a piney forest broken by grassy openings dotted with century plants and Spanish Bayonet lying beneath parapets of scarlet rock scabbed with green lichen and standing into a pale September sky. Eastward above the tops of the trees Animas Peak loomed across the valley, and where the forest opened that way I glimpsed the Animas River where I'd caught trout as a boy and gone swimming while the leaches applied themselves to my sunburned hide and that you could mark from a distance by the big cottonwoods along it and the tin roofs of the ranch houses glinting in the hazy sun. They say you can't go home again, and now I *was* home. It looked different, somehow, but that could have been just a matter of distance, looking down on the valley from high up in the western mountains. Beyond all that rock to the south was Mexico, only a few miles away, and Mexico was what interested me now.

An eight-cylinder truck engine grinding uphill in low gear between canyon walls makes more noise than a tank going through the Eisenhower tunnel. I called a halt and rode forward a way before dismounting, snubbed Quixote to a tree, and walked on through the forest until the white road appeared ahead, winding above a steep ravine up to the pass. Gently, I eased down onto my belly on the dry pine needles and propped myself on my elbows to watch the road. The vibrations grew stronger and I heard gravel crunching under rubber. At the flash of sun on windshield glass beyond the trees I ducked, then rose on my elbows again as the lime-green Bronco passed with a uniformed officer at the wheel and his partner riding shotgun in the passenger seat. Patrolling in the mountains was tough work but I proposed to give them a leg up on the job, since they could miss a couple of dozen aliens tonight and still come out ahead when I was through smuggling sixteen or seventeen of them out of the country; it gave me a patriotic feeling just thinking about it. The white dust cone behind the truck was still spinning apart and sifting into the ravine when I got up from the ground and walked back through the trees to the brigada.

"La migra again," I told Carmen.

"In these mountains? God, what fools! Instead of getting out of our way and letting us do their job for them!"

"They've gone ahead up to the pass. It's only a back road, and then we have a ravine to get across. A few miles more and the Border Patrol will have missed its chance. After that, it will be the Federales' turn."

The brigada rode forward, across the road and down into the ravine which was brushy and very steep. The men were still crossing when a pickup truck pulling a stock trailer came over the pass from the west side and started downhill, clattering loudly in the switchbacks. The rancher waved as he passed and I waved back; it seemed, somehow, like my farewell to the

United States. Even before he was out of sight on the last curve we were up the far side of the ravine and into the trees on the downslope beyond. Open sky showed ahead through the treetops, and the heads of late afternoon storms building above the mountains of Mexico. We rode on several miles and came to an open park in the forest scattered with wildflowers and bordered on one side by a running creek. On the other side, an arm of the mountains made a barrier between the golden sunset in the west and the blue dusk rising on the eastern side of the ridge.

"Well," I said to Carmen.

"Well what?"

"I vote we spend the night in this place and cross in the morning after sunup."

She looked troubled.

"I think we ought to get over right away—tonight."

"The men are tired and the animals are about blown. There's graze here, and water. No telling what we'll encounter on the other side. Also I couldn't see to ride in the dark, last time I tried it."

"The horses can be our eyes," Carmen said.

"They could. If they had an idea of where the hell it is we're supposed to be going."

Light rays fanned the ultraviolet sky behind the mountains, lighting the dry thunderheads from beneath, and the air had an even warmth that felt less like the residual heat of the day than the quality of another country, a different culture already making itself known. Whistling and joking the brigada spread the blankets and brought in firewood, like men who have learned to quit worrying and trust in the future instead. While I was helping Carmen raise the tent I heard a disturbance in the sky overhead and looked up to see John-Wayne clinging like a bear near the top of the tallest pine tree around, the supple spire bent over with his weight.

"Mexico don't look no different from where we're at right now," he reported on his return to earth.

"What did you expect it to look like?"

"Like Mexico, of course."

"Mexico doesn't look as much as it feels," Carmen told him. "It's a different world—a different universe from the United States. You won't be disappointed in Mexico, I promise you."

"We're goin home day after tomorrow, anyway," he said.

All of us were hungry from missing breakfast and eating out of the saddle bags throughout the day. Two of the men caught fingerling trout in the creek with a bucket while the others gathered the ripened fruit of prickly pear and nuts from the cholla growing around. The blue of the forest deepened to black and Animas Peak glowed a deeper red above the golden plain.

"It's like a paradise here," I said.

Carmen glanced, smiling, around the pretty glade and I thought she was beginning to relax at last.

"Paradise lost, perhaps."

"What's the first thing to be done in Mexico?"

"I'm going to send the men home to their families."

"And after that?"

"Take a bath..."

"There won't be water left in Sonora State when John-Wayne is finished showering."

"...and wash my hair and put on new clothes and perfume and go for dinner in one of those quiet little restaurants they have in Mexican towns where you're the only ones eating and the waiter stands all night with his back against the wall holding his tray against his stomach, watching to see when you need something."

"And after?"

"¡Tú sí que eres inquisitivo!" Carmen smiled. "Remember, you have a minor child you're still responsible for."

A single shot sounded from behind the trees on a rise of ground below the cliff.

"It must be either Jackson or a rabbit," I said—an old Civil War joke I didn't expect her to catch.

She was staring uphill toward the line of trees, looking like a sandwich-board prophet who's just seen news of the end of the world flash across the sky.

"That isn't one of ours!"

They hit us fast and hard and in complete silence, except for the gunfire. Too astonished to shout, our men took cover with their weapons on the edge of the park and attempted to return fire as dim shapes advanced from one tree to another through the woods. I pulled Carmen behind a big pine and got off a few sound shots with the revolver while all around the automatic rifles chattered like fireworks on Cinco de Mayo and bullets whined in the air, clipping the branches of trees and socking into the soft resinous trunks. The shooting stopped almost as abruptly as it had begun and was followed by a stillness as profound as the surface of a pool after the last ripple of a tossed pebble has expended itself.

"¡Cabrón!" Carmen exclaimed. "¡Hijo de la chingada! Didn't I say to you that he always strikes from behind? And this time from beyond the grave."

"It isn't your enemies who betray you," I told her, "it's your friends—always your friends. Because friends have faces, while the enemy is always faceless. It isn't the enemy who gets on your nerves and resents you, who you become jealous of and want to see fail, it's your friend. Jeff Davis didn't hate Grant, he hated Joe Johnston. It's how the Trojans lost Troy, and how the South lost the Civil War. It's how every battle in history was lost, every country destroyed, and every cause forfeited. It's the oldest story in the book, and it stinks. It stinks to high heaven."

She wasn't listening. "One knows an ex-lover better than one knows anyone else in the whole world," Carmen said. "Even when he is a dead one as well, knowing that you were only ever just slumming with him during those months after we left Mexico behind."

# BOOK VI
# GUENEVERE

The poor in Mexico have us with them always, so they are used to providing help where it's needed without appearing to think about it very much. The Holguín place in Agua Prieta was a century-old adobe building, painted a flaking pink and falling down behind, on the edge of an expanding arroyo filled with upside-down automobiles and fenced with barb-wire tacked to peeled manzanita sticks snagging the trash and tumbleweed being blown across the desert on a hard wind. On the days when the wind didn't blow the smoke pall from fires burning at the municipal dump covered the city and filled in the valley where it lay, hiding the mountains and the tall smokestacks of the abandoned copper smelter over in Douglas, Arizona. Señor Holguín kept a roping steer in the yard where it chewed sadly on the pancake pear growing up against the wall of the house and also a flock of chickens that, though provided with a comfortable hutch, preferred living in the big house with its owners. Héctor and Concepción Holguín had produced fifteen children in the course of their twenty-five-year marriage, five of whom had died and nine moved away. The remaining child, Arturo, had been among the victims of the lieutenant's revenge attack on the border. The couple, while grieved at the news of their son's death, stoically accepted what in their minds was plainly the will of God. Carmen had requested a Mass said in Arturo's memory in their parish church. It was attended by scores of Holguíns, Apodacas, and others living around, who seemed grateful.

The three of us—Carmen, John-Wayne, and myself—spent ten days with the Holguíns while Carmen attended to the final needs of what remained of the brigada, wiring money from an account she held in Mexico City. A few of the men had left for home already, some were with women in Agua Prieta, others on binges from which they might not sober up for days or weeks. None had bank accounts of their own, some no address. All the time we were with the Holguíns Carmen was beside herself. She was unable to eat and she slept badly, waking in the middle of the night from nightmares in which her men were being slaughtered in ambush. Napoleon, after he'd sacrificed tens of thousands of his troops in Russia, abandoned the remaining army and escaped across Europe in a fancy coach to Paris and his Empress, but Napoleon was not a woman. Understanding, the old couple left us alone much of the time, having offered the use of the single operating vehicle among the four or five hulks parked around in the yard. Every evening after supper señor Holguín produced a glazed earthenware jug and we sat outdoors together in the cooling October twilight drinking homemade tequila before turning in early. Inside, the house was mostly solid wall several feet thick separating small square rooms off a dark hallway about the width of a fissure in a slickrock cliff and deeply scored by the steer who, venturing indoors in search of something better than pancake pear to eat, would retreat hastily backward with a loud clattering of hoofs on finding the passageway too narrow to accommodate his horns. Almost the only furniture was mattresses propped on bricks with Indian blankets thrown over them, a few chairs, and here and there a scarred, peeling santo standing gloomily in unsuspected corners. An exposed pipe in the backyard was the Holguín's water supply, and a collection of rusting buckets their plumbing system. We bathed down in the dry arroyo, John-Wayne and I pouring water over one another's heads while Carmen, climbing down afterward, had to manage for herself. It wasn't what we'd all been looking forward to, but it was something. You don't need Holiday Inn to make you feel like a human being again.

Farther up the arroyo was a brush corral where Tortuga and Baca's horses were penned. On a morning when Carmen had bank work to do I rode with her downtown in Holguín's old truck and walked across the international border into Douglas, where I placed a call from the first pay phone I came to. People don't use the Mexican telephone system if they have a choice between it and talking through tin cans tied to opposite ends of a piece of bailing wire. The voice answering the call sounded unfamiliar and I was on the point of hanging up and redialing when I recognized it as Jody's, after all.

"Hello," I said.

"Hello?"

"It's me. Can't you tell?"

"Am I supposed to recognize your voice after all this time? It must be months. I was thinking just the other day of giving your story to *Unsolved Mysteries.*"

"That would have been a mistake. I'm not a statistic yet. In fact, I'm as much alive as it's possible for any man to be."

"You sound awfully far away—as if you were calling from the moon."

"I'm in Douglas, Arizona. It's a little like the moon, as a matter of fact."

"Well," Jody said. After a long pause she added, "How are you, anyway?"

"I'm doing fine, thanks. Your horse is well, too."

"You found Cortez? Really? You mean you actually *have* him?"

"I have him, all right."

"Why—that's *wonderful*!"

"It's just a little short of miraculous, to be honest with you."

"Is he in Douglas too?"

"He's in Agua Prieta, a few miles from here across the border."

"You mean, in Mexico?"

""Pero sí, señora. En México."

"How did he get all the way to *Mexico*?"

"Somebody rode him there."

"I see."

She seemed less collected now, slightly uncomfortable.

"You're sure he's all right?"

"Sure I'm sure."

"How were you planning to get him through quarantine?"

"Ordinarily there's no problem. Right now, though, there's a contagion of some sort down here. It may take me a couple of weeks to get him a clean bill of health."

"You mustn't let them confiscate him!" she exclaimed.

"Over my dead body," I promised her. "I'll call you again in a couple of days."

The directory holder hung empty below the telephone box, its face scarred where people had been trying to pry quarters from it. I hung the receiver up and walked back through the checkpoint crowded with grandmothers carrying shopping bags on their arms and waving identity cards in the face of the American customs inspector into Agua Prieta, where Carmen waited for me with the truck.

"Did you manage to get through all right on the telephone?" she asked.

"I made the call. I can't tell if I got through, or not."

We went for lunch in a restaurant she'd found off the plaza with whitewashed trees planted along its four sides and a white-painted gazebo at the middle of it. A big American sedan from the Forties was parked across the street with a pretty girl perched on one of its balloon fenders, operating a transistor radio on the hood and sunning herself. When the mozo had cleared away the plates, while we waited for him to bring coffee, I took Carmen's hand across the table and pressed it.

"You're much too beautiful, my darling."

She smiled.

"Too beautiful for what?"

"Too beautiful to wait," I said.

Carmen shook her head.

"The Holguíns do not share our revolutionary thinking. They would not understand, and they would not approve."

"They don't need to know anything about it."

But she was firm.

"We are guests in their house nevertheless. And you have the boy to take care of, first."

John-Wayne had little to do at the Holguíns beyond listening to corrido on the radio and practicing his roping technique on Sr. Holguín's bored and increasingly resentful steer.

"We goin home tomorrow, Dude?" he asked one morning as he coiled the lariat and dropped it through the broken window onto the seat of one of Holguín's inoperative trucks.

"Not tomorrow, no."

"How come, man?"

"Because we still have business to take care of here."

"*I* don't have no business, no place."

"Try being patient for just a little while longer. If you can."

"I can't. It's borin here."

"You were bored on the reservation, too," I reminded him.

"Not like this. This is *awesomely* borin.'"

"Well, you can be grateful anyway that you're not in school. Because school is where you're going, the minute you get home."

I wanted him gone as badly as he wanted to go but there was the matter of the horse to be settled between us first and I was looking forward to settling it the way I'd look forward to gum surgery, or a colonoscopy.

He left the house a couple of afternoons later, saying he wanted to take a walk in to town, and by nine o'clock that evening he hadn't returned. I took Holguín's pickup and drove downtown, looking into all the bars along the strip. There were plenty of Americans hanging around there, none of them of the Native American variety. I went on through the border check to the Douglas bus depot and learned from a crippled-up old saddle stiff sitting on the curb in the dark that the bus for Tucson by way of Bisbee had left an hour ago. I thanked him and drove back into Agua Prieta again, where I stopped on the way out to Holguíns' for a whiskey in one of the better-looking bars. When a couple of men began looking sideways at me and talking in low tones in English about getting the gringo I ostentatiously tipped the bar man five dollars and enjoyed a second whiskey undisturbed. In Mexico five bucks still buys you protection, even if that means only putting a call in to the cops.

John-Wayne rolled in as Carmen and I were getting up the next morning—chastely, in our separate rooms. He looked disheveled, with his hair hanging over his reddened eyes and a whiskey breath.

"What were you up to last night?" I asked as I buttoned my shirt.

"Got drunk."

"Where?"

"At Geronimo's."

"Not at Geronimo's you didn't. I was there myself. Where else did you go?"

John-Wayne didn't answer.

"Just seventy-two hours more and you'd have been kissing Bette hello for the first time in three months."

He looked ashamed, then defiant. Finally he looked very proud.

"I almost went ahead and did it with her—and then I didn't," he said. "I already paid her and she wouldn't give me my money back and I didn't care and I went downstairs and drunk whiskey all night long, stead of gettin laid."

He brushed his hair off his forehead with the back of his hand, rubbed his enflamed eyes, and turned away.

"I was just sick and tired of bein odd man out all the time," he added across his shoulder as he went on through the door to wash up at the pipe.

I decided he'd been corrupted enough and put him on the bus to Tuba City the next morning.

We drove together through Agua Prieta in the coolness of fall that didn't last yet beyond early morning. The big camions loaded with hay and produce rumbled in the narrow streets where vendors were already carving watermelons on the high stepped-up sidewalks and the shopkeepers hosed the stone clean outside their shops. Last year's Christmas decorations hung from the tall iron lamp posts along the central avenue, which was clever of them at city hall since the Day of the Dead was almost here now and another Christmas only two months away. At the border crossing there was the usual early morning mob scene, people waving their MICA and green cards, all of them trying to surge through at once, and a line of vehicles behind them backed up along the chain-link fence that marked the international line. I parked Holguín's truck with its Sonora plates up a side street and walked ahead with John-Wayne to the crossing.

"U.S. citizen?" the customs inspector asked.

"Yes."

"You?" he demanded, looking at John-Wayne.

"Yeah."

"He's more of an American than I am," I told him as we went through. The customs man pretended not to have heard anything.

The bus depot was several blocks north of the crossing. Shopping carts abducted from a nearby supermarket along with a double row of jalopies, one of them burning quietly by itself against the curb, lined the main avenue one street over from the old Gadsden Hotel where Pancho Villa ate once. I pointed out the pale blue façade for John-Wayne.

"Paul Newman made a couple of movies there, years ago."

"Which ones?"

"I don't know. I haven't seen a movie in twenty-five years."

Outside the depot people waiting for the bus sat on their bags with the rest of their luggage arranged around them on the sidewalk. They were Mexicans, mostly, plus what looked like a group of refugees from

Guatemala or El Salvador. The refugees had with them a few clothes in carpet bags and their other possessions in cardboard boxes sealed with tape and tied up with string. They sat very still on top of their luggage, staring into space as if to consider the distance they'd come already or how far yet they had to go. It was forty-five minutes still to departure time, and after purchasing the ticket we went around the corner to the Gadsden and entered through the lobby with its broad curving staircase and polished stone columns. A pretty girl wearing a denim skirt was descending the stairs as we passed underneath, causing John-Wayne to take a sudden, intense architectural interest in the domed skylight directly overhead.

"See anything?" I asked as I pulled back the door into the dark-paneled restaurant.

"Say what, Dude?"

"You don't fool me any," I told him. "I was a young man once, myself. But it isn't the polite thing to do, and you sure as hell don't want to get caught doing it."

We sat up front at the counter and ordered breakfast. The counterman was small, thin, and brown, sharply dressed in black and white, with black hair going gray at the temples and long gray mustaches hanging beside his mouth. I urged John-Wayne to order anything he wanted. He chose the breakfast steak with two eggs over easy, hash brown potatoes, and toast. I asked for hot oatmeal, eggs, and ham. The counterman brought coffee in thick white china mugs like the ones they used to serve you with in Woolworth's when I was a kid, years younger than John-Wayne. The wall clock above the long mirror behind the counter said thirty-six minutes until bus time. Before the hole in the bottom of my stomach could get any bigger I decided to get on with it, jumping in with both feet.

"About the horse," I began.

"You mean, my horse? You goin to bring him with you when you come through, Dude?"

"He isn't yours," I told him.

"What do you mean, he ain't mine? I paid good money for him, didn't I?"

"If I remember rightly, you owe Shorty five-sixths of the purchase price. Only he wasn't Shorty's to sell because Shorty stole him—with your help—at the horse show in Cortez over the Fourth of July weekend. I know, because I was there. The fact is, I almost saw you do it."

I told him the entire story: how Tortuga had been stolen from the boarding stables where Jody had left him overnight and I had traced the thieves to the reservation and then recognized one of them leaving the video store with a couple of movies under his arm. My tailing him from Tuba City to the ranch at Red Lake he already knew about, of course. I was sorry, I said, for seeming to have used him to find his cousin's corral full of stolen horses at the haunted ranch in the juniper woods at Navajo Mountain but that I'd done the only thing I could have done under the circumstances and, besides, we weren't friendly with one another yet. The discovery that he was making installment payments to Shorty had caught me off balance, and I regretted not having informed him of Tortuga's true ownership until now. But Bette, never having expected the present of a horse, would not be disappointed when he returned empty-handed; on the contrary, she'd be overjoyed to see him again after three months. The brown man came with the coffee pot as I was finishing. John-Wayne did not reply when spoken to and the man went ahead anyway and filled his cup and left us.

"I'm sorry," I told him. There didn't seem anything else for me to say.

The food came and John-Wayne pushed his plate away.

"Go ahead and eat," I told him. "You have a long ride on the bus ahead of you."

"What the hell," he said finally. "The white man always breaks his word. Guys that break their word to their woman ain't goin to be able to keep it to no one else." He pulled the plate toward him again and began to eat heartily.

I got out my checkbook and wrote two checks while we ate. The first was in the amount of eighty-five dollars, one-sixth of Tortuga's purchase price from Shorty, the second for three thousand—a grand for every month he'd been in my employ. I tore the checks out of the book, folded them over, and tucked them into the breast pocket of his clean white T-shirt.

"Don't look until you're on the bus," I said. "And for God's sake, don't lose anything."

The bus was already boarding when we returned to the terminal, the pneumatic door swung out and the uniformed driver beside it taking tickets. John-Wayne and I shook hands on the sidewalk. He had on the Bum shorts, new sneakers, and ball cap Carmen had bought him and the kit bag I'd found in a farmacia in Agua Prieta, and he was trying very hard not to blubber. Now that he was really going I was a little teary myself, saying goodbye to the closest thing I ever knew to the son I always wanted and never had.

"Get up there now," I told him, "and find yourself a seat in front behind the driver."

He nodded and turned away, wiping his face with the side of his bare arm. The driver tore out the front part of the ticket and handed him the remainder in its paper wallet. John-Wayne set one foot on the first step, looked around, and waved with the ticket.

"We are the overlords!" he shouted. "Good-bye Dude—I love you, man! Come visit me and Bette on the res!" Then he got up in the bus.

I stayed to watch it drive away in a cloud of diesel fumes. Just before the driver closed the door the Border patrol drove up and took off the Salvadorans along with their carpetbags and boxes tied with string.

---

Hermosillo in Sonora would be a beautiful city even for people who are not in love. There are the wide boulevards leading into the historic heart of the city with its narrow cobbled streets, white-washed walls, and barred windows, the white cathedral rising in tiers like an elaborate wedding cake across the plaza, the palm trees, and the moist soft sky suggesting the nearby presence of water, although the Sea of Cortez is more than a hundred kilometers away. There are the false orange trees ringing like leafy bells with the song of unseen birds and the low gravel hills rising like sand dunes around the urban perimeter. Even the heavy atmosphere, carrying the smells of mesquite smoke and leaded gas, is more pleasant than oppressive, though perhaps you really do need to be in love to appreciate that.

We took the first-class train from Nogales and a cab from the estación to the Hilton Hotel several blocks away. It was just like an American Hilton except for the bottled drinking water in the rooms and the switches that never seemed connected to the designated electrical fixtures. The dining room was full of Mexican ricos and American businessmen down from the States to visit the auto glass factory and the big Ford Motor Company plant. We checked out almost before we had our bags unpacked after Carmen came up from the lobby, dark-eyed and flushed with anger.

"We must leave this minute—right away!"

"What's the matter?"

"The President of Mexico is coming here, tonight! I will cut his heart out with my own hand if I have to spend so much as a single hour under the same roof with that monster!"

I bought a newspaper and she found in the classified section a furnished house for rent in the best part of town. We took a taxi to see it, and it was a very beautiful house.

"But it's a yearly rental. We're only staying three weeks."

"Let them keep the deposit," Carmen said. "It's just six thousand pesos—*much* cheaper than the Hilton at a hundred and fifty dollars a night."

The house, which was a century and a half old, had been built as a mission housing a large complement of priests and brothers and purchased after the turn of the century by a wealthy businessman who restored it and added on an extension. A gravel drive curved away behind the wrought iron gate past cypress trees and privet hedges to the long, low, white house outlined by flower beds and roofed with red tile. The stuccoed walls, three feet thick, embraced a patio open to the front and backed by running arches along an enclosed hallway connecting the two massive wings. Inside, whitewashed ceilings supported by vigas were reflected in the polished hardwood floors and a seemingly endless succession of rooms opened away through arched doorways. There were two grand pianos, a lot of heavy, dark Spanish furniture, hand carved bookcases filled with books bound in gilt-impressed leather, expansive oil paintings covering the walls, candelabra, and dark velvet drapes beside the tall windows. The kitchen from which fifteen or twenty religious had been fed, and which had been modernized since, was floored with Saltillo tile, and so was the master bathroom where you stepped down from an elegant foyer with nidos and stone benches into something like the Baths of Caracalla with five showerheads. In the bedroom adjoining the bath I set the suitcases down on the Zapotec rug at the foot of the bed, a monster in carved mahogany that looked as if it had come over on the boat with Cortez. Carmen stepped up to me and placed both hands on my shoulders, and we exchanged a long, lingering kiss.

"Now, we are alone," she said when we were finished, "at last. Nothing—no one—is between us anymore."

I took her in my arms again and we stood with our mouths fitted together, holding each other upright before Carmen, giving way at last, fell slowly backward across the bed, pulling me down on top of her.

"There aren't any sheets under the spread," I said.

She pointed over my shoulder past the footboard.

"In my suitcase."

A woman like that deserves more success at anything she tries than she ever knew as a military commander. Together we removed the heavy brocade, made up the bed, and replaced the counterpane, folding it neatly down like a blanket at the foot of an army cot.

"I've had enough damned foreplay to satisfy me the rest of my life," Carmen said when everything was ready. "Just take me, Jeb."

---

The house with its thick walls, heavy drapes, and timbered ceilings was as silent and private as the wilderness had been. We spent most of the day there, sleeping late, eating lunch in, and going for supper after nine o'clock according to the Spanish custom. Carmen found a restaurant in the neighborhood where they had a good roast chicken and an even better paella, and we went there most nights because it was a nice place and because going there made it unnecessary to think about going anywhere else. A Tarahumara woman came in every night selling long-stemmed roses with a blood-colored flower and every night I bought one from her and gave it to Carmen and she placed it behind her ear and smiled at me and I took her hand across the table between the water glasses and the ornate silverware. Every night too there was a singer and a pianist to accompany her, and one evening when they had a new chanteuse she came over to our table between sets and explained in a low, nervous voice that the performance was an audition as well. If we liked her singing—really and truly liked it—would we please put a word in for her with the propietario? We assured her that we were already her greatest fans, although Carmen had hardly finished commenting on the superlative badness of her musicianship in addition to her vocal technique. After that, whenever she finished a song we applauded uproariously, crying, "¡Magnífica música!" or "¡Qué canción más linda!" This praise, though it did not improve her singing and the propietario looked dubious, certainly helped her confidence, until, at the end of the evening, she blew us many heartfelt kisses and performed many bows. I tipped her twenty-five American dollars and later, as we were leaving, to make sure of the job Carmen took the propietario aside and thanked him for allowing us a preview of the brilliant young singer who clearly could be expected to make her debut in Mexico City very soon. It didn't cost anything beyond the twenty-five dollars, and it was so wonderful to be in love—really in love—again.

Following that evening we sat in the upstairs part of the restaurant to be away from the music. Tall front windows stood open to the balcony above the traffic crowding in the narrow calle below and through them you could smell the air lifting off the cooling streets of the city and watch the upper half of neon signs winking on and off against the violet dusk. Thinking we were newly-weds the mozo kept a good table waiting for us behind the windows, or perhaps he noted the absence of rings and concluded that we were simply very much in love. The lamps along the walls were covered by half-shades and dimmed to let the night outside into the room, where it became an extension of the city beyond the windows. The soft interior lights reflected from the mirrored supporting columns and the candle fluttering in the blue glass holder between us drew Carmen's lovely features forward and gave her face a dark gypsy look, the way the firelight in the mountains had done.

"A penny for your thoughts, as the English say."

"I was just remembering how it was in the mountains, sitting around the campfire at night."

"It was cold and damp and the ground was hard, that's how it was. And I never did get used to going off into the woods to go baño. But I don't want to think about the wilderness, if you don't mind. It reminds me too much of politics."

"It isn't like politics at all. The wilderness is reality. Politics is just another abstraction."

"Politics is about institutions—about changing them so that they in turn can change people. I don't understand how you can call it abstract. My brigada might have been the beginning of the New Man, the kernel of a new civilization. What could be more concrete—more *real,* and at the same time more visionary—than that?"

"Nothing, maybe. Except it never works. It goes wrong every time, spoiled almost at the outset—primitivism to decadence to deterioration and collapse in a few short steps. We've seen how, you and I. Human beings are just too divided against one another—and against themselves also—for political action ever to be a success, in the long run."

"Is that really what you think?" she asked.

"Yes. It is."

"I disagree," she said, "but let's not talk about it anymore tonight. Except I want to add that, however bad the odds are, the most immoral act in the world is to abandon the struggle and let the forces of reaction prevail."

"You could be right," I admitted. "It always seemed to me I know a whole lot more about women than I do about politics, anyway."

Arriving at the restaurant one evening we found photographers on the stairs and a TV crew setting up beside a speaker's podium and rostrum. Darío, catching sight of us in the doorway, smiled and came forward at once with the menus under his arm to shepherd us back to our table.

""Buenas noches, señores."

"Buenas noches, Darío. ¿Qué pasa aquí?"

Darío said it was a beauty pageant sponsored by the Rotary Club of Hermosillo to select a new Miss Hermosillo for the coming year.

"Should we go?" I asked after Darío had gone away.

"Let's stay and watch for a while. If it's too awful we can leave after a drink or two. You need to see a Spanish beauty contest."

We ordered cocktails and drank them while we waited for the show to begin. Carmen had a martini, a thing I had never seen her do before.

"You're too young to drink martinis," I said.

"I'm old enough to do anything that's fun."

"No one under the age of forty-five drinks martinis."

"In the States, perhaps. Not in Argentina."

"We'll have to go together some time and have fun in Argentina."

The mariachi band that had been lounging on benches behind the maître d's little desk jumped to their feet and began playing as the girls marched in in file down the aisle between the close-set tables and stood behind their chairs for the national anthem of the Republic of Mexico. At the conclusion, they seated themselves and politely applauded the middle-aged gentlemen in tuxedos taking their places on the podium in the glare of the television lights. The girls, though dressed like parrots in an assortment of bright colors, were demure, almost shy seeming.

"Notice how plump most of them are," Carmen whispered. "Much heavier than American beauty contestants."

They nibbled raw vegetables and whispered, giggling, to one another while the introductory speeches were being made and then walked forward when their names were called to take their places in a row across the podium. The girls were Miss Sonora Produce, Miss Sonora Trucking, Miss Sonora Schools, Miss Sonora Plumbing, Miss Sonora Tourism, Miss Sonora Recreation, and so forth: about thirty of them, all with silk sashes coming off the right shoulder and going around under the rib cage. While they were giving their little speeches Darío appeared among the popping flashbulbs carrying our supper high above his head on a tray. I caught his eye and he mimed exhaustion, pretending to wipe the sweat from his forehead with his free hand before lowering the tray onto the table caddy.

"Which one would you vote for, Darío?" Carmen asked him.

He grinned.

"None of them. My mother taught me to stay away from girls who believe themselves beautiful enough to win beauty contests."

Carmen ate prawns, a dozen of them the size of a chicken leg grilled with butter and garlic, and I had sea bass covered with butter and toasted garlic and potatoes au gratin on the side. The fish was fresh from the Sea of Cortez and very good. Darío brought a tossed green salad and a bottle of white wine, wrapped in a linen napkin in a wine bucket. He poured a little of the wine into my glass and observed carefully as I tasted it.

"¿Está bien?"

"Muy bien Darío, gracias."

He vanished among the flashbulbs and the scribblers with their little note pads out, and I raised my glass to Carmen.

"To the most beautiful of all the beautiful women in this room," I offered.

"My God," Carmen said, startled. "The skinniest of them, anyway."

She smiled and we touched glasses.

"Did I mention I was runner-up for Miss Argentina in 1991?" she asked after drinking.

"Miss Argentina—*you*? I mean, with your beauty and all I'm not surprised, but—"

Carmen gave me a helping look.

"I know what you meant. Daddy was determined I should win the title. I was his beautiful little girl, his princess waiting for all the world to acknowledge her. I was to make the best match, marry the richest man in Argentina, and live the rest of my life with nothing to do beyond going to the health club every morning, having my nails done, getting a massage, eating lunch at the club, spending the rest of the day shopping, and the evening wearing the clothes I bought in the afternoon. It's what wealthy Spanish gentlemen expect from their wives."

"Couldn't they just go out and buy a racehorse to pamper instead?"

"Of course they could. Only you can't fuck a racehorse."

Up front a commotion broke out, people cheering, flashbulbs going off, women crying, and the TV cameras panning around.

"Does that mean they have a verdict?" I asked.

"Miss Sonora Plumbing's the winner. The buxom one in the peach-colored dress. She'll make some rich bourgeois the perfect wife one of these days."

The following Sunday they had the last bullfight of the Hermosillo season. The management was offering a matador from Argentina whose work Carmen had seen in the ring some years before in Buenos Aires. "He was a friend of Jorge–my ex-husband," she explained. "Of course, the corrida is terribly counterrevolutionary, but...."

We left for the arena early and sat at a sidewalk café to watch the crowd arrive and listen to the band play pasos dobles from behind the locked gates. The people came by bus and taxi, in pickup trucks covered with dust from the outlying ranchos, boat-like sedans built before the first Middle Eastern gas shortage, and polished late-model European sports cars, while in the parking area vendors hawked straw hats, banderillas with guards placed over their fierce steel points, and taurine figures sculpted in wood and iron. When a car drove up carrying one of the toreros and his cuadrilla the crowd surged around, and there would be an uproar of people climbing on top of it for pictures and autographs. I asked Carmen which was César Salvador's car and she replied, rather loftily, that she had no idea. Some of the women were rigged out in complete going-to-the-bullfight costumes, including usually the broad ribboned hat and no underwear. The sun was scorching in the baked sky; trying to stay cool we drank a lot of white wine, which only made the heat worse. They opened the gates a half hour before fight time and we passed through with the crowd and bought seat cushions for a few pesos from two girls in a booth under the shady overhang of the stadium filled with pigeons. It was glaring hot again in the concrete benches where we dropped the cushions on the numbered seats and sat looking out over the barrera into the arena, where men in white uniforms were dampening the sand with hoses and smoothing it over with rakes. Vendors climbed around in the seats with baskets on their arms calling out, "¡Cocas! ¡Cervezas! ¡Tamales!"

"Dos cervezas, por favor," I told the nearest man.

"Not for me," Carmen said. "I must have gained five pounds this past week."

"Have one anyway and they'll elect you Miss Sonora Cerveza next year."

The crowd applauded as two men in tuxedos carrying trumpets under their arms walked to the center of the arena, bowed very low around themselves, and raised their instruments to play. It was wild music, a passionate lament that rose and fell and stretched itself out before swooping into the harsh, broken rhythms of something like flamenco—triumph alternating with defeat, defiance yielding to submission, death giving way at last and reaffirming the life that transcends it, and something more than life.

"Do you see," Carmen asked as the men tucked their instruments beneath their arms again and withdrew, "how operatic the corrida actually is? We've had the overture already. Now Act One begins."

A Spanish beauty wearing a hoopskirt, bodice, and a wide ribboned hat, seated on a chestnut Arab mare, rode out to applause and made a half-circuit of the arena in dressage. She retired, and after a dramatic pause the entire cuadrilla emerged from the tunnel and stepped forward across the sand, led by the three toreros carrying their dress capes on their arms and behind them the banderilleros with the fighting capes, followed by the picadores on horseback. The toreros, advancing briskly, arrived beneath the President's box and saluted. Then, as the picadores turned and rode out of the arena, they passed on through into the callejón accompanied by the banderilleros.

"Which one is Salvador?" I asked.

"The tall one, older than the others. Isn't he magnificent?"

"He seems to be first man up."

"He is. The senior man always goes first. God, isn't he wonderful!"

"The program calls him the Grand Cyclone."

"Oh," Carmen said happily, "he's *much* better than that."

The bull, a black in perfect condition from the San Miguel de Mimiahuapam Ranch and weighing four hundred-seventy-five kilos, was pretty cyclonic himself. He came charging into the ring with a rosette in the colors of the Mimiahuapam on his right shoulder, circuited partway, and charged straight at Salvador's man when he cited him with the cape. The man slipped behind the burladero with the bull almost on top of him, just before the point of the left horn struck into the wood with a splintering crash.

"See how Salvador watches him," Carmen instructed. "Those blue eyes don't miss a thing. Darling, if I wasn't in love with you already I'd be in love with Salvador—César Salvador."

When the banderilleros had drawn the bull out and exhibited his points, Salavador took him over and cited him from his knees in the sand, close in to the barrera so that when the bull charged he would leave him no escape. He passed him beautifully and very close and the crowd roared out, applauding him.

"That's a young man's trick," Carmen said. "Many young toreros never make middle-aged ones, doing that. Salvador ought to know better. The men following him today are very young, and he is playing up to them in advance. It is very stupid of him because he doesn't need to do it. You will see."

Salvador placed his own banderillas and received another ovation from the crowd. He was in early middle age and only the extreme youth of the toreros who followed him made him seem old by comparison. In the faena he was very good and killed with a single stroke between the shoulder blades. The bull, vomiting blood, went down on its knees and rolled onto its back with its four feet in the air.

"Wasn't he beautiful?" Carmen demanded. "I told you he didn't need to lower himself to the level of the pendejos with those vulgar tricks of theirs."

The crowd, on its feet and shouting, was turned to face the presidential box. The President, a stocky man dressed in a black suit and tie and wearing a black flatbrimmed hat, conferred briefly with himself before holding two handkerchiefs out, one in each hand at arm's length.

"That's fair," Carmen agreed as Salvador's man stepped forward and cut two ears. "He really wasn't quite worth a tail, this time."

When the first of the younger men, who Carmen learned from the man in the seat beside her had only recently made his alternativa, took his bull he too passed him from a kneeling position against the barrera. He was very fast and his movements were beautiful, but after the first calculated danger he worked so cautiously and with so many avoidances that soon the crowd was booing him and calling him a perro. When he killed with the sixth or seventh stroke and after having his sword snapped twice into the air and away by the bull, botas and cushions were already raining down through the blue curved shadow of the ring.

"Pobrecito," Carmen remarked; "wanting to be so daring on so little technique, to be glorious and to live at the same time—showing off for his girlfriend. She's the güera wearing the slinky black dress in the barrera seat, straight down from the President's box. Not only does she not get an ear presented to her by her young man, she'll be lucky not to be hit in the back of the head by a flying cushion."

The third torero was only a novillero, not yet a matador, eighteen or nineteen years old to look at him. Working to upstage his rival he took terrible risks, egged on shamelessly by the crowd until Carmen turned her face away in distress.

"You are about to see this boy die," she said. "Without the possibility of death there is no corrida, but this is not death. It's suicide."

In the end the kid killed fairly well and this time there were no boos and no cushions, only boredom and inattention.

"If he had been killed, the reaction would have been exactly the same," Carmen commented. "You have to know the bullfight crowd to believe it, but it would. Not the aficionados I mean, but the crowd."

"I believe it anyway," I promised her. "Here is your man to take his last bull."

Salvador looked very handsome as he stood resting his forearms on top of the barrera and his chin on his clasped hands, watching the door across the arena marked TORILES. He had a thin face, a long chin, and just enough gray in his hair and the right number of lines beside his eyes to make him irresistible to women. The ribboned queue below the crown of his head was his own hair, I saw, not an artificial pigtail.

As the bull exploded into the arena and the cuadrilla took him in hand, he leaned forward slightly over the wood and lifted his chin from his hands. The bull careered around the ring, striking at the burladero and hooking at the men alternately with his left and right horn, charging at unpredictable moments and eccentric speeds. Salvador watched him. Then he removed his arms from the top of the barrera and stood back a step. Someone handed him a water bottle and he drank from it. Then he wiped his mouth with his hand, accepted the cape from his man, and walked out to meet the bull.

"He's worried," Carmen said. "This is the opposite of what is called a brave bull, one you hope not to draw in the sortillo. It's nearly impossible to look good working a bull like that the way you need to work him if you don't want to leave the ring on a stretcher—even if you're the new El Gallo or Joselito or Belmonte."

Salvador took his time with this bull, trying to get to know him better if it was possible at all for him to do so, and by the start of the tercio de varas he was looking pretty good, considering. The crowd began to boo as the picador rode out.

"I wouldn't blame him if he let the fellow overdo it a bit this time," Carmen said.

But Salvador called the man off before he—and even a part of the crowd—were ready for him to go. The bull stood a little off-center in the ring, pawing the ground and blowing while the red blood pumped in shallow flows over the glossy black shoulders.

"Oh, don't let him try and place the banderillas again," Carmen breathed. "Better a live dog than a dead lion—this one time, anyway!"

The banderilleros, not wishing to be dead dogs either, performed their work conscientiously. But the placement was imperfect and two of the banderillas fell out in the sand almost at once.

"I just want this fight to be over now," Carmen exclaimed. "Let him kill the best he can and be done with it. Anything else isn't worth the risk."

Salvador performed brilliantly with the muleta in the opening part of the faena and this seemed to give him not courage—which he plainly didn't need—but confidence, and finally exhilaration. The crowd was with him again now, with volleys of "olé"'s and much waving of handkerchiefs and hats. When he turned his back at last on the bull and stepped forward to ask the President's permission to kill the uproar cut off as cleanly as a trained chorus, and in the interval of silence that followed the President signaled him to go ahead.

César Salvador and the bull together made a single plastic figure there on the yellow sand, a grouping so dramatic it was impossible to tell whether there was motion in it or not. They stood directly below us and out, so that when the man raised the sword and sighted along it to its downward point I was there, sighting with him. Going in over the horns he crossed with his left hand holding the muleta, and then as the sword went in between the shoulders on its way to the heart the bull brought his head up suddenly and the man with it, impaled on the left horn. The bull tossed Salvador and shook him as if to be rid of him, and when he failed to come off tossed him again and flung him down in the sand where he lay on his back looking up at the bull standing above him and trying to gore so fast that he only bumped his nose in the sand. The men ran in with the capes for the quite and brought the bull off. He followed them away at an easy trot, and as he went Salvador raised himself from the waist as if to watch him go. Then he fell back dead in his blue and gold suit on which his own blood met with the bull's and overran it.

The crowd remained to savor the tragedy while Carmen and I, escaping by the deserted exits, went into a neighborhood bar for several stiff drinks. She was very pale and her hand shook as she raised the martini glass by its narrow stem.

"He didn't cheat," she said. "It was the worst bull anyone could ever draw, but he wouldn't cheat. He gave absolutely the best performance he knew to give."

"I don't believe he suffered, either. Probably he never knew how badly the bull had hit him."

"Probably he didn't. I hope to God not."

I offered her my arm and we walked to a table in the rear of the bar, taking the drinks with us. Seated on the banquette behind the table I held her against me with one arm while she opened her purse and dabbed at her eyes with a handkerchief.

"I'm sorry," she said. "I saw a man killed in the ring before—once, in Buenos Aires. It isn't just Salvador, it's the way life can be—like drawing a bad tarot card."

"I understand," I told her. "It's not going to spoil our time together, is it?"

"No," Carmen said. "I hope not. We mustn't let it. Would you like to go away from here—tomorrow—to the seashore?"

---

The blue sky began overhead and curved away, out and down to meet the water, growing paler and softer until it touched it along the indistinct horizon from where the sea came rolling in undulant creases back to the land, bluer and bluer until it ran in and broke sluggishly on the yellow beach below the massed metal rooftops of Bahía Kino glinting like an open landfill in the late morning sun.

"My God," Carmen said, gazing at the sprawling tin colonia on wheels. "I had no idea it was as bad as this. Just look at all the damned Yankee invaders."

"I'm a damned Yankee invader myself, I guess."

"Not you. You're a Yankee prisoner of war. Do you suppose we can find a restaurant where they serve real food instead of soybean glue in plastic boxes from America?"

"Why don't we have a drink first. If we can discover a good bar they'll be able to tell us where to go for a decent meal."

"Or, if they don't, we won't need it."

"Spoken like a man, sweetheart. You drive, I'll be on the lookout for the good bar."

We came to the waterfront and turned into the frontage road running between the beach and the line of buildings.

"There's one," I said.

"Does it look like the good bar to you?"

"Any bar is a good bar," I explained.

Carmen parked the rental Ford in the row of ancient pickup trucks rotted by the salt air and we went inside where commercial fishermen in ragged bloody clothing and tall rubber boots stood along the bar with their elbows in the spilled beer, slapping the wood when they made a joke and laughing heartily. We sat at a table up front by the window and waited for someone to serve us. When nothing had happened after five minutes I walked back to the bar and stood in between two men drinking beer with shots of tequila. The propietario came along after another minute. Seeing me, he spread his arms wide to grip the inside of the bar with his brown hands.

"Dos martinis secos y agitados—por favor," I told him.

He looked at me, not understanding, and I repeated for him, slowly. The propietario shook his head and put his hands in the air as if he was attempting to lift the roof off the building.

It was the Italian—not my Spanish—he couldn't comprehend. I looked past him to the backbar and saw several bottles of gin imported from the States.

"Ginebra," I told him, "y vermut."

He reached behind himself for the gin bottle, set it on the counter between us, and looked at me. There was no vermouth that I could see in the line of bottles reflected in the long mirror. I instructed him to put ice cubes in two glasses and pour two shots of the gin into each of them. As an afterthought I had him add several drops of tequila. I paid the man for the drinks and returned with the glasses to the table where Carmen sat, watching me.

"We found the good bar, definitely."

"How do you know?"

"The barman doesn't know how to make a martini. Never so much as heard the word, I'd bet."

"That makes it a good bar, does it?"

"It makes it really a Mexican one, anyway."

Carmen tasted her drink.

"This isn't a martini."

"I just got through telling you."

"What is it then?"

"Gin and tequila. Does it taste all right to you?"

"Try it for yourself, and tell me."

I tasted the drink and found it not too terrible, but strange. Probably I'd felt the same way about the first martini I ever had.

"Well?"

"It isn't so bad. Better than a Manhattan, anyway."

"Manhattans are undrinkable. They really *are* for old people. Eighty years and counting."

"What should we call our invention—our noble experiment?"

She considered.

"We could call it a Darién, after Cortez. Bringing Europe and the New World together."

"Why not? To the Darién cocktail, invented this whatever-it-is-day of October, 1999. ¡Salud!"

"Salud."

We drank and sat looking out for a time over Cortez's smooth sea and the white-sailed fishing boats drifting vaguely on it in the pale October sun.

"We're crazy, I suppose," Carmen said. "It's fun for a little while, though. Isn't it?"

"What's crazy about us? Another Darién for you?"

"I think I'd prefer plain gin-on-the-rocks."

"I believe I would, too."

After the third drink Carmen would not be put off from lunch any longer.

"Where would you like to go to eat?"

"You were going to ask the mozo."

"I don't think he'd know, after all."

"They appear to be serving food in the other room back there."

"You want to eat here, then?"

"Let's. Neither one of us has any business driving after two gin-on-the-rocks— and a Darién, of course."

There were three tables in back, two of them occupied. We sat again and waited for someone to notice us. They had no menu and a chalk board standing against the wall was blank and smeary. At one of the tables an Indian couple sat stolidly over the remains of their meal, while three fishermen ate steaks carved from some large fish and drank beer around the other. They kept their caps on while they ate and had their oilskins thrown over the backs of the chairs. When we'd been sitting for some minutes an old woman came from the kitchen with two set-ups and Carmen asked her what there was to eat. The old woman said yellowfin tuna, come in on the boats that morning. Could we see the fish first? Carmen wanted to know. She gave me a significant look as she said it and I got up from the table and followed the woman back to the kitchen to view the tuna lying on a cutting board on the porcelain drainage beside the sink. It was a beautiful fish, firm and pink-fleshed, that would have gone twenty-five or thirty pounds before the first steaks were removed from it. The kitchen was not so beautiful, but I thought I would say nothing about that to Carmen. What she didn't know probably was not going to hurt us and this was Mexico, after all, not San Clemente or Carmel.

"Muy bueno," I told the crone. "Muchas gracias, señora."

"How does it look?" Carmen asked when I was sitting again.

"The fish looks delicious. I wouldn't ask any more questions though, if I were you."

"Oh, let's just go ahead and eat, then," she decided. "I'm starved."

"You are? I'm parched."

"How could you possibly? You've been drinking like a fish since we reached the coast. We both have."

"Maybe we're evolving backward. Our remote ancestors came out of the sea."

"You can devolve if you want to. I believe in positive, creative evolution."

"Does that mean you won't join me in another drink?"

"No. Yes. I might have one more. For my nerves. I'm feeling awfully anxious today, somehow."

We ordered gin from the old woman, not wanting to trust the wine if they had any.

"It's so strange," Carmen said when the drinks came. "Here we are, two healthy people, relatively young, with our lives ahead of us still; well-off, well-fed, knowing how to enjoy life. And yet there's something missing. It's like having everything and nothing at the same time. Something is wrong, and it scares me."

"Life is strange."

"You're being flip," she reproved me. "Do you feel it too? Or is it just me?"

"Of course I feel it. I've felt it all my life. Most of it, anyway."

"It's like a yawning chasm. I wish it would close up or go away. Or something."

"It's just life," I said. "It never goes away until life does, and then it's the grave closing over you."

"What are we talking like this for?" Carmen demanded. She seemed almost in tears; the fourth glass of gin had been a mistake. "Why can't we just be happy together?"

"We are happy. I'm happy. Aren't you?"

"I don't know what happiness is anymore," she said, "or even what love is. But I do know I love you, Jeb."

I reached for her hand under the table and squeezed it.

"I love you too, darling. I love you very, very much."

The old woman approached with two steaming plates that she set down before us without a word.

"Oh good!" Carmen exclaimed. "We can stop talking nonsense now and just—eat!"

The fish with butter, boiled new potatoes, and garlic was superb. While we were eating two of the fishermen at the table across the room got up and left, leaving the third who sat on with his legs crossed and his chin in his hand. Looking up from the meal several times I saw his eyes dart away as if he had been watching us.

"God," Carmen said, putting her napkin to her mouth, "that was a wonderful fish. I'm glad I didn't ask about the kitchen. I feel like a whole new person now. Does it seem to you that fellow has been watching us?"

"He has, absolutely."

"Maybe he wants to sell us something."

"Like what?"

"Make eye contact with him and he'll probably tell you."

I caught the fisherman's eye and smiled encouragingly. He did not return the smile but instead gave a sort of salute, or salaam, rising from his chair as he did so.

"You see?" Carmen asked.

The man came over to our table and stood with his hands in the pockets of his coveralls, looking down at us over his stomach.

"You talk to him," I said. "I need time to recharge my Spanish after eating."

Ordinarily I speak Spanish better than I understand it. These people talk so damn fast. This time I heard the word barco repeated so often in the short conversation that I had already doped out the gist of it before Carmen translated.

"This gentleman has a fishing boat that sleeps four people. He brought his catch in this morning, early, and he's done fishing now for a while. For two hundred American dollars we can charter the boat to one of the islands around here, or any place else we want him to take us for two days."

"Two hundred bucks isn't anything. Is it something you want to do?"

"Oh, I would love it!"

"Tell him yes, then."

He put money down for his meal and left before we could pay the check. It was agreed we should meet him at five o'clock at the boat basin with whatever we were going to need for the two days at sea. There were plenty of provisions aboard already, and we'd be welcome to share with him at the captain's table.

"I'm so excited, darling," Carmen said. "It's just what I needed to fill in the missing place so I can stop feeling anxious and be a complete human being again."

---

Smooth as oil and as quiet the sea passed beneath the vibrating keel and astern, barely scored by the thin wake. Ahead of the boat the sun burned red at the end of its copper track and the Isle of Tiburón, off the starboard bow, foundered in the darkening sea. Pelicans and gulls cried overhead and an offshore breeze carried the pursuing land smells becoming steadily fainter until the odors of smoke, garbage, and rotting fish were overcome finally by the fresh ones of salt and iodine, the clean antiseptic smell of the open sea.

Pedro Piedra's boat, the *Fray Kino*, had two masts rigged with furled sails that could be spread to catch the wind, when it blew. For those times when it did not blow it had a diesel engine that pushed the *Kino* along at ten knots, venting clouds of bitter smoke from the exhaust pipes at the stern above the single propeller. The forward two-thirds of her length were the cargo hatches and masted booms, the last third the wheelhouse with below it the galley and the two berthing compartments. It was a ship-shape, well-cared-for boat and Pedro and his first (and only) mate had hosed down the decks and hatches to be rid of scales and other fish parts before we embarked. He was a short stocky man, very dark, with round brown eyes, a black mustache, and grizzled hair growing on a round head covered most of the time by a black greasy cap, and wearing hip boots over jeans held up by suspenders that curved out over his belly and a striped denim work shirt faded by the sun and stained brown with the blood of many fishes. He smoked a pipe when he was alone or in a silent mood but knocked it out in his talkative moments and used chewing tobacco instead, which allowed him to swear steadily and cheerfully behind the plastic saint suspended just forward of the ship's wheel.

"Who's he have with him up there?" I asked Carmen. "Is it Saint Anthony?"

"Saint Anthony's the patron saint of all travelers. This one would be just for sailors."

"But who is it?"

"I don't recall."

"He's certainly getting an earful, for a saint."

"That's what saints are for," she explained.

"Whoever he is he's getting the job done. For now anyway."

"Do you get seasick, Jeb?" Carmen asked.

"In this weather?"

"I mean when it's rough, of course."

"I don't remember."

"You'd remember if you'd ever been seasick."

"Riding a horse doesn't make me sick. Why should taking a boat?"

"Never mind," she said. "You vaqueros are all alike—insular."

When the outline of the town had faded behind the coagulating lights astern we went forward to watch the water parting smoothly at the bows and feel the wind and sea spray in our faces. In the light of the diving sun Carmen looked bronzed and serene as a carved figurehead staring ahead to the horizon, and beyond it.

"Does this make you happy?" I asked.

"Of course it does. Doesn't it you?"

"Of course. . . . What are you seeing out there?"

"Nothing. I wasn't looking for anything."

I circled her waist with my arms from behind and she laid the back of her head against my shoulder.

"This is so romantic," Carmen said; "like Tristan and Isolde. With Pedro back there as the Watchman."

"They fell in love after drinking the love potion. What's romantic about being drugged?"

"Love *is* a drug. Didn't you know that?"

"Speaking of potions, I'm going to have a small one."

"I will too, then. This breeze has an edge to it already."

I withdrew my arms from around her, brought out the flask, and poured the cap full. Carmen drank it off at a swallow and returned the cap to me.

"Scotch?"

"Bourbon."

"One's French and the other isn't?"

"Not exactly."

"I don't really know anything about hard liquors," Carmen admitted. "I never was much of a drinker—except for wine, of course—before I met you."

"I hate to be the begetter of bad habits," I said. "But it could be I did you a favor this time."

We toasted the sun down and walked aft toward the darkened wheelhouse. The masts still showed against the darkening sky, the top light driving steadily forward among the stars. Carmen took my arm as we made our way carefully along the deck and pressed it to her side.

"I'm starved again," she remarked. "Then, after supper, we'll turn in early, while I've still got a little wiggle left in me. It's what people do at night on shipboard."

"It's what people do at night anyway," I said.

The first mate was a young man in his middle twenties called Ángel who Pedro said was his nephew. Ángel doubled as steward for the voyage and as ship's cook served us a simple but delicious supper of fish chowder and tortillas. We were still eating when he carried a bowl of the chowder to the wheelhouse and remained up there while we gathered the dishes, placed them in the zinc-lined galley sink, and wiped down the table with a rag.

"Come," Carmen said, "before we go ahead and wash up for him, too."

The cabin was snug and clean, the pillows propped, the blanket turned down, the coarse linen sheets stretched tight.

"Like the QE II only cozier," Carmen said. Already she had her sweater and blouse off and was stepping out of her trousers as she spoke. "God, but you're a slow man getting undressed!"

She lay back naked on the narrow bunk, her copper hair spread on the pillow, staring up at me with wide eyes as I got on top, covering her. Carmen clasped me in her arms and held tight, digging into my flesh with her nails.

"Do I feel good to you, Jeb?"

"You feel exquisite, my darling."

"I'm not getting too fat?"

"The bone isn't as close as it used to be, maybe. But the meat is even sweeter."

"My body was never meant to be lazy like this."

"It isn't being lazy now."

"Oh! Please—touch me there, first."

"I was trying not to be slow."

"I don't want you to be slow and I don't want you to be fast, either. I want you to be just—perfect."

"With a woman like you, perfection might actually be possible."

"I know it is. You've been perfect before. Many times. More than perfect—oh!"

"Was that perfect?"

"Oh, Jeb!...Do you feel the boat?..."

"Hold on darling. Just keep holding on."

"I'm holding. Can't you feel how tight? You're not going anywhere 'til I'm done with you. You're not going anywhere away from me—forever!"

---

In the morning there was a low swell running. We lay on our sides, belly to back in the single bunk, bracing against the roll of the boat and looking out through the gray porthole. The woodwork creaked and the steel walls vibrated with the turning propeller shaft. The cabin felt close, and it had a faint animal smell.

"I could spend the whole day lying here," Carmen said. "Why don't we?"

"You wanted to go ashore and see Tiburón."

"Why should I? When all the shark I need is right here in bed with me."

"There's no steward to call. If we don't get up and out of here, we don't get fed."

"That's so." She freed her arm from beneath mine and drew back the hair that had fallen across her face. "I believe I could eat a horse this morning. The sea air seems to have given me an appetite."

Ángel had coffee waiting in the galley. We took the porcelain mugs he gave us and carried them on deck, setting our legs against the boat's easy roll. Already the fog was lifting away from the sea which was changing from slate gray to gray blue as the sun burned through, until the broad base of Isla del Tiburón appeared to starboard and finally its strong blue peaks against a sky of paler blue.

"Like Ararat," Carmen suggested, "while the flood waters were going down."

"Or coming up," I said. "So we want to see Tiburón, after all?"

"Of course we want to see it! As soon as I've had a little something to eat, of course."

For breakfast Ángel gave us scrambled eggs with green chili peppers, wrapped in flour tortillas, and chorizo. Then he climbed to the wheelhouse to relieve Pedro, who joined us in the galley where he poured coffee all around and filled his plate at the stove.

"How long you guys want to spend on the island?" Pedro—whose English turned out to be pretty good so long as he kept it propped up by profanity—asked, taking a chair at the end of the table.

"I don't know," I said. "What's worth seeing over there?"

"Not a goddamn thing," Pedro said. "Not a goddamn thing to see on the goddamn island except the goddamn snakes and the lizards. And the goddamn sea lions."

"Sea lions?" Carmen asked in an interested voice—the voice all men everywhere despair at hearing the women they love use.

"Plenty sea lions. Goddamn sea lions all over the place."

"On the beaches, you mean," she said. "I don't think sea lions care for mountains very much."

"All over the goddamn beaches. Probably in the goddamn mountains too. I never looked."

"I'm certain we're going to want to spend the whole day," Carmen told him.

We went below after breakfast to change into clothes suitable for confronting sea lions and rattlesnakes. Carmen had along old jeans and a pair of wooden sandals with leather thongs. I had the jeans I was wearing and a pair of new cowboy boots I'd bought in Agua Prieta. Besides these we had our jackets and straw Western hats—what John-Wayne called potato chips—and Carmen's bottle of sunscreen lotion. It wasn't much as far as outfitting goes, but Ángel added a box lunch and a gallon of drinking water in a haversack. Pedro put the boat within a hundred yards of the shore and lowered an ancient wooden dinghy, and Carmen and I climbed down while Ángel held the dinghy steady against the *Fray Kino*'s plating. Finally, he waved his pipe at us broadly from behind the wheelhouse glass.

"¡Que lo pasen bien!" he shouted. "We come back at four o'clock to take you off the goddamn island."

It took Ángel only a couple of minutes to bring us to the shore. There was no surf, just the swells like smooth outsized ripples riding in and crumpling on the gentle beach. He ran the prow of the dinghy onto the sand and gave his hand to Carmen who stepped out barefoot into the water, holding her sandals. I removed my boots and jumped, and when we were both ashore he tossed the haversack after us. Then he thrust the blade of the oar hard into the sandy bottom and pushed off in the direction of the fishing boat. Standing on the beach with our shoes in our hands, we watched him go.

"Well, "Carmen said, "here we are again, alone in the desert. A desert isle this time. The Island of Sharks." She looked around at the desert mountains behind us. "It doesn't look like a very likely place for sharks, does it?"

"They're all in the state prison here, wherever that is. At least, I hope they are."

She placed one arm on my shoulder for support as she leaned to fasten her sandals, standing first on one leg and then the other.

"Now that we're here, " I asked, "what is it you'd like to do?"

"Take a walk along the beach and look for sea lions. And other things."

"You think there really are sea lions?"

"Of course I do. Pedro said there were."

"Maybe it's something he tells the tourists."

"We're not tourists," she said. "Anyone can see that."

I drew on my boots and shouldered the haversack and we began walking along the shore just behind where the water started to run backward almost before it had stopped gliding forward up the beach in a series of fanning arcs edged with foam. Pedro had put us off on the south coast of the island west of a peninsula jutting eastward into the sea. For no reason other than its being there, we made for the high, rocky point standing dimly in the haze.

"What time is it?" Carmen wanted to know.

I consulted my watch.

"Ten past ten."

"That's good. We can see lots of sea lions in six hours."

"We haven't seen one, yet."

"No," she agreed, "but I've found some pretty sea shells already. And here's a crab of some sort. What kind do you think he is?"

"I have no idea. I was raised in the desert."

Recalling my promise to take John-Wayne fishing in the Sea of Cortez, I felt a sudden, sharp sadness. He'd been a good kid and a good partner and the next time I saw him again—if I ever did—he'd likely be a man already and we wouldn't recognize each other or, if we did, it wouldn't be the same for either one of us.

Leaving the crab in the shallows Carmen approached me with the shells in her outstretched hand, the palm glowing pink and white from the cold water.

"Aren't they lovely?" she asked.

"They're beautiful."

"These are for you to keep," Carmen said, "to remember me by."

"I don't count on having to remember you, ever."

"Take them anyway," she said. "Put them in your pocket. Wait—let me dry them, first."

We walked farther along the shore under the wheeling seabirds diving and calling to one another. Far out to sea were the fishing boats and early clouds building behind them over Baja California. Lifting higher from the sea, the peninsula was beginning to clarify itself through the saltwater haze.

"How far do you suppose we've come?" Carmen asked.

"A way. Too far to have walked in cowboy boots."

"Why don't you take them off?"

"If I had feet like an African Bushman's, I would."

"We could walk where the water breaks, in the sand, where it would be soft for you."

The breeze from the sea was pleasantly cool but overhead the sun was very hot. I sat on a rock to draw the boots off, peel away my socks, roll them, and stuff them into the tops of them.

"Now I'll have to carry the damn things on my back, in the haversack."

"Leave them there behind the rock and we'll pick them up on our way back."

"If the tide doesn't wash them out to sea first."

"The tide doesn't come in that far."

"I'll carry them."

"You already have enough to bother with. Just put the boots behind the rock there, and they'll be quite safe—trust me."

"Cowboy boots are good for one thing and one thing only, and that's for riding horses."

I set the boots where she'd told me, stuck a piece of driftwood in the sand to mark the place, and we went on together over the firm sand through evenly timed washes of salt water and foam. The cold turned my bare feet pink first, then white, until the numbed soles quit flinching from the irregular patches of pebbled gravel and the toes ceased to curl in on their own. Carmen took my hand in hers and swung it easily between as we walked.

"Doesn't it seem as if our best times together have been away from other people, alone in the wilderness?" she asked.

"Wherever we're together, I'm alone with you."

"It's sweet of you to say it. But nothing lasts forever."

Hand in hand we continued along the water's edge until Carmen stopped short suddenly, pulling me off balance in mid stride.

"What is it?"

"Sea lion!"

"Where?"

"Don't yell like that or you'll scare it. There, ahead of us. Can't you see him?"

"That black object up there? That isn't a sea lion."

"You're legally blind without John-Wayne to see for you, aren't you? Of course it is."

"Well," I said, "there's only one way to find out. Walk straight at him from behind so he doesn't see us coming—very slowly."

We moved up in file, Carmen leading, three steps at a time followed by a pause before taking the next three steps. We'd got up a hundred yards on whatever it was when Carmen turned back, holding her finger to her lips.

"*He's sleeping!*"

The thing ahead of us was in fact a sea lion but it wasn't asleep. It lay half in and half out of the water, a quarter-ton of blackened blubber washed by the salt sea and baked by the sun, the flippers spread and the chin stretched on the sand like a fat and elderly dog.

"It looks dead to me," I said.

"Why would he be dead?" she whispered.

I didn't answer her and we approached the rest of the way at a normal pace until the eye sockets, emptied by birds, were visible and the discoloration of the hide, stretched dangerously tight about the bloated corpse.

"God what a smell," Carmen said, circling to evade the breeze. "He's dead, all right."

"I told you it wasn't really a sea lion," I told her.

"That wasn't philosophy or even semantics, and you know it. It was just a lucky guess—a blind guess, I should say."

"Lead on," I instructed, "and find us some real—some living—lions."

We walked another mile and a half or two miles and found three more of the things, the last of them only recently dead. They lay like the first one, partway out of the water and eyeless, all three corpses staring blankly up at their vacant sea lion heaven. Carmen was discouraged.

"I don't suppose it's worthwhile going any farther. What do you imagine killed them?"

"I don't know. Pollution, probably. Maybe Pedro knows something about it. He made it pretty clear they had God's curse on them, like the rest of the goddamn island."

"He wouldn't have brought us here to see dead sea lions. How far would you say we've come now?"

I looked ahead to the peninsula, a rugged mass of sterile rock, hopeless and gray, pushing into the sea.

"Does five or six miles sound reasonable to you?"

"Anything seems reasonable except going on."

"Shall we go back, then?"

"Let's eat lunch in the hills, away from the nasty ocean," Carmen suggested, "and then start back."

"I can't go climbing around up there barefoot, you know."

"We'll follow the beach as far as your boots," she decided, "and explore in the hills after we've eaten. It's almost four hours still before the boat comes to take us off."

The sea lion carcasses made a kind of gauntlet to run getting back to the rock. I dried my feet on my pantlegs, pulled on the socks, and stepped into the boots. The tide, receding, was drawing away from us along the beach. We turned our backs on the sea and began climbing a dry wash coming down from the mountains among giant cardón cactuses and the ironwood trees and smokethorn shedding their leaves in anticipation of winter. Small bright-colored birds searching for late water jinked among the trees and a short pinkish rattlesnake lay coiled on a rock, enjoying the warmth of the low riding sun.

"Where do you wish to stop and eat?" Carmen asked.

"Anyplace you like. Everywhere in the desert is clean and fresh. Just not on that little rattler over there."

"How about the big ironwood tree ahead?"

"That will be fine."

"The desert air does give one an appetite, doesn't it?"

We sat on a ledge of rock beneath the tree and opened the box lunch Padro had made up for us. In it were half a roast chicken and several flour tortillas, two red pears, apple pastries wrapped separately in waxed paper packets, a container of salsa, and a larger one of red wine. Underneath everything, two small skulls made of hard sugar grinned at us from the bottom of the box.

"El Día de los Muertos," Carmen said.

"It's the end of the month already?"

"The twenty-second, I think. I've been trying not to lose count."

"What difference do the days make anyway?"

"For you, not so much perhaps. Your job is terminado—finished. Mine, on the other hand, is just beginning."

"A woman's work is never done, they say."

Eating lunch beneath the ironwood tree we looked out from under the branches to the glittering sea stretching away from the gravel hills below to the horizon, where a low wall of gray cloud was rising against the yellow-and-blue sky. From our point of elevation the scattered fishing boats, making a three-dimensional pattern on the surface of the sea, appeared to be drawing closer together on a heading toward Bahía Kino or Guaymas.

"There's a storm coming in," I said.

"Do you think so? How can you tell?"

"It looks just the same on the plains of Wyoming in December."

"I don't imagine you thought to bring your harmonica with you," Carmen said.

"Of course I did. Would you like to hear something?"

"Play 'Kathleen Mavourneen'," she suggested.

I gave her the first verse on the harmonica and sang the second a cappella and standing to allow my diaphragm to function as freely as possible above my full belly.

Kathleen Mavourneen! Awake from thy
slumbers!
The blue mountains glow in the sun's
golden light;
Ah! Where is the spell that once hung
on my numbers?
Arise in thy beauty, thou star of
my night;
Arise in thy beauty, thou star of
my night.
Mavourneen, mavourneen, my sad tears
are falling,
To think that from Erin and thee I
must part.
It may be for years, and it may be
forever;
Oh, why art thou silent, thou voice
of my heart;
It may be for years, and it may be
forever;
Oh, why art thou silent, Kathleen
Mavourneen?

I got carried away a little toward the end, and when I finished Carmen was looking at me with tragic eyes and tears running on her cheeks.

"I'm sorry," she said, "I was thinking of Salvador—and the tarot card—again. You sing that beautifully, darling. You do everything beautifully—so very, very beautifully."

Ángel's lunch had been very good. We scattered the chicken bones for the wildlife to enjoy and crumbled the remaining tortillas for the birds. I sent the apple cores as far as I could throw them underhand and crushed the box with the plastic containers in it underfoot.

"Do we want these?"

I held out the two sugar skulls to Carmen.

"I can't think why. They're nothing but pure cane sugar."

I got on my knees and placed the skulls side by side together at the base of the ironwood tree.

"What are you doing, Jeb?"

"Leaving our dry bones to bleach on a desert isle."

She shook her head.

"You have an awfully Mexican imagination, for a Yankee."

I stuffed the garbage in the haversack and we started downhill in the wash.

"I thought we were going back across the hills," Carmen said.

"We'll make better time along the beach. That storm is coming in pretty fast."

Waves were breaking among the rocks as we arrived on the beach. I removed my boots and jammed them into the haversack away from the salt water. The cloud line was half way up the sky now, a dark mass like gray cotton blotting the horizon. Shading my eyes with my hand I squinted against the sun along the curving sand strip.

"I can see the boat," I said.

"That little one, way out there?"

"He's coming in early, figuring we have sense enough to do the same."

"The storm won't sink the boat, will it?"

"No. But it could make putting the dinghy ashore impossible."

"Oh. I see."

We hurried just out of reach of the breaking waves where the sand ended, against the rising wind and wetted by a fine spray. The sun went out overhead and after a time I ceased feeling the pain of stones and gravel under my numbed feet.

"Maybe the storm will wash the beach clean of dead sea lions," Carmen suggested breathlessly.

"Maybe it will."

The boat drew steadily closer inshore, converging on the landing place we were making for.

"If we could get them to see us, could they steer farther up the beach in our direction?" she asked.

"Possibly, they could. But you can't put a boat ashore just anywhere."

The storm covered the entire sky and fat drops of warm rain began falling, pelting through the salt spray. The *Fray Kino* had stopped and lay motionless in the water now, parallel to the shore. In the gathering darkness the dinghy appeared on the lee side, making for the little beach.

"There he is," I said, raising my voice against the wind and seizing Carmen by the arm. "Come on. Let's run for it."

Ángel, dressed in yellow oilskins and wearing an oilskin hat, had the dinghy drawn up on the beach as we approached. I waved, and he raised a wide yellow arm in return. There was half an inch of water already in the bottom of the little boat. I worked the haversack off my shoulders and dropped it onto the forward seat.

"Quite a storm," I said. "I'm glad you made it back here early."

Ángel grinned.

"Is only a—how you say?—chubasco." A squall.

"Need a hand putting the boat in?"

"Gracias, señor, pero no. The wind, he turn offshore five minutes ago. Have the señora get in, por favor, and we go now—right away quickly."

Carmen climbed over the gunwales and I went aboard after her. Ángel walked around to the prow, placed his hands on it, and shoved, holding his back arched like a grayhound's. The boat did not go anywhere.

"What's the matter, Ángel ??"

"Nada, señor."

He shoved again, grunting and with his eyes closed, and one foot skidded suddenly backward on the gravel. I climbed out of the dinghy and waded up to help him.

"The gravel," Ángel said. "We are caught on the gravel. Put your hands here. Put your back into it—así. Uno—dos-tres—*¡empuje!*"

We pushed and the boat slid back a little on the beach, the bottom scraping against the stones.

"Bueno. Otra vez: Uno—dos—tres—"

We pushed again, and the stern half of the dinghy went into the water and came afloat.

"Now I get in," Ángel told me, "and use the oars. You push again hard—one more time—and then you get in, too."

He climbed into the dinghy and took up an oar.

"Can I help?" Carmen asked.

Ángel did not answer, or even look at, her.

"¡Empuje!" he shouted back to me.

I concentrated my entire strength against the prow as Ángel, standing just forward of midships, dug in with the end of the oar and shoved off. The boat gave way suddenly and then with a hollow scraping sound it cleared the beach and was taken by the waves. The offshore wind had turned the boat parallel to the beach and was pushing it broadside out to sea, the following waves slapping against the partly exposed bottom. Ángel had the oars unshipped and was struggling to bring the unweighted bows around against the wind, but its force was too great for him. He shouted something I could not hear as I ran knee deep into the water and stopped to watch the boat with Carmen sitting in the stern carried farther and farther away from me to sea. Ángel dropped one oar to wave me forward and I floundered on toward the boat, feeling the blown spray in my face and the water rising cold around me, the peculiar lightness in my feet and legs. The sea was already chest deep when I seized the gunwale and heaved myself inboard, helped by Carmen supporting me under the armpits. Like a fish I flopped down on the bottom of the dinghy, blowing and spitting, shedding water. While Ángel rowed, Carmen assisted me to an upright position on the seat. The wind and waves were driving us rapidly away from shore in the general direction of the fishing boat, which was already tacking round to pick us up.

"Are you all right, Jeb?" Carmen asked.

"Fine and dandy, thank you. I had no idea the sea was actually as wet as all that, though."

"It looked to me for a minute as if we were going to have to leave you there, alone on our desert isle."

"You'd have returned for me later though—wouldn't you?"

Ángel was laughing as he rowed, dry and warm inside his oilskins. I went ahead and grinned anyway, to show him I could take it.

"What's so funny?" I asked.

"You want to know what's funny?"

"¡Dígame!"

"You looked just like San Pedro trying to walk on water!"

He was still laughing as we pulled around the stern of the *Fray Kino* and into the smoother water on the lee side of the salt-streaked, rust-stained hull.

In the cabin I sat on the edge of the bunk to remove my soaked clothes. The new boots, spoiled by the sea, were already shrinking and stiffening from the salt water. I blew into the harmonica to dry it, hoping it had not been ruined also, and inspected my torn and bloody feet. Carmen sat close beside me with her arm about my shoulders while she inspected the damage, then rose and left the cabin. She was back in minutes carrying an enamel basin filled with hot water, clean cloths, and a bottle of iodine. The roll of the boat caused her to set her feet wide apart in a waddling gait as warm water and soap slopped over the side of the basin.

"This will have you poor feet feeling better in no time," Carmen said. She sat carefully, cradled the basin between her knees, and wetted one of the cloths in the water.

"Are you certain you really *are* all right?" Carmen asked suddenly.

"It's no big deal, just a little blood and skin missing."

"I mean your face," she said, looking concerned.

"What about my face?"

"It's green as a sea turtle's and all puckered up. Just like a turtle's."

"I'm okay," I said.

She brought the basin up in time for me to empty my guts into it—once, twice, and again. When the heaves subsided she set it aside on the floor and placed her two hands bracingly on my shoulders.

"Feeling better now?" Carmen asked.

The blood vessels around my eyes seemed to have burst and my esophagus felt as if someone had been pouring Plumber's Helper down it. My backbone was snapped like a Thanksgiving wishbone and I felt empty as outer space inside.

"I'm all right," I said. "I swallowed too much unboiled seawater is all."

---

The house in Hermosillo, after the hard-edged light and bright space of Tiburón Island and the Sea of Cortez, seemed massively dark and shut in. All that Spanish architecture and furnishings that a month ago had appeared heavily romantic and colorful now felt oppressively gloomy, almost cruel. Both of us felt it I think, I more than Carmen who was familiar with the style. Rather than spend our time at home we began the day by going for coffee and rolls at a café a couple of streets over, then wandered through the city until lunch time looking into the shops, visiting museums of various kinds and occasionally a movie theater. Around two we'd eat lunch in some small, good but inexpensive restaurant and return to the house for a siesta and Carmen's telephone calls to Mexico City. She spent a lot of time on the phone in the late afternoons and was always preoccupied, even a bit distant, afterward. In the evenings we went out again for dinner and often to a nightclub afterward where we drank champagne and cognac and Carmen tried to teach me to tango. Though an accomplished dancer herself she made a very patient teacher—so much so that she nearly succeeded in doing what no woman before her had even come close to doing, which was to teach me to dance anything. We ate and drank an enormous amount and Carmen plumped out until she could no longer fit into the clothes she'd bought when we came down from Agua Prieta.

"You look very handsome with a little weight on you," I told her.

"What do mean, handsome? I'm fat as a pig."

"You're not fat."

"I have a double chin and a belly and hips—I look as if I were painted by Rubens—and you tell me I'm not fat?"

"Just pregnant, perhaps."

"Don't even say it. And if you were doing your job I wouldn't look as if I were pregnant, either."

"You're saying I don't exercise you enough?"

"Too much is never enough. It's your responsibility not to leave me time ever to eat."

"The way to a woman's heart is through—"

She hurled the nightgown she'd been holding in her hand across the double bed at me.

The shortening late October days were hazy and warm but it had begun to be cold at night. Once when the overnight temperature fell below zero the few water pipes in the colonias burst and people in the cardboard cities beyond them were found frozen to death the next morning. Downtown, the pleas of the street people and beggars grew sharper and more insistent. The Tarahumara women sitting crumpled on the sidewalks as if their legs had been cut from under them rolled their eyes up as they lifted their tin cups and sent their children after us for more. One evening when we went for supper we passed an old man with white hair and a white beard below his waist playing on a tall gilded harp within the recessed entry of a jewelry store a couple of streets away from the restaurant. We saw him every night after that and gave him a few pesos each time. The old man played very well, but no one stopped to listen and we never observed anyone else give him money. Several mornings later we passed a beggar lying partly across the cracked sidewalk and partly in the dirt against a chain link fence surrounding a pottery yard. He was rolled in a dirty blanket pulled over his head and surrounded by his shaving things and a rooster pecking at a brown paper sack with an empty wine bottle inside of it. When we came by again an hour and a half later the man was on his feet, supported by a motorcycle cop wearing a brown shirt and military style cap.

Carmen asked the cop what he was doing with the man. The cop said he was charging him with vagrancy. Carmen ordered him to release the fellow and the cop looked surprised. But this is a good neighborhood, he said. She told him it was her neighborhood and ordered him to let go of the man at once. The cop frowned, his shark eyes narrowing and drawing together against the bridge of his nose. If he was not to do his duty as a protector of the public, he suggested, someone must pay. As everyone knows, he added, vagrants have no money. When Carmen ignored this statement and demanded the name and badge number of his captain the cop flinched and seemed to crumple, as if he felt the sky falling on his head. He did not appear angry so much as profoundly shocked, almost terrified. But he did not defy the señora, as a well-trained obedience dog does not defy his mistress. The cop released his hold on the man's collar and Carmen told him to get on his motorcycle, which stood braced against the curb with its motor running, and leave. The officer turned from her without a word, threw a leg over the machine, and shot away in a series of sharp small explosions and a cloud of blue smoke. The vagrant looked dazed, and more scared even than the cop had been. Carmen put twenty thousand pesos in his hand and we walked on without another word.

"¡Vaya país!" she exclaimed—not to me. With a little luck, and in certain circumstances, the class system works just fine sometimes.

The capitol building of the State of Sonora was a massive, partially modernized building facing the cathedral across the plaza with its gazebo and false orange trees. We entered it, and walked about on the tiled floor to view the revolutionary murals on the walls of the great hall. The murals showed heroic workers, naked to the waist, with bulging biceps and dorsal muscles like ships' hawsers, driving tractors, cutting cane, and raising steel beams into place. Done in bright fiesta colors they appeared inappropriate somehow, like Mariachi music in church. Carmen stood back with her arms folded, regarding them critically.

"It's all a lie," she said finally. "Everything in Mexico is a lie, including the revolution. The revolution is the biggest lie of them all. ¡Ay, este país…! "

Outside, a wedding party was emerging from the cathedral. We watched from a wrought-iron bench on the plaza as the limousines drew up before the dazzling white wedding-cake church and the crowd surged through the wide doors, the excited bride's-maids swirling and fluttering and the tuxedoed men forming a kind of review guard on the sidewalk to allow the bride and groom to pass. Cheers and laughter sounded through the rattling rice and drifting confetti and even the disturbed pigeons overhead seemed to celebrate the solemn event, the great good fortune of the newly married couple. Of course, they were really waiting to swoop down on the rice scattered across the paving stones.

"How Daddy would approve," Carmen remarked.

We went for lunch in a neighborhood restaurant and were joined after a quarter of an hour by the wedding party arriving to occupy the banquet room, skylighted with a working fountain at the center of it and lined with potted palms. As the guests seated themselves and mozos in stiff white coats poured champagne the band, dressed in maroon uniforms with gold stripes down the pantleg, took their place up front behind the head tables. From where we sat in an alcove off the big room Carmen and I watched the women in their full skirts maneuver gracefully in the growing crowd. Beribboned, with flowers set in their elaborately coifed hair, they were like people from another century, gay but formal, and deeply serious somehow beneath all the Latin gaiety.

"May I order you a drink, ma'am?" I asked Carmen.

"Certainly you may, kind sir."

"What is your pleasure?"

"Champagne, of course."

"Champagne?"

"Why not? Doesn't Champagne sound good to you?"

"I'll go ahead and order a bottle, then."

Before I could summon him the mozo came into the alcove carrying a bottle wrapped in a towel and with it a couple of crystal flutes. He set the glasses down and poured them full of Champagne and passed on to the couple seated behind us at the next table.

"You see?" Carmen asked. "Champagne is in the air today."

"He must suppose we belong to the wedding party."

"Don't tell him otherwise. Let's see how long it takes him before he catches on."

"Maybe he won't ever catch on."

"We'll get a big complimentary wedding lunch, then." Carmen lifted her glass. "Here's to the happy couple—¡Salud!"

"Salud."

We tasted the Champagne.

"It's an excellent wine," Carmen pronounced appreciatively. "The girl's family must have good taste. And be very rich, of course."

The Mariachi band struck up outside, drowning the laughter and the chink of glass and china. Two couples in formal dress entered and seated themselves farther back in the alcove. The mozo appeared almost immediately to fill their glasses and refill ours. "How could he have mistaken us for members of the wedding party?" Carmen wondered. "We're dressed totally inappropriately."

"Possibly he figures us to be poor relations from the States."

"Actually, I think the restaurant is meant to be closed to the public this afternoon."

"If they had a sign up, I didn't see it. Do you think we ought to leave?"

"Of course we're not going to leave. This is all very enjoyable. And the Champagne really *is* wonderful."

The couple at the next table watched carefully as the mozo set a glace au citron before each of us.

"How lovely," Carmen said. "The Latin American ricos know how to live better than anybody."

In the big room beyond people were rising from the tables to dance as the Maraiachi band resumed playing. The couples seated with us in the alcove were young couples; one of the girls wore an emerald the size of a pigeon's egg, surrounded by diamonds and set in gold, on the ring finger of her right hand. When we'd finished the glace the mozo came again to remove the plates and serve us with an endive salad. The musicians, switching abruptly to a kind of pasodoble rhythm, played on.

"Spanish weddings really are something," I said. "This one is more like a bullfight."

"That's an interesting comparison, wouldn't you say?"

"What I mean is, the two of them sound pretty much the same."

"If marriage is like a bullfight, who is the bull and who the torero?"

"Who was which in your marriage?"

"We won't talk about my marriage, please," Carmen said. "*If* you don't mind."

The mozo brought the entrees and a bottle of vino tinto. All the tables in the alcove were occupied now and the restaurant was filled with noise and the smoke from expensive cigars, swirled by the rapid passage of the mozos and wine stewards. The food had been wonderfully prepared, but neither one of us felt hungry anymore. Carmen took a cigarette from a glass vase behind the flower setting and I held the match while she inhaled. The matchbook was white with the linked initials of the newly-weds embossed in silver on the cover. I'd never known her to smoke a cigarette—or anything—before.

"I didn't know you smoked," I told her.

"I don't. I'm hoping it will help me eat less."

"You're not hungry?"

"Not particularly, just for once. And you?"

"I'm not terribly hungry either."

Her enthusiasm had drained away, leaving her quiet and unhappy seeming, almost morose. Champagne will do that to you if you don't keep drinking. I reached for her hand across the table.

"Are you all right?"

It was limp and unresponsive.

"I'm all right."

"Don't have any more of the Champagne. It only makes you feel good for a little while."

"I don't want more Champagne."

"We can go now, if you wish. I'm ready to leave whenever you are."

"If I don't know what happiness is, how can I ever know about love?" Carmen asked. I couldn't tell whether the question was rhetorical or not.

"*You* know all about happiness. And love too."

I pushed the chair back and stood from the table.

"I'll be back in a minute," I told her, "and then we'll go."

The wedding party was in full swing beyond the alcove. In the men's room there was a line to get to the toilets and another had formed behind the washbasins, mostly mocosos wet-combing their straight Spanish hair in the wide mirror. All the boys had clean-cut, even features and smooth, healthy skins. Jeweled rings sparkled on their brown fingers and the French cuffs falling back into the sleeves of their white tuxedo coats showed slim wrists braceleted by platinum and gold watches. A street beggar seated against the tiled wall with his legs stretched out on the floor held a battered hat upside down on his crossed legs. There wasn't any money in the hat. One of the boys, wiping his face with a paper towel, looked around and saw the old man. The boy wadded the towel in his hands and pitched it overhand into the hat. The other boys laughed and tossed their towels also at the hat. They went out together laughing, leaving the beggar sitting in a half-circle of damp paper balls and banging the door behind them. I gave him five dollars on my way out and started back through the palm trees and the crowded tables to the alcove. Carmen was watching me as I ducked past the velvet hanging. She sat leaning forward on her elbows at the table with her chin propped on her fist, smoking a cigarette. Beside the ashtray with two butts in it was a fresh glass of Champagne. "I thought you wanted to leave now," I reminded her.

"I did. Then the mozo came again with the bottle. It *is* wonderful Champagne."

I drew the chair out and sat sideways to the table, one leg crossed on the other.

"I've had enough Champagne," I said. "Do you suppose they have any brandy to offer?"

"I'm sure they have anything you want. Ask the mozo when you see him again."

When the mozo came I asked him for a Napoleon brandy straight. He brought a double in a balloon glass and poured Champagne for Carmen. She smiled.

"What did I tell you? 'Ask, and it shall be given unto you.'"

It was wonderful brandy. We sat drinking while Carmen smoked and together we watched the dancing through the elbowed curtain. The bride was a busty blonde with dark roots, a red mouth, and skin the color of very light coffee.

"Do you think she's pretty?" Carmen asked.

"She's so-so. Nothing to get excited about. Would you say the groom's a good looking guy?"

The groom was one of those smooth Latin business types you see in newspaper photographs datelined Miami and showing the son of a local radio station owner handing over a check for fifty thousand dollars to fight Castro.

"God no! He's simply Mama's first choice—the poor girl."

"How can you tell? Perhaps it really *is* a love match."

She shook her head.

"Women don't fall in love with men like that, their mothers do."

"Don't women ever love men their parents approve of?"

"Not if they really *are* women," Carmen said.

The brandy suggested a comment here, but I put my foot on its neck and held it down until the urge had passed.

"Bourgeois females aren't actually women," she went on, "anymore than bourgeois males are men. At most they're just immature girls and boys. At worst they're hardly even human beings."

I said, "I'm not a bourgeois male."

"You *are* a romantic, though—aren't you?"

The Emperor Napoleon climbed into the top of my head and stood looking out from it, as if he meant to hold a position there.

"Yes," I agreed, "I *am* a romantic. Guilty as charged, I'm afraid."

She smiled a tight smile, looking past me to the wedding party building toward the climax of its bourgeois bash. The red coal at the end of the cigarette raced toward her mouth as one broken fingernail tapped the stem of the Champagne glass.

"Who chose your husband?" I asked in a casual voice.

"Mother didn't. That I can promise you."

"The mistake was yours, then."

"The mistake was my own."

"You know, you remind me of the man who joined the Mormon Church and when he discovered it was really just a business club for men and a social one for women concluded that all organized religions had to be equally false and dishonest."

"I never said marriage needs to be false or dishonest. Did you ever hear me call it false and dishonest?"

"Not in so many words."

"What words did you hear?"

"It's more a matter of attitudes than words."

"And what is this attitude supposed to be?"

"Pretty cynical, I'd call it."

"You think I'm cynical about marriage?"

"Well, aren't you?"

The mozo returned with the Champagne bottle and I covered my glass with my hand. Carmen's glass was empty again. He filled it for her and passed on to the girl with the emerald and gold ring.

"I'm not cynical about marriage," Carmen said. "I just don't have much to offer anyone just now, do I?"

"Only what every other woman has—for starters."

"Who's being cynical now?"

"I didn't mean that the way it sounded."

She laughed a small, bitter laugh.

"Of course, you didn't. You don't have a cynical bone in your entire body, Jeb Ryder."

"Thanks for making it sound like a compliment."

"You're very welcome....I don't want to fit into the bourgeois world of Argentina or Mexico, or the middle-class one of the United States. I never really wanted a family of my own. All my life I've done what was expected of me, been the good little girl, to please my family, and other people. And now I have work to do—my own work. I need to do what *I* want, for a change."

"Go ahead and do it, then. Who's stopping you?"

"No one is," she said. "I made that promise to myself, years ago."

"We need to leave now," I told her. "This isn't the time or the place to be having this discussion."

"Anyway, we're having it. We should have had it long before."

"When? On Pedro's boat, or Tiburón?"

She was crying suddenly, golden Champagne tears glistening in the corners of her eyes.

"I love you Jeb, I really do. Don't you know I love you? But the timing's all wrong. We're totally at different stages of our lives."

"We can accommodate the timing, somehow."

"And there's your mistress in Colorado, waiting all these months for you to bring her horse back to her."

"Utah. Jody and I never promised one another anything."

"Jody? Her name is Jody? You never told me her name before."

"I didn't think it made any difference. Does it?"

"Look," Carmen said, "here comes the bride."

The girl swept into the alcove and went from table to table, stretching out her arms on the seatbacks as she bent to converse with her guests. She was laughing, and she looked very happy. Carmen and I exchanged glances.

"Come on," I said, "let's get out of here."

"That would be impolite of us." Carmen was amused. "We'll just tell her thank you for the lovely afternoon, and then leave."

When the bride saw us her mouth opened and stretched in a wide red smile like the whale swallowing Jonah. Holding her arms out she greeted us like long-lost friends, kissing Carmen on both cheeks and embracing me around the neck. I gave her a hug in return, letting go as soon as it seemed polite to do so. She felt soft and billowy and smelled sweet as an overturned perfume counter. Champagne and excitement had left her damp with perspiration, and only moderately sober. After chatting with Carmen in rapid-fire Spanish for a minute or so she turned on me again, her red mouth yawning and full of teeth. She had her hand out and I was reaching to shake it when she seized my arm in a grasp like an ironworker's.

"Only once dance before you have to leave," she insisted, in excellent English. "I remember you for being such a *marvelous* dancer! I love all your movies, too."

The band was playing an American number but it might as well have been the Abo Outback Waltz as far as I was concerned. Couples kept bumping us with their hips and knocking us with their elbows, and it was impossible to tell who was supposed to be dancing with who. When I went to take hold of my partner she stepped back and began a kind of jig like a drunken Irishman, and when we came together again the oldfashioned way she rode right over me, pressing me backward with the force of a small tank with a jammed forward gear. Concentrating on my feet I lost the count and the rhythm and fell back to just shuffling my feet around, hoping that one of them would make it into the right place one step in every ten or fifteen. When the music ended I stood stock still like a pig on ice while my partner looked disappointed, and a bit puzzled.

"What time is it?" she asked.

Apparently ours had been the Dance That Wouldn't Die for my hostess as well.

"Five forty-three," I told her.

The girl seemed relieved.

"Oh," she said, "as late as that? I thought it was early for people to be tipsy on the dance floor."

Carmen stood waiting by the door with her overcoat on her arm and a too serious face like an overfilled balloon ready to burst. Silently she handed me the coat, turned, and backed into it while I held the shoulders spread for her. Still without saying a word she slipped her arm into mine and together we went out into the dark street and the wet bright lights. It was raining, fine gray drops slanting through the pink halos around the sodium lights. The doorman came forward under the shelter of the little awning.

"The señor would like a taxi?" he asked.

I nodded. He took an umbrella from the dark place where he'd been standing and stepped out into the street to hail a cab. Carmen let go my arm as it drew up to the curb and bundled in through the door the man held open for her.

"Your wife is a very beautiful lady, señor," the doorman said in a serious voice when she was inside.

I tipped him in American dollars and ducked into the cab after her, pulling the door shut myself so that he and the five single bills in his fist could all go back to being nice and dry and warm together under the awning, out of the black, falling rain.

---

"Hello."

"Hello."

"How are you?"

"I'm fine. How are you?"

"All right. I'm coming home soon."

"Where are you?"

"In Douglas, Arizona. Still."

"You're coming—alone?"

"I'm bringing the horse with me. Can you spare O'Grady for a couple of days?"

"Danny? What do you need him for?"

"My rig is still at Snowflake. We have to get from here to there somehow."

"He's off hauling cows this week."

"Is there someone else you can send?"

"I suppose there must be. I have to think about it."

"Think fast then, and tell me."

"Right now this very minute?"

"There isn't a phone where I'm staying over in Mexico."

"I guess Whitey could drive down and pick you up."

"The old man?"

"Yes."

"See that he's at the house around suppertime tonight. I'll call and give him instructions."

"Did I tell you I bought a new horse?" Jody asked.

The Holguíns as always were up before dawn. I saw the light under the door and smelled tortillas frying in lard. Lying on my side on the single mattress I watched the dawn break through the small window high in the adobe wall. One of the Holguín roosters crowed and was answered by another several houses away. They'd been going at it since three o'clock at least, the Holguín bird beginning with a low-throated call, the other replying in a stepped-up key. Now and then I would hear Carmen cough from the other side of the wall. The coughing stopped before dawn when I heard her door open, and after that the sound of her voice and that of señora Holguín conversing softly together in the kitchen.

Dawn came late, most of the early light sponged up by gray clouds lying across the valley between the mountain ranges. It was cold lying in bed under thin blankets and I rose before the little light there was had gathered in the room and crossed the hall and slapped cold water from the bucket on my face. I returned to the bedroom where I dressed in jeans and a flannel shirt and went on to the kitchen where Carmen and the señora had breakfast waiting. Carmen was pale and she looked as if she hadn't slept much during the night. We sat in the warm kitchen drinking hot coffee and listening to the cold wind scrape like sandpaper against the outside adobe, and after a while Holguín came from watering the steer and feeding the chickens and seated himself at the stove. Then his wife poured more coffee and we ate the flour tortillas browned in lard, fried eggs covered with green chili, and chorizo. The chorizo, señora Holguín explained, was to honor our last meal together in their home.

When we'd finished eating the women cleared the table and Carmen helped the señora with the dishes while I went outside with Holguín to ready the horses. We haltered and tied them and I brought the saddles and other tack and hung them along the iron rail surrounding the corral. Holguín lugged five or six hay bales from the barn and stacked them on the far side of the fence where the horses couldn't reach them.

"You come back and see us again soon, no?"

"I hope so, señor."

"You do not care to live with us here in Mexico?"

"Mexico is a fine place. Sometime, maybe, I will live here."

"You are better off living up there in the States, I think. Life in Mexico can be very hard—very cruel."

"Life is cruel everywhere, Raoul."

"I believe it. But here in Mexico especially it is so. In Mexico the government is very bad. But the Mexican people are very good."

"If they are only half as generous as yourself and your wife they are saints."

He looked pleased by the compliment.

"We are patriots, and the señorita is a great lady. Truly she loves the people of Mexico, my compadres."

"I know she does," I said.

He would not take the money I offered him for the hay.

Holguín backed the truck up to the trailer and I dropped the hitch onto the ball and secured it. We racked the hay bales on the roof and brought the horses up one by one, loaded them in the trailer, and snubbed them. They looked well kept up after five weeks in Holguín's corral to the point where I was—almost—not ashamed to return with them, and their grown-out winter coats gave them additional bulk. Remembering the tack in time I lifted it down from the fence and stowed it in the truck bed, and we were ready to go then.

Carmen came from the house wearing a hat and an old duster of Holguín's that had room for another woman of her size inside it and fell to the undershot heels of her cowboy boots. She had the hat pulled down in front and the corduroy collar turned up as if she was trying hard not to recognize herself. Carmen stood for a moment in the bare dusty yard holding the hatbrim with her fingers against the wind while the canvas skirts of the duster billowed about her. She asked, "Ready?" without looking at me, and we got up on the seat of Holguín's truck together. I started the engine, switched on the lights, and backed the rig around in the yard. The Holguíns stood side by side in the doorway of the house to watch us as we drove away.

The colonias were dark except where lanterns showed behind plastic sheeting stretched over the window holes and in the spacings between the cardboard walls. Dust and trash blew in the streets and the wind smelled of mesquite smoke and kerosene. I braked the truck and geared down into second as we lurched and jounced in the potholed road.

"You'll call me in Agua Prieta when you get the chance?"

"Of course I will."

We reached the end of the colonias and arrived at the paved central avenue running north to the checkpoint. There began to be more traffic, most of it headed, like us, for the border; people going over to Douglas to work or shop, semis from the Mexican interior headed into the United States. The business district was busy with paisanos come in from the surrounding ranches and shopkeepers opening up, people queuing at the ATM machines for early cash.

"What will you do if it doesn't work out at home?"

"I don't know."

A Ford truck and trailer with Utah plates stood parked on the Mexican side between the crossing and the tracks of the Ferrocarriles Nacionales de México. The man inside the cab wore a black hat with a punched-up crown and a white beard.

"There's Whitey waiting for us," I said.

"He looks like something out of central casting. Only, isn't it supposed to be a black beard and a white hat?"

I turned across the southbound lane into the lot and pulled along beside him. The chew inside his underlip gave him a bee-stung look.

"Howdy, Whitey."

"Howdy," he acknowledged, setting *The Last Cowboys* aside on the seat.

"Did you have a good trip down?"

"Nope."

"What happened? Breakdown?"

"Truck was fine. Goddamn Injuns everwhere I looked."

"Well, it's their country. You ready to load some horses?"

He looked up the street, then down it, then back to me again.

"Never saw so many goddamn Meskins in my life, neither."

"The sooner we get started the sooner you won't see them anymore."

Whitey and I handled the hay bales while Carmen transferred the horses from Holguín's trailer to Jody's and secured them for the trip home. She spent a long minute telling Tortuga goodbye, fondling his ears and rubbing his black nose. When she'd finished her eyes were full and her voice shaky. I held the door as she got up on the truck seat and closed it after she'd drawn the skirts of the duster in after her.

"Goodbye, then."

"Goodbye, Jeb. Have a safe trip."

"We intend to."

"Call me if it doesn't work out. You can reach me at this number for another couple of months. I've written it down for you, so you won't forget it." She took a scrap of paper from her pocket and gave it to me. "It's the one I'm using for business from here."

"Would that make any difference?"

"I don't know."

"We'll see, then."

Carmen set two fingers on her lips, and pressed them lightly to my forehead.

“Thank you so very much for all your help.”

“De nada,” I told her.

She put the truck in gear and nosed into the traffic rattling through the business district.

We had no trouble at all at the checkpoint station, where the brand inspections I’d forged for three horses one night at señora Holguín’s kitchen table got the job done, no questions asked.

---

My old rig stood alongside pieces of retired farm machinery and a couple of detached long-haul freight trailers, plainly visible beyond the corrals as we rattled up the long drive leading from the highway to the Baca ranch. Whitey parked on the turnaround and we went together to look for the old man. Señor Baca was at work in the horse barn on the concrete runway between the two lines of stalls, up front by the door in the late afternoon light of the early winter day, putting shoes to a long, gray, red-eyed, and mean-looking Appaloosa. He looked around as we approached, set down the near hind hoof he’d been working on, and turned to face us, holding the new iron shoe in one hand, the hammer in the other, and a nail between his teeth.

“What can I do for you boys?” Baca asked around the nail. Then, recognizing me, he grinned. “Maybe I should ask what can *I* do *you* for? You’re a few days overdue on your rental return, ain’t you?”

We shook hands. Señor Baca was still grinning. His thick gray eyebrows arched toward his balding forehead under the greasy pushed-back railroader’s cap and his large brown eyes also were amused.

“Just a little,” I admitted. “We’re bringing the equipment in undamaged, though, both tanks full.”

Baca fitted the horseshoe carefully over the top of the wooden stall and stuck the hammer in the seat of his pants.

“You must have been havin yourself an adventure.” He looked hard at Whitey. “Give the kid white hairs before his time.”

“John-Wayne’s safely home in Tuba City. Whitey here came down to pick me and the horses up in Agua Prieta.”

“What was you doin away down there in Mexico?”

“It’s a long story,” I told him. “We had unlimited mileage, didn’t we?”

Baca worked hard to get rid of the grin.

"What's the contract I give you say?"

"I don't recall. Mexican car thieves stole all our papers."

Baca removed the shoe nail from his mouth and dropped it in his shirt pocket.

"Why don't we go over and take a look-see at what you guys are wantin to turn in," he suggested.

I stood aside with him while Whitey dropped the bar and led Quixote and Doña Ana from the trailer, while Tortuga stamped his foot and whinnied. The horses' grown-out coats were shaggy over their broad barrels, rounded from Holguín's keeping. Their feet were well-set, their legs straight and sound. Whitey lifted their heads on the lead ropes and brought them forward several paces for a demonstration.

"Horses look all right to me," Baca conceded. "You say you rode them all the way to Mexico?"

"And then some."

"Chasing Indians maybe?"

"Among other things."

"I didn't hardly use your vehicle at all," he said.

"How did it get here?"

"I hotwired it out there on the desert and drove it home before the sheriff's men could get curious about it."

"That was good of you."

"Hell, I knew I could trust you boys. I wasn't worried, I had security. I figured you boys was goin to turn up eventually with them horses. We're on Mexican time around here."

He stepped in front of Whitey and looked in the back end of the trailer.

"That the horse you guys was after?"

"That's the one."

"Ain't much to look at though, is he?"

"Well," I agreed, "he's had a fairly hard year."

Baca and I followed Whitey with the horses to the big corral, where we turned them in with the riding stock. The other horses trotted up to sniff them head and tail and take them into the herd again. I drew my wallet, opened it, and took out five one-hundred-dollar bills.

"For your patience and the inconvenience," I told Baca.

He put his hand up in protest.

"I never missed em. Just a couple less mouths to feed."

"You must have missed them. They're damn good cow ponies."

"What's a couple months more or less? There's all the time in the world."

He went on to the house for the truck keys and returned with a bottle of whiskey and three glasses. I refused to take the keys until he'd accepted the money and rolled it and tucked it into his shirt pocket, and then we all went into the barn and had a drink in Baca's office, where he found a couple of straightback chairs for us and sat with his boots up on the big rolltop desk. Around the office were oak shelves filled with ledgers and flyspecked calendars illustrated with color photographs of nude women. Baca said he'd never been married and kept his own books.

"Say," he inquired as he poured a third time, "did you boys ever meet up with the bruja, all that time you was out there on the desert alone?"

I held the drink up to the naked bulb overhead to admire the whiskey color through the glass.

"Nunca," I told him, and tossed it back in a single swallow.

---

You don't offer whiskey to a sheepherder unless you're crazy—or, of course, he isn't *your* sheepherder. After leaving Baca to put the remaining shoes on his horse backward, we drove the two rigs on to Holbrooke in the dark: myself in the lead with the horse, Whitey following with his high beam on and one headlight out. In Holbrooke we took a motel room together. Whitey went out while I was showering and bought a gallon of firewater in a liquor store down the street that catered to Indians and old saddle stiffs drinking up their Social Security checks. I ordered in from a Chinese restaurant and we sat on the twin beds eating ham fried rice and egg rolls, watching a cop show on television while I rationed the whiskey carefully. Later, I locked the jug away in the tack compartment of the trailer when he wasn't looking. He was up several times in the night to search for it, barking his shins and cussing, and in the morning he had the shakes pretty badly. I brought the jug out and poured him a shot to brush his teeth with, and when he begged for another I let him have it and took one myself.

We went for breakfast at a café across the street from the liquor store and hit the road for home by way of Second Mesa, Piñon, Kayenta, Mexican Hat, Bluff, and Blanding. Whitey kept up all the way to Monticello, where he appeared to fall behind in a snow squall. Since he wasn't pulling a load beyond the empty trailer I wondered why he didn't pass and make it home ahead of me. Thinking of home and other sobering thoughts I forgot about him until, past Monticello and into the pinto bean fields south of the airstrip, I checked the tow mirror and saw only the empty highway unrolling behind. Monticello, being Mormon, is a dry town but Cortez, sixty-five miles away across the Great Sage Plain, is full of sin and deviltry. He'd given me the slip back at the junction, but I didn't care and I didn't have to care. It was why I was pulling the horse myself.

Her cattle grazed spread out across the still green valley running between the red of the canyon walls. Along the creek the cottonwoods were gray and webby, the last golden leaves jittering in the bare crowns, and the sky stretched cold blue overhead, shading to icy white above the purple cliffs beyond the Colorado River. I'd forgotten, in the long interval of summer, how cold it actually gets in southern Utah. Last year's leaves lay drifted across the shoulders beside the blacktop road, and only the stunted evergreens on the rimrock a thousand feet above the valley floor looked alive. When the ranch came in sight finally around the last curve, I felt a sudden pinch in the pit of my stomach. It was as if I'd been away for ever—and, at the same time, as if I'd never left. I turned off the highway across the cattle guard and drove slowly on to the house standing within a crazed pattern of shadow thrown by the low sunlight through the bare branches of the trees. I braked the truck and switched off the engine. Then I sat looking at the house, still with that feeling in my stomach, and after a time Jody came out on the porch and stood with her arms crossed, staring.

She stepped off the porch as I climbed from the truck and came across the turnaround to greet me.

"Hello stranger."

"Hello Jody."

We embraced.

"You've been away a long time."

"I know it."

"It seems like forever to me."

"Me also."

We embraced again, and she seemed to see the trailer then for the first time.

"And who would you happen to have with you in there?" Jody asked.

"An old friend of yours. Who doesn't 'happen' to be anywhere, by the way."

"I can't believe it," she said. "I mean, it all seems like a dream—doesn't it?"

I didn't answer her.

"Are you going to bring him out, so I can have a look at him?"

I opened the rear door, dropped the bar, took hold of the tail, and pulled. Tortuga backed out slowly, setting his off hind foot on the ground and feeling behind himself with the other before he came out the rest of the way in a rush. I let go his tail, seized the trailing rope before he could bolt sideways, and led him away from the trailer, lifting the rope to bring his chin up. The horse responded instantly by assuming the show position: neck arched, tail raised, legs straight; totally collected and looking like something the BLM cowboys had captured in a wild horse drive, using a helicopter and a net.

"That's Cortez?" Jody cried.

"That's the boy," I assured her.

*"What have you done to my horse?"* she cried.

"Chased him for a good thousand, maybe twelve hundred miles. Caught him. Brought him home again."

"He looks *terrible*!"

"You should have seen him four weeks ago, before I built him back up."

On her way around the horse she saw the brand and stopped dead with her hand against her mouth.

"He's ruined! He looks like…like an old range steer!"

I passed on the opportunity to comment.

*"Who threw a brand on this horse?"*

"The Indians who stole him in the first place did it. I'm sorry. It happened before I ever caught up with him."

She looked handsome in her anger but even thinner than I remembered her, and harder somehow.

"I'm sorry," I repeated.

"I can't believe it," Jody said.

"Where do you want me to put him?"

"In his stall, I suppose. Do you remember which one that is?"

"Of course I remember."

"I'll come with you anyway," she said, "and move the new horse out, first."

Streaks of the cold sky showed between the siding but inside the barn was warm, and the warmth had a sweet smell. We shut Tortuga away in the stall and Jody threw two flakes of hay in the rack, while I dragged the hose over and filled the water trough. I dropped the hose and embraced her suddenly, drawing her hard against me and kissing her full on the lips while the hose ran water over the concrete floor. She held rigid and still in my arms before pushing away without having opened her mouth.

"It's going to take me time to get used to you again," Jody said. "Let's go on back to the house now—shall we?"

In my absence, she'd rearranged the furniture to create a kind of organized chaos. Jody fixed a sandwich and we sat at the table in the kitchen while I ate it with a bottle of beer and she drank coffee.

"Where's Dago?" I asked.

"At Cisco, bringing in the last of the cattle. He'll be home tomorrow sometime."

"He's been behaving himself?"

"How do you mean, behaving?"

"Working hard—staying sober?"

"Danny has always been a hard worker. And he's not a drunk, either."

"That's not my recollection."

"It could be your recollection's getting a bit old," she suggested coldly.

"That could be," I agreed.

"Where's Whitey?" Jody asked suddenly.

"I was afraid you'd ask."

"*Where is he?*"

"I lost him. Actually, he lost me, to be exact. It happened somewhere around Monticello. He's probably in Cortez this minute, having himself a high old time."

"God."

She stood from the table, took my plate and the empty bottle, and washed up in the sink while I went back to the bedroom for a nap.

Seated on the bed I removed my boots and overshirt, turned down the counterpane, and stretched out with my head on the pillow. The room smelled of the sachets she kept around, and of herself. I did not fall asleep at once but lay wide awake with my eyes open, thinking. When I had thought as far ahead as it seemed to me I could see, which wasn't very far, I let my eyes close and pretty soon I was asleep. It was not a very good sleep, more a kind of fever in which a variety of anonymous voices and formless ideas contended with one another.

When I awoke the room was dark and it was dark outside except for the arc light above the turnaround. I buttoned the flannel shirt, pulled my boots on, and walked out to the kitchen where Jody was taking a roast from the oven. Coming from behind her I put both arms around her waist, lifted the straw-colored back hair, and kissed her on the nape of the neck.

"Are you glad to see me again after all this time?"

"Of course," she said, "I'm glad to see you."

"You don't act glad. I really am sorry about the horse."

"It isn't the horse. It's just…strange, after so much time."

"Only four months."

"Is that really all it's been? It seems so much longer."

"I got home as quickly as I could."

We had drinks in the parlor, seated together on the sofa before a fire of piñon logs, and after a couple of whiskeys everything began to feel normal again. Jody let me kiss her and put my arm around her shoulders, and pretty soon I was lying on top of her on the sofa, undoing her blouse buttons while she took my lower lip between her teeth and arched her belly up from the cushions against my weight. Abruptly, she pushed me off of her and sat up with her hair in her face and sweat glistening at the hairline.

"Stop, now," Jody said. "You don't want me to burn supper, do you?"

We both drank too much with the meal and went to bed leaving the dishes out on the table and the unwashed pans in the sink. Jody was fairly tipsy. I undressed and lay in bed under the covers waiting for her to come from the bathroom. She came out wearing her nightgown and I tried to talk her into taking it off. When she wouldn't do it I turned out the light and watched her long gray shape climbing into bed with me in the darkness.

"Take your nightgown off, now."

"No."

"Why not?"

"I started my period yesterday."

"I don't care."

"Yes you do."

"Take your nightgown off."

We tried making love but we were both too drunk to do anything and after several attempts we gave it up and went to sleep, Jody lying all the way over on her side of the bed and me against her with one arm behind her head and the other hand resting on her naked belly.

When I awoke in the gray November light I thought I was in the dark Spanish house in Hermosillo. Reaching for Carmen I found her gone from beside me, and then I woke up the rest of the way and it was Jody who was missing from the bed. While I lay waiting for her to return I fell asleep and when I woke for the second time it was full morning, the fall sun through the small-paned windows throwing bright trapezoids on the white-painted walls. I got out of the bed and pulled my pants on, threw cold water in my face, and went looking for Jody in the kitchen. There was fresh coffee in the coffee maker, and I poured myself a cup and drank it. Then I went ahead and drank the rest of the pot, washed it out, and threw the grounds away. Jody was nowhere in the house. I returned to the bedroom and finished dressing. Then I went out to the barns to see what she was up to.

I saw right off that her horse was gone—not Tortuga but her working horse, a tall chestnut thoroughbred. The other horses, penned in their stalls, were still putting away their morning hay. I took the paint I remembered, threw a bridle on him and jumped up onto his bare back, and rode across the creek and up the canyon cutting south between the high mountains on the one side and the mesa on the other. The sun blazed red on the upper half of the eastern wall as it topped the mountains, leaving the bottom still in shadow. The mountain peaks were blue with early snow, and snow lay in patches under the trees growing on the pitched rock terraces above. In the twilight canyon the cold air numbed my feet and stiffened my fingers until I barely felt the reins.

I worked the paint off the bank and down into the dry creek bed where the red sand was thick and kicked him up to a lope, and then a gallop. The paint asked politely for his head. I gave it to him, and together we went flying flat-out up the wash, the curving banks flashing past on either side, the junipers beyond falling back at a slower rate of speed, the high rock walls scrolling by more slowly still in the distance. The hoofs made almost no sound in the sand, so that all I was aware of, leaning forward into the blowing mane, were the wind in my ears and the horse's snorting breath as he plunged ahead, fighting to take the bit in his teeth. I let him run for a mile or so before throttling him down through a lope to an extended trot and finally back to a walk again. Then I turned him and we started for home, the broad shaggy barrel between my legs warming me with its radiant heat. Give a man a good horse and there isn't a thing else he needs in the world except a million square miles of nothing to run it in. I'm talking about Westerners, of course.

The big thoroughbred was in his stall when we arrived at the barn. I put the paint up and went on to the house where Jody sat at the kitchen table with her checkbook open in front of her.

"Hello," she said. "Were you able to scrounge yourself some breakfast?"

"I finished the coffee."

"Don't you want something else?"

"I don't think so."

"I didn't want anything, either. I'm not the least little bit hungry this morning."

"We shouldn't have had so much to drink last night."

I placed a hand under her chin and tilted up her face to kiss it.

"Behave yourself," Jody said, slapping the hand away. "You and I need to have a talk sometime."

"A talk about what?"

"We'll discuss it later."

"Let's talk about it now," I said.

The cell phone she'd acquired while I'd been away rang just then. All the ranchers are getting them now. She took it from her belt and cradled it in the space between the hollow of her shoulder and her ear as she continued to work on the checkbook.

"Hello," Jody said into the phone. "Yes, everything's fine.... He got here yesterday afternoon.... Cortez looks terrible, I'll never be able to show him again. I don't suppose it matters, as busy as we are I don't have time to show anyway.... You're short how many cows?... I'll go with you next week and we'll look for them together.... Of course.... All right.... I'll see you soon, then.... Drive safely.... 'Bye." She pressed the off button on the phone and hitched it again on her belt.

"That was Dago?"

"Um-huh."

"When's he getting back?"

"He's in Moab right now."

"How many cows is he missing?"

"He thinks seven. Maybe eight. We're not sure exactly how many calves there should be."

"We can go looking for them tomorrow, if you wish."

"Mm. What I really could use is some help pruning the orchard this afternoon."

The apple orchard was a couple of acres between the house and the cottonwood trees along the creek. The trees, more or less inferior stock, produced a small, hard green apple that tasted sour. This year's crop, along with most of last year's, lay stored in bins in the cellar for use in baking and for applesauce. Jody hated baking and applesauce takes time to make.

"Is November pruning time in Utah?" I asked.

"It doesn't matter," Jody said. "We're only taking what's already dead."

Black and bleak looking, the trees twisted in straight rows above the still-green grass. A few yellow leaves were left on them, and the windfall apples lay scattered among the fallen leaves between the trees. I carried the ladder from the garage while Jody brought the pruning shears, a handsaw, and a bucket of tree paint. With the sun just past the overhead the Indian summer day was warm, and I shucked my overshirt after the first tree. I pruned and sawed, she handed up the paint bucket and brush, and soon piles of the dead gray branches, dragged together by Jody, appeared between the rows. I was out of shape for the work, but as I sweated and sawed the violence of the action drew something from me, intensifying my assault against the defenseless trees. The harder I worked the more violent I felt, and the angrier, until I could have reduced the entire orchard to stumps and the fallen trees to logs. I stood it for about an hour before I climbed down from the ladder, still with the sharp-pointed tree saw in my hand. Jody stood ten feet away, making a pile of the branches I'd just cut.

"Tell me what it is we have to talk about," I said.

She finished placing them carefully before answering me.

"I really don't think there's anything that needs to be said."

"Why did you tell me there was, then?"

"Do I really have to say it?"

"Yes. You have to say it."

"You want too much," she said. "You've always wanted too much. You've wanted too much from me since the day we first met."

"I've wanted too much?"

"You think this relationship is going to end in marriage. But it isn't."

"I never mentioned marriage, as such. It was you who brought the subject up in the first place."

"I never did. When did I?"

"Many times. Several, anyway."

"If I did it was because I knew you expected it. Men always do."

"I thought it was the woman who wanted marriage, and the man who was scared of making a commitment."

"I'm not scared of marriage."

"You're scared of being married to me."

"Exactly!"

"What is it about me that threatens you so much?"

"I'm not threatened. It's just that you and I don't want the same thing. That's all."

"What do you want?"

"I want to be friends. You want something more."

"You didn't used to want to be just friends."

"Yes I did. I knew from the first time we met that that was all we were ever going to be."

"Why did you insist on fucking me then?"

"It was an experiment—a test-drive around the block."

"There's a name, you know, for women who think the way you do."

She bent so fast I thought she'd tripped before the little green apples started pelting around, striking me in the chest and head, bouncing on the ground and rolling away among the leaves. I let the saw drop and advanced through the hail of fruit to embrace her. With the unexpected strength almost of a strong man she threw me off, her eyes dilated and shining with hate.

"Stop right now or I'll shoot!"

The voice seemed to reach me from a long way off—as far away, I saw, as the corner of the house. Dago O'Grady advanced to the edge of the orchard, a small insignificant-looking man behind the big horse pistol he leveled ahead of himself.

"She don't love you anymore, she loves me. She's my woman now. Show respect, Ryder, or I'll teach you some."

Jody ran to him and he placed one arm protectively about her, holding the pistol leveled. I stood looking at the two of them for a long time, and then I turned and went back to the house. I took my toilet kit from the bathroom and dropped it into my overnight bag, found my coat in the closet, went out to the truck, and drove away from that place, half expecting to see them out on the front porch with their arms around each other to wave goodbye, the happy couple bravely facing the future together 'til death do us part, amen.

"From your form I thought you were an angel; from your acts I know you are a woman." Who said that? It could have been anyone but in fact it's from *Don Quixote,* I believe.

---

Cortez is kangaroo-free in November. I checked into one of the more expensive hotels at the off-season rate and stayed a couple of weeks. There didn't seem to be anything better for me to do.

The weather was mostly gray and cold, or clear and very windy and still cold, and I spent much of every day reading in my room. A couple of times I took the truck and followed the Dolores River back into the San Juan Mountains, and once I found a way in behind Mesa Verde and explored among ruins no tourist ever visited and perhaps no white man either, who can say? The pueblos were decrepit and crumbling and I discovered a strange pleasure walking on the bones of a dead civilization—killed, archaeologists now believe, by its own hand as, indeed, most—if not all—civilizations have died. Now there were only the ravens, coyotes, rattlesnakes, and ground squirrels in these places where men and women of a thousand years ago had gone about their unexamined daily business, while their priests and medicine men attended to the needs of imaginary gods. I ate my suppers out, in the restaurants; a different one each night until I'd run through all of them and had to start over. Going for supper one evening I found every place closed and wondered why until I saw a sign, CLOSED FOR THANKSGIVING DAY, behind one of the plate glass windows.

Most nights after eating I went drinking in the bars, and as there were a good many more saloons in town than restaurants I was able to go about twice as long before coming around again to where I'd started from. The bars were mostly slow and quiet except for the ones the Indians frequented, and I didn't go in many of those. One night as I was having a whiskey at one of the more respectable establishments I saw a familiar face reflected in the backbar mirror, pale with a black punched-up hat above it and a long white beard below. I signaled the barman to buy the face a drink, and after Whitey called along the bar to thank me I went over to where he was and stood with him. He hadn't recognized me at a distance, and when he saw who it was had bought him the drink he looked as if he wished there was no such thing as a free whiskey, almost.

"Hello Whitey."

"'Lo."

"How long have you been around?"

"Since openin time."

"I meant in Cortez."

"I don't know. A long time."

"I thought you'd got turned around and ended up back in Agua Prieta and became a Mexican citizen."

"She send you to take me back there?"

"Not at all. I'm on the lam myself."

I could tell he didn't believe me.

"What you doin in Cortez then?"

"Not a whole lot. Exploring the Indian ruins, mostly."

Whitey looked at me as if he thought I might be crazy.

I bought him another drink and had a second one myself. Then I left and went into the bar across the street for a nightcap. I never saw Whitey again after that. Probably he got scared and moved down to Farmington to do his drinking. If so, I couldn't blame him. Wild horses wouldn't have dragged me back to the Bar Nun Ranch, either.

Alone in the motel room I took the slip of paper Carmen had given me in Agua Prieta from my wallet. Carmen Dominguín was the finest woman I'd ever known. People without hope don't write books, they say. Neither do men who love women—one woman in particular—lack hope. I sat for a while on the edge of the bed by the telephone, holding the paper in my hand. Then I lifted the receiver and dialed the number she'd written down there.

After several failed attempts the call went through and I heard the phone ring once, twice, three times. Perhaps she'd gone out for the evening. There was a click, and then I got a voice—a recorded voice, a woman's voice, her voice—speaking in that soft familiar flutter of Spanish vowels and followed immediately by a robotic one: "Por favor deje un mesanje después del tono." I've always hated leaving messages on recording machines.

"It's me," I said for it. "You wanted me to let you know how it went when I got home. It didn't. Meet me tomorrow evening at the Gadsden Hotel in Douglas. I'll reserve a room for two in both our names. If you get there ahead of me, go ahead and check in first. Te veré pronto, mi amor.

"¡Carmen, te amo!"